On *To Die In Provence*

"Norman Bogner's first thr... ...pp... noir side of Peter Mayle's sweet books about ... Bogner offers a spooky evocation of the horror that can live alongside all that great food and scenery. We first find top copper Michel Danton recovering from shotgun wounds while working in his father's restaurant in Aix, where "fresh strings of Arles sausage and legs of jambon de Bayonne slyly waltzed on their hooks in the window." Michel's father is a tyrant, and his latest lady friend has just dumped him, so he's ready for a new case. Enter Darrell Vernon Boynton, a charming young psychopath called Boy by the women he conquers and the wealthy tourists he murders. Boy is a true descendant of Hannibal Lecter, and the only reason he hasn't eaten any of his victims is that the other food in Provence is too tempting. But be warned: not many other atrocities are beyond his imagination. As Bogner has proven in such previous blockbusters as *Seventh Avenue* and *California Dreamers*, he has the imagination to create nightmare landscapes in all manner of settings—and the writing skills to quickly make us a part of them."
　　　　　　　　　　　　　　—Dick Adler on Amazon.com

"Fans of the Thomas Harris brand of intelligent, fast-paced suspense and hard-edged action should find Bogner's trip to Provence just the ticket. . . . Presents an Aix-en-Provence as picturesque as the one Peter Mayle writes about, but he includes such realities as crooked cops and prostitutes, and ratchets up the suspense levels with . . . a thrill-killer couple who should give even Quentin Tarantino nightmares. *Die*'s cast is large . . . but Bogner manages to present them in full color and dimension. And each fits into his jigsaw puzzle of a plot so meticulously that the end result is picture perfect. While the novel is by turns charming, funny and good-naturedly sexy, there are some sections that explode into extreme violence."　　—*The Los Angeles Times*

"When you pick up *To Die In Provence* you won't put it down until you've finished it. This fast-paced, suspenseful, psychological thriller is a real page-turner, one that kept me on the edge of my chair right to the end. Norman Bogner has drawn extraordinary portraits of two young psychopathic killers who are all too frighteningly real. At the same time he has painted an evocative picture of Aix-en-Provence right down to the tastes and smells as well as the Cezanne-like vistas. Well written and skillfully plotted, the novel is bound to hit the bestseller lists."

—Barbara Taylor Bradford

"Norman Bogner has captured in this brilliantly written novel of suspense the sights, the sounds, flavors and smells of Provence. He has created a remarkable detective and one of the most perverse, frightening villains in contemporary fiction. I couldn't put it down. Plan to stay up all night." —Harold Robbins

"Bogner writes like the devil: scary, intriguing, full of passion, wit and real seductive. His murder most foul is complex and a great read, an intelligent and spine-tingling thriller. It's gourmet stuff concocted by a great chef: it goes down like escargot with a good Pouilly-Fuisse—rich fare, but you'll enjoy it immensely."

—John Nichols, author of *The Milagro Beanfield War*

"*To Die In Provence* is a great read. You can almost taste the flavors and aromas of Provence, almost sit on a terrace and feel the sun. And in this Garden of Eden is a human snake, one of the most terrifying killers to appear in years."
—Barbara D'Amato, author of *Authorized Personnel Only*

"Bogner scores a scary bull's eye with this one, like a baguette straight to the heart. I know I'll be thinking about Boy for some time to come and looking over my shoulder whenever I do. Move over Hannibal Lector, and pass the brie!" —Anthony Bruno, author of *Devil's Food*

"Perfumes, scents, essences; take deep intoxicating breaths."
—Nicholas Freeling

On *Honor Thy Wife*

"The author is an impressive storyteller, weaving threads of mystery through his love story. The dialogue is witty and realistic, his characterizations well drawn. This story of a man and his two loves plays out over twenty-five years, and despite the many sub-plots, the author deftly manages to bring his characters full circle. This complex novel of love and honor is sure to be a crowd pleaser."
—*Book Browser*

"What makes Mr. Bogner's novel a necessary read for fans of relationship dramas is the conversations between the protagonists as truths are revealed. . . . A soap opera that works because Norman Bogner instills flaws, traits, and motives into his prime characters. The story line is entertaining as Terry struggles with his life. . . . This novel will receive honors for a well-written story."
—*Midwest Book Review*

"This intricately plotted novel of family intrigue and ungovernable desire has all the ingredients for a compelling beach read: sex, love, lies, betrayal, hatred, revenge, threats of murder. . . . All the threads are satisfyingly tied up."
—*Publishers Weekly*

THE MADONNA COMPLEX

BY NORMAN BOGNER

THE *M*ADONNA COMPLEX

NORMAN BOGNER

A TOM DOHERTY ASSOCIATES BOOK
NEW YORK

This is a work of fiction. All the characters and events portrayed in this book are either products of the author's imagination or are used fictitiously.

THE MADONNA COMPLEX

A Forge Book
Published by Tom Doherty Associates, LLC
175 Fifth Avenue
New York, NY 10010

www.tor.com

Forge® is a registered trademark of Tom Doherty Associates, LLC.

ISBN: 0-812-57584-9
Library of Congress Catalog Card Number: 00-027161

First edition: August 2000
First mass market edition: April 2002

Printed in the United States of America

0 9 8 7 6 5 4 3 2 1

In loving memory of Jane and Alf Gordon

and Jim Parks
My friend for all seasons

IMMACULATE VENOM BINDS THE FOX'S TEETH.

-HART CRANE

ONE

EDDY SUSPECTED THAT SOMEONE HAD FOUND OUT about him. His face was flushed, and he was sweating as he apprehensively unlocked the door of the apartment. He was startled when he discovered something blocking his entry. He found two large telephone books behind the door and a herd of catalogues and videos imploring him to buy everything from Dean & DeLuca foods to Victoria's Secret lingerie. He could improve his mind with the new *Encarta;* surf the Net free courtesy of friendly AOL, even follow Scientology to wherever L. Ron Hubbard was leading mankind over the millennium.

If that weren't enough to lighten his mood, he would be in a position to surprise his friends with his knowledge of international social affairs by subscribing to *Vanity Fair* for a lifetime. He'd have to tell the porter not to go into the apartment again, and get rid of this junk mail. He was a fastidious man and clutter irritated him.

He stood in the doorway surveying the empty rooms that confronted him like the hands of strangers waiting to be shaken. He then opened the hall closet and removed his telescope and high-powered binoculars. He rooted around the closet and had a vague recollection of a gun. He had purchased one years ago when he had been threatened by some woman's husband, but he couldn't remember who the man was or what the woman was like, but he must have had one of his fast, reckless affairs with her to incite this reaction. Had he brought the gun with him? Perhaps it was lost or stolen.

He set up the tripod by the east window, fixed the telescope, adjusted the sights so that he commanded a clear view of the entrance of the United Nations. He looked at his new Patek Philippe watch that featured a perpetual calendar, a Christmas gift from a man whose software company he had saved from bankruptcy by investing a hundred million dollars.

Barbara was late and he waited anxiously for her to come out. He wondered if she was also looking at her watch and thinking of him. He had bought the same $43,000 watch for her—she had no idea of the price—and given it to her the previous week. When he placed it on her wrist, he had said, "Just remember that every hour that passes is an hour more that I love you." She had kissed him on both cheeks like a distant relative, and when he pulled her close to him in the back of the car, feeling the mold of her breasts under her thin dress, she had pushed him away and replied, "Don't rush me, Teddy. I may not look fragile, but I am. I'll crack and all the Krazy Glue—or you—won't help. I don't bind well."

He wanted to remind her that a ten-month courtship wouldn't be anybody's idea of a rush job.

Teddy's heart began to palpitate when the hands of

the watch read twelve-thirty. He peered through the telescope, then decided to use the binoculars.

He was so intent on adjusting the focus of the glasses that he didn't notice Barbara walking out of the main entrance of the General Assembly and heading down the promenade of the garden. Drops of sweat fell into his eyes as he swung the glasses from side to side, searching for her. She had already reached the Augustinic statue when he caught sight of her. She dropped her handbag and sat down on the grass at the base of the statue, under the olive branch held by the woman rider mounted on a stallion.

Barbara must be waiting for someone, meeting someone. Very clever of her to do it in broad daylight amid hundreds of visitors. No one would notice. She hadn't, however, considered the possibility that he'd be watching her. He had given her a Compaq computer for Christmas, which was tied into his mainframe at the office. VINTAGE was her password and he had already hacked into her e-mail twice that morning. She had the usual monthly message from her former employer in Bordeaux, pleading with her to return. The wine buyers missed her, the orders weak, the staff slumbering. Jealousy had made him despicable; he had relinquished his sanity to desire.

A sudden gust of wind came from the river and blew her boyish, cropped hair into a rooster's comb. He could have wept about her hair. She had had it cut the week before without telling him. It would take at least two years before it would grow back to its former length, down to her waist. Any idea of arranging it beautifully—geometrically, like a Japanese flower display—on his pillow, would have to be suspended until it grew back. It would have just covered the top of her buttocks, and he had a secret vision of lifting it up and kissing her on the small of the back.

Life cheats people in a variety of ways, but none was

more disturbing or insidious for a man like Teddy Franklin than the weeding out of a fantasy. At his global level of society, which had nothing to do with family connections or education background and everything to do with his achievements and the size of his fortune, the women he encountered were either rapacious divorcées or embittered widows. All of them on Prozac or one of its companions. He had gone through a period of hiring different, sylphlike call girls who needed a new wardrobe or coke cash. He employed the women as dinner companions; very, very rarely for intimacy. The new trash on the block would appear at his reserved table at Daniel's or Le Cirque and no one would comment. Too many of the clients owed their dinners, their very solvency, to him.

He had been lonely, adrift for many years, until he met Barbara. In some respects his had been a manageable, predictable existence. Routine had never been his enemy. Unpredictable behavior, especially his own, had become his nemesis. Love and its dangers.

Downstairs, he spied Barbara flicking her short black hair with the back of her hand and smiling. Teddy shifted his glasses and saw a tall man with a thick mustache and Porsche sunglasses, which gave him the cryptic manner of one of those senseless idiots he was always seeing in the foreign films Barbara dragged him to and which worked like sleeping pills.

It was good old Noel, dressed in a designer knockoff suit, who was third secretary to a diplomat in the French delegation. He felt secure with Noel, who had no money and gabbled about his family's property interests, proposed to Barbara and was rejected, and invariably fell back on the secretary pool. Teddy had run a credit check on Noel through the manager of his Paris office: the only property was an apartment on the Avenue Foch owned by Noel's father, a career civil servant in the ministry of economic affairs.

Noel had given Teddy one bad day several months ago when he and Barbara had paused at the reception desk of the Plaza, but they had done nothing more daring than have a drink in the palm court. Barbara, Teddy was glad to see, had ordered tomato juice, which put an end to any plan the Frenchman might have made for getting her loaded then wheeling her into a room.

They took an outside table at the nearby bistro, which had a prix fixe lunch and was not at all conducive to seductions. Noel was pulling in his belt, having come to the conclusion that he wanted more than Barbara's conversation for his money. Teddy had a rare moment of indecision: should he stop for a drink? How could he explain his presence if Barbara saw him? "I was just passing by." She'd know in a minute that he was spying on her, and she'd resent it, possibly punish him by refusing to see him. He didn't dare risk it.

Best to stick to his plan of furnishing the co-op and presenting it to her when the flighty English decorator finished. Barbara would be touched by his thoughtful gesture. Or would she? He'd shift some of the paintings from his townhouse. Who could say no to Vuillard, Matisse, Bonnard? If he had to ask himself this question, doubt was in the air.

How would Barbara express her gratitude? He thought about it for a minute and felt his flesh tingle with excitement. Would she ever say, "Teddy, I love you. I want to marry you"? When he was alone, after they'd been out, he'd say the words to himself, imitating the sonorous timbre of her voice, but it would come out in a reedy falsetto that might have been the cry of agony coming from the tortured Christ in Rouault's painting, which hung on the wall opposite his bed, serving to remind him of the subtle pleasures of lancination.

He put the telescope and the glasses back in the closet and double-locked the door. Except for the size of the rooms, the view of the East River and the UN, which were some compensation for spending 3.6 million for the co-op, the United Nations Plaza had all the glamour of a morgue. Even the elevator men and porters had the ashy faces of people who were constantly exposed to abrasive chemicals.

"Who do I speak to about keeping people out of my apartment?"

"The concierge," the elevator operator said as they sped down to the lobby.

"Concierge," Teddy grumbled. All these new titles exasperated him; salesmen were marketing consultants, boiler-room closers introduced themselves as telemarketing associates. "I'd probably have to make an appointment with him."

"That won't be necessary. I'll give him the message if you like."

"Please do that," Teddy said, handing him a twenty. "It's number ninety-one."

"Decorating coming along, Mr. Franklin?"

"I haven't started yet. And how do you know my name?"

"The staff here all read *Forbes*."

"Really. I never should have given them an interview. And that was five years ago."

"And with all due respect, sir, you must be even richer now."

Teddy's laugh had a snarl. "But I'm unhappier now."

He passed by the bistro against his will, then quickly got into the backseat of his car before the chauffeur could move from behind the wheel.

"Let's go to the office, Frank."

Teddy sank back into the soft, embracing seat. His sapphire Silver Seraph Rolls was about a year old, and the leather smelled strong and fresh, like the river when a breeze blew. It was a good smell. There were others: pine forest, golf greens, malt scotch, wood fires, lavender, and, of course, Barbara, who combined all the smells and made him aware of the pure physical joy of breathing. He looked at his watch. She'd be drinking her coffee, and Noel would be mentally adding up the check and playing with her fingers, as he recounted yet again the splendors of the old family chateau. Barbara would counter with the merciless politics of Bordeaux's vineyards.

But he'd be touching Barbara while he talked; the ooze from his pores would be entering Barbara's body, poisoning her. Teddy lived in constant dread of being poisoned, as though he moved in circles frequented by Borgia heirs whose sole purpose in life was to drop some obscure and deadly henbane into his shrimp cocktail. His irrational fear of receiving a sudden dose of poison stemmed from a childhood experience of having some ham infested with maggots, which resulted in his having his stomach pumped at a nearby hospital and a twenty-four-hour stomachache. He had been nine and now, forty years later, the thought of eating ham made spots dance before his eyes. He picked up the cell phone from the rest and pressed a number on his automatic dialer.

After a minute a voice answered.

"Theodore Franklin and Company."

He had intended to call his private line, but had been careless. "This is Mr. Franklin. Please put my assistant on."

"Yes, sir."

Teddy heard the tension in her voice.

"Mr. Franklin's office."

"Nancy—" The line went dead as they entered the underpass on the FDR Drive. "Hello? Frank, I've lost the goddamn connection."

"Sorry, I would've pulled off."

Mysteriously, Nancy came back on the line.

"We were cut off, Mr. Franklin."

"Never mind. My laptop's down. Give me Intel, Yahoo, MS, Disney, AOL, and the NASDAQ Internet garbage."

He listened to the stock prices she read off. "It looks like someone's been buying big blocks of Yahoo."

"Probably to cover a short position," he said.

"I didn't get that, Mr. Franklin."

"It's not important. If Mr. Pauley wants to know about the activity, tell him a few of the funds got caught with their pants down. I want him to start selling all of our Yahoo at two o'clock sharp in hundred-thousand lots—bang, bang, bang. I want to create some confusion. All these stocks are hot air in any case."

"Yes, sir."

"Any calls for me to return?"

"About forty, and your son phoned. He said to call him after seven because he'll be in court." She paused. "Will you be back this afternoon?"

"I don't think so. I'll catch the close at home."

They were approaching Wall Street and Teddy barked: "Frank, I've changed my mind. Drop me at Trinity Church."

The Rolls-Royce swung, edging its way cautiously through the traffic.

"Don't wait for me. I'll catch a cab," he said as the young chauffeur opened the door for him.

He was twenty-four, just a year older than Teddy's son Robbie. Teddy wondered who'd go farther in life. He admired Frank's pluck and had discovered that the young man was borrowing money and buying on margin.

"We'll be going out at eight."

"When should I pick up Ms. Hickman?"

"Let's see—" He opened a small crocodile wallet that had Barbara's daily schedule typed on it. "She finishes at five, possibly six tonight with all this East Timor stuff she's been translating. Make it seventhirty." He looked at Frank's long, horsey face. "How much Yahoo have you got?"

"Forty-one shares."

"Still buying odd lots."

"I couldn't raise money enough to buy a hundred."

"Unload it."

"I intended to," Frank said, smiling crookedly. "Do you think I ought to go short tomorrow?"

"No, you'll only pick up a few points, and it won't be enough to cover the interest and commissions you'll have to pay." He paused. "But, Frank, your thinking's right."

"Thanks, Mr. Franklin." As he opened the door, he asked incredulously, "Are you going to walk?"

"Either that or start smoking again."

Teddy waited for Frank to pull away before heading for Nassau Street. He couldn't take the chance of having him know where he was going.

Two

THE LUNCHEONETTE WAS NARROW AND REEKED OF burnt coffee and bacon grease. The amenities, such as they were, comprised a few cracked red plastic seats all built too close to the ground so that legroom was restricted, and once a customer had stuffed a sandwich into his face, he left because it was too uncomfortable to linger. The booths were also tightly bunched. Teddy knew the place served as a club of sorts for the messengers on Wall Street. Santana blared from the old jukebox, and a few young men were assaulting the Nintendo games in the back.

Lopez squeezed off a last round of some war game and nodded at him. He hustled in the big office buildings: he brokered teenage girls, dope, automatic weapons, or whatever the Ivy League graduates who pulled down the fat salaries imagined might be pleasurable. Lopez was said to be connected to the Latino gangs.

"Want a coffee, boss?"

Teddy hesitated and inclined his head toward the other boys.

"Don't worry. They're stupid and hardly understand English," he said with authority, to reassure Teddy.

"No, I'll have a can of Diet Coke." Lopez yanked one out of the sputtering refrigerator, snapped it open, and held out a straw.

"How much money did you bring, boss?"

"Five thousand."

Lopez watched him carefully—a boy really—but one who had spent most of his years on the streets of Spanish Harlem when he wasn't locked up. He was a pleasant menace to society and he intrigued Teddy. His grandparents had been part of the large Puerto Rican diaspora in the fifties and their hard work had unfortunately produced Julio Lopez.

"The price of poker has gone up to ten thousand," Lopez said with an impudent smirk.

"You're ridiculous," Teddy responded.

Lopez hadn't expected any disagreement, and he was caught off-balance.

"Don't you Wall Street big shots pay a finder's fee when someone brings you a new issue?"

"What've you been doing, watching *Moneyline*?"

"MTV. Look, Mr. Franklin, I'm entitled to it. I found two guys for you."

"You're going to rake off something, aren't you?"

"Okay, let's make it nine thousand."

"This Coke is flat," Teddy said, shoving the can away.

"You probably know the boss of Coca-Cola. Why don't you call him and ask him not to send the old ones to places like this?"

"Is that what they do?"

"Yeah, and the beer's flat, too. When I take a piss, it's got a better head."

Teddy laughed at these complaints. Lopez scratched

one of the acne patches smoldering on his unshaved chin. There were a number of these self-inflicted scratches on his face, giving it the viscidity of a badly varnished table. Teddy had skillfully negotiated with serpentine billionaires and tycoons for years, and he had learned early that the only way to make a deal was to make an adversary's strength work for him, which was also one of the cardinal principles of self-defense. If he revealed any weakness at the outset with Lopez, he could count on extortion at some later date.

"When you play poker, you don't change the stakes any time you feel like it unless the other players agree."

"You can afford to pay."

"It's not a question of that—we made a deal. Live with it."

"What if I mentioned this to a cop I know."

"Go ahead. I'm glad you told me. I'll have my security guys throw you out the window the next time you make a delivery. A hundred stories. You'll have an aerial view of New York. Just like the MetLife blimp."

"What about me hitting other people when I land?"

"I'll have them do it in the back, over the parking lot. You'll be salsa on the hood of a Dodge."

Lopez digested this bit of intelligence and nodded. He admired Teddy for boxing his ears, and he resolved to use this tactic in his own military campaigns on the streets, where his kids patrolled like jackals. He'd keep the five thousand and let the two foot soldiers split the remaining four.

"Okay, you're *el jefe*. We got a deal."

"I haven't written anything down, so you'll have to remember it all."

"I've got a good memory."

"The building is called the Castilla. And the address is Two Ninety-two Central Park West. The man's name is Dr. Paul Frere. The records are located in a gray steel filing cabinet. Tell the boys to look under *H* for Hickman. Barbara Hickman." Teddy's face clouded with doubt. "They can read, can't they?"

"Oh, sure, Harvard and Yale," Lopez growled.

"Cut it out. Can they read?" Teddy insisted.

"Yeah."

"Okay I want them to take the records and tape recordings of half a dozen other people—but Hickman's the important one."

"I got it. Where do we meet?"

"We don't."

"What about collecting the rest of the money?"

"As you come into the Port Authority Building, you'll find some lockers and phone booths just beyond them. Put the files in a locker, and slip the key into page two hundred forty-eight of the Manhattan phone book. The other four thousand will be there."

Lopez repeated the instructions and, to Teddy's relief, got them all correct. He had a new respect for Lopez, as one predator carefully surveys the territory and strength of another beast of prey before encroaching on its rights or attacking the same victim the other has planned to kill.

"You're sure this hombre won't be home tonight?"

"Positive."

Lopez rehearsed his plan for Teddy, which was straightforward and involved no violence. When he had finished, Teddy patted his shoulder, initiating a camaraderie that touched Lopez deeply in some dark, concealed region where his emotions once lay.

"If it works, there'll be another thousand on the same page of the *Brooklyn* phone book."

Lopez reacted with a puzzled look, which involved furrowing his brow and puckering his lips.

"I don't understand you, Mr. Franklin."

"If you ever make a lot of money, you'll understand."

"Verdad?" Lopez stared at the handsome man with the benign smile. "One last thing, Mr. Franklin. If your security guys would toss me out of a window on your say-so, why don't you ask them to do this?"

"They'll kill for me, but they won't steal."

THREE

THE TAXI WITH ITS OFF-DUTY LIGHT ON STOPPED FOR Barbara outside the United Nations.

"Couldn't resist beautiful woman," the Russian driver observed, offering Barbara a pierogi. He held out a gray carton with grease tattoos. "My mother make, delicious. Or don't you eat meat?"

She took one. It was still warm. "Any vodka?" she asked.

"For that we have to go to Brighton Beach. I have mine own apartment."

"Next time. Eighty-seventh and East End and drop me on the corner."

He pulled the flag down and shot ahead just as the light changed.

"Do you work at United Nations?"

"Yes, I do."

"Could I ask you a stupid question?"

"A lot of people do . . . why be different?"

"What do they do there, I mean, really do?"

"Argue," she said sharply, hoping to prevent further discussion, but the driver continued talking about his life in New York, his family, his fiancée, and his availability on Wednesdays.

When he dropped her off and thanked her for the tip, she leaned in the window. "And don't be following me home. I have a gun and two angry Dobermans."

"Feh," he said. "Nazi dogs."

"What does *feh* mean?"

He spat, then drove off, and she had a new definition to add to her translation list of idioms.

Her apartment was one of four on the ground floor of a retro twenties brownstone that had undergone the whole panoply of modernization: a universe of new plumbing, wiring, cable TV, a stall shower with six throbbing heads, thermostatically controlled heat and air-conditioning, and three invisible neighbors whom she had caught glimpses of only during the Christmas season. Despite the conveniences, the house still retained most of its external old New York character. When she was away from it for any length of time, she always returned with a sense of "This is where I live, *chez moi*"—as the one-room cell at the Brabourne she had once lived in had never been.

The possession of objects, a place to live in, and money in the bank hadn't been important to her, although the money gave her freedom and mobility. She had traveled for some years after graduating from Radcliffe. In a literal sense, this flight to Europe presented an escape. She had been going there since childhood, accompanying her father on his wine-buying tours. She drifted through France, Germany, Italy, and Spain in a Volkswagen. She met a great many people during her stay in Europe, but established no close or binding relationships and slept alone, since no one tempted her. In Munich she managed to pick up the lilting southern accent with its Italian flavor, so that in Cologne the *wirte* in the pension would have sworn that she had been born in Munich. She had the natural gift of mimicry, which she used the way a sniper does his grass, leaves, and camouflaged uniform, as he sits in a tree waiting for his unsuspecting prey.

Teddy had enlisted as her victim, and even though she recognized this, it was hard to think of him in a passive sense. Like most men with money, he had a crack in his character, which he assumed she could repair with some magical elixir. In this respect she was stunned by his naïvete. She had let it go too far. He not only had hopes but also plans for her: homes in three countries, a yacht awaiting her on the Mediterranean for their honeymoon. Such was his determination that she had given up refusing him, despite being touched by his forlorn gestures and despite loving him more than she would admit, even to herself.

Teddy had begun a love affair without finding out how she felt. From her point of view, he was behaving as though this was a financial trade—somewhat speculative, certainly, but one that he could control. He believed he had the resources to manage every eventuality, not to mention her character, hang-ups, and quirks.

As she reached her door, she found her daily bouquet of three dozen yellow roses. In this ongoing romance Teddy pursued her like Napoleon advancing on Moscow. The attached card read, *The time of Flowers*, and was signed *T*.

Her living room was an effusion of color: apricot walls with apple-green moldings; the sofas facing the fireplace were covered in a Provence fabric she had bought in the Souleiado shop in Arles. There were old tables and vases made into lamps, darkish shades, and an assortment of tasteful but inexpensive paintings. Today was Friday, and Monday's pubescent buds had become the darkened petals of a spinster's remembrance secreted in the dusty pages of Eliot's *Four Quartets*, musky but not forgotten, like the memory of first love. Many of her copper kitchen pots now resided in the living room, serving as vases.

The photograph of Laura was hidden behind bulbous dying flowers. Barbara reached up to a kitchen shelf and took down her huge pasta pot, filled it with water, and arranged the new roses. She looked for a place to put them and in despair set them down by the fireplace fender. She picked up Laura's picture, dusted it with her sleeve, and centered it on the mantelpiece.

Laura . . . Laura Sargent. There was no point thinking about her unless, of course, thinking about the dead brought them back to life; perhaps when no one thought about them, they were incontrovertibly gone, their history reduced to a few superficial statistics as irrelevant as those contained in an almanac.

The flowers—the sight of them crowding the room—depressed her. The air was torpid, weighted with a stale pungency and she opened both front windows that faced the street. A couple of nannies were wheeling their charges home from Carl Schurz Park, which ran along the river and led to Gracie Mansion.

Barbara undressed and ran a bath, absentmindedly put in too much of the lemon-verbena bath oil because she was concentrating on making herself a vodka martini, which she mixed with a dash of Pernod instead of Noilly Prat. One of the vintners in Bordeaux had taught her how to flavor vodka so that it had some body, the semblance of a drink with a real taste. The bath was steaming, and as she sipped the ice-cold martini, she cautiously examined herself, then looked away. Dr. Frere had urged her not to be self-conscious, but had forgotten to explain how to break the lifelong modesty indoctrinated by her gentleman father.

"You're not simply beautiful and sensitive, you're an exceptional woman, Barbara. So stop plotting against yourself. In logical terms—and I accept that emotions are seldom a product of reason—what does your downfall mean to anyone but you? No one said you have to do penance because you've got it all."

She had become a sullen, secretive woman; she was loath to change. When she was at Radcliffe, she hadn't been the same person, seldom bummed out, endowed with a cheerful glee about life and its endless possibilities. Laura had changed her personality, remolded it, like a master artist shaping it into her own vision. Frequently when she was at MOMA and she looked at a grotesque Picasso portrait of a woman or *Les Demoiselles d'Avignon* when it had been on exhibition, she could barely catch her breath and she'd dash over to a Renoir and an inner voice would cry, "Once this was what I was like and now I have become a horror. A Picasso woman."

She liked Dr. Paul Frere and was drawn to him as a psychiatrist because his name meant *brother* in French and he was also a Francophile. Dr. Frere—she'd started to call him "Paul" last week—had accepted a dinner invitation from Teddy and was bringing his wife. She hoped that he would be coming because he wanted to be seen with her outside the office. But as usual she had been assailed by doubts and suspected it was Teddy—Teddy in the flesh—who really intrigued him and made him break his ironclad rule of never socializing with patients. Perhaps Frere wanted Teddy to give him some advice on the stock market, let him in on a "special situation," make him a multimillionaire. Why should a psychiatrist, even a very good one, be invulnerable to the magnetic field of the profit motive? What would Freud or Jung do if someone dangled a fortune in front of their eyes? she thought as she dressed for dinner.

She discarded a modest black dress with the high-collared old-maid style she invariably wore, and instead treated her breasts to an outing. No more disguises for her buxom figure. She had bought a pale yellow Lagerfeld plunger on sale the previous month. Against her will, the markdown had taken her prisoner. She knew from experience the problem with these dresses. Men dropped food on their laps and soiled their ties, gawking at her breasts. One of the Arab diplomats who had hit on her at the UN had said after repeated dismissals that she was a candidate for Hooters. Some diplomat.

Promptly at 7:30 the chauffeur rang the doorbell. Frank told her she looked very pretty, without being suggestive, and ushered her into the Rolls. Queen Latifah's sultry rendition of "Lush Life" was on the Macintosh CD player. "I can change it if you don't like it."

"No, it's fine."

"Are you sure?" he insisted.

"Yes, honestly."

"I can change it to the Elvis Costello–Burt Bacharach you mentioned."

"Great." She was going through a revisionist period in her music tastes.

She wished that Teddy wouldn't go overboard with everyone—even the chauffeur—to ensure that she was pleased. Just once, when she was being willful or contrary, couldn't he have the grit to tell her to fuck off?

A PART FROM THE HERD OF COMPANIES TEDDY Franklin controlled, he was a real estate luminary in a smaller, quieter fashion than Donald Trump, whom he referred to as the Trumper and avoided as he did fellow *Forbes* members of the billionaires' league. Teddy wore his wealth silently except at his various homes, which, despite the blandishments of *Architectural Digest*, he refused to have photographed. He threw no charity galas and seldom attended functions. He would simply send off a check and, if an appearance was de rigueur—say for the late Lady Di—he would bestow his assistant on the company.

His house was a sienna brown four-story mansion on Fifth Avenue and Sixty-second Street that he had not had sandblasted and was encrusted with the life and death of the city during the previous eighty-odd years. It had an unprepossessing entry down three steps, leading to a curtailed hallway that in turn brought guests to a gilded Art Deco elevator. Stairs were also a possibility for the active but then the alarm system objected. On the second floor were the gracious public rooms: The copper-hooded kitchen through a swing door; Chippendale dining for a dozen; ultimately a variety of intriguing spaces on different levels and a circular gallery. The quiet Renaissance cove displayed Raphael, Donatello, Bellini, Titian, and a rare, mysterious Giorgione landscape with confused people looking at the sky, which was Teddy's favorite of the group.

The loosely called Impressionist inlet offered Cézanne, Monet, Renoir nudes, a striking Manet of an opera crowd, and Gauguin's later work in Tahiti. For the show at the Tate and later at MOMA, Teddy had loaned the curators three of his Bonnards. He was one of the silent bidders whenever Sotheby's or Christie's had a worthwhile auction. He bought his paintings through a dealer in Zurich whose company he in fact owned.

Teddy's home had been done by Colfax and Fowler of London; the four bedrooms had spiral staircases to guide guests to the roof garden where they'd find the usual gym and sauna; flowers, trees, and a swimming

pool with a retractable skylight. Teddy had in effect
moved country-club amenities to Midtown. When he
wanted to sample the actual scent of seaweed and
brine, his French Puma helicopter was stationed on a
pad atop his office building, and fifteen minutes later
dropped him at his estate on Lily Pond Road in East
Hampton. Of all the domestic chateaux, Barbara preferred the beach house where the rooms faced wondrous ocean dunes, which swirled in the windy
evenings and formed mysterious topiaries. A grass tennis court lounged on the property along with a cro-
quet lawn; the Shinnecock golf club was a dogleg away
and Teddy's yacht was moored at a slip. She had so far
put off visits to his apartment in Paris and the villa in
Antibes. Teddy Franklin didn't stay at hotels or fly
commercial. He had converted a Boeing 727 into a
playground in the sky.

Barbara heard voices filled with rich laughter coming from the central living room and there was
Leonard, Teddy's English butler, in a dinner suit smiling with welcome and placing a glass of champagne in
her hand. Dr. Paul Frere's deep and resonant voice
carried; the skillful listener was telling a joke about
his wife.

". . . Susan still isn't sure why she married a psychiatrist."

"To please my parents," came a cultivated woman's
voice, the English accent mocking.

"Not because he loved you and you him?" Teddy
asked.

"I suppose that might have been relevant," Susan
Frere replied.

"Or irrelevant," Barbara interjected.

She was in the mood for a quick snipe, for Frere's
wife had looked her over like a contractor about to
start spiking a job. Frere had told her that Susan was
addicted to Upper West Side intellectuals, any male in

denim, bearded writers, and Lincoln Center first nights. This coy admission by Dr. Frere came after Barbara began one of their sessions with a long list of her own habitual faults and self-destructive behavior.

The men turned to Barbara, who stood at the threshold under a baroque archway implanted from a looted castle in Reims when Teddy was gathering home furnishings.

"Welcome, Barbara," Dr. Frere said.

Teddy looked at her as though for the first time, enthralled, and Barbara felt he was about to bid on her—no matter what the price was—to add to his collection. He placed an arm around her and lightly kissed her on both cheeks. No fancy emotional stuff in front of the guests. But he was quick to catch his breath before he actually gasped at her plunging neckline. This was the involuntary effect she had on him, both of them powerless to alter the condition of his attraction, which was tidal and murderous in its all-embracing possessiveness. She might have been a land mass and he Magellan on a voyage to circumnavigate it.

Barbara extended her hand to Susan and said, "Hi, I'm Barbara. And I know you're a rare woman."

"How so?"

"You've made a psychiatrist happy and that's a feat."

Everyone laughed and Susan Frere wasn't sure if she was being put on. She was a small, dainty woman with stony, tobacco-leaf eyes that measured everything, but now in Barbara's glow she was disarmed.

"You're very kind to say so."

"Any man who has a framed collage of pictures of his wife on his desk has to be crazy about her."

"Thank you. And I've heard wonderful things about you." She had not been keen to meet her husband's patient, but this one was different—she had captured the celebrated Teddy Franklin and dinner with a billionaire would be an uncommon experience in her life.

Leonard approached with more champagne for the guests.

"Which one is this?" Teddy asked his houseman.

"It's the '59 Krug."

Teddy smiled at Barbara. "We're serving it in Barbara's honor," he announced proudly to his guests. "She told me that Dom and Cristal sell more because they spend a fortune advertising, but they're not as good as Krug."

"Krug is for royalty," Barbara observed. "Is this my father's last case?"

"No, I managed to rescue two more at the auction. And I've got my Paris office scouring France for '61's."

Susan sipped the wine cautiously, peering at Barbara. "Linguist, wine expert, and beautiful."

"Thank you. My father was a wine shipper. I used to travel with him to tastings in Bordeaux, Burgundy, the Loire Valley, and Provence. I think he would have preferred a son, but he was stuck with me."

"He was a great guy," Teddy informed them.

"You're at the United Nations, aren't you?" Susan asked.

"Yes. I'm a translator and a substitute interpreter."

"How many languages do you have to know?"

"One for translator apart from English, and five for interpreting."

"How many do you know?" Susan asked, beginning to sound like a headhunter.

"She's fluent—but really fluent—in six languages, including Russian," Teddy proudly observed, indicating that Barbara was a woman of accomplishment and not merely for his amusement.

"And German, if I'm not mistaken," Frere said.

Barbara nodded, and Susan looked at her grimly, a real fan. A few more like that, and Barbara would wind up with a knife placed neatly between the shoulder blades. "Who's being hostile?" she'd tell Frere. "Your wife just doesn't like me."

"Education is quite meaningless," Barbara said stormily. "It's what you are, what you become."

Her mood had changed. She had refused antidepressants and told Frere what he could do with Lithium. The tension within Barbara welled up like an electric charge as she listened to the innocuous chitchat between Frere and Teddy. One slip of the tongue—a mere hint—and she'd be exposed. She wondered how much Teddy would pay Frere for a little inside information about her. "Nothing complicated, just what makes her tick." Teddy wouldn't pay; he'd work out something practical: "You tell me about Barbara, and I'll give you an insider's tip."

"I had a rough day," Barbara said apologetically.

"You must have them very often," Susan said, "with one crisis after another."

Barbara's paranoia kicked in. Any double meaning? Did she study the records of Frere's patients? Possibly a few, in between poetry readings, but if she had taken even a lingering squint at Barbara's, she would have been surer of herself.

"How did you and Teddy meet?"

"It was very romantic." She always fell back on a kind of hollow pretense when she felt cornered.

"Really?"

"Yes. Teddy agreed to advise me on my dad's lousy investments and we met at his funeral. I guess I became Teddy's client. Not that he has any besides himself." She smiled at Teddy. "Does anything draw people closer together than money, a portfolio?"

"A man's work defines him," Susan said.

"Right. Well, money is Teddy's work. If you ever have the chance of going to his office and watching him analyze a company, you'll see romantic love in its purest form."

"Are you sure of that?"

"No, I'm not sure of anything. That's my problem."

There was a long pause while Susan sipped her Krug, then puffed daintily at her cigarette. "I think he loves you very much."

"He hasn't started to make public confessions, has he?"

"Does he usually?"

"No, not usually. But if he starts, I swear I'll dust him."

Teddy had overheard only part of the conversation.

"I came down to New York from Syracuse when I was young. My father'd worked himself to death on the assembly line for Carrier Air-Conditioning. I thought of all the fans he'd installed in their units and I knew it wasn't for me. I was a twenty-year-old, raw, rough hustler who'd busted out of City College because the courses bored me and I wanted to get rich.

"Eventually I was hired by Merrill Lynch as a broker's assistant because I could type. I noticed that my boss and his associates used to send gifts from Hickman Vintners. I was a glorified gofer, and I would drop off the booze to their clients at Christmas. Eventually Barbara's father, Conrad Hickman, an old-world gentleman, took me under his wing. Connie taught me to appreciate wine and actually gave me a course on all the fine things."

Susan appraised Barbara. "I can see that."

"Susan, I didn't know he had a daughter, or believe me I would have been on the case earlier."

"Teddy became my financial guide. And after the funeral service, he took me and some people out to the River Club. I suppose it was a wake."

"We drank enough to qualify. From sad beginnings, happy endings," Teddy said, offering them a final drink before adjourning for dinner at Le Cirque.

He put his hand on Barbara's bare shoulder. Leonard picked up the signal—leave the master alone—and offered the Freres a quick guided tour through Teddy's kingdom.

Teddy wore bespoke Brioni suits when he was going out; otherwise he was a tweedy Savile Row laird, a peer of the realm. He was about five-eight—she just a bit taller—very broad-shouldered and solidly built; heavy bearded, his straight, black hair, cut short, meandered to gray. He affected a breezy, tactical urbanity, not entirely trustworthy; in his ashy gray eyes, she witnessed a detached alertness, and a seemingly mellow demeanor that screened his domineering nature. She knew he was a predator who possessed the acuity of someone who hunted professionally and with success. He smiled frequently and the echo of a snarled laugh lingered. His voice was velvety with persuasion. From the instant they had met, she sensed she was prey. He never talked anyone into doing anything; they seemed to do it themselves of their own free will. He was merely the guide who always got his way. It was his route or off the cliff. His astute generalship invariably inspired surrender and had evolved into fear on her part.

"Are you happy, Barbara?" Teddy asked.

"As happy as I can be."

"You wanted to have your shrink to dinner, so here he is on a platter."

"Your invitation must've been very compelling."

"I was under the impression you wanted to personalize the relationship, so I delivered him."

She cast off Teddy's hand without seeming to and nervously walked to the Adam fireplace, but he surrounded her. He had the ability found in great basketball players of crowding people with defensive maneuvers, oppressively encircling her, shadowing her every movement.

Teddy was perplexed. "I thought you'd like having dinner with Paul."

"I thought I wanted to. But I feel awkward and nervous. You know, when you establish a patient-doctor relationship with a man, it's hard to change it into something light and frivolous."

"You suggested dinner, didn't you?" Teddy said, as though he'd made a mistake in his appointment book.

"I suggest a lot of silly things. I feel off balance with this situation. Giddy and confused. You see, Teddy, Dr. Frere *knows* me," she said with frightened emphasis. "I've told him things that I don't like about myself. He knows everything about me. And it scares me."

"The context or him?"

"Both."

"I'll get rid of them," Teddy said.

"You just can't."

"Tell me what you want me to do."

"His wife looks at me. It's hard to explain. Up my dress, like my panties aren't clean or something."

"You're imagining it. I'm sure she likes you."

"Everyone does, right?" She tried to goad him.

"Sure they do. What's not to like?"

"What a cross to bear, the world's affection."

"Barbara, you're not making sense. Do you feel okay?"

"Jittery, that's all. Nothing to get hysterical about."

"Frere's helping you, isn't he?"

"I suppose so. Sometimes I feel so good that I could cry, really cry. I'm on a different trip tonight."

Teddy put his arms around her, and she moved back suddenly.

"Sorry. I just want to hold you when you're like this, but you don't like me to. I want to say, 'Baby, it's okay. I'll take care of you.' I'll be your friend and nothing more if that's all you want. That's what I mean when I touch you."

"You smell good."

"Caswell-Massey; I'll send them a thank-you note."

"I like you when you're a smart-ass." She kissed him on the lips, and he made no move to hold her. "Has Paul said *anything* about me?"

"No, of course not. We were talking about the market, and I was explaining commodities to him."

"You didn't try to pump him about me, did you? Because if I thought for a minute you had, I'd walk out of here."

Teddy was growing uncomfortable and eased away. He was never sure whether she was playing games with him, in love in her fashion, or whether she despised him.

"Don't you give me credit for any brains? Naturally, I want to know everything that's gone on with you. But I want to hear it from you. Past and present. Because I want to help you. I wouldn't take a chance of hurting you or doing something that might upset you. Barbara, just remember I'm here whenever you want me. I'm an old pair of shoes you can put on to walk in the rain. I'll never be more, unless you decide to make me more."

She clinked glasses with him, took his hand, kissed his fingers and he was bewildered. He was deeply in love with her and so irrevocably entrapped that he felt that he was the one who needed psychiatric help and not Barbara.

"You know something, darling, with all the languages I have at my fingertips, and my education, there's just one word that sums me up." He waited for the revelation. "I'm dirt."

Like a diner who has swallowed a hair in the soup, Teddy gasped, and turned a fine Mikado yellow, the color of murder and coronaries.

"What? That's one word, one word," he said, flustered, "you could never use about yourself."

"I don't give a fuck. You ought to find a woman who genuinely appreciates you."

"Oh, stop. Don't talk that way," he said as the injured party. "And it's politically incorrect."

She began to laugh at herself, the mad situation, and found herself almost falling in love with him.

Teddy stalked out of the room in pursuit of his wandering guests, who had locked horns over Magritte's *Son of Man* painting. He stood behind his guests and listened to them rail about the mystery of the painting. A man wearing a dark suit jacket, red tie, and a derby has a green apple for a face with the leaf covering the brim of the hat. Teddy didn't want to spoil the Freres' disagreement by telling them that the man was Adam and he was about to enter the garden.

*A*S A TREMULOUS BIRD FREED FROM A TRAP TAKES flight, so Barbara did at Le Cirque while Teddy spooned the truffled risotto into her mouth. She gained confidence and was amused by the establishment's owner, who explained how carefully he selected the wines, bought the food, supervised the kitchen, and justified the prices.

"Quality and originality, they come with a price," Teddy explained to the astonished Freres, who were reading the menu from right to left and were clearly disconcerted by notations like *market price*.

When the owner moved off to another table of diners waving at Teddy, Barbara said, "He runs this place as though it was Rome under Julius Caesar."

"He can afford to. He picks his clients, too."

"What if he doesn't approve of you?" Susan cheeped as her husband shrank back from the folly of the impertinent question.

"Oh, he's very direct. He courteously puts you on the waiting list." Teddy nodded at a group of men waving at him from an adjoining table. "Some people have a right to be here at the center," he said imperiously while pointing out that *Fortune* magazine's feasters were out in force, disposing of millions to the less fortunate and using their fortunes to build schools and hospitals over dinner.

"Do you feel guilty about deciding the futures of other people?" Dr. Paul Frere asked.

"As guilty as Michael Jordan when he won the MVP or David Duval after he'd shot a fifty-nine. Athletes never have to apologize for their excellence; rich people do for making it."

"Is there anything we can't have?" Susan asked.

"Yes, the soufflé. I forgot to order it."

Barbara adored Teddy at this minute, with his giant balls and ego splattering the canvas of life like a Jackson Pollock.

FOUR

W.T. GRANT, THE NIGHT MAN, A VETERAN OF TWENTY years' service, took the elevator up to apartment 9E, which was next door to Dr. Paul Frere's office. Grant was back on duty after a heart attack. As a reward for his long service, he had been given the softest job in the building, the four-to-twelve shift, which left him free to handicap his horses, gossip with the doorman, and put his feet up on the sofa in the small room that served as his nook. He was carrying a pair of gold candlesticks delivered from the antique shop where Mrs. Collins, the tenant in apartment 9E, had purchased them. Mrs. Collins and her husband were out for the evening, and Grant, who took as holy writ the rules and regulations emblazoned on a plaque in his office that stated that the management takes no responsibility for packages left with the porter, decided, as he had countless times before, to deposit the package in the tenant's apartment.

He jangled his passkeys like loose change as he padded down the heavily carpeted hallway, which smelled sour from a recent shampoo he had supervised. He opened the door and placed the candlesticks on the telephone table in the darkened foyer and stopped dead in his tracks when he heard the unmistakable crash of furniture coming from the apartment next door. He had seen Dr. and Mrs. Frere leave at five-thirty. Dr. Frere had even asked him how he was feeling, to which Grant had replied with his characteristic brevity, "Comin' along."

Standing in the darkened foyer, Grant made a herculean effort to remember if he had seen the Freres return. They would have passed him, and he hadn't moved all evening. He always made a point of greeting tenants, coming and going, in the hope of recovering some forgotten tip or to call attention to the fact that he was there to render service. He leaned on the door, shook his head with finality, and listened. With his ear pressed against the wall, the sounds he heard reminded him of the symphonic gnawing rasps of rats. Grant made his way next door and listened in the hallway.

He jangled his keys thoughtfully. If he buzzed the security man who was on his break and there was no one inside, he'd feel like a fool. If the Freres had slipped by his vigilant post without his noticing, he might find himself interrupting a personal scene. The only alternative left was to ring the apartment on the house phone, but that meant a long walk to the front elevator. Grant solved the problem by resorting to his typical course of action, minding his own business. He double-locked 9E, muttered to himself, and started to walk off, when he heard another sound, louder than the first, possibly a lamp smashing, and he came to the conclusion that he must at least ring the doorbell.

He pressed the bell and waited. Two sweating boys

inside, both seventeen, froze when they heard the buzz. They were in Dr. Frere's office, and they had done their work thoroughly. Grant had interrupted them during a tribal rite de passage, which involved systematically tearing books from their bindings, urinating in Frere's desk drawers, and scratching the tops of all tables with a large hydra-headed can opener. The young men advanced to the waiting room, their 9mm automatics steady. Ears pressed behind the door, they heard Grant's heavy breathing. Rafael calmly winked at his friend and held the gun to his own stomach, indicating where he would shoot the intruder. Mario smiled broadly, his gold front teeth capturing the slanting lamplight from the office.

The door opened slowly, and Grant's head—as though emerging from a turtle's shell—came past the edge of the door. His eyes bulged as he took in the broken lamps, tables upended, strewn papers in the office. As he entered, Rafael and Mario confronted him and pointed their automatics at both temples of his head.

In shock, Grant made a strangled, gagging noise. He sounded like he was choking. His knees sagged, and he pivoted around in slow motion, like a drunk falling in a slapstick comedy. As he descended, multicolored spots flickered intensely across his line of vision, and he saw the face of his long dead wife, not as she was in death, but as she had been when he had first seen her as a young girl; the face was in the entrance of a cave, but there was no body, and orange and gold lights shone from her eyes. He tried to smile, but his mouth wouldn't move. Then in the foreground of the cave he noticed two pairs of shiny, pointed black boots, which frightened him and made him recoil. Falling, his head clapped the edge of the long-waisted magazine table. He swerved downward, retreating into darkness.

The two boys stood mutely. Mario closed the door.

"Qué pasa?" Rafael asked.

"Creo es el corazón." Mario shrugged indifferently and sniffed his coke-loaded inhaler. It cleared his head. He stooped down on one knee and listened for signs of life.

"Un ataque cardíaco?" Rafael asked.

"No sé."

"Quizás está muerto?"

"No es importante," Mario replied. He slipped his hand into Grant's pocket and found some loose change, but no folding money. "Eighty-three cents," he said with disgust.

"Tengo dolor en la cabeza," Rafael complained, wagging his head as though to put out a fire inside. He broke open his inhaler and saw he'd run out of blow and licked the residue.

Mario held up an airline kit bag and said, "Nosostros marchamos ahora."

They both felt calm in the street and got into a black Chevy Monte Carlo and cruised up Columbus Avenue, heading to 112th Street. It was only ten o'clock, and they were early for their meeting with Lopez. They bought a couple of beers in the Old San Juan Bar, then ambled outside and sized up a group of girls leaning in a doorway.

When he finally appeared, a half hour late, Lopez seemed to them all the prosperous man of affairs. He wore a black mohair suit, a white silk tie held to his patterned white-on-white shirt by a sword tiepin. He flicked his cigar ash defiantly on a stolen white BMW parked in front of the San Juan.

"You find that thing I wanted?" he asked casually.

"Aqui está," Mario said, brandishing the navy blue gym bag.

"Cut the Spanish," he said peremptorily. "That's why people call us spics. Practice your English, man," the elder statesman advised.

"You got the money?" Mario asked.

"Yeah, right on me. What're you, my banker or something? Walking in the neighborhood with three grand on me and get popped!" He paused to puff his Cuban cigar. "We go an' pick it up now."

"I'll jump the BMW," Rafael said.

"Great idea, we'll ride down to Port Authority in a stolen car, asshole. Get in my Honda. It's clean and I've got papers."

"By the way, Julio, an old black guy came into the apartment," Rafael said.

"And . . . ?"

"Took one look at us and dropped dead," Mario said with a smirk. "We're scary guys."

"Oh, well, that's what happens in this kind of work. The price of doing business."

T EDDY HAD DROPPED OFF THE FRERES AND DISMISSED the chauffeur. He now had Barbara to himself. "Would you like a brandy?"

He waited as she thought about it.

"Yes. Come to my place. I'll give you a grand old Napoleon I salvaged before the auction."

He had never before been invited to her apartment, and the prospect thrilled him. Was any man luckier? He rested his hand on Barbara's knee. She made no attempt to remove his hand, nor did she glare at him. He held his breath, concerned the least movement would alter her mood and once again he would be cast into the graveyard of his fantasies.

"You like touching me," she said.

"Not just for the sake of touching you."

"Really? Then for the sake of what?"

In a logical argument she'd cut his throat with the skill of a surgeon. He wouldn't feel a thing as blood spurted from his jugular.

"Well . . . I can't help loving you. It's such a good feeling."

"Isn't it just the opposite? Isn't it a sweet, nauseating feeling that wells up in the back of your throat like bile?"

"Sometimes," he admitted.

"Wouldn't our relationship be more satisfactory if you could lock me in your safe, like a stock certificate?"

He laughed, embarrassed.

"You could take me out and stroke me whenever you liked. You know there are plenty of women who'd be glad to be in that position."

"What if there are?"

"Find one."

"I've had enough of them over the years. All sizes and shapes."

"And colors?"

"Yes, and colors."

"You treated them well?"

"I try to treat everyone well."

"What was the problem with the world of women at your feet?"

"I never met anyone who had the emotional reality I have with you."

He was a man who took a position, whether buying a stock or exposing his personal vulnerability. She knew he could not live any other way and she admired his daring. He brought grace to his weakness for her.

"Was it like that with your wife?"

"Frances?" He pronounced the name, and it sounded like an echo in a hollow. "For a time, yes. Then she started to die. I was working at another big board house then. Reading the messages I had to deliver. Imagine hiring someone like me for *security* reasons. I got friendly with a broker from one of the small houses, and he used to trade the few bucks in his account and I'd get twenty-five percent. He told me that he was risking his capital. In eighteen months every trade I told him to make was a winner. I wound up with five thousand dollars, quit my job, and took the Stock Exchange test to become a broker. And all the time Frances was dying. She got pregnant around then. And I guess we both thought that was causing her sickness. How Robbie was born I'll never know. It was a miracle. A dying woman giving birth to a child. When he was four, she died."

"Did you ever want to get married again?"

"No. I was never tempted . . . not until ten months, three days, and"—he looked at his watch—"eight hours ago. When Barbara Hickman walked into my office. I thought I was immune to the disease, but maybe my vaccination wore off." He paused to light a cigarette, and she watched his face in the dark car. "I wasn't even hurt when my wife finally died. There wasn't anything I could do, or the doctors. My hands weren't soft anymore. I accepted it. I got a woman to look after Robbie; she was English, and she'd been in love with an Italian and lived in Florence. But he wouldn't divorce his wife, so after five years of teaching English to businessmen, she decided to get out. She was very good to the two of us, and she never interfered or complained about what I did. I always tried to be discreet, and I think I managed it. I had a young boy and an English lady in a small house on Staten Island. I didn't want them to be hurt or put out by . . . you know what I mean."

She gripped his hand tightly.

"You're a good man, really, and a kind man."

They were passing through the park at Eighty-second Street, and Teddy could see several lost souls plying their twisted commerce of drugs, sex, despair.

"Maybe that's true with you and Robbie, and the people I like having around me."

"Most men are shits."

"Well, that's pretty much my reputation on Wall Street. I made five million dollars when I was twenty-seven, and you can't make that sort of money by being kind and gentle. Then I put a group together and we became a gang of greenmailers. You threaten to take over an old-line company, the stock goes up, they don't want to sell, and they pay you a premium to buzz off. You do it enough times and suddenly you're sitting on fifty million." He cleared his throat. "Barbara, I want to ask you something."

"Okay."

"What do you want? I mean, really want?"

He put his arm around her, and she slipped into the hollow of his shoulder. Holding her close like that made him believe he was capable of any human exploit; and the pedigree of happiness was his.

"I'm trying to find out. It's not something that I can just point to, and it's not something . . . well, how can I explain it? Look, it isn't this—a Rolls, or great houses."

"I know, nothing material. That would be too easy. And you're no longer hurting financially."

"No, I'm not, thanks to you. I want answers . . . answers to questions I have about myself."

"Do you feel something—anything!—for me?"

"I feel your love."

"But you—what do *you* feel?"

"Empty."

When they reached Barbara's apartment, she changed her mind and did not invite him to come in.

"It's not that late," he said, despising himself for groveling.

"I think it is for me."

"I'll call you tomorrow. Will you be free?"

"I don't know. Thanks for tonight."

He peered through the latticed, wrought-iron door to make certain that she went directly into her apartment. There was no pleasing her. From his point of view it was an impossible task: money, comfort, travel, a position obviously meant nothing to Barbara. What frustrated him was the certainty that he had almost broken through her armor. Or was he deceiving himself?

FIVE

EDDY FOUND HIMSELF BACK WHERE HE STARTED from, sitting behind his massive partner's desk, running through the junk stocks Connie Hickman had left her. Through bad management and a gambling addiction, Connie's estate came to a bit over forty thousand dollars. Much of his wine inventory had been on credit, and what was left, Teddy told Barbara, should be auctioned. In the ten months, Teddy had run this paltry inheritance into six hundred thousand dollars, all of it legally, by trading the account and investing in several IPOs he controlled.

He turned toward East End Avenue and walked through Carl Schurz Park, which ran along the river and led up to Gracie Mansion. The Triboro Bridge was lit up like a ship at sea, and parades of cars moved relentlessly to Queens. Teddy passed a string of young couples on benches at the guardrail. It was just eleven, and the evening was balmy with a hint of impending rain. His relationship with Barbara was subject from the beginning to these mercurial and quixotic changes of moods, alterations of plans, as though they were votaries serving the god of chaos.

Shortly after attending her father's wake, Teddy had agreed to see Barbara as a favor to Joe Hartman, Connie's lawyer, who had done him a few favors in the early days. He had never handled Connie's account, or been privy to the vintner's bad judgment.

"Barbara needs help, Teddy. Connie's affairs are royally fucked. She's only been back in this country for a few months and she got herself a job at the UN."

"What does she do?"

"Translator, something like that."

Teddy looked out at the city from his aerie on the hundredth floor of the World Trade Center.

"Amazing how little we know about people. I thought with all his pals on the Street—including me—Connie would have been in great shape."

"He was a horse junkie," Joe explained. "He even bought shares of bloodstock from a syndicate who never had anything but claimers."

Teddy sat on the edge of his desk. "The only way people make serious money from horses is to kill them and collect the insurance."

"You should have told Connie that."

"What do you want me to do about his daughter?"

"She needs a hand. That's why I came to see you, Teddy. She's living in this all women's hotel off Lexington. It's a glorified hostel. The Brabourne. She can't even get an apartment."

"Bad credit?"

"No credit. She was working in France as a translator for some wine company."

He had felt an irresolute attraction to her from their first encounter at the funeral. When they got sloshed afterward, the attenuation of her lure expanded, but he thought it best to let grief take its course. Funerals and romance made for a doomed couple.

"Get her to call me for an appointment, Joe."

"Can you see her now? The market's closed."

"It's never closed for me."

"Well, this is a little awkward, Teddy. She's waiting in reception."

"The lioness at the gate." Teddy regarded the sleek lawyer with a smile. "Will you stay?"

"I hope you don't mind, but I'm meeting a client."

"Who you can run the meter on?"

"Yeah, at five hundred an hour, lunch at '21' thrown in."

"Do you fuck him afterward at least?"

Joe laughed. "No, I make promises and direct him to someone at the firm. I am the *signer*."

In an instant, on the closed-circuit monitoring system, Teddy observed Barbara Hickman, in a tailored saffron suit, sail through the large computer room where his drones were ferreting out currency weaknesses throughout the world.

"Your office is fantastic for a broker's," Barbara had said with a shade of sarcasm at their meeting.

His eyes were on the inflated French franc, which was taking a battering, and he spoke without looking at her. He was predicating his currency buy on lower unemployment as his France financial circles would continue to shrink the social entitlements every Frenchman considered his right.

"I am not a broker. Although once upon a time I was. I take positions in commodities, currencies, stocks, and whatever is for sale. I am an investor in markets."

"So that you can manufacture products?" she asked, curious about this man.

"No, it's too dangerous to produce a product. Cars,

for example, are too risky. They're part of cyclical markets and sales depend on low interest. I capitalize on markets. I look for strength or weakness."

"I don't understand."

"A weak company may have assets it doesn't realize it possesses. Real estate, personnel. A strong one is a prisoner of its own energy and capacity. In other words, an investor always expects more from a successful company. If the earnings are excellent but the same as last year, that's construed as flat earnings and people or analysts recommend to the public that they sell something that's perfectly healthy. They don't understand the dimensions and the limitations of growth. If you're six feet tall, you remain six feet and you can't be expected to grow a foot a year." He gestured to the window cavalierly. "The lemmings can't fathom this simple, obvious fact."

"Don't you look at people?"

"Sorry. Not when I smell blood." He pressed a button on a telephone bank and his voice came over the speaker. "Pauley, buy francs. The price is too low and it's due for a rebound."

"How much, Teddy?" came a thick voice.

"Five hundred million. The Bank of France will come in sooner than later to support the franc."

"That was a good call on the Internet stocks, Teddy."

"It was easy to predict a sell-off. Even the clowns who bought this stuff from me eventually want earnings and not an endless waltz on-line."

Barbara strolled around his office, which was used for board meetings and paneled in finely varnished walnut. On the walls were as good a private collection as she had ever seen outside a museum. The Barbizon school was represented by its famous trio, Delacroix, Millet, and Corot, and there were two fine drawings by Egon Schiele of women with their hairy privates exposed, which she looked at with interest and respect for the boldness of the artist and his patron. They were hardly what she expected to find in a financier's office. She ran her finger over a small, exquisite Degas bronze, a ballerina, which was on his desk.

"How come it isn't labeled?" she said of the statue.

"I know what it is. Degas cast three others. This is the first one."

"What's it worth?"

"Why? Do you want to buy it?"

Teddy removed his wire spectacles, which she knew he hadn't bought last week. He slipped in his contacts and noticed her looking at the glasses.

"They're sixteenth-century Italian. The desk is eighteenth-century English and is called a partner's desk. Drawers on both sides and pedestals, the paintings are genuine, and if you want any advice on antiques, I can suggest a few dealers on the Quai de Voltaire in Paris. They'd welcome you with open arms."

She was pleased by his rebuke. "I deserved that."

"Yes, you did." He looked at her with irritation. "If you buy antiques the way your father did stocks, can I also suggest that you find yourself a rich husband and a decorator? Now, how can I help you?"

She was enjoying his brusque, offhand manner, his taking her in hand firmly. "Joe Hartman made this appointment for me. He said you were the best man . . ."

"For what?" Teddy said, giving her a puckish smile, pleased to have handled a filly with sternness.

"I guess lots of things, apart from the stock market."

He pressed a button on his desk and a screen slid down from the ceiling, revealing a breathtaking painting by Seurat—one of the studies for *La Grande Jatte.*

She was flabbergasted; she rose and moved closer to the painting, standing spellbound.

"It's an original?" He nodded. "Not all partner's desks are equipped like yours. Is there a partner?"

"There was ten years ago and then I bought him

out, but I kept the desk to remind me how much I disliked him."

"You own a great Seurat."

"That's one of the reasons I bought francs. I love French painters."

Her interest in him swelled, and she said sweetly and with childlike wonder, "Can I see the rest of the paintings?"

He laughed easily, and she felt comfortable. "I'd have to take you home for that."

She sat down across from him and a vigilance enclosed her. She looked frightened, and very beautiful, Teddy thought, with a kind of quality he had encountered only in paintings: Vermeer, the frozen piercing light that illuminated northern Europe and which made the work of the Dutch school so profoundly moving—its search for the source of light was an artistic quest.

"Is it true that I have just under ten thousand from my father's estate?"

"That's a sorry fact. Joe didn't make it up."

"With friends like you, how could my father have made such disastrous investments?"

"He never took my advice. He preferred horse races."

"He has a stable."

"No. He has nothing."

"His collection of wine . . . ?"

"—is the property of the shippers. What he actually owns, you can auction. I'll buy some and I'll have some people at Sherry's and Sotheby's see what it's worth or if anyone's interested."

She winced and he decided that she needed delicate treatment, but knew she would never ask for it. There was a silence as he considered his next move.

"How about dinner?"

"I'll bore you."

"I'm a speculator."

"Like my father."

"No, not like your *father*," he said firmly. Point for her; so she certainly guessed he was twenty-odd years older than she, and she also sensed he might possibly be vulnerable.

At dinner she said, "I'd never been in a new Rolls-Royce."

She was making him touchy. "Mademoiselle, I am not a parvenu. I did not buy the Rolls last week. I'm also glad you overcame your prejudices. I'd be distressed to hear that you held it against me."

She sniffed her hands. "They still smell of leather and whatever it is they sweat."

"A Rolls doesn't sweat, it just fucking breaks down on the FDR and you really feel like a jerk when it's towed and all the drivers in their Toyotas and Hondas honk and give you the finger."

They had downed a dozen Olympia oysters each and he watched her stack the thin, delicate shells into sets of four, like casino chips. She had begun to endear herself to him and he was not oblivious of the architecture of her bright face, the warp of long, dark hair she toyed with, nor the serpentine legs below the table. Her breasts were simply flagrant, and he thought how nice it would be to have them sitting on his chin at the beach house in East Hampton.

"I think you just might be smarter than me," she said.

It was a stroking he'd heard a million times, but he was prepared to be stroked. "We'll find out, won't we?"

In the stop-start progression-regression, Barbara didn't exactly encourage him, but then again she didn't turn him down. Somewhere within this area of passive acceptance—as what, not a lover, but something akin to the professional suitor—his confusion and the sense of her mysteries were born. He possessed no dormant spirit of romance waiting to be brought to the surface; the closest he ever came to this state was "calculated risk," and this usually involved reading people correctly when a business decision had to be taken. What he had—and what Barbara brought—without his fully realizing it until it was too late and he was a trout going after a lush, multicolored fly—was his disposition to fall in love if the conditions were right. Just as the caterpillar after its diurnal sleep develops into a butterfly when the conditions are right, so Teddy's metamorphosis took place gradually, and the change that involved a degree of unconscious mimicry—a blending—grew like new skin. Her timing was impeccable.

As he stood by the park rail in the greenish entrails of the foggy night, peering anxiously at the swiftly moving tugs herding flatboats to their destination, he recognized that their first meeting was the end of twenty years of detachment.

Perhaps it was the first dinner. You make a spontaneous offer, and your life takes a different course. Maybe it was meant to take the course, diverge, filtering off into small streams. In order to justify his entrapment, he told himself that they had kept off the subject of business and that she was in a difficult position and he must reassure her. She must have been anxious, but she had the smarts to avoid money.

She might have hinted at it when they shook hands in front of the Brabourne. She could have said, "Call me when you've made a decision," or "I'd be grateful for any help." There was nothing of the kind, simply a firm handshake and "I've really enjoyed myself, and I don't think I'll ever forget it. Carve it on my headstone. 'Dinner with T. Franklin. That is all ye need to know.' " She was serious, and he felt oddly moved. It was from some poem that he had read as a schoolboy. She went through the swing door, stopping at the desk, where an older woman had given her her room key, and he stood stock-still, a bit dazed, possibly from the Calvados, possibly not. Something had happened to him, something significant, something that required recovery.

He telephoned a real estate agent he knew from the past and she had just what he was looking for on East Eighty-seventh Street: a large two-bedroom, ground-floor apartment in a brownstone with a fireplace and new plumbing. "Done to the nines, it even has earrings," she said with a real estate shark's laugh. "At four thousand a month, first and last and security, it's a steal." Teddy picked up three thousand of it, instructed the woman to contact Barbara at the Brabourne, rent it, not to bother about her references, or that he was involved. She could, if pressed, mention Joe Hartman's firm.

"Will she believe it's only a thousand a month? We're talking nineteen hundred square feet."

"Tell her it's rent-controlled. And be sure to send me a key and don't tell your new tenant I have one."

"Trust me, Teddy. See no evil—"

*I*T FREQUENTLY OCCURS IN STUD POKER THAT WHEN you have a pair of open aces and you build up the pot, you try to chase out a pair of open sixes and lose to trips. It happens in chess when you play a clever opening and find yourself confronted by the mysterious symmetry of the queen's Indian defense, but mostly it happens in dealing with people: in taking the initiative, you lose it, never regain it, and gear your resources to defense.

He had difficulty sleeping for several nights and at the beginning of the week telephoned Barbara. He heard a jabber of voices in the background.

"I'm in the hall. That's where the phone is," she said when he asked about the noise. "A crew of southerners moved in for the month."

"Is it a dorm?"

"Damn close to it," she replied.

"We never got around to business," he said.

"Is that why you called?" She sounded hurt.

"Partly."

"The fact is, I was going to contact you, but I know how busy you are. I got a lead on an apartment and it's a steal. It's on the Upper East Side."

"That's a good neighborhood. How far are you from the river?"

"A block! Isn't that amazing! And it's rent-controlled. A thousand a month. I can't believe it. Someone from Joe's office had a connection."

"A Good Samaritan."

"Probably the Virgin Mary. Teddy, I feel like dancing."

"Is the Rainbow Room too old-fashioned?" he asked. "Some place downtown—Soho?"

"No, it's perfect. I haven't been there since my dad threw me my sweet-sixteen party. Do they still kiss in the alcoves?"

"Let's find out."

Barbara was waiting outside the Brabourne when his car pulled up. There were several women standing at the entrance gawking at her as the chauffeur opened the door. One of them said, "I didn't know they ran escort services out of here."

"Could I ask you a favor?" she said.

"Sure you can."

"If you pick me up again, can I meet you around the corner?"

"Yes. But why?"

"Oh, these corn pones think I'm a call girl." She started to laugh at the disingenuous expression on his face, lifted up her skirt suddenly, and Teddy leaned away at the blazing flash of her yellow satin panties. He averted his eyes. "Maybe I just am. No harm will come to you. I'm just in the mood to celebrate."

"Oh, I thought I was getting a special bonus."

"Then why'd you look away?"

"I was pretending to be a gentleman."

"You are and you'll do very nicely."

"Barbara," he said with a serious face, "you make me laugh."

She laughed nervously. "The joy of your declining years."

"That's entirely possible."

As they drove down FDR Drive, the wind, heavy with snow, roared, slamming against the car, but she felt very safe for the first time, in years. The security came not from being in the car, but because she was next to Teddy. She genuinely liked him, but she wondered how long she could keep him at arm's length. What she knew with a certainty that the doomed St. Barbara must have felt when she went to embrace Christ was that she had at last found a man she could thoroughly trust.

Six

THE HISS OF SPUTTERING BUS FUMES CANNIBALIZED the air outside the Port Authority Building. Horns bellowed as the sixteen-wheelers came up from Ninth Avenue when Teddy entered the building. It was two in the morning. He stood in the corner by a photo booth to see if anyone looked suspicious or was watching him. He had confidence in Lopez, but he wasn't sure of the boys Lopez had used. They might be lurking in a phone booth or at the all-night coffee counter. He carried extra cash in case they hassled him. But this might not satisfy the boys. They might want more and more and more. Where would it end?

He nervously bit his lips. If he had had Frank make all the arrangements, he would have now been home in bed asleep, the apostle of innocence. Although he believed in delegating jobs, even important ones, he knew the value of secrecy. Frank as a potential enemy would be more formidable than Lopez. Frank knew too much about him as it was.

He sat down at the coffee counter, ordered black coffee, and surveyed the desolate humanity preparing for flight by Greyhound. He counted the future travelers: twenty-eight adults, nine children. All the races were represented, except the American Indian. He couldn't swear for the nationalities. He concentrated on Latino men. Six possibilities. Two were in their fifties; one in his thirties and with his family; one looked about fifteen. This left two boys, early twenties. Both were sullen, with permanently pressed angry creases around the mouth—career city terrorists whose forebears had probably held important posts during the Inquisition and passed on over the centuries an innate virulence to these two distant sons. One was noisily chewing a wad of gum, the other spat gobs of saliva through his teeth. They wore anger like a coat of armor.

Teddy sipped his coffee, a nasty, bitter blend, with rivulets of fat swirling on top. He wondered if he should speak to the two boys: Make a deal quickly and decisively. Perhaps it would be better to wait them out for a while to see if they were really traveling. He picked up a copy of the *News* that had been left on the next seat.

A steely, disembodied voice announced that the bus for Washington, D.C. was leaving in ten minutes. Several people stirred. The two boys, however, made no move to go. One was now cleaning his nails with a toothpick, and the other whistled.

They both stood up for no apparent reason he could detect and headed for the photo booth. The gum-chewer remained outside, while the other one went inside to take his picture. A few minutes later he emerged, whispered to his associate, and they both walked quickly out of the Eighth Avenue door. Teddy left a dollar on the counter and followed them outside. They were running full speed across the street in the direction of Forty-second.

He went back inside the terminal. No one looked up. He passed the photo booth, parted the curtains, and saw that the coin slot had been jimmied open. He was relieved to discover that their ambition had extended to nothing more ambitious than petty larceny. He took some coins out of his pocket and prepared to impersonate the innocent bystander looking up a number in the phone directory before making a call. He turned the pages slowly.

He found the key. It was pressed between the binding on page 248. He palmed it, like a magician astounding children, and moved to the locker section. He didn't know why he was surprised, but the key fit. The locker smelled like a rodent mortuary. He lifted the bag out and wiped his fingerprints off the key with his handkerchief.

His knees were trembling when he reached the street, and he embraced his freedom and good fortune. How could anyone point a finger at a night traveler newly returned from his excursion in Greyhound country?

At home he discovered that he was too exhausted to examine the contents of the bag.

He dozed off and slept fitfully until seven the next morning. When he awoke, the first thing he saw was the airline bag lying on the floor. He dragged himself out of bed, rubbed his head, which began to throb the moment he opened his eyes, and hit the shower.

Leonard had already brought in the newspapers and his breakfast, and stood pondering Teddy's mood.

"Are you going to skip your workout?"

"Yeah."

His hands were shaking while he shaved, and he

nicked himself twice. After he dressed and had his coffee, he started to feel a bit better. He glanced at the *Times* without his usual interest. When Leonard returned to take his tray, Teddy hastily pushed the bag under his bed.

"Frank asked if you're ready to leave."

It was almost nine o'clock, and he was running behind schedule.

"In a few minutes."

There wasn't enough time to go through the bag with any thoroughness, so he just picked at the items, which included three hour-length cartridge tapes and some folders with badly crumpled papers. He picked up one that was headed *Case History of Lawrence T. Gibbons.* Frere's handwriting was cramped, slanted to the right, and barely legible. He'd need one of those magnifying glasses with a light attachment and a portable tape deck. In a sudden fit of despair, he stuffed the papers back into the bag and threw it on the top shelf of his closet. Teddy went into the bathroom to wash his hands. He realized that they weren't dirty, but they felt unclean, as though some noxious and invisible gas had clung to him.

He barely spoke to Frank during the drive downtown. His face was hot and prickly, and he toyed with the air-conditioning control with the obstinacy of a bored child. He wasn't really a Peeping Tom, he thought to himself in a haze of embarrassment, and his only reason for engineering the robbery was that once he possessed the facts about Barbara, he would be better equipped to help her, to understand her problems.

Still, he was overwhelmed by a wave of contrition, and he wished that he had one person, just one person, to whom he could unburden himself—someone who would hear his confession, understand his reasoning, sympathize with his predicament, someone who would absolve him. He had such a person.

"You're the truest friend any man ever had," he had said years ago to his son Robbie, and the years had only enforced that conviction. But to think of confiding this to Robbie verged on madness. Maybe he needed Frere's sympathetic ear even more than Barbara did.

He closed his eyes, and he began to float dreamily toward a bedroom where Barbara waited for him.

"Mr. Franklin." Someone was touching his hand. He opened his eyes. "Are you all right?"

"I . . ." He looked into Frank's raven black-Irish eyes. ". . . Didn't sleep well last night." He got out of the car crisply, his head now clear.

"Those people last night, Dr. Frere and his wife—"

Teddy didn't wait for him to finish and said, "Pick me up at five."

*T*HE FIRST CALL HE MADE WAS TO ROBBIE. HE RE-membered with pleasure the charming apartment on Appleton Street that Robbie lived in, the rooms filled with bookshelves, the CD player humming Baroque music, the plants assiduously watered, the roof garden where his son sometimes held a party.

Teddy was justifiably proud of his son, who was now clerking for a judge; he had recently passed his bar examination. There was no need to tell Robbie to cram during his undergraduate period, because Robbie had graduated Phi Beta Kappa and later was in the law review at Harvard. What also pleased Teddy was the boy's maturity and his belief that he had to work despite being the son of a billionaire, and that neither money nor position was his by droit du seigneur to be exercised with arrogance.

He could have been worthless, Teddy realized, like the sons of several of his friends who frequently asked

Teddy how his boy had turned out so well. Teddy would shrug his shoulders and, without intending to sound sententious, would say, "Respect. It's the foundation of any relationship. Robbie knows that I respect him, and I think that's the key to it." He'd pause to let that sink in and then say with a smile, "Apart from that, my guy's very smart, and he hasn't got that instability you usually find in someone with his intelligence."

After graduation Teddy had bought him a blue Honda, his son's car of choice. Nothing flashy for Robbie. He accepted no money from Teddy, believing with almost puritan obduracy that after a man reaches twenty-one, he must pull his own weight. He allowed Teddy to pay for his skiing holiday in St. Moritz every Christmas, but that was all. When Teddy was at his villa in Antibes during the summer, Robbie worked in his office. Only when Teddy pleaded would he take a week off. It wasn't simply the pride of a young man who wants to prove a point to his elders, but the conviction that he had had advantages Teddy had dutifully given him—education, foreign travel, a position—and that if they were equals, he, Robbie, must show the world that he was more than the son of a rich man.

"I tried to get you yesterday," Robbie said.

"Phone tag is the story of my life. What's up, squire? Can you come down for the weekend?"

"No, I'm tied up. But I'd like you to come up here if you can."

He looked at his organizer. He was free to go, but it would mean being away from Barbara for two days. The thought terrified him.

"I don't know when I can make it."

"Dad, I've got some amazing news."

"I'm listening."

"I wanted you to be the first one to hear. I've asked Elaine to marry me. How's that grab you?"

"Dynamite. I really like her."

"She likes you, too."

"That's great. But how does she feel about you?"

"She loves me, pal."

"You sure?"

"Of who?"

"How you feel?"

"I love her."

"When do you want to get married?"

"Some time in June."

"Robbie."

"Yes?"

"It's just sunk in. I want to see the two of you."

"We want to see you."

"I've got an idea. The two of you drive down next weekend."

"Sounds good."

"I want to buy the engagement ring."

"I thought *I* would."

"That's my prerogative."

"Okay. But nothing too big. Say about the size of a contact lens."

"Let Elaine pick what she wants. Robbie, I'm thrilled for you. Do you think she'd like to go down to East Hampton for the weekend? We can be in town on Friday, take her parents to dinner if you like, and go down Saturday morning."

"You'll have to open the house. Isn't it a hassle?"

"No hassle at all. Just come as soon as you can. Thursday if possible."

"Okay. And thanks."

He was handed a note by his secretary telling him he was late for a meeting.

"So long, Rob. I've got to go."

He hung up the phone, and felt slightly dazed. For the first time in his life he was jealous of his son, who had discovered the perfect, requited love. Perhaps now that he had the information Frere had squeezed out of Barbara, he would be able to establish a final, irrevocable claim to her and hear with his own ears the real music of life.

SEVEN

$\mathcal{O}$N HIS WAY TO LUNCH TEDDY STOPPED OFF AT THE newsstand in the lobby of his building. He bought an early edition of the *Post* and thumbed through the pages. The *Times* had carried nothing about the robbery. Perhaps it was so trivial that it wasn't worth reporting, he thought buoyantly. Just to the side of an advertisement for Viagra on page eight a small, bold headline caught his eye. His eye retreated and his face froze, trapped in the ivory attitude of a death mask. He leaned against the phone booth to prevent himself from falling. He read slowly like a child having difficulty with word sounds.

NIGHT PORTER SLAIN BY MYSTERY INTRUDERS

Police homicide detectives were called last night after W. T. Grant, a night porter, was found dead in the apartment of Dr. Paul Frere, a prominent

New York psychiatrist. The body of the dead man was discovered by Dr. Frere when he and his wife returned last night after dinner with friends. Both Freres knew the porter, who had worked in the building for more than twenty years. In reconstructing the crime, Lieutenant Alvin Field said, "Grant probably caught the burglars ransacking the apartment and put up a struggle." Nothing of value was taken from the apartment, but in typical vandal fashion, the thieves upset the doctor's record cabinet and destroyed his records." This was an act of pure frustration, according to Field. Grant is survived by a thirty-five-year-old daughter, who when informed of her father's death said, "No one cares much about an old black man being murdered, least of all the police."

Teddy stood blinking at the paper, which fluttered in his hands as though in direct path of a wind. His knees began to buckle, and he fell against the lobby wall. He dragged himself to the bank of phones. He could hardly breathe. There was no need for him to reread the story. He crumpled up the paper and dropped it on the floor. He held his hand to his mouth to catch the sickness. He caught it just in time and forced it back down his throat, belching so hard in the process that his chest felt as though it were being struck by a hammer. His head jerked forward, and he rested it against the cool black phone. He lurched into the cocktail lounge at the end of the lobby. It was packed with young traders from the building, and he was swung around as two men hit him accidentally from behind. He didn't hear their apologies, just loud, raucous laughter, slivers of glass abrading his senses.

Men were three deep at the bar, and he was caught

in the middle of the maelstrom. Someone touched his shoulder, and he heard a voice say, "Can I get you a drink, sir?" It was one of the young executives from his office.

"A double Black Label, neat." His voice sounded normal, and he felt secure in the middle of the crowd. In a moment a drink was handed to him. He tipped down the drink without tasting it and left the glass on a table as he retreated to the street exit. He was now forty minutes late for his lunch meeting, and he tried to think calmly of what to do next. He'd have to keep his date.

Another wave of nausea caught him as he came out to the street. He began walking in the wrong direction, away from his destination toward the Battery. He stopped, looked up at clear blue sky, the color of lapis lazuli. He took a deep breath and his dread faded. For a moment he had forgotten *who* he was, and this temporary loss of identity had caused him to panic.

Calmly, rationally, he must plan a course of action; after all, he was Theodore Franklin, a power to be reckoned with in every financial capital from Zurich to Hong Kong. He wasn't some sallow-faced straphanger pummeling his way back and forth on the subway, whose livelihood depended on the boss's occasional smile and pat on the back and whose car and house were at the mercy of a cranky bank manager. If his life started to fall apart, he could always fly to Rio and spend the rest of his life there, immune to the police and the courts. Years ago, after an illegal transaction, he had salted away fifty million in Brazil, fearing that his arrest was imminent. But they hadn't touched him. He had left the money there, investing part of it in prime real estate that had quadrupled in value.

Why should he worry? Lopez was unlikely to go to the police, and the two thieves were murderers, not he. Teddy Franklin never murdered anyone. There was one cardinal rule to adhere to, he reasoned, unaware that he was talking aloud and that passersby were staring at him with amusement: he must not act out of character. He had what incriminating evidence there was safely tucked away in his closet, and the police weren't about to search his house. He looked at his watch. He was now an hour late for his appointment. With deliberate indolence, he strolled over to Broadway.

*B*ARBARA WONDERED WHAT THE COMMOTION WAS AS she looked down the hallway at the gaggle of men in front of Dr. Frere's apartment door. When she was only a few feet away, a tall, bald man with a NYPD gold shield stopped her.

"Where do you think you're going?"

She didn't like his manner or the brusque, authoritative way he extended his arm across the doorway.

"I've got an appointment with Dr. Frere."

Another man, smaller than the first, with a shock of red hair, said, "You a patient?"

"No, I'm the cleaning lady."

"Very funny," said the bald man, wiggling a toothpick in her face.

"What happened?"

Over the long arm in front of her she could see Frere talking to two men inside and a band of yellow police tape. She waved and caught his eye. He came toward her, shaking his head from side to side.

"It's all right," he informed the tall man. "She's a patient." He took her hand and led her back to the elevator.

"You going to be long?" another detective asked.

"Just a minute."

"We've had a multiple homicide in the Bronx and we don't have time."

"I'll be right back." He whispered to Barbara, "I've had police here all day and most of last night."

Barbara gave him a blank stare.

"After Teddy's chauffeur took us home, we found the night man dead in our apartment. You can imagine the shock."

"What was he doing there?"

"The police believe he caught some thieves ransacking the apartment, put up a fight, and was killed."

She pursed her lips in fright, "Oh, my God! It's like some awful tabloid story. It's a good thing you and Susan weren't there."

"If we were, I would have said, 'Take anything you like. I don't want to see your face, just steal all you want and go.' But Mr. Grant came from a different school. I guess he felt he owed the tenants some special obligation. Just terrible. And all for absolutely nothing."

"Do you mean that nothing was stolen?"

He brushed his damp hair off his forehead. "Some records, I think. Looks like yours is among the missing. I don't know, maybe they're still here. I don't think they meant to steal the records of strangers. That was just vandalism, pure and simple. They didn't take any of Susan's furs or jewelry, and I don't suppose they realized that the de Kooning and the Rothko were worth more than all the contents put together."

She was stunned, and her mouth trembled. In the background someone was shouting something about the Bronx again.

"My records?" Barbara said, dumbfounded. "That belongs to me—*us*—it's something private. It's me, my life." She was shouting. "I trusted you!" and her hands jerked frantically as though they had an independent life.

"Barbara, it'll be okay," Dr. Frere said, nodding impatiently at the detectives who were waiting. "I'm sure they haven't bothered to look at *your* record. They probably dropped it into a trash can."

"That's me. I'm in a trash can. Oh, Christ, Paul. I'm through, I really am."

"Barbara, you're overreacting. A kind old man was murdered. You're alive, he's not. Records can be replaced," he continued, losing his customary self-possession.

"What's that supposed to mean?"

"I'll see you tomorrow. If there's still a problem, my service will contact you."

She was relieved to find that Frere had lost his god-like stature. He could tell her how to act in a crisis, but his own behavior bore little resemblance to the lofty philosopher-king. She sensed that their relationship had changed because he had allowed her privacy to be violated. What right had he to expect her to keep her end of the bargain? She hailed a taxi and gave her home address. As the taxi floated down York Avenue, she caught sight of a bar that she had wanted to go into for months. It was called the York House and it had a Union Jack in the window. The bitter was Whitbread's, served unchilled, in tankards, and the place was filled with femmes fatales secretaries, cruising for a dinner.

A few gym slugs made room for her at the bar, and the dry vodka martini she ordered was half price, served in a vessel the size of a small vase because it was before seven. She sipped her half-price martini, lit a cigarette and heard Sinead O'Connor bleating on the jukebox. She tuned into half a dozen partially intelligible conversations, which ranged from the Stanley Cup on TV to Phil Jackson's contract with the Lakers. The new surroundings and the drink relaxed her.

A man behind asked, "All alone?"

"I was till now."

"Can I buy you another one of those?"

"And then what, the ferry to Staten Island?" she responded without turning. "Or are you heading up to Westport to see your wife and girlfriend."

"None of the above. I was thinking L'Absinthe for dinner and small talk. It's just a few blocks away and very good."

"I know. I live in the neighborhood," she said, finishing her drink and signaling the bartender for a refill. "Your French accent is pretty good," she observed, finally spinning around and facing a well-dressed, smiling man, somewhere in his thirties. "I didn't expect you to be this attractive *and* hunting."

He extended his hand. "My name is Alex Hammond. I am single, AIDS-free, not hunting. I work for a living with difficult people, and I'm happy to meet you."

"I am Barbara and a ball-breaker. How do you do?"

At this they both laughed and he sat beside her when the crowd began to disperse. She liked the vapor of him, which surprised her, and that he wasn't pumped up with steroids or iron. He was slender and smelled of a pleasant after-office aftershave. Lime, she thought. Royall Lyme, if she was not mistaken, out of fashion but agreeable. Conrad Hickman had used it. Alex had the mandatory professional suit, but it was unfussy and summery. The rest of him comprised an untouched-by-surgery grand nose, chestnut eyes, manicured nails, the quarter moons unscathed. He was a neatly sculpted man, with careless, thick hair, and large, straight, eggshell teeth.

"I'm a ball-breaker myself—in court only—and I insist on buying this round."

"Take yes for an answer."

He flagged down the bartender and did the air squiggle to put her drink on his check.

"Were you waiting for someone, Barbara?"

"Not now that you've come into my life."

"If you sing sweet enough, I'll take you to the opera on Saturday night. Good member seats and I have a pair."

"Thank God for grateful clients."

"Well, this one—his ass isn't in jail for life—so yes, you could say he was beholden."

"Anything more, Alex?"

"Sturgeon from the Carnegie Deli for a Sunday morning wake-up call."

"I'll bring my juicer."

"We'll spend every Saturday shopping at Dean and Deluca."

"Eli's. I don't shop, I buy," she said.

They touched glasses and laughed at their badinage.

Teddy had phoned her six times during the day, and even though she had let him twist her arm for a dinner date, she was definitely going to stand him up. He pursued her relentlessly, and he was smothering her. They were due for an argument, she decided, another hollow, pointless victory for her. If only he had the guts to stop treating her as the vestal virgin, his Madonna, she would have gone to bed with him. If it worked, his suffering would be at an end and she might think of marrying him. Life wasn't really as complicated as he perceived her part in it to be.

"What's your story, Barbara?"

"I have many. I don't know. I haven't made my mind up yet. And if I don't get to the ladies' quickly, you're going to have wet shoes."

She patched up her makeup and squirted some Naphcon A into her eyes. The idea of picking up a strange man excited her. It also took her mind off the theft of her records.

When she returned, Alex was waiting with out-stretched hungry hands beside their bar stools. They finished their drinks, but something was nagging at him.

"Barbara, what do you really do?"

"I'm . . . well . . . I do outcalls."

"What?"

He failed to contain his shock, shook his head ruefully as though this couldn't be true. She'd have to tell Frere that she was having her *Laura* fantasy again: The universal womb for legions of men and women. When she didn't set the record straight, idling to amuse herself at his expense—men in general—she realized that he had taken the bait.

"But why?" he protested. "Why would someone as attractive as you . . . ?"

She touched his hand to soothe him and knew he was on the verge of asking her price. She spared him the embarrassment.

"I work at the United Nations as a translator, and I think you're really kind of neat because you haven't been scared off."

"Do you want to scare me off?"

"Ask me after dinner. I'll pay my own way though if you don't mind."

He didn't ask her to explain. If he had, she would have walked out.

"Are you married?" he asked.

"Nope."

"I was, but I'm divorced. Are you divorced?"

"Who'd marry a wacko like me?"

At dinner she had sweetbreads in a rich, creamy mushroom sauce and checked out the terrain by allowing him to order the wine. He passed the test with a sassy Gevry Chambertin. She liked a man who could carve a wine list without her pedantic assistance.

"Do you like it?"

"Yes, and it's good value."

"So you know about wine also."

"Family business."

"You're a woman of many talents."

"And few friends," she said.

"That's probably out of choice."

"Or maybe because I'm not very good at making them. I had a friend once—oh, never mind." She stopped suddenly, catching herself about to betray a confidence.

"What'd you do, chip a tooth?"

"No, about to waffle."

"I don't mind."

"I do."

The bill came and she whipped out her American Express before he could catch her. Teddy had sold her Internet stocks and made her what she considered a staggering profit.

"I had a good week in the stock market," she explained, "and you're probably paying alimony."

"As a matter of fact, I'm not. My ex-wife makes a fortune. She's a model."

"Runway?"

"She started that way. Then she hit a home run— Armani and *Vogue*."

"Is that a happy ending?"

"I suppose. I didn't get my heart broken," he said.

"Why'd you get divorced?"

"She was promiscuous and I was loyal, and the combination never succeeds in achieving more than grief. I know couples who try it out—sometimes it works for years. Then one day the husband finds the wife in their bedroom or at a party or God knows where on her knees with someone he more than likely knows. Friends as a rule make the best lovers. They've been subjected to the same seduction as the husband and usually at the same time, so they're good investments, and if they are friends, they belong to the same economic class. They're also safe. The photographer she's living with isn't as lucky. He calls me for advice."

"Maybe I'll call you, too," she said.

"That what's it come to, huh? Or," he added quickly, "are you afraid of your old man?"

"Sometimes, yes, he frightens me."

His mouth dropped, and he gave a good imitation of someone whose feelings were hurt. "That's not very encouraging."

"Can't you take a joke?"

"Sure I can." He decided that she had initially told the truth and was now covering her tracks.

"I don't know." She held his hand. "Aren't there guys who can romance a girl with humor and make love and have a good, deep belly laugh about it without all this soul-searching?"

"There probably are. I suppose I'm looking for trouble."

"Aren't we all?"

They waited for the doorman to get them a taxi and he dropped her off first. Alex took her to the door. She fished for her keys and he pulled out a penlight. A tug passing down the river rent the silence with a thick, hoarse blast from its horn.

"Thanks for dinner," he said when she found them.

"You're welcome. Don't I get a kiss good night for my investment?" He took her in his arms, but the ironic smile on her face extinguished the intimation of passion. "Come on, don't be stingy."

He brushed her lips lightly as she continued to smile, and when she said good night, she was laughing.

"You will call?" he asked.

"Count on it." As an afterthought, she asked, "Alex, do you have a legal specialty?"

"Yes. But I don't think you'd need me."

"Why?"

"Most cases I do involve violent rich people . . . mostly murder. I guess that's my specialty."

"So you're not a public defender."

"I don't think it would pay for my co-op."

Eight

TEDDY HID BEHIND THE BLINDS IN BARBARA'S APARTment watching her and a strange man on the street. Teddy had been there for three hours. The cab pulled away from the curb. Teddy walked into her bedroom. The plant light was on and he touched her white matelasse bedspread and lay his head for a moment on her pillow, the soft Egyptian cotton fragrant with her. Her short, sheer nightgown hung over the sunny yellow chaise longue beside the fireplace.

He wasn't quite certain how she'd react when he confronted her. He heard her at the fridge, ice cubes dropping in a glass, the hiss of a bottle of soda being opened. There'd be an argument, a violent one, culminating in her death. He'd take sole responsibility for this murder, the planning and the perpetration. Perhaps that's what she really wanted—an assassin. He was relieved that the man she'd been with hadn't come in, since that would have meant another murder.

He cast his mind back to Christmas, and he was overcome with the remorse and sickness that comes from loving too much and unexpectedly. Like most shrewd men, he was capable of self-deception on a grand scale, and the deception invariably was induced by someone he thought himself wiser than. It was compounded of the simplest materials: innocence, unself-conscious behavior, and a lack of affectation, all qualities that Barbara had mastered and appeared to possess.

He brought her to his office party at La Cote Basque. The elegant banquet room was afloat in champagne, truffled foie gras, tubs of caviar, and crammed full of his executives and their wives. It had been a remarkable financial year for the company, and his team of managing directors had been rewarded with bonuses that ranged from one to five million dollars. Teddy believed in sharing wealth on a grand scale, it was the only way to keep the good people who ferreted out information and brought in new companies to take public.

He had tried to slip in unnoticed with Barbara, have a quick drink with his troops, then disappear for an intimate dinner with her. But his entrance was observed by everyone, and a buzz went around. Teddy had never brought a woman to an office bash. He made the rounds, introducing Barbara as a new client, and since this assembly comprised financial wizards, the master sorcerer's ravishing lady had to be very well connected, certainly an heiress. Where the rumor began it was impossible to discover, but by the time Teddy and Barbara had their champagne flutes refilled, the word was out. DuPont and Getty were co-favorites. No one could have imagined him with a lesser light, certainly not a translator at the UN, scrambling for a roof over her head that Teddy had covertly arranged.

"You pick stocks like women, Mr. Franklin," one of

the new hires said drunkenly.

Bemused, Teddy just nodded and smiled, and Barbara shook his arm.

"They'll have us engaged by New Year's eve," he said, considering the possibility.

"Is that an offer?" she asked.

"No, a rumor."

"Do rumors ever turn out to be true?"

"Sure. When enough people believe them."

She stood next to him, slowly sipping her drink, and the impression she created was that of a young aristocrat whose manner kept people at a respectful distance. She wasn't cold, but detached. She listened attentively to people planning ski trips to Sun Valley and Aspen. They received invitations but diplomatically declined. Teddy had a noticeable glow. Some men acquire possessions for their psychological value as ego struts. Teddy didn't; he used everything he owned, and this gave him a distinctive style. They stayed only an hour.

When he picked up her velvet coat at the checkroom, she slipped into the alcove and put her head on his shoulder. He knew then that he had finished second best in the race they were running. If he opened up, though, he might never regain what appeared to be his dominant position. He wanted to touch her but held back. The torture was exquisite. She turned and kissed him. Her mouth tasted winey and she began to passionately devour him. He was giddy with excitement. He was choking, swallowing her, and he would have been happy to die just then.

"Why'd you do that?" he asked.

"I wanted to save you the embarrassment."

"Of what?"

"Making a pass. You looked sort of, well . . . uncertain."

"You're very special, Barbara. I'm overwhelmed

with happiness."

She masked her cynicism. "We're both very special people," she replied. It didn't matter how she responded. He was blundering through passion, oblivious of irony.

"Do you think the age thing makes a difference?" he asked.

"If you let it, it will. I mean, it only becomes a hang-up if it's in your mind."

"Can we make love?"

She pulled away, shaking her head angrily, and he recoiled as though a bullet had pierced his skin.

"I don't take requests like that," she said.

"I didn't mean to."

She gripped him by both arms and shook him.

"Don't say you didn't mean to. You're a fucking liar. You meant to. What do you want, my permission? Why didn't you raise your hand to ask?"

He was stumped and frightened. Unaccustomed to disagreement, he was powerless to argue. It was simpler to put some money down on the table, cut a deal, and do whatever he wanted with a woman.

"What were you trying to be? Courteous!" She spat the word out.

"I don't know what I was trying to be. Obviously I was wrong."

Outside, he started for the car, and she ran after him.

"Do you always run away from a fight?"

"When I can't win, yes, I take a hike."

"You ran."

"Winning a fight with you isn't very important because if I win, what do I win? I'm falling in love with you. It's that simple."

"What a shitty thing to say!" She dropped her head, staring at her shoes like a mourner at a funeral. "What am I supposed to do about that?"

"Nothing."

"Teddy, there're some things you don't ask. You steal them." She was calmer now. "You pretend you've got a gun in your hand and the gun gives you the power to take what you want."

She kept him off balance, and he didn't know how to continue the conversation. Then, unexpectedly, she began to cry, and he was as unprepared for it as he had been for her mood swing. First aggressively tender, then retreating and defensive.

"Do you want me to apologize?" she said.

"No, Barbara, you're right."

"When we were inside, I felt sort of liberated from myself. I wanted to be with you."

He opened the car door for her. When he had given Frank the night off, at the party, he had been overcome by the excitement of bringing her home for a private dinner he had arranged without the staff. Gravlax, caviar, steak tartare, and Grey Goose vodka, her drink of choice. He waited for her to get into the car, but she didn't move.

"I read a poem a long time ago. There's a man swimming, and he gets a cramp. He's way out, and he starts to wave his hand frantically as he goes under. His family and friends are on the beach, and they see him waving. Do you know what they do? They wave back. They think he's waving and they just watch. Then they don't see him."

He had eased her into the car while she was talking, and she seemed confused and disoriented when he put the key in the ignition.

"I'll help you."

"When I was in Europe . . . all the time I was there . . . I kept thinking something's wrong with me, something's very wrong. I kept traveling. If I kept moving, it was all right, but whenever I got to wherever I was going, I knew I didn't want to be there."

"We'll find someone to help you."

"I'm afraid." She replied in a toneless voice. "If somebody tells you that I'd be better off if I went away somewhere, that it would be best, please don't let me go." She was crying again, and he stopped the car in the middle of the street.

"Oh, my God! Is that what you think I'd do?"

He held her very close to him and tightly.

"I swear, if I had to go into a sanatorium, I'd kill myself. I really would. I've got to get out of my hotel as soon as possible. Last night, I had a horrible experience at the Brabourne. When I came in, I passed a room in the hall, next to mine. The door was partly open, and there were two young women in bed really going at it. It was horrible, made me sick to my stomach. But I stayed there and watched, and this morning I saw the girls in the elevator, and they knowingly smirked at me! They knew I was watching. They did it for my benefit, leaving the door ajar. If I had a gun, I would have shot them both right there in the elevator."

"I'll call somebody tomorrow."

"I can't wait to get into the apartment. Have some privacy."

"Do you want to go there now? Or stay over at my house?"

"No, I don't think that would be a good idea," she said in a daze. He had never been with anyone who confounded him like she did. "Teddy, when you've found a doctor—psychiatrist—you won't ask him questions or pry. Promise me you won't."

"Of course not. Get it out of your head."

"Swear you won't."

"I never take an oath except in court. My word is more binding to me."

She considered this for a moment as though breaking it down into some code she and she alone could understand. She removed the glove from his hand and kissed his fingers, giving him chills. Embar-

rassed, he moved his hand away and kissed her forehead, then her nose and cheeks and briefly her
mouth. When he tried to pull away, she held his neck
tightly.

"Can we go to Rockefeller Plaza and watch the ice-
skating?"

He was perplexed but yielded. "If that's what you'd
like."

"And we could have a *rhum chaud.*"

"Of course."

"I love hot buttered rum. I used to go to the
Rhumerie every night when I went to Paris. It was
right around the corner from my hotel on the Rue de
Buci. I stayed at a hotel called the Jeanne d'Arc. Isn't
that a scream? I was on the fourth floor, and I could
see the church in St. Germain. The man in the room
next door said he was in hiding. I didn't believe him
until one day there was a terrific noise—in the hallway,
men with boots tramping up the stairs, and I heard
metal clangs. Gendarmes! Somebody'd shot the man
next door. I didn't hear a thing. The murderer used a
silencer, and he escaped in the métro. The gendarmes
couldn't find him, and they were furious. They gave
all the cars parked on the street tickets."

"Did you get out of the hotel?"

"No, the view was too good."

At her insistence, he rented a pair of skates for her
at Rockefeller Center and watched her swirling around
the rink. She was a graceful skater, and she could
moved elegantly. They drank hot rums and she gave
him a glassy smile. Then she went back on the ice and
something dark that she had clung to was released
and she gaily skated. She was the last one to leave the
rink. Her sweater was soaked with sweat and her eyes
unfocused. If he hadn't been with her for hours, he
would have thought she was drugged. When he helped
her off with her skates, he saw that her toes were

bleeding where the hard leather of the skate had rubbed them.

"Didn't it hurt when you were skating?"

"At the beginning, but *ooooooooh,* I feel so much better." Her feet were too swollen for her to wear her shoes, and she walked barefoot back to the car. He took her home. He had given the staff the night off. At home he prepared a basin of warm water with Epsom salts, and she soaked her feet. He could see that the water stung her raw, red toes, but she never complained. She showered in his bathroom and fell asleep in his bed, Persephone at peace. He slept fitfully in the guest room.

Now in her apartment, everything had changed. The doomed courtship had come to an end. He got up from her bed and his hand went immediately to his pocket. The gun was there, the metal warm and sticky. It was an ugly, snub-nosed .38, and the short barrel was oily.

He stealthily opened the bedroom door a few inches. The indignity of being naive, Teddy angrily thought. For ten months she had tantalized him, and he had been too enthralled to consider this possibility or understand exactly what kind of person she was. She'd been seeing other men on the sly and kept him dancing.

He was relieved the man had not come in so that he could have the pleasure of making Barbara suffer before he killed her. He didn't want to have to kill a stranger. He knew that Barbara had led the man on with her deadly combination of ingenuousness and worldly treachery. He'd become another spoke on her wheel.

Teddy had no plan of escape or thought of concealing the crime. He'd call his lawyer, explain the situation, and then make a statement to the police. He dreaded to think what was on the tape recordings

Frere had made. He had listened to about thirty seconds and had been so overcome by remorse that he could not continue.

He eased the door open a bit more and, like some Cyclops, pressed his eye hard against the door. When he saw her, she was standing in her bra and panties looking into the full-length mirror alongside the fireplace. He saw her in profile. Slowly she dropped her panties, then unhooked her bra and tossed it on a chair with her dress.

He couldn't believe what he was seeing. She was touching herself, running her fingers over her breasts as though she were a man exciting and caressing a woman. With her thumb and index finger she gently rubbed her nipples until they were full and pointed. She seemed to be humming as her excitement became unendurable. Her nipples had grown like a man's erection. She lay down on the sofa, legs spread wide and fingered her clitoris, groaning with the intoxication of this game. In a few moments, she got up and started for the bedroom.

Teddy sank down on the edge of the bed. His breathing was irregular and loud, and he thought in a panic that he might be having a heart attack. The gun was heavy, and he couldn't keep it steady. He held his right wrist firmly with his left hand. The room had two bed lamps and no master switch. She'd have to pass him to turn one on.

The door opened and she stood in silhouette, a goddess risen from the dead. She swayed slightly on the balls of her feet. He could smell her. She saw him almost at once, and she looked at the gun pointed at her.

"Teddy . . ." Her voice quavered nervously.

"Scared?"

"For a second I was. It could have been a burglar or a maniac."

He walked toward her. With inordinate delicacy, he

placed the gun on the night table.

"Why are you persecuting me?" she asked.

"I've lost my mind."

She stared at him, he wasn't certain with disgust or provocation. "Did you see me in the other room?"

"Yes."

"Why didn't you stop me?"

"You were having too much fun."

"Was I?"

He slapped her across the face. She fell back and the imprint of his palm scored her cheek. She dropped to her knees.

"Why don't you hit me with a belt?" She defiantly turned her bare buttocks to him. "Put me across your knee."

He seized her hair in his fist and yanked her close to him.

"You're mad," he said in a breaking voice; then put his arms around her bare shoulders. He lifted her to the bed. He expected her to scream but she behaved with a bewildering confidence. He wondered if she was in shock.

"Teddy, do you want to hurt me? I deserve it."

She seemed to be a guileless young girl, and he held her head in the crook of his arm.

"I wanted to kill you . . . and myself," he added.

"Oh, Teddy, why?"

"I'm cracking up."

"Bad dreams about me?"

"All the time," he admitted.

She pressed her naked body against him, slipped her arm around his neck and pulled him close to her face.

"Teddy, I wanted it to be this way. Fuck me. Be diabolical with me," she said with premeditation. "Teddy, fuck me so good I'll never forget it."

NINE

$\mathcal{L}$ ILY POND ROAD FACED THE SEA, AND IT ATTRACTED the big money in East Hampton. The older families, some of whom had been spending their summers in the town since the turn of the century, preferred Hands Creek Road and Egypt Lane because they were quieter and attracted fewer tourists. Robbie Franklin had taken his fiancée Elaine on a circuitous route, leaving the Montauk Highway at Bridgehampton and heading north to Sag Harbor.

The place names were magical to him—Barcelona Point, Shelter Island, Alewive Bridge Road—conjuring up a vision of whaling ships, rum-drunk sailors, hostile Indians furtively hiding, and the pure gold of his first kiss at the age of fourteen in the shell of a rowboat beached down the coast at Napeague. The girl had been plump, thirteen, and on the fiery perimeter of inquisitive pubescence, and she kissed with her mouth open, a trick she had acquired the previous summer in France from a fifteen-year-old Italian, who, as she described it, had mastered all the suave wiles and angles of the professional courtier.

Robbie hadn't thought about her for years, but the magic of the moment had lived with him and been reborn in Elaine, who, at twenty-two—as a result of some quixotic whim of his—remained a virgin. She reminded him of a daisy, perhaps because of her coloring: Wheat-sheaf hair and eyes as brown as coffee beans. She was a tall girl and slender as a blade of grass, with a covey of freckles on her nose and the promise of permanent childhood on her face. She had survived braces on her teeth, a proper Catholic upbringing, four years at Mount Holyoke, and despite her love of freedom and willful independence, she had never used drugs or slept with a man.

It was a blustery day, and they could feel the swirling winds rock the car. Robbie drove his Honda as if it were a horse he had taught to jump. He slowed the car to a stop, and they got out, went up to the guardrail, and looked out at the empty beach. The sand was the color of oatmeal. It was blowing in from the sea, and they had to cup a hand over their eyes. Robbie pointed to a small patch of land just visible over the drifting horizon.

"That's North Haven to the left, and up over there is Shelter Island. The Sound becomes Gardiners Bay. We sail there every summer."

She had spent summers in Nantucket, and during her teens her father had bought a rotting white-elephant Tudor mansion in Newport with rolling lawns, a gazebo, and topiary gardens in the style of Capability Brown, all of which had been overgrown and shapeless when they had moved in. It had settled into a comfortable, crumbling desuetude, but the Westins had rescued it. Robbie had spent his summer vacation there, enjoying it more than his own house because there were fewer conveniences than he had on Lily Pond Road.

"You've been very quiet," Elaine said. "Something bothering you?"

"I've been enjoying the scenery. I always like the drive down."

He was incapable of dissembling, and the lie registered on his face like poison ivy. He had stopped off at the house in New York to pick up some clothes, and he had hoped to surprise his father, but had been told by Leonard that Teddy had already left for East Hampton with Ms. Hickman. He hadn't expected that there'd be anyone else down for the weekend, and he was puzzled and uneasy about Ms. Hickman, whom Leonard had described as "a close friend of your father's." He knew that his father had had a woman for months, but he had never met her, and he had never had any desire to establish contact with her. If his father entertained any serious intentions, he would have been introduced to her months ago. Hickman was probably some old maid who was a business connection, and Teddy was probably laying the groundwork for some deal. Still, he regarded her presence as an invasion of privacy at what he had hoped would turn out to be a family weekend. He wanted Teddy and Elaine to spend some time alone.

Eight-foot whitecaps thundered on the beach. "Rob, look at that sea!"

The wind became fierce and carried salt spray with it, and Elaine's hair blew across her face. He led her back to the car. As they continued the drive, he had a fit of conscience about his attitude toward the visitor he didn't even know. He and Teddy usually agreed on people and if she weren't the kind of person who'd fit in with them, he was certain that Teddy wouldn't have invited her. He hated himself for being so selfish, especially since he was so happy. He wanted to share

Elaine with his father, believing with a touching innocence that happiness was similar to group sports and could be enjoyed like sailing. He made up his mind about Ms. Hickman: He would like her and so would Elaine.

"My father's brought somebody with him," he said. "A woman."

"Has he?"

"He's still a young man. He'll be fifty next year."

"I don't mind, but you seem to."

"He hasn't pledged himself to a life of celibacy."

"I'm glad to hear that. It'd be a waste of a very attractive man."

He visualized his father's barrel chest, the muscular arms and flat waist, his youthful bearing.

"He's usually pretty cool about it all."

"Cool or discreet?"

"Discreet then."

"So what's worrying you, Rob?"

"Stupid really. I wanted it to be the three of us, and it's sort of thrown me."

"Hey, if your father's asked her down, she's probably lovely. But you'd know more about that than I would."

"We've never talked about his personal life. I mean, he hasn't made a point of keeping it some big secret. He just never mentions it."

Despite a lack of evidence or logic, Robbie had misgivings about the weekend, which for lack of a better reason he blamed on the new relationship he and Teddy were about to begin. After all, he was going to be a married man soon, and his father would be the intruder, the odd member. For all his life he had taken his father at face value, but he realized that he knew very little about the actual man he loved above all other men. Some things you take on trust, but with Teddy everything was on trust. At the root of his anxiety was his fear that Elaine and Teddy would not get along, find fault with each other, and that a choice would be thrust on him. He would hate to be faced with divided loyalties. As some men require a healthy push into the howling, predatory world, so he required approval, which always brought out his best. He communicated his lack of confidence to Elaine.

"It'll work out all right, Rob. We'll like each other."

"You're pretty good at reading me."

"It'd be a hell of a relationship if I wasn't. I'm going to be your wife, have our children, and if I can't feel what you feel, then there'd be something awfully wrong with the messages you send me."

"I want things to go perfect with my father. I guess what worries me is that I'm trying to predict his reactions. I don't mean the stuff about 'Great, kid, you're getting married; let me buy the ring.' That's not important."

"He can't love me the way you do."

"But will he love you, period?"

"Does it matter?"

"To me. I've come to the conclusion that I really don't know him."

"Is there any reason why you should?"

"No. Just my ego."

He turned onto the hard-pebble circular driveway.

"Good God, is that the house?"

"What'd you expect, a log cabin?"

"Christ, we live like peasants compared to you. My cup overfloweth."

He kissed her on the tip of her nose.

"We love peasants."

TEN

THE HOUSE WAS SET BACK FROM THE ROAD SEVERAL hundred yards; over its colonial pillars, ivy and honeysuckle grew as tenaciously as snakes in a Greek bas-relief. The house was monolithic and constructed to withstand changes of fashion and heavy winters. It came out to embrace you like a grizzly bear, immutable and overpowering, the home of a baron or an English squire who wears his wealth as proudly as a woman her diamonds.

"Home sweet home," she said gaily.

"For quiet weekends and meditation," he replied, feeling more secure. He took their suitcases from the trunk, but stopped when a tall man he hadn't seen before trotted from the house.

"I'll take them. I'm the new houseman, Basil, sir," he said, his accent English. "I'm Leonard's nephew from Surrey."

Robbie shook his hand. "Hi, I'm Robbie Franklin.

And this is Elaine Westin. We use first names with everyone. How long've you been here, Basil?"

"Your father hired my wife and me a few months back. He performed magic with the green cards."

As they started inside, Robbie said, "Where's my father?"

"Gone for a walk with Ms. Hickman."

Robbie shook his head and tried not to show his irritation. "Didn't he get my message?"

"Yes. Leonard called to say you were en route."

*I*N A RELATIONSHIP WHERE THERE IS A DEGREE OF IN-timacy and a struggle for the dominant position is also taking place, it is relatively easy to hold back secrets about yourself, which might force you to yield ground and take a temporary backseat. It is harder, however, to hold back an attack on your opponent, especially when your intelligence is reliable and you are certain of gaining a distinct advantage and assuming an unassailable ascendancy. This was Teddy's problem, and twice he had caught himself as he was about to make a slip, and twice Barbara had prevented him by interrupting at just the right moment. His strength was her ignorance, and it was difficult to accept this as a mere defensive weapon, when it could be used to win the war. He had to tread carefully.

Despite the fact that he was happy, had won Barbara, and had demonstrated a sexual prowess and mastery over her that was intoxicating, he felt a continual gnawing dissatisfaction with the means he had used. There was no further mention of Grant, the robbery, or Dr. Paul Frere. He had two schemes: one was an anonymous settlement—by way of compensation—to Grant's daughter; the other involved a degree of danger and might expose him to never-ending blackmail. Every day he searched the newspapers for an additional mention of the burglary and Grant's murder, but the news had moved on to other fresher, more dramatic felonies.

Teddy chided himself. He had been thinking about Grant's death in an emotional way. That was all wrong and foolish. Grant was beginning to assume the spectral importance of a family skeleton, who could pop up at any time from Lopez and his friends. The more Teddy thought about the time factor, the more convinced he became of the necessity of seeing Lopez and finding out if his tracks were permanently covered. Emotionally and from a personal standpoint, Grant was coarse feed.

When there had been a run on the Asian currencies in Thailand and Malaysia, initiated by one of his peers, Teddy had taken part in the banquet. Millions had lost their jobs, homes were foreclosed, factories closed, banks failed, governments fell, families were torn apart, and people died. Some were murdered, some committed suicide, others had heart attacks and entire populations went hungry. Was it his fault, or his colleagues in the high-stakes financial circles they played in, that the people of these nations couldn't keep their houses in order?

Was it his fault that an old man had a miserable, unskilled job and defended property that was worthless—except for Barbara's psychiatric records? None of it mattered. He regretted that the old man was present on this occasion, but wasn't the life he had led prior to this event been a meaningless disaster? No one seemed to understand that the only world that counted was the world of the individual, and the world that individual created. Teddy doubted that his account was overdrawn in God's bank. God had only to look at himself to discover the true failure, the true evil. In the mirror of these cosmic catastrophes, God might see Satan.

Teddy was his own world and pleased with his creation.

In considering Barbara, the emotional content filled every channel of his mind. Theirs was the music of sexual derangement. She had struck chords of such deep, secret congress that it made him both her slave and conqueror. He had never possessed or been possessed by a woman as voluptuous and savagely imaginative as Barbara. She would choke off his orgasm and torture him, forcing him to hold back, maintaining his erection while she sucked her own breasts and him at the same time. He would bind her or she him and they would grope at each other with just their tongues. Hers was an unflagging appetite so pronounced in its deviousness that he was jealous of every second she had breathed without him.

She had a small waist, her dress label said 23 inches, her bra was 36DD, the shape and swell of her buttocks were like those of a Phidias statue. It was as if he had been given the goddess Diana. Barbara's short hair gave him a voyeur's view of her mouth and head, the beatific expression on her face when she sucked every drop of sperm out of him and he saw it glistening on her teeth like beads before she would run her tongue over them and swallow it. He was no less generous with her and explored every part of her. They were making love three or four times a day. In fugitive moments, thoughts of her expertise, the wonder of her sexual techniques, stormed through his consciousness, but he dismissed them, yielding to the pleasures of the present. He couldn't restrain himself, or keep his hands off her, even in the company of his staff, who turned a blind eye.

Under any circumstances but these he would have been delighted with a weekend with his son and Elaine, but the throbbing of his body was like a biological defense against welcome.

The water was choppy, the color of a blue marlin, and looked dangerous and uninviting. Teddy wore a thick fisherman's turtleneck sweater and a corduroy jacket and was starting to feel the chill seep into his bones. He refused to admit it, though, because Barbara didn't complain and she was wearing only a denim skirt and a thin suede jacket. He had offered her his jacket, but she had refused, and he was thankful that she had.

He and Barbara had been walking on the beach for more than an hour, and he had enjoyed every second of it. They had spoken only a few words during the time, and neither felt compelled to talk. He took her arm suddenly, led her behind a sand dune. He unzipped his fly, lifted up her beach dress, and rammed it into her from behind. Although she craved rough sex, she hated both herself and Teddy for reading her desire. In mere moments, come spurted out of him and he growled like a wild animal.

"You're perfect. You were born to fuck," he said turning her face in his palms and kissing her.

"My solitary virtue is a vice."

"It's ours."

"I should always live near water," she said, splashing her thighs with seawater. "It makes me feel secure."

"We can live anywhere you like."

"But not out here all year round?"

"It's not very convenient for me. But we could get out of the city every weekend."

"I'm a water sign. Scorpio."

"What about living in my house? Make it your own."

"It's very beautiful, Teddy, but it's your palace. You can always tell about a man from his toys."

"What can you tell from mine?"

"You're like a magician. I can see you as a boy inventor with a Gilbert chemistry set trying to make disappearing ink."

"I used to play Monopoly. Ridiculous for a grown man to admit, but I never lost a game, and I must've played thousands of times. I was a Monopoly hustler." He wondered if he ought to tell her that she was going to be rich in her own right. He had been trading her account. "I've bought some stuff for you."

"For my birthday or what?"

"No, as your financial adviser."

"How much have I got?" she asked, without any real interest.

"When the market closes on Monday, you'll have your first million. Free and clear, no entangling alliances."

She stopped in her tracks, shaking her head in disbelief. "That's impossible."

"I want you to be comfortable, have choices. Quit your job. World peace doesn't depend on you translating French for the ambassador."

"The truth is, I really enjoy what I'm doing. Just like you do."

"I've given you the kind of independence that only comes with real money."

"Will I be able to tell you to go screw yourself, if I want to?"

"You did that when you were broke, so I don't think it'll make much difference." He paused, looking worried. "If that's what you've got in mind . . ."

"Then what?" She taunted him. "Will you dump me on the street?"

"No, that'd be too gentle."

"You are serious?"

"Well, my darling Barbara," he said sweetly, "I was ready to blow your fucking head off before we went to bed. What do you think I'd do now if you walked out?"

"I'm not going to, so plan on torturing me after cocktails. I want you to get me off all night," she said, kissing him.

"We may have to be civilized. My son and his fiancée," he said with a glum smile.

Gulls cawed just above them and made a right-angle turn toward a boat that was cruising along the shoreline.

"How do you think your son's going to feel about us?"

He had grave doubts about Robbie's reaction, but he refused to reveal his uncertainty.

"He'll be surprised, naturally, but I'm sure very happy."

"Does it matter if he doesn't like me?"

"Why should you think that he won't?"

"My natural lack of confidence. After all, you suddenly wheel me into the daylight, and he'll wonder what a woman, twenty-nine on her next birthday, is doing with his father?"

"A twenty-eight-year-old woman with a million dollars to her name doesn't have to kiss ass. You have what's known as 'fuck-you money.' "

"Is that why you made it for me?"

"I had no definite motive." He considered this for a moment. "Actually, I wanted you to have some security. Now, don't worry about Robbie. We have a wonderful friendship and you won't affect it in any way. He's terrific and he wants his old man to be happy."

"Teddy, you're being naive now."

"Just hopeful."

"What's his girl like?"

"Sweet and inexperienced and good for him. Her parents are kind of . . . oh, I guess you'd say, well connected, social. They have a few bucks. He's got an architectural firm. They design up-market shopping centers and commercial buildings in New England."

"I'm looking forward to the company of a woman."

He regarded her warily. "Do me a favor, will you?"

"For a million bucks, if you ask me to comb her hair, scrub her back, sew her dresses, manicure her nails, and lend her my birth-control pills, I'll do it."

He flushed with embarrassment.

"Oh, stop. You see, she's lived a sheltered life, close family and, very proper, so just be nice."

"What does being nice mean?"

He cleared his throat, kicked an old can, and locked his arm in hers.

"Please don't swear."

"Teddy, you're beautiful." She gave him a wicked look. "Now, let me get this clear in my head. I'm not supposed to use words like *fuck, shit, suck*, in front of them?"

"Er. . . . yes."

"You realize I'll deal a blow to feminism forever."

"You are a lady."

"And you're an animal."

"Your animal."

"You know something? Until I began to see Dr. Frere I was an uptight, politically correct bitch and that's a fact."

"Oh, come on. I didn't mean it to sound like I'm a censor."

"Well, look. Now that I'm closing in for almost a year with Paul Frere, I've reached that happy stage of saying just what I'm thinking and feeling at any given moment. At least that was how I felt before my records vanished." Teddy looked away. "Frere said open the sluice gates. Don't hold back with people. If they object, then drop them. You and Frere seem to be in mild conflict."

"Barbara, give me a break. I just don't want them to get the wrong impression of you or go into your psychiatric history."

"And you're an expert on that, aren't you?"

He heard the accusation and froze. Could she possibly know, and were she and Frere testing him? He'd have to be extremely careful.

"I don't know a damned thing about your case history, and I don't want to know, unless you want to tell me about it."

"Oh, you silent, suffering, noble heart."

"Barbara, what's wrong? I mean all of a sudden—"

She put her arms around him and clutched his head against her breasts.

"Teddy, I'm so scared your son won't like me and think I got my hooks into you for all the wrong reasons. You know, some awful career bitch who's slept with half of New York to get a guy."

"I love you. Isn't that the important thing? People're going to gossip, believe all sorts of twisted things, but that can't be helped."

"That's what worries me."

"We have 'drop-dead money' and we love each other. Nothing matters to me but you."

ELEVEN

*B*ARBARA OBSERVED THE YOUNG COUPLE SITTING IN the living room in front of the fireplace. They had drinks in their hands and were whispering. She darted up the stairs before they spotted her. She insisted on changing before coming in to meet them, and Teddy with his hands outstretched, reluctant to be alone, let her escape to her bedroom. He turned and walked into the splendor of summery Matisses, Dufy, and the countryside of Cézanne's Provence. Robbie opened his arms and grasped Teddy in a bear hug. Suddenly there was no pretense in seeing Robbie; the physical presence of his son called up all the feelings of love he felt toward him.

He kissed Elaine on both cheeks and said, "Welcome to the family."

She kissed him, and he placed his arms around their shoulders and beamed with the sunshine that Robbie always inspired in him.

"Now where do you guys want to live after Robbie finishes his clerking?" he asked.

"My family is lobbying hard for Boston."

Teddy concealed his disappointment, and was relieved when Robbie said, "I'm taking the bar exam in New York, Elaine. We've discussed this."

Teddy played peacemaker. "Take the Massachusetts bar as well."

"Maybe we can keep your apartment in Boston to please my parents."

"That's a plan," Robbie replied.

"Good," Teddy said jovially. He would give them the co-op at United Nations Plaza as a wedding present. "For a moment I was worried about this being an issue. You see, I'm going to need Robbie in New York." They both gazed at Teddy nervously. "So I'm glad this is settled. Serious money requires serious obligations. My fortune isn't an abstraction, Lainie. There are companies, investments, land, and thousands of people and their families who depend on me."

Basil appeared carrying champagne, chilled glasses, and a tray of dim sum. Teddy had hired a new Chinese chef from Hong Kong for the summer.

He raised his glass. "To my golden couple and your happiness."

Elaine's luminous dark eyes had the suggestion of tears. She held Teddy's hand. "You're the kindest, most thoughtful man I've ever known. And now I know where Robbie got it from."

"I bred him as well as I could. For years, we were just two lonely bachelors waiting for our sirens to come along."

Teddy caught the sound of his own voice. He sounded hearty, successful, with the tactful humor of a socialite. It was Teddy in his pre-Barbara days, and he thought: You can keep that Teddy, I like the new one better. But it was the image that Robbie knew and

loved, and he fell into the role of paterfamilias with
ease. He had a vision of himself: White-haired, eighty,
the ancient patriarch dandling whining brats on his
lap and pursuing health in obscure watering places,
receiving injections of synthetic genes, someone's
glands he had bought so that he could sink painlessly
into the final chaos of senility.

Fifteen good, prime years with Barbara, he thought.
Maybe he had twenty years left, filled with excitement,
lovemaking, and the tantalizing joy she had brought
to him. He suddenly wondered how Elaine would react if he told her that he was responsible for killing an
old man. She'd run for her life, leaving Robbie with
his crazy father. He waited anxiously for Barbara to
appear.

Had Robbie made love to Elaine yet? he wondered.
Probably not. It was improper unless you were married. The sexual revolution had bypassed the Westins.
If Robbie had wheeled Elaine into bed already, how
good was it? Probably an old conventional lay, not like
himself and Barbara. Reflecting on the evening he
had attacked Barbara, he invisibly patted himself on
the back; it was worth it. He could have gladly blown
his brains out afterward. It wouldn't have mattered.
Some men never know the danger of lovemaking on
this level. He picked up fragments of their plans—"If
it's a boy, we'd like to call him Teddy Junior"—and he
had a wave of self-disgust and despised himself for his
shabby, misplaced contempt.

"Have you got an actual date in mind?" he caught
himself asking. He wondered if his profound lack of interest communicated itself to them. He supposed not.

"We thought the eighteenth of June. I told my
mother and she said it was perfect if it fits in with your
plans."

Lainie was really sweet and thoughtful in her concern for Robbie. He could have brought home some

lowlife and given him an ultimatum—"Love me, love my dog"—since the scions of good families were doing this more often than not. It was fashionable to tell your parents to go fuck themselves. He hated himself for criticizing the young people's propriety. What rights did a murderer have?

"I've arranged for you to pick out your ring at Winston's," he said.

"Dad, Lainie's got an old ring her grandmother left her. It's not terribly valuable, but she wants it to be her engagement ring until I can afford to buy her one."

"Forget it. As Lainie's future father-in-law, I demand certain privileges. You can afford to buy it right now with your own money."

"But it's not *my* money—it's money you've settled on me."

"Rob, don't make it sound like criminal behavior."

"Who said anything about criminal?"

"Well, then, why're you trying to make me feel guilty? Really, Rob, this conversation is starting to irritate me."

"Teddy, thank you. It's settled. I'll go to Winston's on Monday."

"Sensible girl." He decided to amplify his position. "Look, Rob, if I got hit by a car or developed a fatal disease and dropped off, you'd stand to inherit a lot of money, wouldn't you? Would you live in some dump if that happened, or give it all to charity, or what? It's our money. Do you think Lainie's folks would stand for it? So just relax, and don't think I'm stealing your manhood by *doing* a few things for you."

Robbie nodded his head thoughtfully. Teddy had to love the boy, his spirit and the absence of those vanities that money incites in young men.

"You drive a Honda when you can have God knows what—a Ferrari, an Aston Martin? You haven't bought yourself a decent suit in two years; you eat your meals in dives; you work every summer for peanuts—you won't let me do a thing for you. What're you trying to prove? That you're the better man, that you can make it without my help?" Robbie was about to speak, but Teddy waved him down. "You *are* the better man. I admit it. So the contest is over. You won. I concede, you beat me fair and square at my own game."

"I just don't like flash. But maybe I *have* been too cautious," Robbie admitted.

"Hallelujah! Now let's get started on the champagne. We've got a case to kill and only a weekend to do it in."

Where the hell was Barbara? He had a terrible fear that she had packed her bag and was attempting to sneak out of the house. Robbie had heard that there was a guest and hadn't even asked about her. Basil came in, carrying a folded piece of writing paper on a silver tray. Teddy's heart began to palpitate erratically. He glanced at the note:

Sorry, I don't think I can make it. Come to bed. He scribbled on the bottom in a nervous, angular scrawl. *I'll drag you down. I mean it.* He handed it back to Basil.

"Would you give this to her, please?"

He was restless and filled Elaine's glass, then his son's.

"If I'm not being inquisitive," Elaine asked, "who is the mystery woman?"

"She's no mystery. I've invited her down, and she's a bit nervous about meeting you both."

"Who is she?" Robbie asked.

"Remember my wine merchant, Connie Hickman?"

"Sure. He had a shop near Wall Street."

"He died last year and I met his daughter Barbara at the memorial service."

"What does she do?" Robbie pressed.

"She's a translator at the UN."

"Have you asked her to do some translating for you?" Elaine asked so seriously that Teddy could not contain his laughter.

"She's doing a bit more for me, sweetheart."

Robbie gave him a puzzled glance, and Elaine leaned forward, propping herself on the edge of the deep leather armchair.

"Like what?" Robbie asked.

Teddy wanted to run out of the room, make the two of them disappear. He had played the scene several times in his mind, but the actual confrontation completely unsettled him.

"I'm going to marry her."

"Are you serious, Teddy?"

"Yes, I'm always serious about marriage."

He resented the remark and thought that Elaine herself, an interloper, ought to mind her own business. He had imagined it would be easier to tell Robbie with Elaine present, but he was wrong. He waited, with a mixture of disquiet and positive excitement, for Robbie to speak.

"Maybe I better leave the two of you to—"

"No, stay, honey," Robbie said.

"Well, if you're sure that you and your father don't think I'm interfering, I'd like to stay, since I'm practically a member of the family."

Robbie appeared more startled than dismayed by his father's announcement, and Teddy knew that he had handled the whole thing tactlessly. Robbie sucked in his cheeks and played with the forelock of his hair, a sign, Teddy remembered, of childhood agitation.

"I'm sort of breathless," he said. "I'm happy for you."

"Are you, Rob?"

"Sure, why shouldn't I be?"

"I don't know. You don't look pleased."

"Why didn't you tell me you were seeing someone?"

"Was I supposed to?"

"Of course not. I just would have liked to have met her before today."

"It's not something sudden. I've wanted to marry her for months. It's just worked out *today*. I thought this would be a good time to tell you. We both had some good news."

"How long have you known—?"

"Barbara. It's almost a year."

"You played it pretty close to the vest."

"I didn't want it to be premature and find that it wasn't going to happen."

"Sort of like a business deal. No leaks."

Teddy smiled. "You know me."

Robbie extended his hand, and Teddy took it anxiously and clasped it with both hands.

"I was very anxious about how you'd take it."

"I'm as happy for you as you are for me."

Elaine smiled at them. But she had the unnerving suspicion that she had finished second in a beauty contest. Her plans about being the confidante and queen in Teddy's hive were now unrealistic. Sunday morning brunches with the lonely billionaire who would adore her as much as his son were part of the fantasy she had constructed. She'd be damned, though, if she'd be the one who'd sit with her back to the room when the four of them went out to dinner. Her claim was an earlier one, she knew, but her position was weaker, and she wondered how she could establish her ascendancy over Barbara. The daughter of a wine salesman.

Her weekend was spoiled, but she was determined to make it absolutely clear to Hickman that she didn't want any maternal advice or a big sister. How many men had Barbara had before grabbing Teddy? They're like children, these middle-aged widowers. Obviously, Teddy was sleeping with her; when you bought that kind of a toy, you made dead certain that you enjoyed playing with it, especially on rainy days. Elaine wanted to cry because her happiness with Robbie now seemed irrelevant to Teddy. Like most women, she concealed her self-interest skillfully until it was threatened.

"Barbara should fit in nicely. Let's see, Lainie, you're twenty-two, Rob is twenty-three, and Barbara is"—they waited apprehensively—"senior. She'll be twenty-nine. It's going to be a merry band."

"I'm going upstairs to change," Elaine said, getting up from the chair and quickly walking out of the room so that Robbie's "What's wrong . . . ?" went unanswered.

"Is something bothering Elaine?"

"No, I think she's knocked out from the drive."

"I hope that's all," Teddy said suspiciously. "I wouldn't want her to feel that her position's changed and that Barbara's going to compete with her. I really want them to be friends. Lainie'll be good for Barbara."

"What about her *own* friends?"

"Her own friends?" The notion puzzled Teddy. "She hasn't got any. I'm her friends."

"That's a big responsibility."

"I'm prepared to assume it. Rob, I'd consider it more than just a kindness if you and Lainie made a special effort to draw her out."

"Are you going to tell me any more about her?"

"No, Barbara'll do that."

"I'm going to grab a shower, Dad, and lie down for a while."

"Okay. We'll have dinner at eight and drinks at seven-thirty. And, Rob . . ."

"Yes?"

"You're a very kind man; please show Barbara why I'm so proud of you."

"Do I get a medal for it?"

"No, just my gratitude."

"I'm sorry. I didn't mean that."

Teddy embraced him then walked with him up the wide, spiraling oak staircase.

"You don't have to apologize to me."

"I guess I'm a little rattled myself."

"We're both shrinking grooms," he said solemnly. "Oh, I've moved you out of your room and next to Lainie."

"We haven't—"

"What you have or haven't done is your own business, not mine. What you may *want* to do is still less my business."

"Are you suggesting—?"

"Absolutely nothing. I'm only trying to be a good host." At last his son smiled at him, and he knew that he'd won a temporary victory. The rest would be up to Barbara. If they didn't get along or disliked each other, he'd suffer, but not nearly as much as he would without Barbara, a prospect that was to be feared more than death.

TWELVE

TEDDY KNOCKED ON BARBARA'S DOOR FOR A MINUTE, and when she didn't answer, he walked in. She was sitting at the window seat with her back to him, a cross, spoiled child banished to her room and paying back her parent with a case of the sulks. He touched her hair, and she twisted her head away from him.

"Why didn't you come down?" She didn't answer. "It was damn rude."

"Don't play schoolteacher with me."

"Then don't send me stupid notes."

"How's the happy couple?"

"They're fine. They only wanted to meet you, and you could've come down just to have a drink."

"Yes, sir."

"Oh, Barb, give in a little, will you?"

"Don't call me 'Barb.' My father used to, and he's dead, and I liked the name when he used it because it was as a friend and not 'Barb, you're a naughty girl.' "

"I don't know what the hell we're quarreling about."

"I don't know either. Maybe because I feel like I'm in the way and that I don't enjoy cornball announcements like engagements. I mean, what the hell is an engagement anyway?"

"If we got married first, Rob might feel we were stealing his thunder."

"Oh, shit, all these conventions are one goddamned bore. I've got to float around like a fiancée for months."

"I agree with you."

" 'Meet my fiancée.' It's a fucking musical, that's what it is. A musical with no score, just a lot of sentimental lyrics that rhyme." She put a hand to her mouth and mocked him. "Oh, I forgot, I'm not supposed to swear. It's very coarse, isn't it? Not refined like giving you a blow job."

He'd never known such helplessness, such an inextricably difficult situation, and for a moment he wished that he'd never met Barbara or that he had and she had died tragically and he could spend his life mourning her, tapping women on the shoulder at bars and parties who he mistakenly thought were reincarnations of Barbara. To placate her was, he discovered, a losing tactic, but he felt tired at the moment and old, ready for a sauna, a massage, and an evening of old movies on TV, with a bowl of fruit on the night table.

"What do you want me to do?"

"Just call me a dumb cunt."

"Take it as read."

"This isn't a board meeting you're presiding over."

"Okay, you're . . . a dumb cunt," he said, hating the sound of the word.

She opened her arms to him, and he sat squashed at the window seat beside her. She shook his hand, as though sealing a business deal.

"Now we can be friends."

"I love you madly, Barbara."

"I had such an urge for you when you were down-stairs pouring champagne and looking very lord of the manor. I could have just jumped on you."

"I'm glad you didn't."

"Miss Westin wouldn't have approved, would she?"

"Probably not."

"Is she religious?"

"Convent educated."

"I used to see girls like her all the time. Blond hair, preppy, plaid kilts, books covered with the school name, like it was a big deal. That didn't prevent them from playing with themselves in the dorm. All so dishonest and rah-rah and getting laid by every football player."

"She's not like that at all."

"No? Well, she reminds me of them. Westchester country clubs, and abortions at fifteen. They'd prance into my dad's shop with their parents and their junior Gucci bags while I was carrying cases of wine and they'd look at me like I was underprivileged." He kissed her fingers. "Am I a bitch, Teddy?"

"Yes, absolutely. One hundred percent honest bitch."

"I'm glad you said *honest*. It's just that when I see a girl like Elaine, I get out my flamethrower."

"You don't need it."

He started to unbutton her blouse.

"A fast and furious one before dinner?"

He looked at his watch. It was five o'clock. "There's plenty of time."

"Can we have a bath together afterward?"

"Why not?"

"Am I really good for you?"

He was starting to perspire, and his knees jerked reflexively.

"I was like a sleepwalker when I met you."

She lifted up her skirt and said, "Happiness is *no* panties."

They used the large sunken bath in his room. She turned on the Jacuzzi and roared with childlike pleasure.

"I hope to hell Rob doesn't knock on the door."

"He won't."

"How do you know?"

"I put a sign on the door: 'Out to lunch.' "

"You didn't."

"Take a look."

"Oh, Christ, what'll he say?"

"Not a thing. He'll just know he may have to wait awhile for his inheritance."

She began to blow soap bubbles at him playfully, a child having a game with a parent. She sat in between his legs in the bath and he stroked her back with the sponge. Her vellum skin glistened in the water, and he slipped his hands beneath her breasts and arched them, toying with the nipples. She sighed with pleasure.

She had a small waist, and her body was extremely firm without being muscular or worked to death. He slipped his head under her arm and kissed her wet, soapy neck. Reality never quite lived up to the expectations of fantasy except at that moment, Teddy reflected. His winter of sorrow, of agonizing uncertainty, his inability to touch the dark side of Barbara's mind, had now in the warm water become the tangible velvet, the soft skin of life. They were breathing the same air, sitting in the same water, and for the first time since he had known her, he believed that they were communicating on a common level; most of the time he was excluded, but now he was at the very center of her universe.

One of the disadvantages of contentment is the leveling off of the erratic sexual peaks of desire: to

achieve one's goal, one's purpose, is to lose it at exactly the same moment. Teddy was like a marksman
who scores a succession of bull's-eyes at fifty yards and
then discovers that because his skills are secure, he
must extend his range to a hundred yards and repeat
the exercise until he is proficient.

The relationship he wanted with Barbara took the
form of an infinitely erotic progression. If he rounded
out the picture of conventional life—children, friendship, travel, security, the entire composite perfume of
the elusive love life—he would find something lack-
ing. He would want more. It wasn't simply ownership
he was after, but the complete possession of the core
of her being, every thought in her mind, every sensation she had ever experienced, the sum total of her
existence.

He wondered if Barbara had had some instinctive
perception of his aims and had fought him without
knowing why she was fighting, but because of his
greater force had given him a small part of herself
while concealing the core, simply to pause in the action and regroup her forces. Did she understand his
quest, which was nothing less than the pursuit of the
lover, mother, sister she embodied for him? The ultimate, complex Madonna, who at various times
emerged in the myriad and interchangeable roles of
Demeter, Athena, Aphrodite, and the queen, Diana,
the stalking, graceful, omniscient huntress who in another manifestation was the doomed and martyred
Barbara, standing at the three windows that overlooked the light-spangled courtyard where her father
would reveal her destiny, the last vision?

He sat on the stool and dried her toes. He had a dis-
tracted expression on his face.

"You look like a boy when you're not thinking about
anything special," she said. "All the lines go."

"I didn't know I had any lines. Plastic surgery isn't an option for me."

"Shit, no, Teddy. It would erase your character. I like your face. It's a graph of everything you are. In the next life I want to be born with your Roman nose. Why hasn't Robbie got it?"

"His mother won that battle."

"His mother won most of the battles. He's not like you at all, Teddy. I mean, in looks. I was sitting on the staircase watching you all. He's kind of nice and straight, and he'll still have that collegiate-manner style when he's forty."

He kissed her ankle. "Let's get down to important things. Do you like powder on your feet?"

"Only if it isn't Estée Lauder or some fancy French crap. Johnson and Johnson baby powder is my brand."

He took the container from the medicine cabinet and powdered her feet, then helped her on with a blue Japanese kimono.

"I love this robe," she said.

"They come from the Oriental Hotel in Bangkok. I get a dozen every year. I'll put it on your Christmas list."

She rubbed the robe. "It's the ultimate in sexiness, not like chiffon or lace negligees that women always buy one size smaller so their tits slink out like rabbits' noses. My tits are size thirty-six, and finally I'm proud of them, and I don't have to make them look bigger or sexier than they are. For years, I was self-conscious."

He laughed. "I love every inch of them and you have every reason to be proud. I'm glad I make you proud of them. You're the most dazzling woman in the world."

"Does that mean I'm a good fuck?"

"The best," he said with an animal purr. "You're the only honest, gutsy woman I've ever known."

She reflected for a moment on her last visit to Dr. Frere and the panic she felt about her missing records.

"You can thank Dr. Frere for that. I was so frightened and cowardly about myself when I first started seeing him. Someday I'll tell you about it."

Teddy no longer had any desire to probe through her past. He owned her now. "How about June twenty-fifth for a wedding date?"

"What's wrong with Halloween or Guy Fawkes Day?" She enjoyed ragging him. No one else had the nerve.

"It's the week after Robbie and Elaine."

"Is that when we come of age?"

"It's just more convenient."

"There you go, plotting and scheming. Can I call you Theodore after June twenty-fifth?"

"No, you can't."

"Okay, then, I give in."

"We'll have any kind of wedding you'd like."

"I want minstrels and acrobats, jugglers, magicians, and I'd like sides of venison, saddles of mutton, barons of beef, so that it looks like the court of Henry the Eighth. How about trying that on the banqueting department at the Plaza, or the Carlyle? We'll get Bobby Short to sing for us."

"Let's get serious, Barbara. Do you really want a big wedding?"

"Why not, are you cutting corners? Don't you want to show me off to all your fat old friends?"

"Not particularly. I thought we could have a quiet civil ceremony, then a reception at a hotel or restaurant. Do you like the Four Seasons, Lutèce, the Carlyle? One of my houses? Pick a place, a country. You've got *me*, which means you've got the world by the balls."

She put on her high-cut yellow panties, fastened her bra, straightened the straps, buttoned a white linen blouse and slipped on her skirt. She looked so young and pure; her face had a healthy outdoor sheen that would be tan in another day.

"There, I'm respectable."

"In theory," he replied, now in seersucker trousers and a navy blue Armani shirt and a pale blue blazer.

"What a pair we are," she said with a lascivious glint in her eyes.

"Help!" he moaned.

"That's what you need when you want to marry somebody younger."

He caressed her, cherishing every moment he was with her. "I love you."

"For real?"

"Let's get going." He slapped her on the backside. "We have guests."

"You go first and break the ice."

THIRTEEN

$\mathcal{B}$ARBARA STOOD TIMOROUSLY ON THE LANDING OF the stairs, straining to listen to them talk. She had lost her nerve, and her bravado with Teddy had vanished. Their voices carried through the darkened hallway, but all she heard was a confused gabble of sound. She descended slowly and with ceremony. Three heads in the lamplit living room turned as she approached, swishing. She walked with the extreme concentration of a bride frightened of tripping over her train. No one said anything, either, she thought, out of irritation because she was late or because she had done something wrong and they were deciding on a suitable punishment.

She stopped at the doorway. Teddy came toward her, took her hand, the high priest about to initiate the young couple before him into the twin mysteries of fire and blood, so that their union would be blessed. Teddy pulled her along into the room but felt her resisting. Robbie and Elaine rose. Their faces, she thought, revealed impatience and puzzlement. Robbie's hair was straight and carefully parted on the right side, and his eyes were a dusty gray, attentive to risks. He shook her hand, and his long, reedy fingers were cool and surprisingly strong.

"Hello, Barbara, I'm Robert."

"Robbie," Teddy said in a manner that was both affectionate and corrective.

"Hello, Robbie."

Elaine's face was half shadowed by the setting sun. Reluctant to give ground, she waited for Barbara to come to her. Barbara detected the talons of jealousy emerging as though from a bat's claws. As she came closer, Elaine's features became clearly visible. For a moment Barbara lost her voice, and realized that she was staring disconcertingly at Elaine, who said, "Have we met?"

"No, I don't think so."

"Maybe we've seen each other, then?" Elaine insisted.

"I went to Radcliffe years ago."

"It might have been at some restaurant or at a museum."

"That's possible."

"I'm sure. Like generations ago."

"I left Boston after college, and I haven't been back."

"Barbara Hickman." She pronounced the name as though it were the answer to a riddle. "I can't figure out the association, but I've got one. Did you always wear your hair short?"

"No, I had it cut recently."

"I wouldn't be surprised if we knew some of the same people."

"Could be." Barbara held her hands behind her back to prevent anyone from seeing them shaking. She'd give Elaine a false scent. "I used to go to the usual student hangouts." She never had.

"Probably I saw you in one of them."

"Can I have a vodka on the rocks with a twist?" Barbara said to Basil, who was lingering patiently by her side. Her voice had a tremor in it, and she tried to control it. Fortunately, the lighting gave her an advantage once she was seated; it was diffuse and coming from a lamp at the other end of the sofa. Except for the nose, which was a bit shorter than she remembered, Barbara might have been sitting next to Laura Sargent, and the thought—although shocking because Laura was dead—was strangely comforting. Possibly Barbara could now reveal what had been unspoken.

"We've got a double celebration ahead of us," Elaine said, picturing herself as bride and maid of honor, unless Barbara had a best friend destined for the part.

"I hope so."

"You must be thrilled."

"I am, it's just that"—Teddy hovered—"I wasn't sure that this was the best time to make any announcements. You came first. . . ."

"I told you she was thoughtful," Teddy interjected.

"Robbie, I'd like you to know that I really tried to put your father off until the two of you were settled."

"I'm glad you didn't."

"So here we are, two professional fiancées with our guys."

"Is my hair okay?" Elaine whispered.

"Yes. It's fine."

"I thought the way you keep looking at me that it was messed."

"No, you look quite lovely."

"I feel lovely."

"Barbara, I've got something very important to ask you," Teddy said, addressing her as if she were a member of the board.

"Well, let's live without mystery."

"Are you up to getting drunk before dinner?"

There was an edge to Robbie's laughter, and Elaine lifted her glass forthrightly and said, "I nominate Robbie as toastmaster."

"Do us proud, Rob."

Robbie cleared his voice. "To strangers and friends."

"I'd like to say how happy I am about becoming a member of your family."

"And we're lucky to have you," Teddy said, seizing the top of Barbara's chair to steady himself.

Eventually dinner was followed by an erratic rubber of bridge, which Teddy yawned his way through. He made his apologies, sipped his cognac serenely as though it contained magical properties, and left the trio of young people to discuss their plans. Elaine struggled to keep her eyes open, pecked Robbie on the mouth before disappearing upstairs into one of the wings of the rambling house.

Barbara was wary of the young lawyer and decided to confront the issue. "Don't you like me?"

"Is it important or relevant?"

"Very. I want to be your friend."

"You're going to be my stepmother," he said as though swallowing poison.

"Ah, come on, don't be silly."

"I'm your stepson or soon will be. It makes me feel a little awkward. Sort of a strange sensation to look at a woman like you and think of you in that way."

"Then why bother?"

"It's a fact of life and a legal reality."

"Don't talk shit. What do you think I'm going to do: boss you around, give advice, or cut off your allowance?"

"No, I'm independent of you and my father."

She knew that this would never be a comfortable situation either with Teddy's family or his friends.

"Rich, single men don't marry women from their age group."

"Do you have any evidence of that?"

"They may date them or drag them out as an armpiece, but they don't like fucking them," Barbara said.

"Exactly," he said.

"Is that supposed to mean that I'm a clever schemer with some kind of master plan?"

"I'm not the best judge of that. Although you have convinced me that you have a gift for irony and understatement."

"In what way?" she snarled.

"When you call my father rich, it's like saying Tiffany sells trinkets."

"Okay, you drew blood."

"I really don't know what you expect me to say, Barbara. I'm in a state of shock."

"You're a good actor."

"I love my father very much, and I wouldn't want to make him feel uncomfortable."

"Well, then, we're on the same side."

"Time will tell."

She lit a cigarette and he batted the smoke away from his face.

"Don't you want to be my friend?"

"We don't know a damn thing about each other. Maybe we're temperamentally out of tune."

"Are you willing to find out?"

"Of course I am. I don't have much choice. I'm engaged, Teddy's engaged. It's a fait accompli. We can celebrate our anniversaries together."

She had seldom encountered personal success by going out of her way to please people and the toll of failure registered at this moment. Robbie's animosity had a viperish sting, but then again he was a newly minted lawyer who had charged out of Harvard.

"We'll try to be civil," she said.

"If you're going to hustle me, you'll have to do better than that."

She got up from the card table, white-faced and tense.

"Good night, Barbara."

She wanted to cry but held back. "Give me a chance, will you?"

"I apologize," he said coldly. "I've behaved badly."

"You know, it hasn't been easy for me. Your father's behaved like a lunatic the last few weeks."

"Don't you dare talk about him like that to me."

"I have to talk to someone."

"Well, I'm the wrong one. I think you're an astonishingly beautiful woman, well educated, obviously very shrewd, and you've caught the great white shark."

"I caught—? You don't get it, do you?"

"I'm sure it's been a great strain on your resources and I hope the two of you are going to be extremely happy."

She began to cry and ran out of the room. Robbie stood there numb, a graven statue. His body ached with tiredness, and his left eye began to twitch from the strain. He had put on an Academy Award–winning performance at dinner and deferred to her about everything, even the wine, which she talked about for ten minutes the way some emotionally unstable women do about their cats. She had spoken five different languages, and he had only caught a few words of French, which he had only half understood.

On top of it all, he didn't know why, at that precise moment—maybe the house or the sea air or earlier the sounds of fun and games coming from his father's bedroom—something had created a desire in him for

Elaine that made his knees go weak. His shoulders caved in, and he slumped forward as he walked upstairs to his suite. As he began to undress in his bathroom, he heard a whining staccato of breathless gasps coming from the upstairs deck.

He ran the water full blast, hoping Barbara would hear it and stop crying. Limply, he dragged himself into the shower. He heard nothing now but the cascading water slapping against the tiles. He dried himself in the shower and put on a pair of shorts. She was still crying, and he was overcome by a wave of sympathy for her. She was unsure of herself, vulnerable, and possibly not a tough nut who was out for a free ride. He combed his hair, came out into the hallway and found her still on the deck. She was in a sheer white nightdress, and her face had a crazy zigzag of half-wet tears. Her eyes were black from the running mascara.

"Barbara, let's forget what happened." He held out his hand. "I was really out of line."

"Thank you. I never had a plan or a scheme. And I'd rather end this with your father than come between you."

He nodded mournfully. She kissed him on the cheek, and he felt the swell of her breasts, their thickness and depth, the weight and power of her body, and the warmth of her breath on his cheek. She smelled of honey, and he was oddly frightened of her. A thought flashed through his mind, and he stepped back suddenly as though avoiding the thrust of a knife.

"I feel better now," she said. "You're so generous."

Robbie went into his room, turned off the light, and climbed into bed. The sound of the waves crashing down on the beach calmed him. He turned on his left side and almost at once drifted to sleep when, without realizing it, he found himself staring at the shadows dancing on the ceiling. Voices from the next room hung listlessly, like drowsy flies in the air, and he tried to shut them out, but he could almost hear the conversation.

He continued to listen. He got out of bed and pressed his ear to the wall. He hated himself at that moment, since he had never before in his life attempted to invade the privacy of other people and had thought until this moment that he was incapable of it. The voices stopped, but other, more unnerving sounds took their place. He heard Barbara groan, and then his father grunting. Sweat ran into his eyes, even though the night air was cool and his window was open. The harder he tried to ignore the intense noises, the harder his ears fought to detect them. Something about their lovemaking struck him as distasteful, unclean, and he wished that he could punish his father and Barbara for their indecency.

The word *indecency* made him swallow rapidly, and he said aloud, "I'm a goddamned hypocrite."

The sexual aspect of their relationship didn't worry or surprise him; he took that for granted like abortions, kids smoking crack, the gay world, and all the other former taboos. What had happened was less obvious and much more upsetting, since it tore a sizable hole in the long-standing relationship he had with his father. He objected to the *manner* of the affair, a fine point perhaps, but he was a young man with an elaborate network of delicate feelings which, because of the times he lived in, seemed somewhat anachronistic. He didn't like to put himself in a seat of judgment.

The moans, sibilant sighs, and low, languid moans, continued unabated until he found himself lost in some pleasure garden of whores and uninitiated teenagers, all of whom extended their arms and lifted up their dresses to snare him.

He leaped off his bed and furiously stalked around the room; wild, breathing heavily, inconsolable. He opened his door and strode down the cold, long corridor that snaked into different wings of the house. He could find his way anywhere blindfolded. There was a light on in the living room, and he gripped the banister tightly and headed downstairs. He opened the liquor cabinet, pulled out a bottle of fifty-year-old Napoleon brandy, and poured himself an enormous drink. It went down smoothly, and he sat down on a chaise lounge. It was almost three o'clock, and he knew that he wouldn't be able to sleep that night.

He bolted back upstairs, this time in a rush, purposively, with a plan. Outside Elaine's door, he turned the knob slowly, cautiously.

He had a vision of Barbara naked, waiting, compliant.

He dropped his shorts and slipped into bed with Elaine. She turned over on her side, her back to him, then, suddenly shocked, swung her head over her shoulder and opened her eyes.

"Robbie?"

"Yes." He had slipped his hand under her nightgown, and his fingers glided down her belly.

"What're you doing?"

He lifted up her nightgown and began to kiss her breasts.

"Robbie, please."

"Please what?"

"*Don't.*" It was an order, but he ignored it.

Was this how a rapist felt? She pushed his head away and held his shoulders at arm's length. "Why now?"

"Because I want to."

"I don't understand. We're in your father's house."

"What's that got to do with it?"

"Look, we've waited."

"I'm tired of waiting."

To preserve Elaine's virginity, he had an out-call service send over a fresh recruit once a week.

"What?" There was an edge of panic in her voice now, which excited him even more. "Whose idea was it to wait? We've had so many opportunities in your apartment, in mine. Last summer at my house. I wanted to. I couldn't think of anything else but having you. But here? Now? Your father and that—what's her name—just down the hall—"

"She's screwing his brains out."

"Don't talk like that."

"Like what, for Christ's sake?"

"It's me, Elaine, not some whore from south Boston. I don't like it."

"I want to make love to you, right now."

"Can't you wait just till we get back to Boston? We'll be alone. Don't you want it to be nice the first time?"

He pushed her arms down and she twisted her head from side to side. He forced her thighs apart by digging into the soft flesh.

"She's fucking him," he protested.

"I don't care. If you want a fuck, maybe she can accommodate you, too." Elaine was too angry for tears, and he released her. "I'm very tight. The first time it's bound to hurt me. I don't give a damn about that, but can't we do it romantically and with some privacy? Can't we, Rob? Is it asking too much?"

"Forget it."

"Please, not this way. I'll move in with you when we get back, anything. I don't feel any guilt, and I don't care about what my family says."

He thought of any number of arguments, but none of them was as strong as hers.

"Do you want to stay with me tonight?" she asked.

"And do what, talk?"

She began to cry with such deep forlornness that

her pain tore through him, but he was incapable of consoling her at that moment.

"She's ruined everything . . . that slut," he heard Elaine say as he left the room.

FOURTEEN

*R*OBBIE SAT IN A ROCKING CHAIR ON THE UPSTAIRS deck facing the ocean. Except for the continued thundering cascade of the rough sea and the squeaks from the rocker, the house was quiet. Beyond the low horizon a thin gossamer veil of gray light swept up from the east. It was almost five o'clock in the morning. He couldn't remember ever feeling such a mixture of sadness and depression. When he tried to close his eyes, he imagined for a moment that he had awakened from a drugged sleep. Something had been removed or lost, and he knew he'd react logically, calmly, if he could find out exactly what had been done. Family conflict was not a natural part of his experience, and he was unprepared to fight. Somewhere along the line in the last twelve hours, the rational process of his life had become entwined with a mysterious black seed that threatened the orchard: Black apples would grow on the branches of black trees, and the infected trees would kill all the others in the orchard until they prevailed, glowering, tempting.

He had to make it up with Lainie. Even if she forgave him—and she would, he was certain of it—the rest of their life together would be shadowed by what had happened. To consider it purely in the light of a sexual attack was to oversimplify the situation, since the sex aspect of it was rather unimportant, he realized. He wanted Barbara and had turned to Elaine, and the damage had been done right before their eyes.

He nodded off, sleeping fitfully for an hour. He stood up, stretched, his bones cracked, and he decided to get dressed and go for a walk on the beach to clear his head. He caught something out of the corner of his eye, a movement beyond the sand dunes at the water's edge. He wondered if a lack of sleep had made him see things that didn't exist. A head bobbed up, but he couldn't tell whether it was a man or woman. He craned his neck and recognized Barbara. She hadn't spotted him, and he froze. She had on a bathrobe, and she sat down on the beach and put on a pair of flippers and a mask with a snorkel attached to it. He wondered if he ought to join her for a swim. She dropped the robe and stood there naked. He recoiled, backing away to the French windows. She turned, full view to the house, unself-consciously to see that she was unobserved, but he got the impression that she wanted to be seen, to tantalize whoever might be watching.

Was it some kind of erotic ritual that she performed for his father's benefit, or to entice him? He thought of closing his eyes, but he couldn't. Before he realized what he was doing his hand slipped into the fly of his pajamas. She turned around, facing the sea, and walked in, then dived into a wave expertly, a kingfisher after food. She came up quickly and did a smooth

crawl in the direction of the barrier of rocks that separated their private beach from the public on the western side of the property. She swam with rhythm and a
fine sense of timing. As she climbed to the rocks, a
wave crashed down on her back and she lost her foot-
ing. He hoped she'd hit her head and was lying unconscious at the point of death, water filling her lungs,
a final death gasp, then oblivion, to be discovered eye-
less and bloated on some beach down the coast with
the rest of the driftwood and jetsam. The vision of her
dead, naked body excited him, then terrified him, and
he wanted to go to her, but he'd never get there in
time. He caught sight of her closer to the beach, on
the edge of the rocks, with bits of moss wrapped
around her breasts and legs. She took off the snorkel
and stretched out, obscuring his view.

It was after six, and she'd been on the rocks for half
an hour before she put on her snorkel and eased herself back into the water. Swimming with the tide now,
she was close to shore in a few minutes. When the water was only up to her thighs, she removed the flippers
and mask and walked in. She smiled, and he twisted
behind the glass doors, suspecting that she had known
he was watching. Then she surprised him by waving,
and he peered below him, spotting Elaine in a bikini.
Elaine ran toward her, gesticulating wildly as though
announcing that the house was on fire. Barbara did
not move; she threw the mask and flippers on the
beach. She stood her ground, and when Elaine
reached her, he heard the loud rasp of shock and
anger as her mouth moved, snapping open and closed
like a hen pecking her cock. He couldn't hear a word.
When Elaine stopped, Barbara said something and
laughed.

Elaine, quivering, stood over her, waving angrily. He
could see Barbara's lips moving again, her face set,

implacable; then with a perfunctory shrug, she turned away. Something was said and the two women apparently found some common ground. Elaine turned toward the house—she couldn't have seen him—and instead of the look of outrage he expected, he discovered that she was also smiling. Barbara wrapped an arm around Elaine's waist. Robbie was perplexed by Elaine's behavior.

Elaine dropped her pants, and unhooked the catch of her top. It fell off her, and she, too, was naked and ran into the water, alongside Barbara. The two swam for a few minutes, then returned to the beach to dry themselves with large towels. Elaine rested her head on Barbara's lap, while Barbara vigorously dried her long blond hair with what appeared to be maternal affection. Before heading back to the house, Elaine threw her bikini into the sea and was rewarded with a pat on the back by her new instructor.

Robbie lay on his bed, dazed, a witness to an event he neither understood nor could discuss. At nine a knock on his door informed him that breakfast was about to be served, and he stirred himself, feeling weak as his feet touched the floor and he dressed.

"Finian Haddie and kippers," his father announced when he came into the dining room. Teddy was red-faced, healthy, and rested, like a victorious athlete after the game. "How'd you sleep?"

"Not very well," Robbie admitted. He was incapable of making small-change conversation, but Teddy was not to be put off.

"How about a ride out to Gurney's for lunch?"

"I think I'd better start back after breakfast."

"You're kidding!"

"No. I'm not. I've got to spend some time at the law library."

"Can't it wait?"

"I'm working on a case for the judge."

Teddy was incensed by the sudden change of plan but decided against forcing the issue. He'd appeal to Elaine.

Robbie heard the women's voices, and he turned to look upstairs. There was a high, shrill giggle, recognizably Elaine's, which was followed by a low, heavy, throaty laugh, which belonged to his tormentor. Could he ask Elaine what Barbara had said—it must have been persuasive—to get her to remove her bikini? But if he did, it would be an admission of spying or—worse still—voyeurism. He'd have to use a more indirect technique. The difficulty there, however, was that he was essentially honest and he played games of deception awkwardly. Elaine, now dressed in shorts and T-shirt, kissed him on the cheek, and Barbara kissed his father. Good mornings were accompanied by another bout of schoolgirl giggles.

"I'm starving," Elaine said. "We had a swim real early."

"Why didn't you invite me?" Teddy asked.

"You were still sleeping."

"We went in bare-ass," Barbara said with a wicked smile. She turned to Robbie. "Did you enjoy the show?"

"Hardly."

"Hardly? That's lawyers' babble," Barbara persisted, "and ambiguous."

Elaine turned to Barbara, her new ally. "Maybe he was pretending to be asleep while he watched."

The tone of the conversation was distasteful to Teddy and he slunk into his *Wall Street Journal.*

"What would I have seen?" Robbie said a bit too heatedly, betraying his lawyerly poker face.

"The X-rated show," Elaine replied.

"Or the two of us with our secret lover."

"Hey, where does that put me"—Teddy said, roused, affably pointing to Robbie—"or rather, *us*?"

Robbie knew that if he played her game, he would finish second best. He had to warn his father about this perverse woman. But how did he go about it, without suggesting that he himself was attracted to her? If only he and Elaine had stayed in Boston that weekend, none of this would have happened. He picked at his food indifferently.

Or would it have happened at another time? Was it possible to elude an event if you avoided it, or was the universe so spatially constructed that the event was there and it would catch up with you at some point in time, which was, he had been taught in a philosophy course, an arbitrary device for counting that which did not exist? The women had worked up an appetite and were having seconds.

"Rob wants to leave after breakfast," Teddy informed Elaine.

She screwed up her face. Her urchin expression, and Robbie always found this endearing. "Oh, no, do we have to?"

"I've got some research to do at the library."

"Couldn't you become a great lawyer five minutes later?" Barbara asked. "Come on, Teddy," Barbara pleaded in a child's voice, "show him who's boss. Give him hell."

"We've never had that kind of relationship. Right, Rob?" The soft, limpid gray eyes covered his face. Teddy at his most persuasive, asking a favor, and because this seldom happened, he couldn't refuse. The ladies waited for him to back off, but without much apprehension.

Robbie found himself fascinated by this bizarre and dangerous woman and he decided he would remain if only to see how far she would take them all in her reckless quest for peril.

"I guess it'll keep till I get back."

"You self-sacrificing scholar," Barbara said derisively.

"He really is a scholar"—Teddy, the proud papa—"Phi Beta, and editor of the *Law Review*."

FIFTEEN

$\mathcal{T}$HE FOUR OF THEM WENT SAILING AFTER BREAKFAST: Teddy the helmsman, Robbie in charge of sails. It was a warm day, but windy, and they were making eight knots an hour. Robbie moved acrobatically from one side of the boat to the other, taking no notice of either Barbara or Elaine, who lay on the deck sunning themselves. He caught the disturbing, erotic scent of their sweaty bodies. Teddy controlled the small mizzen just forward of the rudderpost. He wore a captain's hat, larded with gold braid, and Robbie thought he looked foolish, playing a role.

Despite their lack of family resemblance, the women behaved like two sisters with a long history of mutual understanding and a shorthand vocabulary, comprehensible only to the initiated. Barbara had begun to call Elaine *chérie*. Robbie slipped a knot to hold the mainsail when the wind became constant, then cupped his hand around his lighter and lit a cigarette.

The exercise had made him relax, diverted his mind, and he was glad not to have to talk. The women were whispering, and from time to time he'd hear one of them laugh. Barbara had on a Rio string bikini. She had unsnapped the strap of her top and dropped it forward so that she wouldn't get a line. She lifted herself up on one elbow to turn and for an instant exposed her breasts. He didn't want to look, but he did. His hands tightened around the rope and burned his soft palms. She blinked her eyes in the sun, slowly lifted up her top, and caught his gaze. He turned away abruptly, but she had known he was observing her every move and probably did it to taunt him, he thought. Could he be imagining all this? No one else seemed to notice anything suggestive or perverse in her behavior.

"Good work, sailor," she said.

"As long as you're enjoying yourself," he replied shortly.

"*And* as long as you are, too," she said, rolling over, this time holding her top.

A wave caromed over the side and drenched him.

"Where'd that come from?" Teddy shouted.

"You better change, Rob," Elaine said.

He had worn a pair of white trousers instead of swimming trunks like his father.

"I've got a pair of dry trunks below," Teddy said.

"It's okay."

He kicked off his Rockports and squeezed the water from his trouser legs. He sat down on the deck, put on a pair of sunglasses and rubbed some sunscreen on his face. He was sorry that he hadn't left as he'd intended. A comparison between the two women was inevitable, and although he made a mental effort to avoid it, he found himself weighing them both up as though he had a choice between them. What struck him mostly about Barbara was a cunning talent for spotting a man's weakness, making him aware of the fact, then pricking away until she drew blood. She was cleverer than he, and she proceeded to victimize him. If she had set out to seduce him, she had succeeded, and he wished that now, with a complete victory over both Elaine and himself, she'd desist or else bring it all to the surface and say, "Well, I won that game, didn't I?" He let his fingers' trail through the water, then rose because his sodden pants were uncomfortable, and went down to the cabin to change. Barbara curled her toes when he passed her. Was this some kind of signal?

Just as he was tying the cords in his trunks, she appeared.

"I thought you were mixing me a drink," she said.

"You didn't ask for one."

"I took it for granted. Next time I'll spell it out for you."

"Just ask."

"Are you sore at me or something?"

"Should I be?"

"I thought we patched things up last night."

"We did."

"That sounds awfully tentative."

She was inches away from him, and he could see the white line just under her suit. If he moved toward her, he'd be on top of her, and he was tempted to move, force her back on the bar. He reached for a bottle of Ketel One just behind her.

"There's some ice in the bucket."

He had to touch her, lean over her, to get it, and he was too aroused to trust himself, so he pointed.

"Shall I get it?"

"That's the general idea."

She set the bucket on the bar shelf and touched him. He moved back, banging his head against a low-hanging door.

"Did you hurt yourself?"

"I've got a thick skull. I'll live."

"Robbie, you're not upset with me . . . something I've done or said?"

"Why do you have to be reassured every five minutes?"

"That's the way I am."

"Is that what I have to do to please you?"

"Not if you don't want to. It's an awkward situation for all of us, but me, I'm the real stranger, so maybe I've been acting a little outré."

His body trembled with rage. "What the hell do you want from us? You're going to be ass-deep in one of the great American fortunes. Every whim you ever had will be fulfilled. Houses, clothes, chauffeurs, a position."

She appeared genuinely shocked. "Are you serious? I'm not in this for the money. I like what I'm doing and I'm crazy about your father. He thrills me. I didn't think he would turn me on after I met him. But I've become his obsession and a certain responsibility goes with that."

"What exactly are you doing with him—apart from the obvious?"

"We play. Teddy's a very fine game-player, almost as good as I am."

"You must have had a great teacher."

Barbara nodded and for a moment she seemed dazed by reflection. "I guess I had the best, but I didn't realize it at the time—while the game was being played"—she broke off—"I had no idea that it was a match and that I was in over my head with a world-class performer. It was like chess and I accepted the *poisoned* pawn."

She had an earnest look on her face; her short black hair enhanced the sultry femininity she gave off like an animal odor; her damp face had a feral beauty. Robbie thought he'd never before seen or met a woman as desirable and as deadly. Unaccustomed to

divided loyalties, dissembling, and ambiguous relationships, he had chanced upon an area that was to-
tally new. He stirred the martinis.

"What's the object of the game?"

"Winning is worthless unless your adversary is your
equal."

"So everything is game theory with you?"

"At this moment I'd really like a piece of lemon."

He cut the lemon into segments and dropped a
piece into her hand, consciously avoiding contact. She
chewed it, spitting the skin into her palm.

"You and Elaine have gotten very friendly."

"I knew she wouldn't be a real problem."

"Is that the way you think of people, as problems?"

"Of course I do. You're about to practice law. Aren't
people just a collection of their problems?"

"Am I a problem?"

She stared at him. "At the moment, I guess you are.
But I'll find out why. I always do."

"That's reassuring. I wouldn't like to be the exception to your rule."

"I'll uncover the solution when I'm prepared to
take the trouble to find out."

"That's a decision I'll leave to you."

He smiled, pleased that he had won the exchange.
He handed her the drink, placed three empty glasses
on a tray with the martini pitcher, and waited for her
to get out of his way. She refused to yield, even though
she saw him waiting to get past.

"I'll have to give you some serious thought or possibly more than that."

"I'll settle for the thought."

"But you really want more, don't you?"

She got out of his way, waved her arm ceremoni-
ously, like a waiter ushering a woman to her seat, and
spit a lemon pip at his back.

"Let's use water guns next time, so I've got an even break," he said.

"Next time, my dear, you can fuck off."

"Next time, Barbara, we'll use blowguns."

SIXTEEN

$\mathcal{R}$OBBIE CELEBRATED HIS VICTORY BY GETTING VERY drunk, surprising Teddy and positively shocking Elaine, who had never seen him this way.

"I think we'd better get him back to the house," Teddy said to his manservant when they had docked and Robbie was snoring down below.

"Leave it to Basil, sir."

When Elaine followed Basil, Teddy turned to Barbara.

"Did you guys have a beef or what?"

"No, I adore him."

"What happened to him?"

She took Teddy's arm while they walked from the dock and smiled with charming sedateness.

"Some men get very jittery when they're going to get married."

"I won't."

"I wasn't talking about you . . . we'll see."

Notwithstanding the adroit way Barbara had acquitted herself of any blame, Teddy sensed a deep antagonism between his son and his treasure. Possibly Robbie and Elaine had had an argument and Robbie was blaming Barbara. Out of character for Robbie. Then the ugly worm of doubt arose about someone one loves and can never suspect of betrayal. While they were below decks, had Robbie made a suggestion to Barbara? The prospect was as unlikely as *his* making a suggestion to Elaine. The other alternative was too distasteful to contemplate, except as a ripple of paranoia, but certainly more credible. Barbara, *his* Barbara, had attempted to seduce Robbie and had been turned down, and Robbie, unable to cope with the shock of Teddy's marriage and the apostasy Barbara had revealed, had for the first time in memory gotten drunk. No, this equation was unbalanced. Another factor was in play.

The analytical Teddy Franklin sought a solution, dismissing the hidden motives and susceptibilities of his son, whom he knew as well as his liquidity that his laptop revealed every second of every day. But in a financial investigation Teddy always uncovered hidden factors, either in a company's favor or to its detriment. With Robbie he stopped short, accepting what he saw as all there was to see. In Barbara, he had discovered his poison and his antidote. More of her was never enough, the two inextricably involved, one useless without the other, a perfect symbiotic balance, as necessary to his living as a heartbeat. Yes, Barbara was toxic and he thrived on it.

Everything about her excited and interested him: Her quirks and instability, the sharpness of her vision and her tongue. His sexual satisfaction was complete. He wanted to treat it all as a problem of company reorganization, but he was haunted by the knowledge that eventually a choice would have to be made between logic and madness. If his understanding of Barbara increased, his sympathies extended, he'd be in a better position to help her and at the same time prevent a split with Robbie.

Reluctantly, he thought of the tapes he had, but not of the dead man. He made up his mind to listen to them carefully and find the key to the enigma of her personality. What he failed to recognize or admit was that in understanding Barbara he might find the reasons behind his own motives.

What also puzzled Teddy—as much as the hostility that had sprung up between them—was the remarkable degree of affection that had grown out of nowhere between Barbara and Elaine, who acted like old friends, friends with a common interest and a history of shared experience. He had expected them to compete, to attack each other as adversaries. He couldn't find anything particularly remarkable about Elaine, and he wondered what attracted Barbara.

Toward evening, but still bleary-eyed, Robbie and Elaine packed themselves into his Honda and Teddy had a moment of confusion over where his loyalties really lay. But in spite of himself, he was relieved of the burden of choosing between them for the time being. He watched Robbie's car pull out, with a mixture of regret and bad conscience.

He had Barbara all to himself now. When she had come back from the beach still wet and with seaweed between her toes, he had kissed her feet. He gorged on his Botticelli mermaid fresh from the sea. Each time they were together he discovered exciting facets of her personality, and she always succeeded in making it new and different. She had gone upstairs to change, and when he went up, he was surprised not to find her. He looked in the bathroom, then systematically went through all the rooms, calling softly, "I'm coming to get you."

At the end of the corridor, with one bedroom to go, his tension mounted as he pressed his ear to the door to listen. He opened the door, but she wasn't in there, either. Then, without knowing why, he started to panic. He rushed into the master bedroom, looked under the bed, in the closets, in the bathroom. On the medicine-cabinet mirror, he spotted a lipstick scrawl, and at the same moment he heard a car engine turn over, then, with a screech of tires, tear out of the driveway. He ran to the window just as the Range Rover he kept down there roared onto Lily Pond Road.

"Basil . . . Basil!" he shouted frantically.

The writing on the mirror said: *I've got to get away. Taken car. Sorry B.*

Basil appeared, unaware of what had happened.

"Why'd you let her leave?" he demanded.

The Englishman was for once without an answer.

"I didn't know what she was doing. Taking a drive?"

"Didn't you see her carrying a suitcase?"

"No, she didn't take one."

Teddy flopped into a chair. "You mean she left her clothes?" he asked hopefully.

"I assume so."

"Maybe she'll be back then," Teddy said, as though Basil held some magical power over Barbara's movements.

Teddy yanked open the dresser drawers that Barbara had used. She had left everything, sweaters, lingerie, a nightgown. He lifted up the pillow on the bed and found the nightgown she slept in. It had her scent. He slumped down on the bed, the nightgown across his lap, and prayed for her to return. There were stains on the nightgown, his semen, stiff and crusty. He rolled the nightgown up into a ball and threw it into the fireplace. Then he kicked off his loafers and lay on the bed. He thought of pursuing her, but that would be a pointless exercise, since she might become angry enough to call off their engagement. He dare not take the chance. She'd call him when *she* was ready to see him and not a minute before. No explanations, no apologies, just pure ungovernable impulse. Because he loved her, he'd give in, go to her, powerless to reproach her. He needed some edge to regain the ascendant position, some knowledge of a weakness so that he could control her.

Seventeen

$\mathcal{B}$ARBARA FOLLOWED ROBBIE'S CAR. BEFORE HE LEFT, she had heard him mention to Elaine that he'd be staying at the corporate suite Teddy kept at the Hotel Carlyle. He drove very fast, weaving in and out of the traffic. Finally, she lost him on the Triboro Bridge. It was just eight o'clock, and when she got through the tollbooth, she caught sight of his car on the FDR Drive.

The weekend expedition had proved one thing to her: she didn't belong with Teddy. He was too overpowering and would stifle her. He was always pawing her, feeling her up, and only as a sexual object did she have any value. What made the situation difficult was that she genuinely liked him—at times adored him—but she needed something more. That morning she had pleaded with him to hurt her in bed, but he had already come and was drifting back to sleep. It had been good the first time when he struck her and there was the threat of the gun. When they made love now, she closed her eyes and had fantasies of the gun.

She didn't know why she was following Robbie and Elaine. It just seemed like something she had to do, a compulsive act. She wondered if Robbie would have the guts to sleep with Elaine now. Elaine had confessed to her on the beach that she was still a virgin, and Barbara had become oddly stimulated by the revelation. That had come after she had persuaded Elaine to take off her suit. She hadn't expected Elaine to give in, and yet it was all so natural. She had said matter-of-factly, "It'll free you for the rest of your life and you'll never be so self-conscious again."

She was tempted to turn off at Ninety-sixth Street and go home, but at the last moment decided to continue the game. She headed west to the Hotel Carlyle. She parked across the street and spotted Elaine in Robbie's Honda, with a doorman hovering. Robbie appeared and Elaine rushed out of the car. She opened the back door and pulled out a carry bag. Their acrimonious voices carried, and Elaine gestured angrily. She turned to the doorman who had stood back and he signaled for a cab. Robbie turned away furiously and went into the hotel as the taxi drove off.

Elaine might return, but somehow Barbara doubted it. There had been an attitude of desperation, of escape, as she left. She wondered how serious their argument had been and judged it to have been a bad one. What was Robbie doing, thinking, alone? Barbara didn't hate him, but by now he probably detested her. She had come between him and his father, upset the balance he and Elaine maintained, possibly on the verge of some unconsidered and final act that would change the direction of his life.

She knew how he felt, assailed by doubts, and determined to find some way of paying her back for what she'd done to him. She had aroused violent feelings in Robbie, and he had not been prepared to cope with them.

She walked into the hotel lobby and went to the registration desk, where a smiling assistant manager welcomed her.

"Is Robert Franklin in the bar or the restaurant?"

"No, madam, he's gone up to the suite."

"Would you call him and tell him Elaine wants to see him upstairs."

*B*ARBARA GOT OUT OF THE ELEVATOR ON THE PENT-house floor, stood in the corridor, confounded and hesitant. She stared at the doorbell to the suite and listened for sounds of life. The lights were off inside and the door suddenly sprang open.

"So you decided to stop acting like a princess?" Robbie said.

"I never have so I probably won't."

He peered at her quizzically as though his sense of geography had revealed itself as wildly inaccurate. It was almost as if he couldn't quite identify her.

"Barbara?"

"Can I come in?"

He stepped aside, letting her pass by, his head pivoting like a ball on a string.

"Is this the Carlyle, or am I really cracking up?"

"I followed you here."

"Followed? What do you mean?"

"I left just after you."

"Is my father with you?"

"No. I checked out."

They progressed slowly from the entry through the large double doors of a living room, the plush decor faintly old-fashioned. It had the tinkle of society cocktail parties and worthy fund-raisers presided over by Chanel women.

"I'm sorry, but I don't understand. I may be a bit hung over but—"

"I didn't want to stay with him any longer. That's all there is to it."

"You had an argument?"

"No, we didn't."

"What's going on? Are you still getting married?"

"It's impossible to say right now."

"Oh, shit. Is it because of me . . . something I said today? Because if it is, I apologize. I had no business interfering in his life, especially after he told me he'd never been happier. You see it—or rather you—came out of the blue. We have to get used to this new situation. I'm not much of a drinker and I know I must've been out of line. We better call my father and tell him you're here."

"Please don't."

She sat down in a deep club chair facing the window, beside an elegant wooden table. Robbie retied the belt of his bathrobe. From behind him, there was the sound of the shower.

"Can I have a drink?"

"Drink?" He opened a mirrored credenza bar and dozens of glasses and bottles glistened. "From sherry to champagne."

"Vodka will do me."

He opened the bar fridge and took out an iced bottle of Belvedere and fixed drinks for both of them.

"Why did you come here?"

"I'm not sure."

"You must've had a reason."

"I saw Lainie running for a taxi."

"Oh . . . We had a beef. A bad one. The fact is, we've had more quarrels this weekend than in the last year."

"It's my fault."

"What makes you say that, Barbara? I'm not sure I understand."

She stared at him. She seemed disturbed to him, her deep green eyes unable to focus on any object. Even though she was looking at him, it was through him.

"Elaine is a lot like Laura."

"Who is?" She was making him jittery, and he was worried about her doing something dangerous.

"Elaine reminds me of Laura, my college roommate. There's a strong physical resemblance. That's why I persuaded her to take her bikini off. I wanted to look at her."

"Barbara, why're you talking to me this way?"

"I want to be open with you. The trouble with me is that I invariably wind up doing what other people want me to do. After they've lost the battle, given up hope, I do exactly what they've been fighting for. I start to feel sorry for them, lose my self-control, and then pray for forgiveness."

He seemed to demur. "On the other hand, you have a natural gift for seducing people."

"I do my best to repress that side of me."

"Not with very much success."

"Are you going to turn the water off?"

He left the room and came back in a moment. She had already poured herself another drink.

"Are you hungry? Want me to call room service? Or we could go down to the bar."

"What do you want to do?"

"Have a drink, eat a steak."

"Is that exactly what you're thinking? What you've got in mind?"

He was mystified by her. The effect she was having on him was hazardous. "Yes, I guess so."

"Do you have to guess? Aren't you certain?"

Her ambiguity troubled him.

"No, I *don't* have to guess," he said angrily. "Why're you putting me on the spot?"

"Be honest."

His vocal cords moved, but he couldn't make a sound.

"Are you putting me down again?" he demanded, crossing the room toward her. "Because if you are, I'm not going to stand for it."

"I wasn't putting you down."

"Which car did you take?"

"The Range Rover."

"I'll call Leonard and run you home, then drop off the car."

"I don't want you to run me home." She stretched out on the sofa with her drink. "How'd you sleep last night?"

"Badly."

"Well, that's what I call progress. I slept badly, too."

"Really?"

She nodded. "I had to give your father a command performance—with encores."

Robbie began to tremble. "Why did you, if you didn't want to?"

"I thought I explained why. I got tired of arguing, and it didn't affect me one way or the other, because I was thinking about something else."

He put his hands over his ears, and she got up and pulled his hands down.

"I don't want to hear another word. And I want you to get the hell out of here."

"I sent out clues to you. Couldn't you follow them?"

"Clues . . . What are you talking about?"

"This morning . . . you were watching me on the beach. I know when someone's watching me. I like it."

"I did not see you."

"Don't lie to me!" she shouted at the top of her voice.

He helplessly slumped against the wall. "Tell me what's going on with you!"

"I'm here because you wanted me."

In the forest of her chilly, byzantine logic, she had seduced Robbie and caused a break with Elaine, which had its roots in sexual restraint. She was obligated to compensate Robbie for her own transgressions. In a sense, she recognized that she had projected herself into Laura and evolved into Elaine's shield.

"Oh, no, this isn't happening."

"You want to fuck me, don't you?" she continued, breaching his defenses, his sense of right and wrong. He didn't answer, and she cornered him, then clung to him.

"Act like a man. Tell the truth. Come on."

"Yes." He shoved her away, and she fell back against a glass table. She regained her balance and cocked her head to the side. "I'm sorry, I didn't mean to push you that hard," he said.

She smiled. "Have you decided what you really want from me?"

He felt almost feverish and couldn't continue the conversation. Finally, he forced the words out.

"I'd say it was up to you."

"We're going to make love and forget it ever happened."

"Is that a condition?"

"Yes, it is."

"I can't accept it, just like that."

"Good-bye," she said, walking away.

He grabbed her, spun her around just as she was about to open the door.

"Okay, I accept the condition. But what do I get for accepting it?"

"Me, that's all."

He nodded dumbly, like a horse shaking off flies.

"Do you think Elaine might come back?" she asked.

"No, not tonight."

"Why not?"

"Because I said I didn't want her . . . and I didn't. But you know that, don't you?"

She nestled in his arms, then swiveled around so that her back rested against his chest. He kissed her neck and she moved his hands over her breasts and emitted a low, tortured cry, trapped by his desire and the authority of her deceit.

"Robbie, do it slowly, do everything slowly, and make me suffer for what I'm doing."

"Has anyone killed for you?" he asked, caught in the delirium of the moment.

"Yes," she replied, guiding his hand along her damp, bare thighs.

*H*E WAS VERY RELAXED AND HAD A BOYISH COMPLAcency afterward when they were in bed. She imagined he would have played a trumpet, smoked a cigar, or walked on a roof ledge to impress her with his mastery. His fingers toyed with her nipples as he basked in the sunshine of conquest. She had insisted on him blindfolding her and he had torn up a pillowcase and she still wore it.

She said, "When you think of a triangle—close your eyes and think of the form—do you physically see a triangle?"

"Yes, I do," Robbie said.

"I can't. I just see angles—all of them, acute, obtuse, right, but never the whole triangle. They're always sharp angles with points. Never the totality."

"What about a circle?" he asked. "Can you visualize one?"

"No. It just becomes a series of intersecting arcs and then they become flowers. They're always orange. It's my favorite color. I'm happy when I see something orange; clothes, the sky, or an orange. I never eat oranges, though. There's something sacrilegious about eating them."

"Why?"

"I don't know. There're some things I don't want to investigate. I just accept them."

"Would you like to go out somewhere now?"

"I'm not sure. Would you?"

"Uh-huh."

"Okay. Then we'll go somewhere."

She sat up. He ran his fingers along the small of her back and kissed her.

"Would you hand me my clothes?" Barbara asked.

"But how can you get dressed if you can't see what you're doing?"

"I'm used to it."

"Blindfolded?"

"Yes, it's easy."

"Why don't you take the blindfold off?"

"I'd rather not."

"Do you hate yourself, or just me?"

"It's just something I've got to do. Don't ask me why."

He regarded her with awe. "You are out of my league and probably everyone else's as a game player. You've pretended that I was the dominant one"—he laughed without bitterness and at himself—"and I did everything you told me to do."

"I do really like you."

"Barbara, am I supposed to forget this ever happened? Is that what you want?"

"Well, did it happen?" she asked.

"What do you want me to say to that?"

"Whatever comes into your mind."

"It happened."

"When I take my blindfold off, I'll wipe it out. I'll see the room, the bed, the dresser, that green chaise longue, and I'll tell myself that nothing happened.

It'll be your word against mine, and I won't accept your word when I know different."

"Barbara, I don't understand."

"Do you have to understand everything?"

"It's a habit."

"Well, then, can't you accept the fact that my habits, my behavior, might be different?"

"I can, but I don't want to."

"I'd like you to try."

He handed her her bra, the badly creased linen skirt, her denim shirt; she hadn't worn panties. He watched her fingers deftly move over catches and snaps as though she could see what she was doing.

"Did you really come?" he asked.

"Does it matter?"

"Yes, it does. It's very important."

"For what, your ego?"

"Is there anything else?"

"A lot more."

"I want to know, did you come?"

"Robbie, where were you?"

"Here, but I wasn't sure. Tell me, did you?"

"Yes."

"Has anyone. Have you ever . . . ?"

"Say what you mean."

"I'm embarrassed." He waited for her to help him, but she refused. She put on her sandals and he stooped to kiss her feet.

"Why don't you stop this? I'm not going to give you a grade."

"I want to know. . . . Has anyone done what I have for you?"

"Yes," she said.

He was humbled. "I see."

"Are you going to ask if it was better?"

"I'm afraid to."

"Don't be afraid. They're only words."

"Not actions?"

"Not now, only words," she said.

"What about what you did, was it special? Was I special?"

"Yes, very special."

"Can we continue . . . I want to be with you, Barbara."

She was fully dressed, and she untied the blindfold.

"Is that some kind of proposal?"

"Yes, it's a proposal."

"I'm spoken for, and so are you."

"Could you love me?"

"No, and stop being so sentimental."

He glared at her. "Do you love anybody?"

"Yes, I suppose . . . your father."

"What about the things you do with him?"

"Really, Robbie, what's so interesting about my sex life?"

"I just have to know." He knew he was flirting with disaster, but the lawyer in him forced questions he had no right to ask. "Does he make you happy?"

"Why not ask him?"

"Should I? Are you daring me? Would you like that?"

"Do what you have to."

"I'm so puzzled by you. I simply don't know what I should do."

"Do nothing, then."

"But I've got to talk to Elaine, explain to her."

She was growing weary. "Explain what? In fact, I don't see what I've got to do with it all. You're going to marry Elaine. I got you excited on the boat and she's a virgin. You were bewildered and I knew that the two of you would have a problem. She told me on the beach that she was *saving* herself for your wedding night and that you agreed. I caused the trouble and I came to you to accept my responsibility."

He was thunderstruck by the insidiousness of her rationale. "I hate you now, I really do," he said, pulling on his trousers.

"That's natural."

He threw his arms around her and squeezed her so tightly that she began to gasp.

"Please say you felt something."

"I felt something, all right. Now good night."

"You are crazy," he said with the glimmer of an insight.

"That's right, I am."

EIGHTEEN

$\mathcal{B}$ARBARA LEFT TEDDY'S RANGE ROVER IN THE NO-
parking space in front of his townhouse. She
put the keys in the mailbox, flagged down a taxi and
arrived at her apartment a few minutes later. In the
distance, she spied a figure lurking around the entrance and assumed it was Teddy. She suspected he'd
let her cool off for a day or two before seeing her, but
apparently he had changed his strategy. As she moved
closer, she made out a woman.

"Christ, you scared me—I thought it was a prowler.
What are you doing here?"

"Barbara, I'm sorry. I just didn't know what to do or
where to go," Elaine said timidly.

"How'd you find me?"

"I called Teddy's house and Leonard gave me your
address. He said you had left just after us."

"Was Teddy at home?"

"No, he's still at the beach. Can I come in?"

"Of course."

"I missed the train back to Boston, and I couldn't face going to the airport for the shuttle. I'm so confused about everything."

"I see."

When they were in the apartment—now free of Teddy's roses and in their place a bunch of peonies in a jade green vase—Elaine spun around, regarding the sensual surroundings with pleasure. "Your place is beautiful. It's like a little piece of France."

"Thank you. It's the one thing Teddy didn't do for me. Can I get you something, Lainie, a drink, a glass of wine?"

"A glass of white if you've got a bottle open."

"Fine. I'll just be a minute."

Barbara slipped off her clothes, dumped them in the bathroom hamper and put on a short, red silk robe. She was hot and uncomfortable. In the kitchen, she opened a bottle of Mersault, handed glasses to Elaine and they went into the living room.

"Do you want to know what happened? Why I'm here?"

"If you want to discuss it."

"I had a fight with Robbie and walked out. The minute I did, I was sorry, but I couldn't go back, could I? I mean, would you have gone back?"

"I don't know."

"He's staying at the Carlyle in a suite Teddy keeps there. Robbie wanted me to spend the night with him." There was a childlike fragility about her that touched Barbara. "He hurt me terribly. Barbara, I'm not a woman of the world. Maybe I'm wrong for him and we just found out."

"No, don't even think such a thing."

"I saw a side of him that frightened me."

"He's anxious. Look, neither of you were prepared to meet me, and the fact is Teddy and I have a very strong sexual relationship. It sort of tipped the balance for Robbie."

She pondered this, but her alarm did not dissipate. "I don't want to disappoint Robbie. That's what scares me. Do you remember what you said to me on the beach this morning?"

"Not exactly."

Elaine's face tightened in disappointment. "You told me I was the sister you always wanted."

"Yes, of course. I'm just tired and not thinking."

"I can't discuss this stuff with my mother."

"Let's talk tomorrow. I'm beat."

"I'm sure you've got your own problems. Maybe we can help each other. Isn't that possible, Barbara?"

"We'll help each other," she said lifelessly.

"Can I stay over? I can sleep here in the living room on the sofa."

"You won't be comfortable. I've got a king-sized bed. Come on."

"Are you sure it won't put you out?"

"No, it'll be okay."

"You looked so beautiful this morning when you came out of the ocean. I thought for a minute that you could've been Botticelli's model for *La Primavera*. Your hair's shorter, naturally, but you're even more beautiful than the woman in the painting."

Barbara leaned forward and kissed her tenderly on the lips.

"God, I adore you," Elaine said. "I grew up with three brothers. Football players. The house was always full of sports equipment and my father only had time for his boys. My mother was always running to one church event after another."

"Touchdowns and crosses," Barbara said with amusement.

"That's about it. Barbara, I wish we were real sisters. . . ."

"Yes, that would be nice."

Barbara turned and went into the bathroom. She ran the bath, dosed it with Vitabath, and sat down on a stool to wait for the tub to fill up.

"Are you going to have a bath now?"

"We both will."

Barbara reflected for a moment on the damage she had done. How could she ever explain her behavior to Elaine? There were some things about herself, she thought, that she couldn't admit even to God. If she were face to face with Him and everything she'd done or thought was known—even then, she'd still deny it. Elaine, naked, appeared in the doorway and Barbara beckoned her.

"Barbara, you're a dream."

NINETEEN

*B*ARBARA WAS AWAKE AT FOUR IN THE MORNING. SHE gazed at the splash of blond hair, the cherub mouth, freckled face, sunlined skin, the slender limbs, the quiet child whose back she had washed with a loofah and whose man she had stolen. Elaine was a perfect model of docility, who lent herself to the role of an adopted child. Barbara made herself a cup of Earl Grey tea, and glanced at the *New Statesman,* to which she subscribed. It was three weeks old. She read a few book reviews. She loved the silences punctuated only by the mournful horns of the riverboat traffic. On Sunday there would be a continual movement of flatboats and tugs racing ahead at high speed in order to reach their ports by Monday morning. She had always wanted a house that overlooked the river, where she could install an enormous window so that she could see the boats whenever she liked.

If she married Teddy, she'd have her window. But

could she have a second life, a secret one, contiguous to the public one with him? She doubted if she could continue to be consciously amoral while married to Teddy. No, that would be impossible: she would become an unfaithful wife, immoral, not to be trusted, an embarrassment to her husband. The only trust she required was the trust she had in herself. She had paid dearly for her rights, but the transaction was one-sided, putting money into one pocket from the other. No questions asked, no explanations demanded. She shared when she was inclined to share, and not because of prior claims, or binding contracts.

She tiptoed back into the bedroom. Elaine was sleeping soundlessly, the perfect slave whose life span was a form of bondage and indentured service. Reared by uptight parents who righteously equipped her for marriage, children, grandchildren, dotage, the exquisite serenity of suburban intrigue. She and Robbie would merge into a *House Beautiful* ideal, a golden couple with an ivy-covered, gabled house in Greenwich admired by readers who sought the ecstasy of the ordinary.

Robbie had disappointed her, as all the others had. He had received a gift and had become quarrelsome, shocked that Christmas wasn't a seven-day-a-week holiday, presided over by a league of shopkeepers. What she had given was unique, custom-made, and what he had really wanted was an assembly-line product, which he could pick up a bit cheaper if he waited for the January sales. He'd find there were ten million Elaines, not necessarily cheap, certainly predictable, made to last, and with the manufacturer's warranty.

And yet there was something warm and pleasant about Elaine, which made her stand out a bit, even if she was still assembly-line merchandise; but of its kind, good value for money, and exactly what Robbie needed. Barbara sat down in her desk chair by her writing table and wondered how she could communicate with Elaine. Was it possible to re-create her, make her into Laura Sargent? Apart from a superficial resemblance around the mouth and coloring, the two were different. Laura's hair had been whiter, longer; she had worn strange, unmatching, impulsive color combinations that were always striking and original. She had had a quirky sense of humor, a razzle-dazzle way of half shutting her faded-blue eyes, a presence that informed people that here was someone unique. When you met Elaine, you were observing a lithograph, unnumbered at that. Laura had had a vision of the world in which she saw people as fish, some swimming together in a school, others in deeper water hiding under rocks, camouflaging themselves with bits of moss and sea plants; then there were the hunters and the prey.

It had been an elaborate system, and Laura had classified everyone she had ever met as some form of marine life. Barbara smiled weakly when she remembered her saying, "The lowest of the low is your oyster. It can't even get rid of its shit. Pearls grow, and people buy them, and why would anyone want oyster shit when it's bad luck as well?"

Elaine awoke, languidly stretching and smiling.

Barbara's eyes burned from lack of sleep in the semidarkness. Her memories of now-dead happy times crept through her mind like assassins. They killed the present, destroyed living time, shutting life into a closet of motionless air from which all the oxygen had been used. Tears rolled down her face, and she covered her mouth to stop herself from making a noise. Elaine sat up in bed.

"Barbara, what's wrong?"

"Nothing. Go to sleep."

Elaine got out of bed and padded on the bare cold parquet. She put an arm around Barbara, and Barbara closed her eyes and rested her face on the warm, bare flesh of her neck.

"Can't you tell me, please?"

"I can't. Don't make me."

"You'll feel better; honestly you will. Listen to me, will you?"

Barbara shuddered convulsively, and Elaine held her tighter.

"Tell me, Barbara, and it'll be all right."

"I was thinking of my friend, and you remind me of her. You look a bit like her." She was overcome by a wave of racking sobs. "She was very special; special, you know, and different and original, and I loved her."

"Don't you see her anymore?"

"She's dead. But I do see her . . . I *do*. And I remember, and you're not like her really, and I was comparing the two of you."

"I came out second best, I suppose."

"Yes, you did," she admitted a bit uncomfortably, surprised by Elaine's self-possession.

"I don't mind."

"I thought I was stronger than you."

"You are, but that doesn't mean you're stronger all the time." Elaine held both her hands and made her rise. "Shall I make us some coffee?"

"I had some."

"Are you upset because of something you did?"

"No. I did everything I could, everything she wanted. I gave her everything. It's just that she's dead, and I can't seem to get over it."

Barbara left the room and returned with the photograph of Laura that stood on her mantelpiece.

"I noticed it when I came in. The eyes bothered me. They're so innocent and surprised."

"Laura wasn't prepared for life, but in an another

sense she was more prepared than anyone I've ever known. She could see through people. I don't mean simply understanding people and their motives. But if she spent five minutes—just five minutes—with you, she'd know everything that was important to know, and she was sympathetic and had remarkable perceptions. She was a classics scholar doing graduate work at Harvard. She was two years older than me."

"Were you like her?"

Barbara laughed, startling Elaine, who sat on the edge of the bed holding the silver-framed photograph, which shone and was free of dust or tarnish.

"I became her—she made me into her—I was a willing pupil."

"You imitated her?"

"I was her. I once bleached my hair snow-white. I did everything to be like her. I copied her style of dressing; I affected a Southern accent like hers. In fact, if you met us both for the first time, you would have thought we were twins. We became the twin sisters neither of us'd had."

"That sort of spooks me."

"It started as a joke, it really did; then it got serious. Once, before the Christmas vacation in my junior year, we took off a week early and applied for jobs. You know there are a million little jobs at Christmas, and we got eleven jobs. We used to take turns going to them. We had four different jobs in one department store and—"

A terrifying gasp-howl, which developed into a frenetic shriek, suddenly came from Barbara's mouth, and Elaine jumped up, frightened. She'd never heard a sound like it. Then it stopped when she held Barbara's head against her bed-warm chest.

"Barbara, it'll be all right," Elaine cooed like a mother to her nightmare-ridden child.

"I was so happy, so happy. Oh, Christ, I was happy then."

Elaine tucked her into bed and folded the blanket across her arms; she made a pair of neat hospital corners and redid the crumpled undersheet. Then she slid in beside her. Barbara stretched out her hand, and Elaine held it. She moved Barbara's head against her shoulder and massaged her forehead with her fingers.

"The comfort of a woman," Barbara said, "there's nothing like it. It's holy."

TWENTY

HE SOUND OF THE SUNDAY PAPERS THUMPING against the door awoke Barbara. It was after ten. She showered and dressed without disturbing Elaine. She opened the kitchen window and took a deep breath. It was a clear, bright day and the humidity was tolerable. She put on the coffee and set a tray down on her desk. Elaine stirred, stretched her arms, and had a half smile on her face.

"I had a lovely dream," she said.

"I didn't mean to make so much noise."

"It was over—the dream. It was about Robbie, our wedding night. The coffee smells good. I don't know where my toothbrush is."

"I've got an extra one. It's in the medicine cabinet."

Elaine pressed Barbara's hand affectionately when she passed her.

"Feel better?"

"Yes. Thanks to you. I'm sorry, I just lost it."

"See, it was fate that brought me here. I wouldn't've liked you getting so depressed without me being here. Anything could've happened."

"I think we're going to be friends," Barbara said a bit self-consciously.

"I'm not Laura."

"No, you're not. Maybe one Laura is enough for anyone."

"I'm not sure I understand that," Elaine said, making a scrunching sound as she bit into the toast.

"Never mind."

"No, come on, tell."

"Laura knew everything about me. She sensed what I was feeling, and at times it got very wearing. She'd pick my brain. I was like a subject she was studying and finally mastered."

$\mathscr{B}$ARBARA SKIMMED THROUGH SIX POUNDS OF *New York Times*, while Elaine dressed in the bedroom. Barbara heard the phone click and ignored it, although she had an instinctive urge to eavesdrop. In any case, she'd soon find out what had been said, for Elaine—even more than she—had a compulsion to confide, to seek approval. The phone clicked again.

"I called Robbie. I had to," she said.

They were walking along the promenade fronting Carl Schurz Park. Three ferries crammed with people slowly meandered past. The slate gray water was choppy and the tide fast, with dirty green, irregular waves.

"He was waiting for my call. Didn't sleep all night."

A group of under-tens played ball at the entrance of the park. The playground looked like a camp for displaced grandparents. Sunday fathers with elaborate Japanese video cameras taped their children. She could tell which parents were divorced, or about to be, or living apart, by the desperate efforts they made with their sullen, uncomprehending children.

"Robbie was shocked that I stayed with you. He thought you'd still be in East Hampton with his father. He also asked if you'd heard from Teddy. I didn't tell him."

Barbara was gratified by the news, but she had anticipated Robbie's reaction. No, he was not about to challenge Teddy to a duel or shatter his life because of a good fuck. His common sense and legal training had kicked in.

A few couples in the grass enclosure adjacent to the mayor's mansion were completing unfinished unpleasant business from Saturday night. Policemen diligently ticketed cars in front of the park. Radios played a medley of hip-hop and rap.

"Rob's going to pick me up around three-thirty, and we'll drive back to Boston. I really love him. I feel as if I've lived a lifetime since Friday."

Tomorrow I'll feel better, Barbara thought. Tomorrow I'll confess, and Dr. Frere will tell me why I went wrong, and we'll talk about self-control. She gravely wondered about her missing records. Perhaps during the burglary they had simply been mislaid. Barbara stopped by the rail and looked down over the embankment. Water clapped against the side, making small black-gray eddies.

"I'll miss you, Barbara, but we'll see each other. Maybe you can come up to Boston one weekend. There're like three or four parties every weekend, but if they're a bore, we don't have to go. Rob's fed up with them."

At Eightieth Street the promenade was less crowded, and they sat down on a bench.

"I think I know why Robbie and I had our argument. He wouldn't admit it, but you and Teddy sort of shocked him. He wasn't expecting anything like this, and it shook him up. He's still a kid in some ways. He thinks you hate him. Maybe I shouldn't ask."

Elaine considered the matter for a few minutes while Barbara stared at the water, smiling distantly. Then, because Barbara seemed so attentive and passive, she said, "You and Teddy haven't had anything serious happen? I'd hate for that to happen, and I guess I'm motivated by self-interest, but I can't help it. I feel I can count on you, Barbara, and there're people and relatives I've known all my life who wouldn't give a damn." She paused; then, because Barbara continued to look straight ahead of her, she got up and stood in front of her. "Aren't you talking to me?"

"I like being quiet. I heard everything."

"You look depressed."

"I'm not. I'm glad we spent time together."

"The way you say it it's as if it won't happen again. Did I get on your nerves?"

"No. You sleep like a little doll, without moving."

"Do I? It must've been uncomfortable for you."

"No, I loved having you next to me."

"I have an image of Sunday mornings with Rob. Very early, Sunday mornings, before church, my parents were always alone, and it was sort of nice, even when we were old enough to realize what they were doing. But this morning it was odd. I didn't wish Robbie was there with me, instead of you. I sort of thought—it'll sound crazy, and I don't mean it to be ugly—well, that I was a man and you were my girl. I looked at you sleeping, too. I looked at your body, and I wished it was mine. That Robbie could find me in bed with your body. I'd still be me, but . . . well . . . with your body for him to look at."

"You're very pretty."

"Me? I'm all tree branches."

Barbara hugged her. "I'm enchanted by you, Lainie."

"I'm just a dumb virgin," she said disconsolately. "This morning I felt safe. You were beside me."

$\mathcal{R}$OBBIE WAS WAITING OUTSIDE HER APARTMENT IN A warlike mood. He leaned against his car reading the sports section. Elaine caught sight of him as they turned the corner, and she ran ahead of Barbara and fell on him. He appeared surprised, and he allowed himself to be hugged and pecked on both cheeks. Over Elaine's shoulder he watched Barbara coming toward him, and when Elaine moved her head, blocking her out, he nudged her away.

"Are you still upset, Rob? I'm sorry, it's just that I'm so glad—so glad—you're not angry. You're not, are you?"

"Shouldn't you be the one?"

"I don't know who's right or wrong. Can we forget it?" As Barbara approached, she whispered, "Be sweet to her. She's been wonderful to me."

"She's wonderful to everyone," he said sullenly. "Hello, Barbara."

She nodded to him with the detachment usually reserved for neighbors one spends one's life avoiding.

"I'll make us a drink or some coffee if you've got time."

"I don't know. Do we, Rob?"

"Sure, a half hour one way or the other won't matter. Thanks, Barbara. If it's no trouble."

She opened the door and led them in. On the entryway steps, a man sat studying a map.

"Well, patience pays off. My mother always told me it would," the man said, folding the map, squeezing a bunch of violets tightly in his fist, and treading heavily down.

"Hi, Alex," Barbara said.

"You never called. That's a lawsuit at my firm."

"I was waiting for my lottery results. How are you?"

"Ten minutes older." He turned to Robbie, extended his hand, and said, "Hi, my name's Alex Hammond."

"Robert Franklin," Robbie said suspiciously, "and this is Elaine Westin."

"Have I come at a bad time, Barbara?"

"No, we were just on our way in," she said. "Please join us. Robbie, will you get Elaine's stuff in the bedroom?" Barbara said in an imperious voice. "It's on the bed."

Robbie felt as though his ribs had cracked, and he shook his head uncertainly and followed her hand, which pointed in the direction of the bedroom.

"Would you get some ice and the wine out, Lainie? I'll just be a minute," she said, going after Robbie.

Robbie picked up Elaine's bag at the side of the bed. "Is this where it all happens, Barbara?" he asked, pressing down on the bed. "It smells of you."

"Lower your voice."

"You really like to fuck with people's heads."

"Grow up. Your fiancée's in the other room."

She had called his bluff and he became imploring. "Don't you care about me at all?"

"What's that got to do with anything?"

"I can't just write off last night, pretend it didn't happen. Who is this guy?"

"A friend. Look, pick up her stuff and go. I've answered your questions."

"Just one more."

"Don't bother."

"I'm going to. Has he fucked you?"

"If I tell you the truth, will you leave?"

"Do I have any choice?"

"No, not really." She looked at him with affection. "No, he hasn't."

"Is he going to?"

"I don't know. Why, is it important?" She had a tired, resigned expression.

"My father's going to kill you, you know that. And you'll deserve it."

"Get out, Robbie."

"Barbara, I hope you do die for what you've done."

She shrugged apathetically. "I died years ago."

His hand went under her skirt, and she pressed her lips against his. He was a dried leaf in an old book. He clasped her chin in a vise, forcing her mouth open.

"Be a good boy, now, and go."

"I've got your cunt smell on my fingers."

"Well, hit the first gas station and wash it off in the john."

"What did you think last night when I was eating your pussy?"

"That it's been done before by experts."

"But wasn't I good?"

"I liked it."

Tears formed in the corners of her eyes, and she wiped them with the back of her knuckles.

"I can't stand all this smutty talk from you and making myself sound like I was rough trade. I gave you a part of myself. A gift, Robbie."

He picked up Elaine's bag and left the room.

"I didn't want to interrupt," Elaine said. "I assumed you were talking about Teddy."

Alex rattled the ice cubes in his empty glass. He sat in a high-backed chair like a referee at a tennis match. He rose when he saw Barbara.

"I sort of drifted into a family thing, I think," Alex said. Elaine hugged Barbara, kissed her, and Robbie waited for his turn, his back to Alex. He gave her a fraternal kiss on the cheek.

"Everything seems to take the form of a drama in your life, Barbara."

"My father and Barbara are engaged, pal," Robbie said.

"Thanks for the FYI. Actually, I'm relieved to hear it. I thought I was losing my mind when I got the idea that Barbara was wandering around unattached. Lucky in court, unlucky outside."

"Good-bye," Barbara said, ushering Robbie and Elaine to the door.

"You'll keep in touch, Barbara. Promise me you will."

"I will."

When they left, Barbara remained at the door as though searching her memory for a magic word that would close the door to the past.

"The ice tastes great here."

"I have a filter. The liquor is in the walnut cabinet below."

Alex got up, opened the cabinet, and poured himself a healthy shot of Black Label. Unfettered by his lawyer's suit, he presented an entirely different vision, the carefree Sunday bachelor in Armani blue jeans and a denim shirt. His hair was tousled by the wind and there was a friendly, easy grace about him. She liked him better than she had remembered.

"I phoned you all weekend. Who would have thought you were listed? I really didn't mean to walk into something that wasn't my business."

"I'm glad you stopped by," she said, drinking most of the scotch in his glass.

"You look like you've had quite a weekend."

"Bags under my eyes?"

"No, just rattled."

She sat down on the floor at his feet, saying noth-

ing, and he knew he had to talk about anything to
keep her from asking him to leave when he had finished his drink.

"Is it true about you getting married?"

"I've changed my mind."

"There's not very much I know about you and less
that I understand."

"Maybe it's better that way." She took his glass and
shook the ice cubes, dropped one into her mouth,
and sucked it. "I beat you for your drink." She fixed
him another one. "I didn't want to be alone today."

"Neither did I. But I didn't come just for the company."

"Did you ever have a feeling—without anything to
back it up—that you were going to find yourself in a
lot of trouble?"

"Whenever I go to court, I get it. Undefinable fears
that usually turn out to be surprise witnesses or someone whose story you've heard sixty-three times changing it when he's on the stand. I'm afraid of what I can't
prepare for, so most of the time I'm anticipating disaster—somebody's life or freedom." He laughed to himself. "I suppose it comes out sounding like *Law and
Order,* or Court TV."

"Are you good at what you do?"

"Well, yes, I am. Pretty good. The juries think so.
You can't try murder cases without a big ego."

"Did you win any new cases?"

"As it happens, I didn't. But I got the charge reduced to manslaughter. Barbara, is there anything
you'd like to do today?"

"I can't think what."

"Who was that guy defending you for, himself or his
father?"

"Maybe both," she replied.

He laughed uneasily. "Seems you've had a busy
weekend, driving a father and son insane."

"I thought you told me you like to know the answers before you ask leading questions."

"I've got a natural inclination to elicit information."

"Yes, don't *elicit* information, and don't talk legalese."

"Point taken. I've got an appointment to see a house in Rye. Like to tag along and get me crazy?"

TWENTY-ONE

$\mathcal{A}$ LEX HAD A NEW FOUR-LITER S-JAGUAR IN BRITISH racing green and he drove it as though he was Dale Earnhardt testing it in Daytona for ESPN. They flew by traffic on the Westchester Parkway and she loved the exhilaration of the high speed, which was such a stark contrast from the way Teddy's chauffeur handled the Rolls-Royce in which she always felt like an elderly woman cosseted by a male nurse. She thumbed through his CD collection and liked his music selection. With surprise she found Debussy's string quartet, which she and Laura listened to constantly when they were at Radcliffe. It seemed to ease the pressure and she found herself relaxing. She didn't talk, and he didn't force her. In forty minutes he turned off on Greentree Avenue.

"I went to the St. Regis the other night with a friend. We were at Georgetown Law together. I haven't been out in ages and he's from North Carolina with a small-town practice and he wanted some nightlife. And who should be there but my ex-wife. It's so interesting to observe people when they don't see you. I hadn't run into her before, and I got the most peculiar sensation in my chest, which became a pain as the evening wore on. She was sitting in a booth, and I was against the wall, so she'd have to physically come by to see me.

"I watched her dancing. Wiggling her ass, pushing up against this guy. I guess she and the photographer she left me for had finally broken up. I could see the look of surprise in the man's eyes, like when you're in a store and you buy something for five dollars and the salesperson gives you change with an extra twenty. There's a moment of conflict. You've got the store's money in your hand and what you've bought, and you're not sure what to do.

"My ex's date was maybe about sixty. He'd taken her out expecting very little in return and discovered that she was a whore. At first the man didn't know how to react, but after she made it obvious that there wasn't going to be any problem at the end of the night, he got bolder. Like in a geometric progression that keeps doubling itself. Now this was not out of jealousy . . . but I couldn't stop watching.

"After the second bottle of Cristal, she ordered a third one, and I could see she'd had too much to drink. The man slipped his hand between her legs, she kissed him on the ear, and they continued drinking. I wasn't so much disgusted as horrified that I'd been married to this cheap lush, that I'd shared my emotions with her. Going to bed was the least important part. I'd given her my confidence, really worked to make myself a good lawyer, and she was one of the reasons I had as much juice and drive as I did.

"She wobbled out, doesn't know me from the dead. She's juiced, slurring her words, and my pal from

North Carolina looks her over, turns to me with a big
smile and says, 'Alex, this is glamour . . . this is what it's
all about, boy.' When we were outside, he turned to
me and said, 'This evening was one of the all-timers,
one of the unforgettables.' "

"Is that why you've decided to see me?" Barbara
asked. "Because you're no longer looking for trouble?"

"Oh, come on, Barbara, I know a killer when I see
one."

She laughed, leaned over and kissed him.

"Make 'em laugh and they drop their pants."

"Alex, that's not true. I only *drop* 'em when I'm depressed and there's no reason to live, so it doesn't
matter."

"I'll have to reverse my approach," he said with a
theatrical sigh.

The house was on the corner, Rye Tudor, with small
latticed windows and a fair-sized lawn. A man waited
outside.

"Why'd you tell me about your ex?" Barbara asked.

"Because I felt rotten, and telling you made me feel
less rotten."

"You weren't planning on an exchange of confidences, were you?"

"No, Barbara, I was not. You'll tell me what you want
me to know when you're ready." He helped her out of
the car. "Your legs are too long," he said.

"I've been a hard-luck child all my life."

The real estate agent came toward them, jingling
the keys.

"Mr. Hammond?"

"Yes. Can I have a look around on my own?"

"Sure. I've got to see a few people now. Could you
leave the keys in the security box?"

"Be glad to."

"I think you and your wife will like this one, Mr.
Hammond."

The house smelled of old flowers, log fires, family lunches, and children.

"You didn't bother to correct him," Barbara said.

"I save time that way. Why explain things to people who don't care one way or the other? He seemed a pleasant enough guy. I thought we were going to get one of those overbearing women who'd give us the tour and never stop talking about using the fourth bedroom as a playroom."

The downstairs area consisted of a kitchen, dining room, and a den that overlooked an acre of cultivated fruit orchard, apple and cherry trees. There was also a greenhouse, barbecue pit, gazebo, and swing. Barbara opened the rear door and made for the swing. She held tightly onto the rusty chains, and started to swing. Alex roamed around upstairs through bedrooms with beamed ceilings, inspecting bathrooms, finally arriving in the living room, which overlooked the back garden.

He heard Barbara singing and pushed open the French doors that led to a porch. Barbara had a strange, disconcerting innocence in the garden, like a girl home from a school holiday who was on the point of moving from childhood into the world of adults. It hadn't occurred to him that she had a soft, green side that she kept concealed under a hard shell. He had a transient image of himself and Barbara with two small boys and a baby daughter sitting by the Christmas tree in the living room, which was aglow with candles and had a mound of presents at the base. He was thirty-seven and tired of the bachelor life: the one-week stands with lonely women constantly checking on their sleeping children. He had been a regular at minimalist apartments, opening the wine he had brought, sitting on stools at the kitchen counter for casual dinners. Buying a house in Rye and living out of the city, he decided, was the only way to escape from desolate bars and pickups. But Barbara had been a pickup. Possibly she might turn out to be different.

When she saw him come toward her, she stopped singing.

"Suddenly, I felt happy," she said.

"Do I get any credit for it?"

"Yes, I enjoy being with you. Are you going to buy the house?"

"I'm thinking of it. I could flip my co-op, net out a million, rent an apartment in the city and come here weekends and holidays when I'm not working. It would be an investment and a different life."

"You can hunt for a wife at the country club."

"Do I need another one?" He was disconcerted by her flippancy because of his intense attraction.

She abandoned the swing, picked up her shoes, and leaned on his shoulder while she stepped into them.

"It's too big for me, but on the other hand, the smaller ones always seem poky and inconvenient."

"I haven't lived in a house. We had an apartment on the west side, which made it easy for my dad to get to his wine shop. I went to Dalton. In those days everyone I knew lived in apartments."

"Did you miss not having a house?"

"Are you sounding me out?"

"I don't know. Am I?"

"I couldn't see myself stuck up here becoming a suburban matriarch. I'm too impolitic, in any case."

"If you had kids . . ."

"I'm not a family person. I don't want responsibilities. Where I am now, I'm ten minutes from the UN and I've got the river, which is important to me."

"The Sound's down the street," he said, by way of an offer.

"If I were you, I'd stay single and not get involved,

or else marry some twenty-year-old kid who has a shorter life story than mine. Somebody dependable, who thinks you're more interesting than she is and who'll tolerate an occasional evening out so that you can romance some lady you've stashed away from the old days. That's male nirvana, Alex."

"Is that such an awful existence?"

"No, it's a viable career for lots of women."

"Not you?"

"The maternal instinct was stillborn in me."

"I can't believe you mean that. What do *you* want?"

"I don't answer personal questions on Sunday afternoons in Rye, New York, just a block from the Sound."

"Are you putting me on?"

"Yeah, can't you take it?"

He offered to show her around the house, but she declined, and they drove to the country club, which was a perfect display window for all the bored unathletic drunks and failed Romeos for fifty miles around. She didn't like the looks she got, so she sat in a corner with her back to the room and faced the eighteenth green. Alex's friends were still on the golf course, and she would have liked to leave, but there was no way of getting back to the city without him. And yet she felt a peculiar, illogical affection for him; his personal life seemed to be conducted with the same degree of clumsy blundering as everyone else's. Two men waved at Alex from a golf cart.

"It won't take long," Alex said. "I've got to see this guy. I going to tell him that I've found out a few things that will help his son."

"What did his son do?"

"He's been accused of raping a girl."

"Did he?"

"Personally, I don't think so. But the jury will decide."

"No DNA?"

"Nada."

"Is this what you're working on now?"

"This and eight other cases. Let's see . . . two murders, one armed robbery, a self-defense, a narcotics, an attempted murder—"

"Now you can add a rape to your list."

"Yes, it sort of makes Sunday, doesn't it?"

"How do you keep them all straight?"

"They're all at different stages of preparation. And I have to take this one, because this man's a friend."

"Would you have taken it if you knew the boy was guilty?"

"Yes. But he's not. So it makes it easier."

"I'm really impressed. I really am."

"Well, just because I behave like an ass in my personal life doesn't mean to say that I'm not good at my work."

"I drew that conclusion."

The man, whose name was Brooks, stared at Barbara over his drink during their meeting, trying to place her. He was accompanied by his family lawyer, a middle-aged cigar smoker who appeared to do most of his work on golf courses. She watched Alex and listened to him with admiration as he outlined the case. He didn't go into details because he realized Brooks was uncomfortable with her there, and they agreed to meet at his office when Alex would have more details. As Brooks got up to leave, he spoke to Barbara.

"You wouldn't have anything to do with Wall Street, would you?"

"No," she said, anxious to leave.

"But we've met. I'm sure we have."

"Are you in business?"

"I'm with a hedge fund. The Cornwall Group."

"Doesn't ring a bell. My friend and financial adviser—I guess I could call him my adviser—is Teddy Franklin."

Brooks's face registered a combination of surprise and delight.

"I knew I'd met you. It was at a Christmas party at La Cote Basque last year. In fact, I spoke to Teddy just this week, and he told me he was getting married. You're Barbara."

"Yes."

He extended his hand and Barbara shook it. "Lucky Teddy, he's been on his own for years. I suppose his time has come."

"For what?" Barbara asked.

"Happiness. Good luck to you."

On the drive back, Alex sourly avoided talking to her. He answered Barbara's questions with a curt yes or no, refusing to elaborate.

"Hey, why're you so moody?" she asked as they pulled into her street.

"You damn well know why. You sandbagged me. Made a fool out of me."

"Why?"

"You didn't mention Franklin before."

"Do you know him?"

"Nobody knows him, but everyone's heard about him."

"Something bad?"

He laughed nervously. "It's not possible that you're this naive. Teddy Franklin's a monolith."

"Of course, he's enormously rich. I know that."

"Rich? Try one of *Forbes*'s five richest. He's got billions. Don't you read newspapers?"

"Yes, but not financial papers. Until recently, I was living in France."

"My God, Barbara, doesn't it scare you to be close to so much money?"

"No, should it? Christ, you act like you've never heard of money."

"It's the power that goes with it."

"I haven't noticed it. In fact, he's very ordinary in a lot of ways, with the usual hang-ups."

"Are you one of his hang-ups?"

"What if I am?"

"Did you break up with him—walk out or something?"

She became hesitant. The skin on his face tightened. What attracted her most to Alex was his easy manners, the naturalness he struck, but they had been displaced by irritable tension. At the club with Brooks he had been in command, logical, with a clear path he could take. She found it difficult to believe that men like Teddy and Alex—and Robbie for that matter— were so vulnerable. Even Frere was awkward and unsure of himself when a social instinct was needed. People behaved out of character; they lost confidence, and the thought reassured her and strengthened her ego.

"Don't you want to tell me?" he asked insistently.

"Well, okay, I walked out on him . . . not irresponsibly, either. It was just that he wanted me for a particular reason, and I decided I didn't want him for the same reason. You see, all this crap about money, this fear of not having it or of having it, isn't important to me. I don't fall on my knees because a god has entered the room. I've got other things that worry me. Frighten me. Like getting old, dying, not having a family. I had a friend once, a real friend, but that's something I can't go into. She was important. She's dead. I feel myself drifting. I don't have a center. That's the problem—not whether I break my engagement, or if the man's on *Forbes*'s rich bastard list. You ought to know about people with no center, when you're sitting in court with murderers and rapists. If they knew where it was, they wouldn't be in court, would they?"

"Barbara, you don't seem to understand that you're

in trouble—not police trouble. It's even worse. Don't you know what kind of reputation Franklin's got? You don't mess around with people like him."

"What is he, some kind of racketeer?"

"It's more serious than that. He's respectable. He buys people, business, officials—whatever he wants. He takes over a company, twenty thousand people lose their jobs. He's a stone killer."

"How would you know?"

"How would I know?"

They had reached her street and he found a spot near her apartment.

"Will you come in?" she asked.

Alex acted as though the invitation was fraught with danger. "I may as well."

"Don't let me force you."

"Oh, Barbara, you're living in a dream world. You really are."

Twenty-two

$\mathcal{S}$INCE MOVING IN, BARBARA ONLY OCCASIONALLY shopped for food. Teddy was always there like a grand piano crying "play me." In the early days, when she hadn't accepted a dinner invitation, someone would be at the door delivering food she hadn't ordered: from Eli's, Dean & Deluca, or some restaurant, compliments of the invisible pianoforte. In the year closing in that she had known Teddy, she had never cooked for him. It never would have occurred to him to ask, especially since he always raided restaurants whenever he heard of a chef who wanted an easier life and more money. He thought the lechery of her appetite was purely sexual.

As the daughter of a widower, and after years of living in France, Barbara had become an excellent cook. With Alex scanning through her music library and selecting Brahms's Third Symphony, she scraped together some vegetables and chunks of Provence herbed sausage and produced a peasant omelette, along with a bottle of cold, crisp Sancerre. She liked doing things for Alex. It was almost like having someone of her own. Her pressures floated into the wasteland of activity.

They avoided the subject of Teddy. But they were conscious of his presence; his very absence, like some dark, evanescent symbol of ultimate judgment, sword in hand, lay threateningly over their heads. In the flesh he was mortal, in spirit, an avenger. Barbara had never thought of Teddy before with anything resembling physical fear, but now, because of Alex's reaction, she became aware of a nameless dread that she identified with Teddy, who dominated everything. When Teddy had tried to kill her, she knew her willingness to have sex with him would assuage him.

She and Alex ate her impromptu dinner, watching TV. Couldn't the two of them be any young couple in America? she wondered. She imagined Alex eating ropey sandwiches and drinking coffee out of containers in obscure hotels all over the country. He'd be someone to worry about, someone to be loyal to. What was more, the glimpse she'd seen of his work impressed her. She admired the fact that he had the capacity to suffer as she had. His relationship with his wife proved it. He hadn't made any attempt to make a move on her. She had liked kissing him the first time, and she could imagine herself waking up in the same bed with him without having a grand mal seizure.

They watched Roger Ebert pan movies, then struggled with Mike Wallace trying to comprehend the sociopathic behavior of a neo-Nazi convict who had burned a black family to death. Nothing in the news enlightened them. Afterward, with a familiarity Barbara found endearing, Alex proceeded to divide up the *Times*, and they both read for an hour. He was making life easy for her, ordinary. Alex slipped off his shoes and stretched out on the couch. She switched on the reading lamp, and he nodded thanks.

"Why'd you come today?" she asked, when they exchanged papers.

"Something stuck to me the first time. Usually I'm a hit-and-run man. I found myself thinking about you when I was away, and I got the idea that I had something to come back to. I'd planned to spend the weekend in Chicago, where I'm cocounsel on a case. I've got a preliminary hearing there."

"You were going to say something more about Teddy—in the car."

"Was I?"

"Don't be shy. Is it something I shouldn't know?"

"I've been thinking about it. It's hard to decide what I ought to do and what I should do. Actually, I have a conflict of interest. I'm stacking the cards against myself."

She laid her head on his lap and looked up at him. "I'm not going to force you to betray any confidences."

"I'm in an impossible position," he said. "There've been all sorts of times in the past when I've had a conflict of interest, which really amounts to this: do I do what's best for my client, or is my first loyalty to the community that I'm part of? Usually the client wins, and in most cases there isn't any real struggle, or else I don't take the case. But there've been times when I've believed a man was innocent and at some time during the trial I discover that he's guilty, but the state doesn't know any more than it did when it first started.

"Then I'm forced to persuade twelve honest jurors that my client ought to go free. If I've got a strong case, the defendant gets off."

His voice trailed off, and she was left waiting. He stared vacantly at the floor.

"Are you trying to say you know something criminal about Teddy?"

"I am. And what I know is privileged, and I can't divulge it to anyone."

"There you go, using words like *divulge.*"

"Well, you're making me act like a lawyer and not someone you're spending time with. I want to keep seeing you, and this might affect it."

"It won't!" she said with a fervor that encouraged him.

Men in trouble, she thought, always look better to a woman. Handsome. Alex was shockingly charming without being needy. She adored him.

"All this guy talk about my ex . . . well, I was hurt. I don't want it to happen again." He lit one of her old Gauloises. "Shit, you make men smoke." He cautiously touched her hair without bad intentions. "I want whatever happens between us to have a development . . . a slow, natural development, which will make a decision one way or the other inevitable, like Brahms's Third Symphony."

"I'm glad you're being honest. It's too romantic, but I love Brahms."

"Thank Clara Schumann."

Male awareness struck a blow for her. She wanted to take her clothes off but desisted.

"Barbara, our meeting was a fluke—an accident. I don't want anything else to be accidental or for you to hear about something that makes you look at me in a different way."

His voice resonated with an advocate's tenor and she was thrilled. He shifted his legs, and remained becalmed and held her hand. He kissed it, and she felt another surge of affection for him.

"Barbara, I'm *involved* with Teddy Franklin."

"How?"

"In a sense, I work for him."

"You what?"

"Well, not directly. But what it amounts to is that

he's a part owner of my firm: McCartt, Badgley, Knox, Doty, and Associates. I'm the Associates."

"What about the other partners?"

"They've got a piece of the firm, but Teddy is the boss. Legally, contractually, in every way. You're one of the few people outside the practice who knows now. Twelve years ago, our Mr. Franklin was in a lot of trouble. . . . Have you ever heard of the Archer case?"

"No. It sounds ominous."

"It happened in South Carolina. Dolores Archer was a beautiful young widow who inherited a privately held chemical company from her husband. I had been with the firm a little over a year. Teddy went down to Hilton Head where she had an estate. He wanted to buy Archer Chemicals. So he courted her. He spent a good deal of time down there, got involved with some golf-resort developers and made an investment. From what I learned, that was really chump change for him. He did it because of Dolores. They became lovers and there was talk of Teddy marrying her."

"I wonder why he didn't."

"We'll never know, because she was murdered. Teddy and she had been together hours before—he admitted that at the inquest. But he had an alibi. He was on his private jet flying back to New York at the time of the murder. Dolores's trustees didn't know what to do with the company. Since she had agreed to sell him her holdings, they went ahead with the sale.

"Teddy Franklin bought out the minority shareholders and three years later, he managed to create a bidding war between two chemical giants for the company, and he walked away with a few hundred million in profit.

"Naturally, he needed a criminal lawyer and he picked my boss. After the case ended, Teddy decided that what he wanted was his own firm of specialists. Lawyers to deal with contracts, someone on investments, someone on real estate, and he had a unique idea. Why bother to pay staff lawyers you can't control when you could handpick a few who'd be loyal, put your interests first, and who could give you valuable inside information about other people you brought to the firm?

"He found Dennis Doty at Princeton, McCartt at Stanford, Jeralyn Badgley at Yale, and Harold Knox in Oklahoma. All four top of their classes, and he offered them the unheard-of starting salary of five hundred thousand a year as a draw to go into business. They had offices and support staff, foreign and domestic.

"They had previously clerked for a year for Supreme Court justices, then worked for major Wall Street firms. When they were ready, he opened 'their' office, became their number-one client, and dragged forty or fifty other clients with him. Just the fact of his moving to another firm created a big noise. When I got out of Georgetown, I was recruited, and I clerked there for almost two years. Eventually I wanted to leave because I was interested in criminal law, but they liked me, thought I was too good to lose, and offered me a substantial raise."

Barbara listened carefully, mouth agape.

"The firm's position was: you never know when you might need a criminal lawyer, and it would be better for all concerned if he were a member of the family."

"But you're all very successful now. Couldn't you all walk out and start your own firm?"

"Of course, we all could, but why should we? We've got a reputation and very important clients. The *right* ones."

"What's a 'right' client?"

"Bank presidents. Major corporations, and then there's the bandit department that I now run for people like Jack Brooks and his hedge fund. His son got in trouble. He called me. Why should any one of us leave? We get the best information—Teddy Franklin has made everyone millionaires. It's a very happy arrangement. Money is filtered out into shell companies that are used as offshore tax shelters. We know about takeovers, initial public offerings, months before anything happens. Everyone picks up stock slowly, and then when there's a public announcement, everyone's out, smiling, with monster profits."

"But is any of this illegal?"

"It's illegal, dishonest, unethical, and profitable."

"And you're part of it?"

"Don't look so shocked."

"I can't help it. It sounds like an octopus."

"Barbara, that's what I meant when I said you don't know anything about Franklin. No one's ever known him to be seriously interested in a woman since Dolores Archer."

"Did they ever find the killer?"

Alex pondered the question and wanted to dodge it, but the haunted expression in her eyes forced him to reconsider. "No, it was a professional job and there were rumors."

Now her anxiety clasped him. "You must tell me, Alex."

"That Dolores Archer changed her mind about selling the company to Teddy and he had her put to sleep."

Barbara trembled. "I'm actually engaged to him. I had misgivings from the moment I met him, but he overpowered me. He's obsessed with me. No matter what I do, he won't leave me alone."

Alex nodded gloomily. "This is serious shit, Barbara. You can't just drop him like anybody else."

"Well, what do I do?" she asked, throwing up her hands, her voice edged with panic.

"God knows."

"He's paying for my psychotherapy. He controls my

money." She laughed. "My father was broke. You see, I'd been living in Bordeaux since I graduated from Radcliffe. I did see my dad whenever he came to France on a wine-buying trip, but I hadn't been back to the States until he died. I was in shock. His estate was a mess. I had no money and then my father's lawyer took me to see Teddy. In less than a year, Teddy invested the money for me and he told me this weekend that I had made my first million. For all I know he's been giving me his money."

Alex was flabbergasted.

"Does he love you?"

She nodded.

"And you?"

"I don't know. I'm confused. I thought I did, then something bugged me and I thought: Oh, no, it's not working; I've got to get out. So I did just that. I took his car and drove off."

Alex looked at his watch, got up from the sofa, and put on his shoes.

"I've got to head home and pack. I'm catching an early flight tomorrow to Chicago."

She clung to him and kissed him at the door.

"Alex, will I see you when you get back?"

"I'd like that very much."

"In the meantime," she asked in a quavering voice, "what shall I do?"

"Come to terms with Teddy, whatever they are."

TWENTY-THREE

EDDY NEVER REMEMBERED FALLING DOWN. THE
last recollection he retained was of one of his
paintings, an intimate Bonnard nude in a greenish
blue bathtub. He had stared at it for more than an
hour, steadily drinking vodka until he was drawn into
the sensual painting. The image of the woman turned
spidery, the painting blurred, and he staggered against
the wall.

Leonard found him at the foot of the gallery stairs.
The blood on the jagged gash over his eye had con-
gealed and turned a blue black color. Leonard was
calm but resolute and drove him to New York Hospital, where an attending physician took X rays and
stitched his forehead. The X rays were negative and
he advised Teddy to stay in bed for a day, prescribed
Vicodin and told him not to drink. Apart from the
dull throb when the local wore off and the nuisance of

the bandage, Teddy began to feel better when they arrived home.

Leonard helped him undress in the bedroom, fussed and fretted and offered a host of home remedies: everything from foot baths to Beecham's Powders. He was dismayed when Teddy demanded a bucket of ice and a bottle of vodka.

"There's no reasoning with you. I've got a mind to call Ms. Hickman and have her deal with you. I've never seen you drink this way!"

"Leonard, please don't call anyone."

In all the years he had been with Teddy, he had never seen him so bereft and helpless. When Leonard finally departed, Teddy poured himself a drink and grew despondent. He lay back on his regal bed, surrounded by his paintings: Manet's *Rouen Cathedral*, Bonnard's *Girl in the Bathtub*, Degas's *Ballerina*, and an ink drawing Tchelitchew had made for *Hide and Seek*, which was his favorite. He saw himself as king on a throne in his treasure house, inconsolable, alone, because his faithless queen had deserted him. The shrike of paranoia cawed through his mind. Did Barbara have another man?

He took a pad and pen from his desk and made a list of the assets Barbara would possess with him.

Love, Money, Position, Loyalty, Understanding, Jewelry, Paintings, Travel, a Yacht, Houses, Cars, a Family, Friendship, Time—my time—all the time remaining to me.

Had he left something off the list? He scanned it, pointing with his pen and ticking off the various services, possessions, she'd be heir to when they were married. He's settle a hundred million on her in the premarital agreement and that would put an end to any lawsuits if she ever considered divorce. He couldn't imagine what he'd missed.

He refilled his glass, dropped a couple of ice cubes

in, and drank it down in one long swallow. *What* did she want? He was physically attractive and most important, sensitive to her needs. He wondered if she objected to the frequency of his lovemaking, but he'd been selfless and considerate, waiting, waiting, waiting for her, until his body almost exploded with the pain of holding back. They'd made love seven times over the weekend, and he was certain that she'd had orgasms each time. No, their lovemaking was perfect, a grand slam. What had possessed her to leave him?

She couldn't blame *him* for her psychological problems. Dr. Frere had convinced him that they were making progress and that she'd emerge with a stronger, more secure personality. She'd be confident, emotionally stable. Teddy was certain that Barbara cared for him and at times must have felt some emotion approximating love. He had been only a few blocks away from her apartment when he was at the hospital, but had been afraid to drop in. He had never been so off-balance in any situation.

Perhaps she had been upset by Robbie and Elaine, but apart from Robbie's unpredictable drunkenness on the boat, there hadn't been anything peculiar or noticeably strained in their meeting. His head ached, and his vision blurred for a moment, and he discovered that for the first time in years—since his wife's death—he was in tears. Barbara wasn't simply a woman he loved, he realized, who could be replaced by another pretty face or a willing, compliant body: Barbara was his *life*. He turned on his side and sobbed inconsolably.

He heard Leonard knocking at the door and he forced himself to stop and said, "I'm all right. Please go to bed, Leonard."

Teddy sensed that continuing the pursuit would inevitably lead to the same cul-de-sac. She had to return to him without pressure. He'd fought with himself against calling her. He took out a Polaroid he'd taken of her sleeping, and he set it down on his side table under the lamp. Eyes tightly closed, her fingers gripping the blanket, in the midst of some dream he could not penetrate, she fought to elude a phantom. Was *he* the phantom?

With a mixture of apprehension and revulsion he opened the bag that contained the tapes and records that W. T. Grant had died for. He slipped tape number one into the deck and pressed the *play* button.

"January twelfth. I am about to see Barbara Hickman," Frere began. "She was referred to me by an old friend, Dr. Benjamin Cohen, who was acting on behalf of a patient of his who has agreed to pay her bills. According to Dr. Cohen, Hickman is a woman of twenty-eight, well educated, a linguist, very beautiful and suffering from some as-yet undiagnosed mental condition. Please note, there are to be no insurance claims or forms filled out for Ms. Hickman.

"Ah, you're here early. Please take a seat and get comfortable. Start where you like," Dr. Frere said in an amiable voice.

"With a word or what?" Barbara answered.

"I just want you to be relaxed, and we're not going to play word-association games or give you Rorschach tests or anything like that."

"Okay." There was a pause. "Can I smoke this?"

"What is it?"

"What it looks like."

"Marijuana?"

"Right."

"I'm not against it, but I'd rather you avoided drugs of any kind when we start. If I find that they're necessary, I'll prescribe something. In any case, legally I can't prescribe marijuana."

"I used to play a game at college . . . with my friend and roommate, Laura Sargent."

"What kind of game?"

"Oh, it was parlor psychology."

"There're a lot of those. If it makes things easier, we can try it. Why don't you start there?"

"It's called 'I live in a forest.' "

Frere began to laugh, and so did Barbara, and Teddy got the impression that the sluice gates would now open.

"I remember that one."

"It was a riot," Barbara said. "There's a straightforward way of playing, but we did it for a year, and it got very sophisticated and we used variations." She halted, coughed. "I suppose you know what the questions represent?"

"Why don't you tell me?"

"Okay. But first I'd like to explain something: toward the end—before Laura died—the game got very deep and it turned ugly. We were completely honest— at least I was—and we used to act out our fantasies. I didn't think I had fantasies till then, but a mysterious thing happened. Laura was able to transfer her fantasies to me. She took me over. Do you understand what I mean?"

"She was someone you admired."

"Yes, greatly admired. Emotionally, she was stronger than I was. But I didn't know that at the beginning." Teddy heard her snuffling, then a lighter clicked and Barbara said, "Thanks. Can you bear the smell of Gauloises?"

"I still smoke a pipe, but not in the office."

"Can I ask you something, Dr. Frere?"

"Yes, whatever you like."

"How much do you charge?"

"Two hundred and fifty dollars an hour."

"Teddy's agreed to pay all the bills?"

"Yes, he has. It's something we don't have to discuss."

"Have you some kind of deal, an agreement with him?"

"What're you suggesting?"

"Telling him about me—if you find out something?"

"No, of course not. I'd never do anything like that. Don't even think of it."

"Will he pressure you?"

"I can't imagine why he'd do such a thing . . . and if he does, I'll explain that our relationship is a confidential one. Barbara, Mr. Franklin is a very smart, sophisticated man. He's not going to be a problem. You can tell him what you like, but I'd prefer you not discuss what goes on here. This is a process and it can affect your treatment. You might say something to him that could be useful to us."

"Do you think I'm ever going to be all right?"

"I can't answer that until I find what *you* think is wrong. It may, in fact, be nothing serious. Let's see if we can find out."

"When you do, will you be able to let me know?"

"I'll try to. Let me put it to you this way: 'Our doubt is our passion and our passion is our task.' Henry James said that about writing fiction. I mean it in the sense of ferreting out the truth. . . . You were about to tell me about this game you and Laura, I believe, played."

Teddy heard Barbara sigh and had a vision of her chest expanded and that lost, puzzled look on her face.

"I live in a forest. Now, Dr. Frere, you say, 'What does the forest look like?' "

"What does the forest look like?"

"It's dark with giant redwoods, hundreds of feet high, and I'm in the high grass. You can't see me because I'm lying prone beneath the shoots. I'm hiding.

I'm wearing only a T-shirt and panties. It's an ugly forest with stinging nettles, poison ivy, and omnivorous plants that open and close. The animals don't go near the plants because the plants open up and eat the animals. I saw a fox swallowed by a plant. Its head started to dissolve. The plant was generating some kind of heat and melting the fox. The forest frightens me. But I can't move. I think if I try to escape, one of the plants will eat me, or a tree will fall on me. So I keep stockstill. That way I can maintain equilibrium."

After a pause, Frere said, "Now you see a bear. What do you do?"

"Oh, so you do know the game?" Barbara sounded pleased.

"Yes, I do. I don't want to divert you or force you to play it. Now what happens when you see the bear? What do you do?"

"Well, the bear is ferocious and he comes after me and I want to run away from it, but I'm afraid to move because of the trees, plants, and snakes; but I have to, or else I'll be eaten. There's a large hollow in one of the safe trees, where wolves live. I see that the mother has gone off to hunt for food for her cubs. I creep forward on my hands and knees and slip into the hollow.

"The bear watches me, and he moves closer, but he can't get into the hollow. He growls, and I can hear him scratching the tree trunk with his claws. There's a strong odor of animal inside the hollow and a dead squirrel, which two wolf cubs are tearing apart. The wolf cubs growl at me and bare their teeth and they move closer to me. I hear the bear furiously grunting outside, and I have nowhere to go.

"The cubs begin to nuzzle me, forcing themselves against my breasts and clawing my T-shirt. I realize they've torn my T-shirt and I cover myself with my arms. They snuggle next to my bare flesh. They want to be comforted and I realize they're only playing. Then they begin licking my breasts and sniffing between my thighs. I open my arms to show that I'm friendly and I hold them in my arms. They begin licking my nipples hard, but they're not actually hurting me. And I like the feeling they're giving me. I feel safe and needed, protected by them."

"So the sensation is pleasing?"

"Note the patient nods," Frere said.

"You're recording this?"

"Yes, I also make case notes afterwards. Now, as I recall, eventually the bear goes off into the woods and you can leave, you wander around the forest because you know the mother wolf is coming back. You find something on the ground. What is it, and what is your reaction?"

"I always find the same thing."

"What is it?"

"A black apple."

"Why not a green apple or a red one? And why do you think it's an apple?"

"Because you see, I really do *live* in this forest, and I know that the other kinds of apples won't grow. I tried to grow them, and the seedling trees died. The moment they were planted. But the black-apple trees thrive here every season of the year. They have a kind of—I don't know what they call them. It isn't a stem. It's a primitive tail covered with a slithery skin. It feels like a mucous membrane.

"Yes, it's a membrane. Soft, silky, and wet. Like a vagina."

"But it has the shape of a penis?"

"Yes. The tree itself grows in a kind of translucent membrane. I saw it in a dream. I watched it growing. And when you walk, the apples are all over the ground. You can't help stepping on them, and they get soft and turn rotten, and they have a fetid odor, like tooth decay.

"Well, I pick up this apple and my fingers are sucked in and they meld in this shapeless mass. Now, this part of it never changes. You see, when I first played it with Laura, I always saw it and picked up the black apple, and when I tried to fantasize what I picked up, it was always the same thing. The oozing black apple. Laura said it was something else and I didn't want to give myself away."

"Do you know what this part means?" Frere asked.

"Of course," she said in a cocksure way. "The object you find is the loved one."

Frere cleared his voice and apologized for his cold and they made another appointment.

Teddy poured himself a drink, and, as he was about to change the tape, he heard Frere say:

"Sexual components are marked and suggestive with dead friend, but the passion is still alive. Laura becomes the eidetic transference, an icon of wish fulfillment and role reversal. We'll see."

Twenty-four

Session Two: Barbara Hickman. She is in good spirits and anxious to talk. Very animated.

"Now, Barbara, as I recall, after you've left the wolves' den in this fable, you have to make a decision. There is a body of water you have to get across. How do you do it, or don't you bother to cross it?"

"It's an ocean, and it's primeval. I can see caves with people in them, and there are orange and green colors on the rocks that make them sparkle. I think that's how they get light because there is no sun. Then I see rainbow crystals. I dive in, and the water gets rough. The waves are very high. The weather is changing, funnels of wind form and it looks like a tsunami heading toward me. I can't swim back to shore or dive under it and I'm trapped. The wave relentlessly advances, and I start to choke, and somehow it passes over me. I'm thrust in a tube like a surfer and hurtling

to the ocean floor. The tube breaks and crabs start rip-
ping my toes off. Then suddenly I barrel up to the surface and I can see the sky. It's milky blue gray, and I
start to swim. I'm an excellent swimmer. I was the hun-
dred-yard freestyle champion when I was at Dalton. I
love being in the water because I've got confidence in
myself. That's what I don't understand about the wave.
I've been in all sorts of rough water, but this wave keeps
coming at me."

"What happens?"

"I just keep swimming, and I see the shore. But what
I have to go through to get to the shore. Snapping tur-
tles, eels that give electric shocks. Water snakes. And
the moss and slime and sludge on the rocks. It looks
like someone's guts that have just been removed in an
operating room . . . but I get there."

"That's very good, Barbara," Frere said. "I didn't
think for a minute we'd get that far this afternoon."

"Do you really mean it?"

"I'm enormously pleased with you."

"Oh, I'm so glad. I was sure that I'd disappoint you."

"Do you worry about disappointing people?"

"Doesn't everyone? People have had such high expectations."

"There are demands that are made that you can't
fulfill. Sometimes they're not worth the trouble.
Other times we accede to them and it upsets our balance. I've had a cancellation. This flu is really hitting
everyone. Would you like to reenact the last part of
the forest? Are you up to it?"

"Oh, yes."

"Are you feeling tired? If you'd rather we stopped—"

"No, I'm relieved to talk to you and discuss my part
in this way. I don't have to give so damn many explanations. *You* understand."

"Let's go on with this voyage of discovery. We're go-

ing to try to map it; then we'll see where we're going,
and we won't get lost, and the ocean will become navi-
gable. But it'll take some time."

"As long as you think I'll get to the other side."

"You will. Now you see a house. What does the
house look like, and what do you do?"

"It's a white house with a white brick wall, and it's
got Virginia creeper growing over it. Smoke's coming from the chimney, and the house frightens me in
a way that the wave never did. The house is in-
scrutable, ominous, and my stomach's churning
from nerves. I'm trembling. I don't want to go toward the house, but somehow, I don't know what—
impulse—some message from inside, pulls me closer.

"There's a window, and I see a shriveled old lady sitting in profile, and she's got on a white-lace cap and a
red velvet dress. The light hits her head in a peculiar
way, but the light source is concealed. It's almost as
though the old woman was the subject of a Vermeer
painting. I lean in closer, and she's sewing, and the
window's open, and I peer in. She has someone's head
on her lap! She's sewing the eyelids! It's a woman's
head, and on the table are other heads—men,
women, children, all staring with a dumb, dead, animal expression—and they're waiting to have their eyelids sewn. I duck away and start to run, and as I run, I
wet my pants, and I can't control myself. I've become
incontinent. It's humiliating, and I feel I'm debasing
myself and I, *ooh* . . ."

"You can stop, Barbara."

"No, the urine is golden and it's mine and it's squirt-
ing on the old lady's face and she can't sew the eyelids.
And I'm pleased that I've stopped her needle from
closing Laura's eyes."

"Laura?"

"What? Did I say *Laura*?"

"That's fine, Barbara."

Teddy heard a whimper and a long agonized groan of despair.

"I'm wrung out, Dr. Frere."

"Aren't you sleeping well?"

"Pretty well, most of the time."

"Do you need anything? I can prescribe Restorils or Xanax if you're feeling anxious."

"No, not really. I can manage."

"Good. Well, I'll see you on Monday then."

"May I ask you something, Dr. Frere?"

"Certainly."

"What are you going to do this afternoon?"

"I promised to go to a movie with my wife."

"And tonight . . . are you going out with friends?"

"Nothing special. We'll probably stop at Zabar's and take out some food."

"That sounds so ordinary . . . I thought—"

"What did you think?"

"Oh, I don't know."

"Have you got some plans?"

"Yes . . . Teddy," she said in a sullen voice. Teddy flinched at the sound of his name. She made it sound unpleasant, like an injection.

"Probably something glamorous."

"Yes, glamorous. An auction at Sotheby's. Teddy has his eye on some drawings by Egon Schiele. They looked obscene in the catalogue."

"Why?"

"Oh, they're women sitting with their legs wide open and everything is on display. They're so angry."

"Sotheby's, that's a different world from mine. Good-bye. Have a good weekend, Barbara."

"Thanks. You, too."

"Barbara, for the time being, would you desist from using marijuana or any drugs unless I prescribe them?"

"Okay."

Teddy detected reluctance on her part.

A couple of chairs were shuffled, and the tape ended.

*T*EDDY REMEMBERED THE AFTERNOON VERY CLEARLY. He had sat in his car reading a series of reports on the recent acquisition of an Internet company that a client of his had brought to him. He had at that point known Barbara for two months and had realized after only a few weeks that he had fallen in love with her. He had already found her the apartment on Eighty-seventh Street. He had heard of Frere through the recommendation of Dr. Cohen. It was after the Christmas party that Teddy decided she needed a psychiatrist.

In his mind he saw her coming out of Frere's building and looking for a taxi. They had agreed to meet at his house, then go to lunch.

"Pull up, Frank," Teddy ordered his chauffeur.

The Rolls cut in front of her, and her face lit up with surprise and affection. He got out of the car.

"Rich Uncle decided to come for his young, beautiful ward," he said. He hated to put himself in that position, but he noticed that she liked him better and relaxed more when he treated himself with some degree of irony.

"Beautiful young ward thanks her uncle for being so thoughtful."

"How did it go with Dr. Frere?"

"I'm a bit whacked but starved."

"That sounds healthy."

"And by the way, have I told you today how lovely you are and how elegant you look?"

"I had a shipment of suits from London. It's my new Doug Hayward suit," he said.

"Stand up and let's have a good look."

"I can't stand in the car."

"Try." He did stand up as far as he could. "It's beautiful." She flung her arms around him and pulled him down. "You look younger and gorgeous. Not at all like a Wall Street tycoon. Like a satyr. Now all we have to do is find you the right woman."

"Really?"

"There's a drop-dead beautiful woman on the staff of the French ambassador. A sister translator. She's divorced, no kids and looks like Juliette Binoche."

"Does she do windows on scaffolds?"

"I don't know about that. But I could introduce you two at sea level," Barbara said.

He leaned on her shoulder and felt his youth return. The exhale of Barbara's breath, the sweetness, her breasts rising in the leather environs of his Rolls and her moment of pondering when she smiled and stroked his arm as she leaned into him, allowing him to flourish in the forest of her long hair.

"Maybe, I'll wait for you to grow up."

TWENTY-FIVE

*T*EDDY MOVED THE TAPE RECORDER TO THE SIDE table by his chair. He anxiously turned the tape over and started it. Frere's voice, a bit heavy and his nose clogged with a cold, came over.

"Barbara Hickman is a skillful liar. Yesterday's session was the third, and she came well prepared, like an actress who is a good study. In fact, what she gave was a performance. She came prepared to play a game, which indicates a high degree of competitive spirit, and I assume that she's read quite a bit of the available psychiatric literature. I can expect strong resistance to therapy. The problem at this time is twofold: to analyze the various symbols and determine whether they really exist in her mind. Or whether they belong to someone else. Is she testing me to see if I'll fall into a trap she's laid? She's played this game very often with her friend Laura, who appears at this point to be the most important person in her past.

"Susan," Frere called out, "can you make the TV lower? I can't hear myself."

"Some of the elements of the game no doubt have a certain psychological validity. Even if she was pretending to me, what she selected in her performance is revealing. She sees life as dark, unpromising, and without hope, and from her manner and the doleful expression on her face I can well believe this pessimistic outlook. Who does the plant swallow in this cannibalistic forest? A fox. Who is the fox? Someone clever. Is it Barbara or Laura? Is it some memory of unsuccessful coitus or her loss of virginity, which may have been painful and sordid?

"The bear is less helpful, although it indicates that she is afraid of life and has retreated from it. But her retreat from life is really a retreat from herself. She is attacked by wolf cubs in the hollow of the tree. This could be any number of things—a prenatal memory or search for her mother in the womb, or hollow of the tree. The wolf cubs are significant, and the action of sucking her breasts indicates some degree of psychosexual infantilism. Why two cubs? Did she have a twin or a brother or sister? And was there a battle for the mother's affections? Some kind of sibling rivalry? She's extremely self-conscious about her appearance and her bosom. I noticed the way she kept covering herself with her arms and her habit of running her fingers along the tops of her thighs. Of course, she and Laura are the cubs.

"Black apples. She finds death in the forest in place of a loved one. The loved one is dead, and the act of producing the black apples is important. A sheath is placed over the tree—a contraceptive—and during the growth of the tree, black or dead apples fall off. The act of coitus is an act of death and possibly painful to her, suggestions of some form of dyspareunia and anesthetic sexual life.

"The body of water turns out to be an ocean. Her sexual life is tempestuous. The wave almost kills her, but she survives it because she's an expert swimmer, so perhaps she has some ideal in her sexual life. Perhaps this is what she is looking for, and her willingness to swim in an ocean of this kind indicates that she is prepared to try to achieve it even though the odds are against it. The primeval stereotypic symbols of snakes, et cetera, reveal the rough passage she had to undertake to get to the other side. Society's standard of normality. Crabs tear off her toes. Here she sees herself as a man who is emasculated by her sexual drives, and this ambivalence at such a critical stage is significant. Was she ever forced to play a man's role?

"The white house she recognizes as the house of death. She is curious about death, but her life impulses prevent her from investigating further. The old lady is sewing a woman's eyelids—her dead friend Laura's? But this excites her, and she is ashamed of herself because this brings on an orgasm, and she runs away because she is embarrassed by orgasm. This, however, is an affirmation of life.

"Laura appears to be the key to a number of mysteries in her mind. What was the relationship, really? There are indications that some homosexual attachment evolved. But to what degree? In her disclosures of herself and Laura they both appear as heterosexual. She was shocked by the ordinariness of my amusements. She thinks that most people must live at a feverish pitch to enjoy themselves. Her relationship with Franklin seems to be one-sided at this moment. He may be a stopgap. She is frightened that I might communicate with him.

"Although she gave no indication of compulsion neurosis or the use of any system, I suspect that they will emerge later on and reveal some type of fetishism. I wonder . . . just wonder if some of her behavior patterns have been initiated by her friend Laura and whether there hasn't been some transference of neurosis. Please type Monday A.M."

TEDDY FLICKED OFF THE RECORDER SWITCH. HIS chest and ribs felt sore, black-and-blue, and bile welled in the back of his throat. He looked at his watch. It was four in the morning, and his head was clear. He rinsed his mouth in the bathroom, washed his face carefully to avoid wetting his bandage. He looked at his face—dark gray pouches, eyes watering and bloodshot, his mouth carved out of stone, hard and set. In his desolation he felt closer to Barbara than ever before. He was sharing the essence of her life.

In search of a path to Barbara, he found himself in a swamp filled with snakes and crocodiles; the only way to get across was through the quicksand. The small change of Barbara's confidences created a sense of forlornness in him. Grant was dead; Barbara had left him only the landscape of her mind, burned-out craters, ghosts of memory.

For a long time he had been convinced that human beings were incorruptible unless they actively made a choice to seek corruption, and this had led him to a position in which morality existed only as a concept defined by an individual's actions. But here on the tapes he heard for the first time the progress of human destruction, as real and objective as a plane crash. He couldn't bear to listen to more, and yet he grimly perceived that only in this way could he gain a complete understanding of Barbara, help her, and in the process of helping her, he knew with certainty he himself would be destroyed.

Some men court tragedy as they would a woman, tenaciously and with knowledge of doom, and in the very act of self-immolation they lead themselves to expect some higher, ill-defined transcendence. He knew that without Barbara he could survive in a manner of speaking, find substitutes, live his life, plot new financial intrigues, but that would be all, and his life cycle would repeat itself uneventfully. His behavior was unrecognizable because he hadn't ever been so irresponsible and irrational and was shaped by the trap Barbara had created for him.

He picked up the tapes, examined the neatly typed labels, and dropped all but one on the floor. The one he retained and stared at like a man on the ledge of a skyscraper watching the people below before plunging down. It was labeled *Laura.*

Teddy listened to Barbara weeping and was moved by her sadness.

"Laura was the closest friend I've ever had. I'm sorry, Doctor."

"It's all right, Barbara. Nothing to be ashamed of. You lost a friend."

She cleared her voice but continued to whimper.

"I can't help it. I lose control when I think about her. Oh, shit, what's life all about? I mean except for my father, there was no one else."

Teddy had a recollection of the photograph of Laura he had seen in Barbara's apartment dozens of times, and because of its familiarity, it had receded into his memory; a piece of furniture that you dust off and never notice. He recalled a tall blond-haired girl with a strong oval face and an upturned nose standing in front of a campus building. She had a mocking, knowing smile that suggested that she was bored and yet haughty, and perfectly aware of how attractive a model she was.

It must have been summer; she was wearing a red tank top, white shorts, and dirty tennis sneakers. She had well-curved legs, which on the photo appeared somewhat muscular, like a dancer's. But what he remembered best were her eyes, which disturbed him, and when he casually remarked about them, Barbara had said, "When Laura looks at you, she shuts out the whole world and makes you her world." The color of the eyes was almost Prussian blue, so dark that even in the color photograph they gave the impression of being black; at a glance there seemed to be no eyes at all, just cavernous sockets. It was a face at once beautiful and chilling.

When Barbara had moved into the apartment, the first thing she did was to place the photograph prominently on the middle of the mantelpiece, so that the face struck you as soon as you entered the room. Barbara examined the photograph from all angles of the room and kept adjusting it so that it was dead center, and he found himself listening to what he thought were a lot of pointless college tales, stories about Laura's exploits and brilliance. The only facts he could recall with any clarity were that she came from a town or a farm outside Birmingham, Alabama, and that she had died shortly after Barbara graduated.

"I've always been a good chess player, and when I was sixteen, I won the school championship," Barbara told Frere with some pride. "My father taught me to play when I was seven, and the game always excited and amused me. Because you're pitting your imagination and skill against someone else's and there isn't any element of luck and chance. Anyone who believes you have to be a mathematician to be a good chess player is full of shit." She laughed. "I feel better when I can swear. It's easier. I think things, and instead of bottling them up, I can say them, and somehow I'm relieved they're out of my system. Teddy doesn't like it much, though. He freezes and he gets a shocked look on his face. What will she say or do next?"

"We're treating you, not him. He can look after himself very well," Frere said tartly.

"But what am I going to do with him? He keeps proposing, and there are times when I think: What the hell, why not? What've I got to lose?"

"I really believe you ought to hold up—"

"Marriage?"

"No. Making up your mind. You're not ready to make a decision of this kind. Not yet."

"Will I ever be?"

"Of course you will. But now isn't the time."

"He's got such a big investment in me. . . . I mean, your bills and all sorts of other things, like clothes he buys me. He wanted to buy me an engagement ring at Winston's."

"I'm glad you're making decisions so rationally."

"You see, I've been feeling better . . . in myself, and I assume he has a lot to do with it, and I'm grateful."

"You should feel more than *gratitude*."

"I do, some of the time."

"Barbara, I'm not going to make up your mind for you. All I can do is counsel you. Wait, for your benefit and his. You're not ready to assume the responsibility of marriage, and he's more than twenty years older than you. He can afford the indulgence, but you can't. If it doesn't work—and I'm not saying it won't or can't—he can just write you a check and he's free. But what about you? Where does that leave you?"

"I guess you're right. I almost blew my cool the other night and went to bed with him."

"I'm glad you didn't."

"I feel he's suffering, and I can relieve his pain by fucking him. After all, he deserves it, if it's so important."

"Did you feel any irresistible desire?"

"No. It's sort of paying off my debt."

"Well, don't. It's not a debt, and you're not a prostitute who can work out a rate of exchange as simple as that."

"I've been going to church again."

"Are you comfortable in church now?"

"More than I've been. I get close to believing, but then something, almost a presence that I can touch, gets between me and Christ, and I say, 'Barbara, you fucking little hypocrite, trying to find absolution.' But there is something, though, in my heart for the church . . . for what it could be, its capacity for goodness. But then, well, I see a nun, and she has Laura's face, and I know it's futile."

Dr. Frere cleared his voice, and Teddy heard the rustling of papers. "I'm a bit unclear about the time element. When did you meet Laura?"

"In the middle of my junior year. We'd run into each other at the library and the gym we belonged to. I guess we were circling each other. We started hanging out before and after class at Starbucks. Then having a drink or a dinner a few times a week. I was miserable in the room I had and Laura said she'd lucked into an apartment on Brattle Street and I could move in after the Christmas break. She helped me pack up. From the beginning I was enthralled by her.

"She was a classics scholar in graduate school at Harvard, scrimping by on fellowship. And I was a French language and literature major and I hoped to go on to grad school."

"What about Laura's background?"

"She was raised in an orphanage, then when she was twelve a family called Gadsden adopted her. They had a farm in Anniston, a few hundred acres, and they raised cotton and some fruit and vegetables. The Gadsdens had five sons, and they were all working the farm, and Mrs. Gadsden needed help with the cooking and her chores, so they went down to the orphanage, looked for a big, strong girl and found Laura. Like buying cattle. They signed some papers and got themselves a slave.

"Laura spent five years with them, and how she managed to go to school, score fifteen-eighty on the SATs, and win a scholarship is one of the wonders of all time. She was always used to getting up early, but they had her up at four every morning, an hour earlier than everyone so that she could get her work done before going to school at eight. We went down there the Easter of my senior year.

"Well, this poor young girl worked like an animal on the farm, and the family never liked her because she wasn't one of them. They were the real rock-bottom illiterate white-trash farmers who were Klan members. They'd beat Laura, and actually burned her once on the buttocks with a branding iron. Just to amuse themselves. The eldest boy, some creep called Cal, and the father took turns with her, torturing her and screwing her. Mrs. Gadsden found out about it, and she used to beat Laura with a mule whip, and she got the three younger boys to keep an eye on Laura, which meant that she was systematically raped every day.

"Have you ever wanted to murder anyone? Rhetorical question. Well, I suppose you never have, but when I heard what Laura had been through, I could've killed them all and never thought twice about it. When she won her scholarship, they refused to let her go, and she went to the state authorities in Montgomery and actually saw one of the governor's aides and told him what they'd done and some kind of court hassle started. But it was a county affair, and even though she was allowed to take the scholarship, nothing ever happened to the Gadsdens. It was the word of seven people against one, and the Gadsdens knew the sheriff, and the judge used to get his vegetables for nothing from them for years, and the case was thrown out because of lack of evidence. But Laura, thank God, escaped."

"Did she tell you all this when you first met?"

"No, she had to be able to trust me. It took time for me to win her confidence. She never spoke about it until much later. Then it all came out again in horrible detail. You see, basically she was a secretive person. She gave the impression of being open and extroverted, but she kept things to herself . . . things that shouldn't happen to a human being."

"Why are you smiling, Barbara?"

"I was just thinking of the good times, and there were so many of them with her."

"At school?"

"Yes, we hung out with a great bunch of guys and we used to give parties a lot in our apartment every month. Wine, beer bashes, smoke some dope, very occasionally acid, and stay up all night and talk and confide in each other, and Laura was the purest, most honest person I've ever known, but in the same breath I want to say that if not for her, I wouldn't be in the position I'm in now. Here with you. I'd have my problems like everyone else. You see Laura introduced me to all sorts of things . . . other worlds."

"Like what?"

"That's how, or I suppose why, we went down to Anniston. You see, Laura told me that when she was tripping, she'd had a vision, and I was part of the vision, and we were on the Gadsden farm together. So over Easter we flew down and rented a car.

"She drove us from the airport to the farm. I can still see the hilly dirt road, fields of vegetables at dusk, the scent of fertilizer, the large, rambling dark farmhouse beyond. She said, 'Here it is in all its beastly glory.' And about a hundred yards ahead of us there was a barn and a pigpen alongside of it. We walked, and she was carrying something. I didn't know what. I heard the sows groaning, smelled the cattle dung. 'I've hidden on every inch of this place one time or another,' she said. 'There are hidin' places that none of those bastards knew because they never had to do any hidin'.'

"We got to the barn, which was a big square building with a slanted roof. 'It's got a corrugated iron roof. Gets to be a hundred and twenty on the heat index in summer; and when it's cold, your bones freeze. Lots of wind here because it's open. The forest begins about a mile or so behind the house. I used to sleep in the hayloft.' We were by the pigpen, and there were about a hundred pigs squealing. 'I've got a special pig story for you, Barbara. I'll tell you about it one day. Cal and Drew loved those pigs. Yeah, they sure loved 'em.' She pushed the barn door, and it swung open. And she touched some mule whips as if they were old friends and remembrance sweet.

"Then she picked up a can of gasoline and dribbled it on the floor. She'd been carrying it when we left the car. 'We'll go down to the hedges over there after I light it. I built myself a rock hideout out there. You can't be seen.' She lit a match and the fire started at once. It was fast, and there were shrieking, crackling noises as though the barn were a person.

"We ran, and she found her rock sanctuary, and we slid down to the ground, which was muddy, and we watched the most beautiful colors. Minutes later men ran out in their underwear and started to shout, and an old woman was screaming. Their faces were hewn out of stone. And Laura put her arm around me and said, 'Barbara, isn't it beautiful? Do you see me? My face right in the center of the flames?' I looked, and I did see her face, or I imagined I saw it. 'Barbara, I'm a little girl there.' And it was the face of a little girl. 'You're watching me, Barb. And I'm being reborn. Right before your eyes. Out of the flames a new Laura is made by God.'

"And, yes, I did watch a new child walk out of the fire, and the Gadsdens screeching and everything and

I felt that I was part of the universe, part of creation in the Garden of Eden, and my spirit left my body and entered Laura's body.

"We ran back to the car. When she turned, the fire was out of hand, spreading everywhere, twisting in a wild dance through the fields and she said: '*Decies repetita placebit.* It's from Horace, Barbara. Though ten times repeated, it will continue to please.' "

TWENTY-SIX

*W*HEN WE WERE BACK AT RADCLIFFE, I BEGAN TO
feel that an unconscious seduction had begun
between Laura and myself. Or maybe I imagined the
whole thing. You see, there was this quality of sensuality about her that I had blocked out. She seemed to
possess some forbidden knowledge that attracted me.
She could just snap her fingers and she could have
anyone she wanted, and it wasn't simply because she
was so feminine and pretty. When you were with her
you had a chance to discover something about yourself. How can I put it? She made a contribution to
your life. I guess a lot of men who took her out had
one idea in mind—to go to bed with her. She was completely amoral. If she wanted a man, she just went with
him. Because of her background, you couldn't judge
her by normal society standards. Does that sound as if
I'm condemning her? I wouldn't want to."

"No, you're not condemning her."

"But there are some things about people who are close to you that you should never find out."

"That's something you've carefully, and I might say cleverly, avoided telling me."

Barbara's voice cracked. She began to sob. At that moment, Teddy wanted to be with her, tell her that he'd protect her, that she need never cry again.

"It's what this is all about, isn't it, Barbara? Laura's death. Your relationship," Frere said.

"Oh, dear God, I'm so ashamed I want to die. God forgive me. Please, I swear it wasn't my fault. I fought with her."

"You do want to tell me," Frere insisted.

"I can't tell anybody."

"Look, once it's out, you'll feel better. We'll be able to look at it objectively."

"*Objectively*? What the fuck does that mean? *Objectively*. She killed herself, and it was my fault. That's *objectively*."

"Why weren't you arrested?"

"I pulled the trigger or made her do it. But no, no, no, no, I can't. I won't! Please, I beg you, let's not talk about this. Don't ask me any more questions."

"If I told you that you had cancer and that I was a surgeon who could operate successfully on you, so that you could go on living, would you let me?"

"Not this. I'd rather die."

There was a pause and Barbara seemed to regain her self-control.

"After I graduated at the beginning of June, and the partying had ended, and the last bottle of Krug champagne my father had brought was empty, Laura and I faced the inevitable separation that always hung over us. I had the option of spending a year at the Sorbonne in the fall, and taking some tutorials at Oxford over the summer, but she had to remain in Boston. She was still writing her dissertation on Horace's *Odes*.

We'd paid the rent on the apartment till the end of June and I kept putting off my packing. We didn't talk about it much; it was simply too painful.

"One afternoon we bought some cold lobsters, made a salad, fixed a picnic, iced the last of the Bâtard Montrachets and drove down to Marblehead for a day at the beach. She was retranslating Horace and I was rereading Stendhal's *Le Rouge et le noir*. We were both moody and I guess you could say sullen. There was no longer anything we could say to amuse each other.

"When we got back to the apartment, I took a shower, then she did. I put on an Annie Lennox CD and I . . ."

Teddy heard a sound that he could not identify. It didn't sound human. A cry, a gasp, disintegrating in the maw of some private vision of hell. He felt like a space traveler searching for the secret knowledge of life, out of his time continuum in a land populated by prehistoric monsters. The noises, what was making those noises? He shrank back deep into the soft leather chair.

"What is it, Barbara?"

"I'm afraid of where this is leading. It's a door I don't want to open."

"You were listening to music."

"The door of Laura's room is open."

"You've been in her room before."

"Not often. We respected each other's space."

"It's so damned steaming hot in the apartment. The air-conditioner is grinding and shorting on and off in a brownout. I switch on the fan. I pick up the Sorbonne bulletin and thumb through it. I start reading an article about Hillary Clinton in the *Times*. I go to the fridge and get some ice cubes and make two monster gin and tonics. It's hot. Sweat's dripping off me. There're books all over the place. I cram some in a carton. Then I start dragging my dresses from the bedroom and fling them on the sofa. I wonder if any of my clothes will work for Laura. I can sew well, and possibly take in some of the skirts and slacks. She's a six, I'm an eight.

" 'I've fixed you a drink, Laura.' "

" 'Thanks, baby.' "

"She's towel-drying her hair. 'Welcome to my Conair sixteen-hundred.' "

" 'I already did. It blew, but thanks,' Laura says.

"She's missed a spot on the back of her neck. I take the towel and dry her there. Her figure is a work of art. She has a long neck and a wonderfully recessed S curve, fanning from her buttocks up to her head, like the snaking of a country road. She is so willowy. I'm in a funk, depressed now that college is over and that we're splitting up. And I feel incredibly tender toward her. Whenever I see those scars on her backside, I wince. She is really a knockout . . . and radiant . . . While I'm drying her and looking at her, I had to give her a hug. And I kissed the nape of the neck. She turns around and smiles at me and kisses me on the cheek.

" 'You're my angel, Barbara. Do you think if we were sisters we'd be any closer?'

" 'No, we couldn't be.'

" 'You are my family, Barbara. Mother, father, brother, sister all in one person.'

" 'You know I feel the same way.'

" 'Do you?'

"She had something rolled up in a piece of newspaper behind the sofa.

" 'Hel-lo, what's cooking?'

" 'The queen of cuisine scored some hash from Said's Tandori in south Boston.'

" 'Start cooking, Mama.'

" 'Chop-chop! Get the bong, Barbara. And load it with the dregs of your father's famous ole cognac. After this I could work as a chef in a Michelin three-star restaurant. We got enough for dessert and then some.' I sit down in the high-backed chair and watch her with fascination, rubbing body lotion on my dry skin. 'Viens, ma soeur. We're going to have ourselves a bacchanal. Ooh, that gin and tonic does taste good and refreshin'.'

"I have the first hit and the second and wow, I'm on a . . . Ha-ha-ha-ha-ha. I'm getting high just talking about it, Dr. Frere."

"You're doing fine, Barbara."

"Thanks. Laura puts on k.d. lang and we're cruising. What a voice! Sort of slips between my thighs and enters my spirit and has carnal knowledge of me.

"*Wheeeeeeeeeeeeee*. Oh, it's good. Better than acid. I'm sort of . . . sort of . . . you know, in control but I feel so high. We are getting royally smashed, drinking and smoking fine, fine hash.

" 'I'm climbing up there, Laura.'

" 'Women who are Phi Beta Kappa and summa deserve the best.'

" 'You were Phi Beta in your junior year.'

" 'Pure luck. Life in a universe of chance.'

"I'm stoned out of my head already. Double, then triple vision, then blurs. I see Laura's mouth moving. I take another hit.

" 'Oh, Laura, this is beautiful. I feel so good. It's not like a trip, and yet it is. I've got more control.' "

"Are you thinking of anything specifically, Barbara?" Frere interjected.

"I can't see straight. I'm smiling, and I'm conscious of little things. The fan blowing on my legs, my face muscles moving, my lips are dry. I take a drink and I can feel myself swallowing. My throat's so parched. Laura's got her feet up on the sofa, and she's staring at me. Then I hear her making a sound. She's crying. I make a tremendous effort, and I get out of the chair. I go to her, sit by the side of her feet. Her toenails have black polish on them, and they remind me of the apples. I see ten black apples, but they're really her toenails.

" 'What is it, Laura? Tell me.'

" 'They've killed a pig.'

" 'Who?'

" 'Drew and Cal. They're just outside the barn. I hear them laughing. I've been there only a week. I can't make out what they're sayin'. They come into the barn. I'm in a stall milking a cow. There are three cows. I don't understand what they're doing. But I'm scared. They call me, "Laurie, Laurie, we know you're hidin'. Laurie, come out." I don't know what I should do. I'm too frightened to move. Drew stoops down, and I'm huddled in a corner. He sees me, wags his finger. I get up. My knees're shakin'. Cal comes from behind me. He pulls my hair. I see the stuck pig on the wooden block. They lead me to the wooden block; then they tie my hands behind my back. I try to scream, but I can't. And they start painting me with the pig's blood. My face, my arms. They unbutton my dress. I'm not wearin' anything underneath. I don't have any underwear on. I washed the only set I had that evening. They're dripping blood all over me and smearing me. Then Drew whips out his cock, and he pushes it inside me. *Agggh.* It hurts. I'm standing, and he's pushing it hard. And Cal gets behind me, and he spreads my ass, and he pushes inside me, and they're hurtin' me so bad. Oh, God, no. Barbara, Barbara, don't leave me.'

" 'I won't. I never will.'

" 'I love you, Barbara. From my gut, my soul, inside me—I love you. I've never loved anyone in my life. Now you'll be going. I have loved and lost. Darling, I can't think of anything else but the way I feel about you. When I've been out with a man . . . it was always *you, you.* You, I was thinking of you. It's been tearing me apart.'

"We look at each other. I'm coming down a bit and I have to get back to the high or I'll crash. I'm so shocked. What can I do to make Laura feel better? I pass her the bong and she reloads it. She takes a couple of hits, and falls back on my dresses. Shit, this time it's serious, the hash, stronger than before. It really hits me. I can't focus. What's Laura said to me? I can't concentrate on words . . . just images. Laura gets up. She moves slowly, dreamlike. I'm in a trance. She's swaying on her feet. I start to black out. I'm on a boat that's rocking. Laura vanishes for a while and comes back with a studded belt. Everything is getting hazy. Oh, yeah, I'm high, flying. She's touching me.

" 'I want you to beat the living shit out of me, Barbara.'

" 'I love you. How could I hurt you?'

"She puts the belt in my hand. I'm so weak I can't do anything.

" 'Barbara, we're going to live together in Paris or Oxford, aren't we?'

" 'Sure we are.'

" 'You won't leave me? I couldn't live here without you.'

" 'No, we'll be together. No, don't do that.'

" 'I've got to. I can't help myself.'

"I'm so drowsy I can't lift my head. What am I holding in my hand? It's leather.

"I push her away, but she's so strong. Then I get mad and I lash out with the belt. I start to cry. She's got this red welt on her shoulder.

" 'I'm sorry. I didn't mean to hurt you.'

"She can't stop touching me; and I jump away. I skin my knee on a packing case. She starts to kiss me. Now

I'm lying on the rug on my back. The smoke's blue. It makes such pretty shapes. Oh, I like to twirl my finger through the rings. I touch her head and I feel her hair and her head is between my legs and I feel her tongue pushing into me and it's so good and it doesn't hurt and then I hold her head tight and I want her to get further inside me. But it's forbidden. What I'm doing is forbidden.

"*'Aiiiiiiiiiiiiiii*, I'm coming.'

"I'm sopping wet . . . she kisses my breasts. I have never been so aroused. She pushes her fingers one by one inside me. I think about shoving her away. But I don't have the will. Her tongue and fingers are inside me and she is frantic. I can't stop now and she guides my hand to her and we are in a crazy scissors configuration and I am doing her. She has flipped me over and her tongue is in my anus and I am buried between her long legs, licking her pussy. But then she takes my fingers and moves them into her and she wants them all and I realize I have all five fingers in her, and she seizes my palm and shapes my hand into a fist and forces me to go into her up to my wrist.

"Even in my drugged state, I am afraid of hurting her, damaging her. But she wants my fist in deeper and she is rocking, gyrating and screaming as she orgasms. I don't know how long we continued, maybe for hours. She couldn't get enough. I was her prisoner and the prisoner of my own pleasure. Eventually I passed out.

"She was an early riser, dressed by six, said she was heading out for breakfast and would hook up with me later when she left the library. I spent the day in bed, sleeping, dreaming. I couldn't imagine what I would do. I had no energy. I had these irreconcilable thoughts. Did I want to just get my gear together and leave? No note, nothing. But I felt chained to her. The last thing I wanted to do was face her and discuss what had happened. We had nowhere to go in this relationship."

"Were you angry with her, yourself?" Frere asked.

"No, it was an issue I couldn't address in any terms. You see, I had never experienced anything like that. It was so irrational, as pleasure always is. I was in territory beyond myself. I wasn't sulky or outraged. After all I was a participant, and an active one. I could have stopped it."

TWENTY-SEVEN

I HUNG AROUND FOR A COUPLE MORE DAYS, SLACKING, unable to concentrate. Laura was her usual diligent self, working at the library, polishing her Horace translations on the computer, rewriting, chatting on the phone with her faculty adviser. I finally found the energy to get myself organized. We never said a word about our evening. It almost seemed as though it was an illusion, a different reality possibly, nothing palpable.

"I rented a Windstar and was going to drive down to New York, move my stuff into the apartment with Dad and spend a little time with him. I sent a fax to Oxford, Somerville College, confirming that I would attend the Colette seminar in mid-July, then I thought when that was finished at the end of August, I'd head for Paris, call some of my father's friends who had offered to help me find digs and do my year at the Sorbonne.

"The night before I was going to leave, Laura asked

me to go out to dinner with her and of course I wanted that very much. Everything was normal between us. It was like, 'Hello, where have I been . . . ? Nothing so terrible happened, right?' Two roommates who are crazy about each other had some terrific smoke and got it on. Big deal. I'm not freaking out or going to sweat it for the rest of my life, nor is Laura. We did it, had a ball, and it'll be a special memory. If I want to get morose, depressed, that's my problem. You know: beating my breast. She seduced me—'Oh, how could she?'—that kind of crap.

"Laura had made a reservation at Maison Robert which is an old-line, blue-blood, Boston establishment. Wonderful food, eighteen-foot-high ceilings, arch windows, with a glorious view of the historical neighborhood. She knew that I liked it. It's pricey, and Laura is always in debt. So it's going to be my treat, but she insists she's going to pay. Out comes my navy blue Prada with the jewel neckline. She's wearing a new Dolce and Gabbana dark green suit with a chrome yellow silk blouse. I think she saved for years to buy it. We are gorgeous. We don't have to hail cabs, they're stacked up as we walk down Brattle Street. The guys are yelling from car windows. We are a sight; glorious, young, and life is filled with guarantees.

"We drink champagne in the wine bar, then it's upstairs in the Bonhomme Richard Room and I carve the wine list."

"*Carve?*" Frere asked.

"It's an expression in the trade. I can pick the best-value wine on a list, which that evening was a tart, frosty, Sancerre that went perfectly with our Dover sole. We are debating about splitting crepes with strawberries when someone waves at Laura. She excuses herself, gets up from the table and goes to the other end of the room where two women are having their coffee. I order the crepes and two espressos.

Laura is still talking. When dessert arrives, she returns, laughing, and in a high good humor.

" 'Who are they?' I ask.

" 'Candace Paige and Jill Graystone, as in Paige and Graystone Communications.'

" 'Loaded,' I observe.

" 'They want for nothing. Anyway, Candy asked us over for a nightcap. She has a house on Louisburg Square.' "

" 'My God, Beacon Hill. How'd you meet them?'

" 'At a charity function. They're old Radcliffe girls and they had a bash to raise money for the theater.'

"Laura has already sneakily paid the check while she was visiting the ladies. I thought she was maxed out on her credit cards and I'm ready to use my AmEx. Unnecessary. Apparently it cleared. She's so alive and filled with mischief. As the ladies are leaving, I'm introduced. They are very elegant, mid- to late thirties I guess. Candy is a soft, luminous redhead, and Jill has beautifully cut black hair and an olive complexion. They are friendly, exquisite women, and both are wearing serious pearls. Nothing ostentatious. No flashy diamonds.

"We tell them we don't need a ride, we'll walk over. It's only five minutes and the weather is balmy, with a fresh breeze from the Charles. It's a perfect summer evening and when we arrive, Candy opens the door. The house is a Federal gem and it has been restored with what I can only call discretion. Everything costs a fortune but nothing growls: the clock in the hallway is a seventeenth-century longcase with flowered marquetry; the commodes are Cobbs, on the walls are some wonderful paintings. A Holbein portrait, Ingres, David. I am simply spellbound.

" 'We're in the sitting room upstairs,' Candace says. 'You can see the whole square . . . and the liquor's up there, too.'

"She is so gracious, and although I have been in beautiful homes with my father, this is something very special. A piece of history. I am captivated. Beside an Adam fireplace, Jill is lounging on a soft pink velvet Empire sofa. She looks like she belongs in court. She smiles and I sit beside her.

" 'Our guys are in London cooking up their deals.'

" 'And knowing them,' Candace says, 'exploring the underworld. They are a pair to draw to, restless satyrs. If it wears a skirt, they'll be happy to help a lady remove it.' She turns to me. 'We have cognac, Marc, Armagnac, champagne—anything your heart desires, Barbara.'

"I settle for a balloon of Armagnac, which the hostess brings over. The lighting is dazzling, low and magical. I hear some New Age music coming from a speaker. Jill asks about myself, my plans. She has an olive Mediterranean hue to her skin with delicate doe-like features and a curious, enigmatic smile. On the other side of the room, Candy and Laura are talking.

"It's about eleven now and we're on our third round of drinks and we are all mellow. Laura has surprised me again. I never knew she had friends like these two. She has always seemed to be in such a rush to complete a paper, or go to a class that I never believed she had the time to kick back and just enjoy herself.

" 'Candy, I've had a CRAFT moment,' Jill says out of the blue, opens up her handbag and takes out a bottle.

" 'Craft?' Laura asks.

" 'Yes, Laura. That's Beacon Hill for *can't remember a fucking thing*. I am only thirty-eight and my mind is already gone!' We all start laughing. 'My *man* made a delivery as I was rushing out to meet Candy at Robert's. We have the finest ecstasy in Boston, or the world, for all I know.'

"Jill comes around the room with her bottle of pills

and hands us all a couple of them. I am about to demur. I have never taken ecstasy. Yes, I've done acid
about half a dozen times. I occasionally smoke grass.
The hash evening with Laura was not something I do
on a regular basis. I didn't graduate summa cum laude
by being stoned. The three women down their pills,
the music changes to very soothing Segovia playing
the classical guitar. They are all waiting for me. It's like
an initiation.

"I'm planning on an early start down to New York,
getting my stuff moved back to the apartment, and
they all just look at me like I've committed a terrible
breach of manners. What the hell, it's my last night
and I've told them all about my imminent Europe
trip, and done my party turn by explaining that
Flaubert used the sonata form as his structure for
Madame Bovary. Why should I be such a bore, so high
and mighty in this bewitching company? I am sitting
in the great court of Beacon Hill's aristocracy. I toss
back two pills, and the three ladies applaud and cheer.

" 'We are a merry group,' Candy says.

"The music continues—Carole King oldies from *Ta-
pestry,* which have a special meaning for every woman.
It's shuffled with k.d. and Joan Baez. The ecstasy has
kicked in and I'm floating, adrift, looking out the window at the square and imagining what it must have
been like during the Revolutionary War—our soldiers
fighting the redcoats for America's freedom, the
sound of cannons. I become part of the history in this
golden company. I don't know how long I was there;
but when I turned around the women had vanished. I
thought Candy might be giving Laura a tour of her
treasure house.

"I look for them, not exactly spying. I hear something from upstairs, shakily walk up the broad staircase. I've just noticed that Candy has an elevator, but

I'm at the halfway point and continue up. I call out for Laura first, then Candy, and Jill. There is no response and I hear voices coming from a room. I see light from underneath and muffled sounds—laughter. The door is oversized and might have come from a castle. It has a fantastic bas-relief, carvings of Bacchus and his maidens.

"I am *afraid* of the door and back away. I fight against my uneasiness because I'm probably being foolish and it's the ecstasy that's making me a little paranoid . . . and yet I'm happy I took it. In my heart of hearts, I'm glad we accepted the invitation. It's become a festive adieu with Laura. Having the women as company took the pressure off. We're not two sad sacks in tears.

"I'm trembling as I turn the doorknob. Laughter from within. Now I'm more secure. I knock. More laughter. My wariness is vanishing, I think, but then an air of dread creeps over me. I enter the room.

"The Three Graces are lying naked on an immense, canopied bed with a red velvet curtain. It's as though they're waiting for Raphael or Renoir to paint them and they're simply models having a chat and a giggle, killing time. They have an aura. It's as if they're being served at an inviting, sumptuous banquet. It is a feast of women. A painting, yes. I'd never seen anything like this, except in a Titian painting. The vision is something beyond lasciviousness. It engulfs me.

"The dissolute scent of summer heat and roses is overpowering, but then something heavier, something primal is present that transcends it, swallows it. It's a dense humidity, an alluring fog. These women have created a fragrance of themselves. I've entered a forbidden world. The women's eyes are choking on me.

"The moment I'm inside Laura gets off the bed. She kisses and hugs me, swivels around me, places her arms around me from behind and begins to undress me. My dress is off, my bra is unhooked. Candy and Jill have beckoning smiles. Laura is embracing me and I'm being moved closer and closer to the bed. I'm placed at the edge, and Jill caresses me, kisses my shoulders, puts her tongue in my ear. Laura is licking my neck. It's all very tender and caring. I'm trying to maintain my focal point, but I can't. I've lost Candy. Then I see her. She's on her knees and twisting my panties. She has my thighs spread and she works her tongue from one side to the other and takes the crotch of the panties and rubs it against my clitoris.

"I don't have the will or energy to get up, protest or scream. Laura opens my mouth with a kiss and under her tongue she has another ecstasy pill, which she feeds into my mouth and then she pulls away and dribbles some brandy from glass, which I swallow. My throat is burning. I'm now eased on my back and the women are very sensitive, kissing me, whispering reassuring words. Candy is slowly easing down my panties one leg at a time, all the while kissing my thighs.

"Then the three of them become very serious as though they had special areas they wanted to explore. I'm turned and I find Candy between my legs probing with her tongue and fingers inside me. Jill is across me on an angle and she is sucking my clitoris, building it into an erection. Laura is behind me and her tongue snakes into my anus and she has her finger in it and as she pushes her finger deeper, I have a climax. I am in the derangement of ecstasy—not the drug but the moment—beyond thought, morality. I am the victim of my own gratification. Nothing is more important or urgent than the supple bodies entwined with mine.

"Positions gradually change and Jill is over me, her wet pussy is on my chin, and she says: 'Get into it, Barbara. It loves you.' Laura is sucking my nipples, swallowing, gagging on my breasts as she tries to take one all the way down her throat. Candy is strapping on a black dildo, adjusting it carefully around her thighs and waist. She toys with me, probes delicately and slips inside me. Teasing me with it. She starts slowly, getting in deeper, then when she's all in and knows I'm secure, she starts pumping it in me harder and harder, and it's like a great guy screwing me. Like when Teddy does me and it's magnificent, blotting out everything but the two of us.

"The four of us churn, bash, pound, our flesh battering each other; we keep at it, changing partners as though we're a quartet of ballerinas doing pirouettes. I'm doing Candy with the dildo and she wants to be hurt. Jill is walloping Laura with a double-headed monster that goes into her vagina and anus. The wrath of it, the wrath.

"I have a disastrous admission to make. In spite of the violence of our lovemaking, it was also an expression of the caring and the generosity of these women.

"Later, I was on my knees, crawling from one to the other. I did them all as they sat on this huge bed with their legs dangling. I kept at it. I was besotted by my diligence and made them weep, until they all came and came. I was inexhaustible, and I'm not going to cop out and say, 'Yes, oh, my God, I was drugged, loaded,' because that's pathetic, an *indecent* rationalization. I loved what they gave me. And I reciprocated in kind. I was fisted, buggered with a dildo, and I performed for the three of them. It was a sexual recital, a foursome who gave everything we could put out. Enabling, you might say, but the *act* and not the drug was ecstasy.

"We finished in a final binge, a spree of—I was the star of their night, *my* night. Your innocent, fucked-up patient loved every moment of it—and that's the truth, Dr. Frere. My loving Teddy, who changes worlds, believes *I* am the world. He has no idea of who I am and what I am capable of doing. I'm afraid for him."

TWENTY-EIGHT

*I*N THAT MOMENT OF CONFESSION, TEDDY LOVED HER more than he had realized. It was not simply the rampant sexuality she exuded, the other side she had exposed to the doctor, but the flagrant honesty within her.

"I don't know how I got home. I woke up in the afternoon with the hangover from hell. I heard Laura clacking away on her computer. I had a quick shower and pulled it together. I thought Laura had gone out when all at once there was something . . . coming out of her bedroom. A black sleeve protrudes.

"Doctor, Dr. Frere, I'm choking. I've got something caught in my throat."

"There's nothing in your throat!" Frere said. "Nothing. Absolutely nothing. You're imagining it. It's all right. Tell me about the black sleeve."

"There is a shadowy figure with black sleeves and a headdress, moving toward me . . . white collar. Oh, mother of God! It's Laura wearing a black habit. *She's dressed as a nun!* Why? I don't understand. She slips off the elastic band of a large portfolio. Pictures are mounted, others spill out. I've got the pictures in my hand. A stack of them. There must be hundreds. In some she's wearing leather, latex, and a dildo. In others she's naked and bound.

"I scream. 'I can't stand it!'

" 'Look at me. Look at me!'

"I turn my head up to see her face. She has this abandoned, solitary expression. Her eyes are blank.

" 'If I didn't love you, I couldn't show these pictures. But now, here is your classics scholar.' She goes on: 'Si vis me flere, dolendum est primum ipsi tibi.' I am confounded and she translates this. 'Barbara, if you desire my tears, you must first feel the anguish yourself.'

"The pictures of Laura are on my lap. She flips through them as if she has savored every humiliating image of herself. Each picture is different. Now there's a sleeve missing. It's torn off. Then the collar. She's standing on a bed. She is performing, swallowing a . . .

" 'Laura, I can't go on.'

"She forces them on me, holding them at eye level. They're horrible. She's naked, and she's with a man. A woman. And another with a group. And she's in bed with someone else. She's got her hands and head in pillory. She's licking a leather boot. A woman's beating her. And I drop the pictures. It's not true. It couldn't be her.

" 'Why, Laura, why?'

" 'Did you ever once ask me how I lived? How I managed to support myself?'

" 'When did you start this?'

" 'Two years. With an outcall service.'

" 'No, no!'

" 'Barbara, you are the only child of a rich widower,

a gentleman wine merchant, who spoiled you,' she
says, taunting me. 'I'm rabble, trash, a lowlife—that's
my illustrious background. You saw it. I am the girl
they buttfucked in the pigpen when I had the curse.
Now how do you think I live? On my grant? Do you
know what that buys?'

"I retreat. I don't know what I can say to counter
this. In a crazy way, I am more in love with her than
ever. My voice is quavering when I ask. 'Last night—
with Candy and Jill—was that arranged?'

" 'Of course. I can make the rent for July and don't
have to move to a goddamn single. I can catch my
breath and hunt around for a roommate. It was a two-
thousand-dollar trick! Top dollar! That's three times
more than I ever got from either of them for a one-on-
one. Believe me, they can afford it. It's loose change to
them.'

" 'You fucking pig. You sick, sick, sick animal. Why'd
you do it to me?'

" 'Didn't you like it, Barbara? You got turned out,
my dear. It's not exactly the stuff of Greek tragedy, so
don't act as if you're Electra. You had your pussy done
by experts and gave as good as you got. You may not
know it yet, but you are a natural for this line of work.
Jill and Candy, they are breast fetishists and yours are
spectacular.'

"I am beside myself with such deep rage—a wrath—
I never knew existed within me.

" 'I did it because I trusted you and loved you. You
did this to me. I was your friend, your sister. I could've
accepted anything, but not this.'

" 'What is this, nun's melancholy slathered with remorse?' She strips off the nun's habit and stands there
naked, arching her back like a cat, daring me. 'Yeah,
sure, I'm sure you'll be thinkin' of me punting down
the river at Oxford and when you drive to Paris in the
new car your father bought you, princess.'

" 'Laura, I hate your fucking guts. If I had one wish in life that could come true, it's that those men on the farm had killed you. I'm only sorry that you lived to meet me. If there's a god or a devil who controls this life, I only hope he makes you suffer more than you did when you were a kid.'

"She's standing there. She lowers her head. Her face is so white. Sickly white like after you vomit. She nods her head. She keeps doing it. Her bravado has perished. And my anger reaches a crescendo.

" 'You're a beast, Laura.'

" 'I took a chance. I had to. I couldn't keep on wondering. It preyed on my mind for two years. You see, Barbara, I thought you loved me as much as I loved you.'

" 'Well, I don't. I did love you, but not this way, not in this perverse, deranged way. Those pictures weren't just for money. You enjoyed it.'

" 'I knew this was going to happen,' she says. Laura is standing there in the middle of the room. Her head low, swaying. She can't look at me. 'I had to make you turn on me, because I couldn't survive. I know . . . it's unforgivable, isn't it, Barbara?'

"My hands are shaking so badly. I want her to die. I want that so much.

" 'Unforgivable? I hope you go straight to hell.'

" 'Admit one thing, Barbara, and you'll be all right for the rest of your life. Know one grain of truth. You enjoyed it. Loved every minute of it.'

"There was a roll of quarters on the table that we always kept out for the parking meters. I picked them up, put them in my palm, clenched my fist, and smashed her across the face. She reeled through the room and then went down like a dead weight.

"I wander through Cambridge for hours. I'm disoriented. Roaming. I buy a bottle of vodka and finally I check into a motel, watch TV, drink from the bottle, pass out, wake up in the middle of the night, make myself a pot of the junk coffee they put on the bathroom sink. It's undrinkable. I'm still dressed in jeans and a tank top. I look like what I am: a hungover slut. I grab some breakfast at a coffee shop. It's about six-thirty. I'm trying to pull it together to load up the van and drive to New York. No shower, nothing. Just get the fuck out of Boston and never come back, never revisit my trophy years. I can't wait to see my dad, then get on a flight and vanish in Europe.

"In my rush to escape from Laura, I have naturally forgotten my keys. There's an envelope stuck under the mat. Keys are inside and a note I don't bother to read. I open the door, crumple the note and come into the living room. Nothing's been moved or changed. I notice Laura lit a fire. It's still smoldering. I see bits of charred photos. I go into my room, collect my things. I don't hear or see her, and I don't want to . . .

"That's when I have a change of heart. I'm a wreck. I can't leave this woman. I have to tell her."

Teddy waited, as did Dr. Frere.

"Go on, Barbara. You're almost there," Frere says kindly.

Barbara is sobbing. There is a lost, plaintive bleakness, a choking, as though she is being strangled.

"I . . . I had an epiphany that was divine, mystical. I found out the truth about myself. I call out her name, 'Laura, Laura. I'm not going to Europe. I'm staying with you and we'll always be together. If you want me to go on dates with you, I will. I love you.' I barge into her bedroom. She's not there. I look around. I shove open the bathroom door.

"She's lying in the tub. There's no water in it. She's so very white. It's as if her flesh has been bleached. Her mouth is open. There's a butcher knife beside her thigh. Her wrists have enormous gashes. I can't bear to look at her any longer. As I turn, screaming, I see on the mirror of the medicine chest a crude heart scrawled in blood.

LS
LOVES
BH

"I read the crumpled note Laura had left for me. It's a quote from T. S. Eliot. *In my beginning is my end. . . .*

"I close Laura's mouth, and kiss her cold, blue lips, and for a moment she looks better. More like Laura.

"I've got to do something. You know, *do*. I call the police. I answer lots of questions in a blur. Nothing about what happened, our intimacy, the other women, Laura's other life. Our fight.

"My dad flies up, has my stuff transferred to a moving company and I leave for Europe and only come back when I learn he's died.

"There is no endless summer in Oxford for me, or digs in Paris, or the year at the Sorbonne. I drive for months all through Europe, restlessly, until I wind up in Bordeaux. My father and I have been in contact and he's found a job for me as a translator with a vineyard. I do their foreign business and when I come home to wind up my father's affairs and discover he's broke, I'm introduced to Teddy Franklin.

"You see, Dr. Frere, it's not simply a question of discovering how deeply sexual I am, it's how I can use my sexuality that horrifies me. In my case, it's clear that the prey is the hunter. Until I met Teddy, I have had no affairs. I have been celibate. I haven't even masturbated during this period. It's as though sex is a foreign country and I pretend I don't speak the language."

TWENTY-NINE

TEDDY STOOD AT THE WINDOW IN THE BARE APARTment overlooking the UN. The August mugginess exploded into a thrashing thunderstorm. Below him the few pedestrians were dashing for cover with newspapers draped over their heads to shield themselves from the torrent. The bandage over his eye was seeping and made the stitches throb. He had called his office and informed his assistant that he would not be coming in. He'd had an accident, he said, unaware of the irony lurking below the surface. His heavy schedule of meetings for the week seemed remote and unreal. It was impossible to contemplate sitting around a table discussing anything as trivial as global-currency markets and corporate earnings. Words and numbers on computer printouts belonged to that meaningless jumble he had mistaken for life, not to mention passion.

He had received his money's worth on the tapes. He

had sought a confidence, but had been rewarded with secrets, private forbidden knowledge. A confidant gives advice, he does not usually interfere. But Teddy had to act. With this in mind—and now it wasn't simply a question of what to do with Barbara—he had taken a quarter of a million dollars in cash out of his safe deposit box.

He dialed the number that directory assistance had given him, the number that belonged to the late and anonymous W. T. Grant. Justice is an abstract concept in law; in day-to-day living it usually amounts to dollars and cents, and Teddy was prepared to pay compensation. A woman answered the phone.

"Hello," Teddy said, surprised at the roughness of his voice. "Is this Mr. Grant's home?"

"Yes."

"Can I speak to him?" he asked with ill-disguised innocence.

"Is this a joke or something?"

"No, it's not."

"Well, he's dead. He was murdered!" the woman said sharply.

Teddy was startled by the word. Full of venom, alarm, accusation. A concrete, indisputable fact directed at him.

"I'd heard something . . . but I wasn't sure."

"Well, I'm his daughter, and I saw his body. Murdered." The word hit him again, and he had a dizzy sensation. "Now, who is this?"

"I'm a tenant in the building."

"Are you?"

"Yes, I am."

"What's your name?" she asked suspiciously.

"It's not important."

"Then what do you want?"

"To help."

"Why, have you got a bad conscience about the old

black man who used to carry your packages?"

"No, not me," he said after a moment.

"Why don't you tell me your name?"

"I'd prefer not to. Are you living at the same address? Two ninety-five One-hundred and Thirty-fifth Street?"

"Why do you want to know?"

"I just told you. I want to do something."

"If it's to send flowers, you can stick them up your ass. If you're the doctor, I hope you never sleep a peaceful night. He got killed protecting your property. Is property worth somebody's life?"

"I wouldn't know. I'm not the doctor."

"You killed him, didn't you?"

"I . . ." He recoiled in terror. His hand shook and he almost dropped his cell phone.

"I'm calling the police, mister. We'll find you, don't worry. I'll never forget your voice."

Teddy clicked off the power of the cell phone. How could she know? He had to set her straight. He dialed her number again, but the line was busy. He put on a pair of latex gloves and sat down on the floor. With his left hand he printed out Grant's name and address on a large Jiffy envelope. He put the bills inside and pressed down the fold of the self-sealing envelope. The police had no clue to his identity or that of the boys who'd committed the robbery. No, he was safe, unknown, uninvolved.

He heard her voice at the other end again.

"I just spoke to you a few minutes ago."

"I know who you are," she said ominously.

"Well, I want to explain. I wasn't responsible."

"That's your story. Why bother to call if it wasn't bugging you?"

"I wanted to send some money. Your father once did me a favor."

"Yeah, what kind?"

"It was personal, between the two of us."

"Listen, mister, I know when people lie. I was weaned on lies like this. I'm not some dumb black woman. You killed him, and you want to settle with your conscience."

"Why do you keep saying that?"

"Because if you were a friend, you would've been at his funeral."

"I was out of the country."

"That's another lie!" she shouted.

"How do you know?"

"I can hear it in your breathing. You can't control your breathing because you're lying through your teeth."

"Well, then there's nothing—"

"Are you going to send money?" She changed her tone.

"I want to."

"We need it real bad. The funeral's set us back more than we can afford."

She sounded more reasonable now. Probably anger that she couldn't direct at any source until he called.

"I'm going to send you some money today."

"Thanks a lot." She was boxing cleverly now.

"I hope you get some pleasure out of the money."

"Sounds like a whole lot."

"You'll be surprised. Good-bye."

"I hope I get a chance to meet you."

"That's not possible."

He mailed the envelope in an office building around the corner. He wondered if he was thinking rationally, since everything he was doing had the crazy-quilt pattern of a dream. He stood in the doorway by a coffee kiosk, dazed, staring at people being churned out of the revolving door. They were dripping wet, and hustled to the elevators. It would be more sensible to phone Barbara rather than barge into her office at the UN, but she might not want to see him, and he couldn't tolerate a curt rebuff on the phone. Black tumescent clouds brought another downpour.

He wasn't certain where she had her office, so he headed for the General Assembly building. Crowds hovered around the entrance, and security guards directed them to the guides and ticket lines. He could see his apartment window from the entrance, and he had a vision of himself in front of the fireplace with Barbara. They could use the apartment for entertaining her friends and his business acquaintances if she continued to work there. It was really convenient to have an apartment there.

He was shoved by a heavyset man with a burred haircut and a camcorder dangling like a monkey from his neck. The man shrugged his shoulders apologetically. Teddy saw schoolchildren lined up against the wall and a teacher counting them. He recalled being inside once before to meet someone, but like most New Yorkers, he had never actually attended a session of the General Assembly, which he relegated to that tour package of sights that out-of-towners had on their New York itineraries. He saw a sign pointing to the cafeteria on the lower level, and he took the escalator down.

It was ten o'clock, and Barbara would be arriving at her office. He found a seat at the counter and ordered coffee. His hand trembled when he lifted the cup, and he spilled some coffee in his saucer and mopped it up with a napkin. The fluorescent lighting was making him dizzy, and he had difficulty seeing, barely visualizing the contours of people's faces. He had a thundering pain in his ears. He was dehydrated from his drinking bout, and he realized that the only thing he could do to combat his depression and hangover was to return home and sweat it out in his gym and then have his trainer and masseur come by. But at the moment the physical energy required merely to remove his clothes was beyond him.

Some people specialize in rehearsing what they plan to say, but Teddy played it all by ear, creating his point of view out of the weaknesses he detected in other people's arguments. In this respect he was more than a match for Barbara if she allowed him to say his piece. He couldn't get the image of Laura out of his mind. Had Barbara told the truth, or had she cleverly dissembled? She must have sensed some peculiarity in Laura's behavior. God, he couldn't believe it, didn't want to, because it altered the romantic ideal he had constructed.

Spangles of light danced before his eyes. What he knew with certainty was that he could not permit Barbara to walk out on him. Yet one part of him wanted exactly that, for he had accidentally perceived that the role of heroic suffering suited him and provided a deep and harrowing form of pleasure, which he could not fully comprehend. In a sense, she had freed him from the routine of his life, added a new dimension to it. Instead of appearing at a business meeting scheduled for that morning, he was lurking around the General Assembly like a criminal.

For the past twenty-five years he had been trapped in a jungle of balance sheets, company reports, lawyers, accountants, boring company executives eager to improve their prospects, and he had fought them all with the skill of a military commander, forming alliances when they were expedient and breaking them when they had outlived their usefulness. He had never been more conscious of the power he exerted until he was involved in a situation that deprived him of it.

The receptionist at the information desk informed him that Barbara had her office in the Secretariat and suggested that he call first to see if she was free. He wrote down her office number and walked back into the rain-swept street. In the lobby of the Secretariat he was stopped by two men who sat at a switchboard.

"Please state your business," one of the men said.

"I want to see Ms. Hickman."

He ran his finger along a telephone index. "Extension one-five-oh-eight. Who shall I say is calling?"

"I'd rather you didn't call. I'm her"—he found himself floundering—"her father, and I want to surprise her."

"Sign the book, please."

Teddy signed his name as Conrad Hickman and was handed a pass.

"That's on the fifteenth floor."

"Thank you."

The high-speed elevator made his stomach grumble. On the fifteenth floor he stopped at the watercooler and handed his pass to a clerk who directed him down a long corridor. His legs felt weak, and he leaned against the wall. He located her room number and saw a black plaque with her name:

B. HICKMAN, TRANSLATOR

Teddy knocked on the door and heard a peremptory "come." It was not Barbara's voice. He opened the door cautiously and found himself in a small cubicle with a glass partition.

"Is this Ms. Hickman's office?"

"Yes, it is. She's just about to leave."

"Her job?"

"No, she's going to the General Assembly."

"I'd like to see her."

"Can I have your name, please?"

"I—" He stumbled, then walked by the woman's desk and knocked on Barbara's door. The glass was opaque, and he could see only a form.

"Yes, I'm on my way."

He opened the door, and she looked up, surprised.

"Teddy, what're you doing here?"

"You should know."

"What happened to your head?" she said, springing to her feet and coming toward him. "My poor Teddy." She touched his face with the palm of her hand. The secretary peered into the room suspiciously. "It's okay, Joan." The door closed behind him.

"I fell down the stairs. . . . Saturday night. After you left me."

"Oh, Christ! Is it bad?"

"Just a few stitches."

"I was going to call you to suggest we have a drink."

"Why didn't you?"

"If you want to know the truth, I was scared. . . ." She picked up her laptop and a batch of folders. "I've got to run now. They're short an interpreter, and I was asked to come down."

"Can we have lunch?"

"I'm meeting somebody."

"Cancel it."

"I can't."

"For me?"

She hesitated, nodded reluctantly, and squeezed his hand tightly.

"All right."

She instructed her secretary to contact her lunch date and say that she had to cancel because she'd been called to the General Assembly. Teddy held her arm as they walked to the elevator.

"Is Wall Street closed down?" she asked.

"No, it isn't."

"Aren't you a busy man?"

"You know damn well I am."

"This must be important."

"Is anything more important than you?"

She let the conversation die as he waited anxiously for her to continue.

"Please, not now. I've got to keep my mind clear."

"When will I see you?"

"At the lunch recess. I'll meet you in the visitors gallery."

THIRTY

HE SPENT THE REST OF THE MORNING SITTING ALONGside four priests and tried to follow a discussion about East Timor and Kosovo. He saw Barbara sitting in a glass booth with earphones on and a microphone hanging from her neck. Watching her work, he couldn't believe that she was his Barbara. The last thing he would have accused her of was competence, and it only went to show, he reflected, just how little he really understood her. He read about the UN from time to time when there was a big story, but like many people, he considered the enterprise a failure. What surprised him was the degree of seriousness she showed in her job, but it also relegated her to that ill-defined world of skillful office workers who attend to their menial tasks with a profound show of devotion and loyalty that never ceases to shock the employer when it is brought to his attention.

For all her luster, she might be one of a hundred

clerks in his office, possibly ensconced in the stock-transfer department, or an accounting drone whose obscure existence and function or—at its worst—whose life or death made no difference to the effective running of his office. Despite this attempt to circumscribe Barbara, he knew that she somehow transcended the limits he placed on her. Still, it was an exercise that fascinated him. If he could find out how to neutralize her power, he would once again be in a position of authority, but at the same moment he realized that denigrating her was a useless and desperate form of self-destruction. It had never occurred to him before to try to place her in some larger context so that she would lose her shape and individuality, merging with the gray amorphous mass of humanity that he towered over by reason of his money and authority in financial circles. He was at the center, she on the perimeter, and he wondered if—instead of drawing her in—she had, in fact, pulled him out.

They had lunch at the restaurant on the fifth floor, antiseptic chicken salad, thick slices of roast beef. Not exactly the menu that T. Franklin and Company served daily in the boardroom, but Teddy had no interest in the food. He drank a glass of tomato juice, suppressed a belch, and watched Barbara carve through her roast beef. She had been detached, uncommunicative, and guarded since she had sat down.

"You should've stayed in bed today," she said.

"I had a reason to get up. You know, the way you put it this morning—well, you didn't put it; it was a throwaway about calling me to suggest we meet for a drink. That really upsets me. We are engaged," he added.

He was more anxious than he showed and threw her the bait. She didn't take it but simply continued eating.

"Barbara, I'm not some guy who picked you up at a party. Your behavior is a fucking insult."

"Don't swear at me."

"You do all the time. Look, if you want to pick a fight with me, you can have the common decency to tell me where I stand or what I've done wrong."

"This is not going to work out."

"Stop playing around. A human being is sitting opposite you."

"An important one with a lot of money."

"I didn't say that. Barbara, what's happened? I simply don't understand. I'm willing to try. Can't you talk to me? Is it that hard?"

"You scare me, and make me nervous."

"*Nervous?* That's the understatement of the century. Do you want to call it off?"

She nodded, and tears dripped down her cheeks.

"I think I do," she said. "It's not that I don't love you."

"Then why? If you love me?"

"I'm the wrong woman for you or anyone else."

"I'm prepared to take the chance."

"I'll wind up in a psychiatric ward. I can't take the chance."

"Is that Dr. Frere's advice?"

"No. It's my personal belief. He doesn't make up my mind for me."

"I thought he did everything."

"Let's cut out the innuendos."

"Did Robbie upset you? I mean, you don't have to see him if you don't want to," he said with growing desperation.

Barbara touched his hand affectionately. "Don't blame Robbie. I upset him and he and Elaine had a fight." She felt Teddy's tenderness but spurned it. "I'm the problem. I'm sick. . . . I don't think I'll ever get better. I'm sure of that."

"Barbara, my darling, I have the time, the money, the love, the patience—anything that'll make you better. I'll see you through this."

"For a brilliant man, you do talk a lot of crap. Didn't

you once tell me that only a coward doesn't cut his losses? The first loss hurts like hell, but it's better than waiting for a bloodbath. Teddy, I don't want to destroy your dignity. And I'm watching myself do exactly that. It's very painful not to be in control of myself emotionally and damaging to everyone who tries to help."

"Barbara, I can't cut you." He shuddered. "Do you want other lovers? Is that it?"

She became guarded. "I don't know what I want."

"But not me?" He swallowed some ice water to prevent his voice from cracking. "I've got an apartment near here."

"What?"

"At United Nations Plaza. It's an eight-room co-op. I bought it. There's still no furniture inside. I bought it for you, but I was afraid to offer it to you."

"Teddy, what's this about?"

"I go there every day to spy on you. To watch you." He could see that she was wary. "Are you serious?"

"And I follow you when you go to lunch with Noel or other diplomats. I was at the Plaza when he took you there. I was sitting in the palm court when you came out of the oak room."

She was incredulous. "You spy on me?"

"I can't help it. Your deceit grows in me like a tumor. I'm being eaten alive."

She got up from the table, and he seized her wrist and forced her back down to her chair.

"Please stay."

"You're frightening me."

"I scare myself. I've done terrible things, Barbara. Because I love you. I'm destroying everything. My life is breaking up."

Self-preservation took on the armor of hostility within her and she lashed out at him.

"That's what I can't stand. You're eating me bit by bit. I can't . . . I feel like my life is being consumed, vanishing. Dr. Frere takes part of me, and you take the rest. Do you understand? I'm afraid there won't be anything left. I'll disappear. You've taken me over. I'm like one of your treasures and you want to hoard me, lock me in a safe."

"I wanted to help you."

"Teddy, you're a cannibal."

"Barbara, we both are. Now listen to me for a minute." He was trying to think logically. "Let's find out exactly what you want. Is it money, love, position, sex, success? What is it? *Decide* what you want, and I'll provide it."

She could see that he had lost the solid grounding that had drawn her to him. "You're not making sense. I'm not looking for a bunch of brand names or possessions. I want myself, my privacy. To see if I can ever have a personal life. You've become an obstacle. At times I feel that I'm floating on a dead sea and whenever I turn there's you on the bridge of a battle-ship commanding a flotilla of ships that are closing in on me."

"Be reasonable. Just let me have something. Be with me." His voice grew in strength and conviction. "Live with me. Marry me. Anything you want."

"I think we've got to end it." She shook her head tearfully. "You're much too strong for me."

"You can't. Barbara, I'd rather you were dead and me with you."

"What is it? Why me?"

For a moment, he appeared amused. "That's like asking what the source of life is. How do I know? You are beautiful. I have never had such sexual satisfac-tion. I have never had anyone make me dance, chal-lenge me the way you do. You excite me. I'm like a kid all day long, waiting to see you. You define my for-tune. It means nothing to me without you. What does all the money, the maneuvering, mean to me personally if the woman I love more than myself turns me away? It's a joke. I don't want a woman—a fuck—I want you."

She suddenly remembered the story Alex had told her about Teddy's affair with a wealthy woman whose company he wanted to buy. He had arranged her murder and fleeced the heirs to buy the company she controlled. The emotional appeal of his persuasiveness yielded to a bleak coldness, like a lawyer analyzing evidence, the case against his client.

"Do I wind up with a bullet in my head like Dolores Archer?"

It took a few moments for Teddy's monomania to select another channel. His earnest pleading gave way to a worldly amusement.

"Oh, my God. Who is investigating who? Has my darling been cruising the Internet for scandal? No, you're probably a member in good standing with the Friends of the New York Public Library." He laughed at himself. "Where's my head? Oh, fifteen stitches and Percocets. You must have the research department of the United Nations on my case. Give me a break, Barbara.

"Dolores Archer was a fall-down, slovenly, Southern-belle drunk. I wouldn't have gone to bed with her if George Steinbrenner gave me the Yankees. Dolores, the loveliest thing about her was her name. She let it be known to the gossip columnists who used to mooch package holidays from her property company in Hilton Head that I was *courting* her. All I wanted was her chemical company and she got a premium payoff from me."

"You then sold the company and made millions of dollars."

"The Archer case indeed. *Our* research is inexact, it would seem. I made two billion. Because when I laid it off, I kept stock options in the company that smoth-

ered it in its corporate arms. My lawyers hired a re-
tired New York homicide crew who found out that
some condo manager bounced Dolores. The police in
South Carolina couldn't prove it, so I was a convenient, glamorous suspect. Okay? If I was the criminal it
was a crime without love, gain, opportunity. I did it
just for the thrill of it."

"You make me laugh."

"No small achievement."

And now Teddy was no longer threatening to her,
she thought. He was easy, a bruised man she adored,
charting his hidden past as she had to Dr. Frere. She
leaned over and kissed him below his war wound and
loved him. Her mercurial emotions hopped around,
but she remained determined to extend her breathing room.

"Teddy, listen to me now," she began as though she
were his mentor, "there are women all over the world,"
she said giddily, "who'd be thrilled to have you on any
terms. You are a charming, handsome man, a wonderful lover. You can get yourself serviced twenty-four
hours a day if you like. Magnificent women with perfect, gym-tortured bodies."

The suggestion brought out something angry and
rancid.

He nodded. "Yes, Barbara, I thought the same thing
at one time: if you turn a woman upside down they're
all the same. Right? Wrong. I met you, and you're not
at all like anyone else."

"That's what I'm trying to save."

He felt faint, staring vacantly ahead. He thought he
heard an explosion. Was it inside his head? The people in the restaurant were losing their shapes, disintegrating before him.

"Where's the noise coming from?" he shouted.

"There is no noise."

"It was a bang. A gun went off."

She touched his hand and looked into his eyes. She'd seen that grave expression before—in Laura's eyes—and it frightened her. The drugged pupils, and she realized he was not drugged, but collapsing. The sense of him falling apart disturbed her.

"You should be in the hospital. You might have a concussion."

"I'm fine. Marvelous. Never happier, Barbara . . . We're finally talking. We have to close."

She couldn't keep up with him. "You're the expert on closing."

Once a source of pride, this talent demeaned him and the entrapment was hers, not his. "Barbara, honest answer now. Do I make you happy in bed?"

"No one does," she snapped.

"Is that true? No qualifications?" She was silent. "I mean, wasn't there one person who made you feel phenomenal? It was so good that you could've died?"

She tilted her head back, grimaced, and tremulously ran her fingers through her short hair. "I'm not clear about this. Whatever you're implying, I don't like it."

"Come on, give it up. You know exactly what I'm talking about, Barbara. I know everything. This isn't judgment day. It's our millennium. Imagine it's the court of the Sun King. We can create one, like Louis the fourteenth. We'll be the patrons of artists. Design homes with architects, evolve into a better society, do wonderful things. I am capable of doing that . . . *we* are. Be with me. I need my queen," he said imperiously. "I have bought millions of acres of virgin forest land all over the world. Trees are one of the commodities—the natural resources—that are irreplaceable. It will be your forest and all the trees will bear golden apples. Not black ones."

They were drinking cappuccinos amid a thinning crowd. A wave of sickness overcame her.

"Don't, for God's sake. You're making me crazy."

Teddy was revived, kissing her cheek, aggressive again through the doom she had heard.

"Imagine it isn't me—Teddy. Come on, let's put it on the table. It's really very simple: you want another woman. Imagine you're lying on a sofa and you're a little high on ecstasy, the dope of the week. Whatever you like."

She began to cry, and people at other tables leaving the dining room turned to look at them.

"What're you saying to me? Why should you talk to me about that?"

"It was Laura's fault. You weren't to blame," Teddy said with encouragement. "Hey, you want ecstasy, I'll get it for you."

"You bastard! How do you know all this?"

"Barbara," he said, slipping his hand on her thigh, greedy for the touch of her, "I also live in a forest with Laura and Candy and Jill. They're not the only ones. To some degree, we're all in the forest."

Barbara felt faint, groaning, as the implications became clear. She had a sick, sweet taste at the back of her throat, and she put her hand over her mouth to prevent herself from vomiting. She pressed her palm against the table for leverage to stand up.

"Don't, please, Teddy, for God's sake."

"You know that the fact that you had a night with some women isn't what's been eating at you all these years. Or even that Laura deceived you." Her mouth trembled and her skin turned ashy. "You blame yourself for Laura's suicide. Don't you realize you weren't responsible? You're the innocent one."

Barbara screamed and rushed from the table through a crowd of people, and he followed, knocking a woman to the side. He grabbed hold of her dress collar, and his knuckles dug into the back of her neck. A crowd stared in amazement at them. He pulled her along the corridor away from the crowd to an alcove.

"You're insane," she said. "Let me go."

"We'll find another Laura. Someone who looks exactly like her, and you'll teach her to speak like Laura. We'll create another Laura. She'll make love to you."

The very idea of it, an *offer*, disgusted Barbara, but she forced herself to maintain her composure.

"You took the tapes from Frere?"

He was affable. "Of course I did."

"We were all out to dinner."

"I arranged it," he said in a low, menacing voice that terrified her more than his violence.

"And they killed the porter."

"No one knows."

"They'll find out . . . the police."

"Only if you tell them." He pressed her against the wall, locking her tightly in his arms.

"Don't hurt me, please. I swear I won't tell anyone. I've got to get back. They'll send someone to look for me. Please, Teddy."

"Do you love me?"

"Yes, yes, I do." She studied his intent eyes. "Where are the tapes now?"

"In my bedroom at the town house. No one's going to disturb them."

"Will you give them to me?"

"Naturally." He stroked her face tenderly. "Do you know what I've done for you?"

"Yes. Please, let me leave now. I beg you."

He relaxed his grip, took her hand, and accompanied her toward the elevator.

"We'll be all right. Don't worry," he said. "You won't say a word."

"I won't."

"I'll be in the visitors gallery. I'll wait for you. We'll go to my house together."

"Yes."

"I'll check on what we need for a marriage license."

"Yes, do that."

"Do you want me to get someone to travel with us? We'll say she's our assistant. Would you like that?"

"No, don't. I just want you."

"Barbara, you've saved my life."

*F*ROM THE VISITORS GALLERY, HE WATCHED HER TALK-ing excitedly to a man. The man nodded and Barbara took off her headphones. Teddy realized that he never should have let her go back. The sooner they were married, the more secure he would be. She got up from her seat, and he found himself also rising as though the two movements were regulated by a single power switch. A woman nodded, sat down in her place and put on headphones.

Teddy raced down the gallery steps. He had no way of knowing which exit she'd take. Probably the one used for personnel. He wandered around the lobby, then decided to wait near the Secretariat. Was she phoning the police at that moment?

Obviously she was trying to get away from him. Where would she go? He had to anticipate her move-ments. Outside, he signaled a taxi and gave the driver Dr. Frere's address.

THIRTY-ONE

EDDY SAT ON A PARK BENCH OPPOSITE FRERE'S building on Central Park West. A curdled sun had appeared and the rays seemed to hiss over the sodden grass and puddles of water that had collected. Even the dripping water on the bench slats was warm to the touch.

He had started to think clearly and had worked out a plan of action. As soon as he saw Barbara, he would call his secretary and tell her to make immediate arrangements for his plane to fly them to Maryland where there was no waiting period. At the Baltimore airport a justice of the peace would marry them, and they would return, change for the evening, and have a celebration dinner at Cipriani. He typed in the details in his Palm Pilot notebook.

Iced Krug '59 on plane, Beluga caviar, twelve dozen red roses, orchids, pick up diamond ring at Winston's and wedding bands. Inform lawyers and office staff. Honeymoon:

Paris, London, Hong Kong, Antibes, Rome, Venice. For Med cruise wire for yacht berthed in Cannes.

Had he forgotten anything?

Inform Public Relations, Holman and Graham, to prepare immediately a press handout for Wall Street Journal *and* Times *and wire services.* Dignified! *Details of Barbara's impressive education and UN position. Arrange photo sitting with Avedon . . . Check availability.*

His confidence buoyed dizzily to the surface, and he continued writing, peering up birdlike as people alighted from taxis and cars at the entrance of the building.

There was no doubt in his mind that she'd tell Frere at some time, or maybe she wouldn't if he could bring enough pressure to bear. Legally and morally he'd be in a stronger position with Barbara when they were married. How would Frere react? Would he call the police, exposing Teddy, or would he be prepared to forget it all for a few million dollars. He had confidence in Frere's avarice. Yet another possibility presented itself. He could deny any knowledge of the robbery and say that Barbara had made it up after a vindictive argument. Ultimately, this would mean giving up all claims to her. No, that was impossible.

Evidence. He had to get rid of it. The word crawled down his spine, and he jumped up. He ran across the street, jumping in front of a taxi that just missed hitting him. He gave his home address. The tapes were stacked on his bedside table. Leonard might have cleaned up the room and put them away with his music DVDs in the storage cabinet at the bottom of the stereo unit. If only he hadn't been in such a rush to see Barbara. What was he doing riding around the city in cabs? He was just about to call his chauffeur when the taxi cruised around several police cars double-parked in front of his house.

Several cops were at his front door, chatting. He tried his home number on the cell phone, then had to get out of the cab to use it. A cop was watching him. Teddy clicked off, handed the driver a hundred-dollar bill and told him to stop at the next phone booth they passed.

"Leonard, just say yes or no. Are the police there?"

"Yes, *my dear.*" In a whisper he added. "Just leaving. 'Bye, Lieutenant."

"Can you talk?"

"Almost. What's happened, Mr. Franklin? I don't understand. Are you in trouble?"

"Not really."

"They had a search warrant and went through the entire house. The lieutenant said I had to call him if I heard from you or saw you. I'm frightened, Mr. Franklin."

"Did they take anything?"

"Yes. I went around with them. They took a photograph of you and some tape cassettes from your bedroom."

"Oh, Christ!"

"Is there anything about national security on the tapes? Did Ms. Hickman take something from the United Nations?"

"No, Leonard."

"I hadn't touched anything inside. I thought you wanted me to leave them out."

"It's not your fault. Leonard, you're not to mention that I spoke to you. Where's Frank?"

"He's had to go with the police. What are you going to do, Mr. Franklin?"

"I don't know."

"Is there any way I can help?"

"No, I'll be in touch."

He hung up, stood dazed at the telephone, then called his office, and asked for his assistant.

"Nancy, it's me. Can you speak? Is there anyone with you?"

"Yes, *Dad*. I'd like to meet you for a drink."

"Detectives?"

"Yes."

"Are they going through my office?"

"Absolutely."

"Can you tell me anything more?"

There was a silence at the other end, and Teddy grew apprehensive.

"Nancy, Nancy, are you there?"

"Yes, they're in with Mr. Pauley. Mr. Franklin, there's total chaos. The rumors are crazy. I heard someone say you were a flight risk and they've alerted your pilot and the airport. A man from the district attorney's office is here with other detectives and they have a team of computer people checking the mainframe. Did we do something illegal?"

"No, I'll straighten everything out."

He slammed down the phone, looked at his watch. It was ten minutes to two. He gave the driver the address of his bank on Wall Street.

At two-forty, Teddy made his way into the vault area, signed his card and with a guard unlocked his large safe deposit box. He carried it into a private room along with a night deposit bag. He had not counted the money after sending the cash to Grant's daughter. He shoved stacks of hundreds into the bag.

When he left the bank, he hurried down Nassau Street and went into a luggage shop, bought a carryall and a large training bag, transferring the night deposit bag into it when the salesman was waiting on another customer. Once outside, he lost himself in the milling crowd and clambered down to the subway, bought some tokens and crammed himself into a car that was going uptown. Amid the sweltering bodies he had avoided for most of his adult life, he tried to come up with some plan.

It then dawned on him that his platinum credit cards with unlimited lines were useless and his cell phone would be tracked. He couldn't rent a car or take a chance of buying a plane ticket. He got off the train at Times Square, lost and bewildered. When he hit daylight on the street, he walked west down gentrified Forty-second Street. He stopped off in a clothing store, bought a size forty seersucker jacket, some khakis, and a Yankee baseball cap. He realized the police would be looking for a man with a bandage over his eye, and he bit his lip so hard that it bled when he tore off the adhesive strips. The wound was clean and he pushed his cap low on his forehead to conceal it. He left his blazer and trousers in the changing room and headed for Port Authority rather than chance the train.

He would go to Boston and contact Robbie. Perhaps his son could help him devise a plan.

TEDDY COULDN'T BELIEVE THAT THIS WAS THE NEW world he had entered. No golden parachute accompanied his fall from grace. He recalled the buoyant excitement of his appearance in the Port Authority Building, the culmination of a successful crime by an amateur. Somewhere in the logic of his existence, events had conspired to upset the unique balance that money and confidence had created.

He bought a one-way ticket to Boston, picked up a limp tuna sandwich and ate it while waiting for the departure announcement. He was confronted with an ignominious vision of himself standing in a seedy, rank-smelling police station, surrounded by TV reporters, tabloid photographers, and puzzled policemen, all trying to probe his mind, invade his privacy, and expose him to the mass curiosity of a public whose diet consisted of the protein of violence and the agony of strangers. It would be better to blow his head off.

His bus was called in Spanish and English. He made his way to the gate, falling into step with two old ladies. He included himself among America's lost tribe and was now a member of an anonymous community of fugitives. He'd call Robbie from a pay phone when he reached Boston. Pride had taught him caution in business, and he had no illusions of police incompetence. He'd have to be very careful. As he slid into a window seat on the bus, he had an electric shock of joy and discovery. Barbara had acted positively; she had reversed their roles and become the aggressor. He had aroused an emotion in her: Revenge.

He did not feel exploited or the subject of injustice. Even his momentary sadness and cri de coeur vanished when the bus grumbled out of the depot; he came to the conclusion that she had, in demanding vindication, demonstrated that she loved him. He knew with unprovable certainty that finally he was master and that in any future extension of their relationship he would be in control.

The periphery of New England rolled by—the towns one drives through and past, obscure hamlets made corporeal by their AAA signs: Buckland, Tolland, Stafford Springs, Mashapaug, Bramanville, all in green-and-white metal decor whose presence in the world is defined by how far south they are from Worcester and how many miles from Boston.

Teddy dozed, then awoke at Richardson Corners and was told by the woman sitting next to him that they were close to Worcester. She noticed the gash above his eye, said that she was a nurse and opened a small black plastic kit and offered him a tube of antiseptic cream, which he accepted with the delight of a confirmed cynic discovering humanity. He applied the cream with a piece of gauze she provided him with. Her name, he learned, was Ellen, and she had married one of her patients only to find that healthy, he was indolent, unfaithful, and a tempestuous alcoholic.

She was returning to the family bosom in Roxbury. To hold up his end, he confessed to being a bookkeeper. He closed his eyes, hoping to terminate the conversation, when it occurred to him that she considered him a prospect; she promised to guide him through the treacherous waters of Back Bay.

At the Boston terminal he carried her suitcase, as well as his own, hoping to demonstrate to any observant detectives who might be on a stakeout that he was married, a gentleman, and poor. He left Ellen outside a drugstore a block from the station; she had printed her address with schoolteacher legibility in his notebook.

The police might be with Robbie at that moment. They certainly would have contacted him. Someone in the office was bound to inform the detectives that he had a son in Boston. The Boston police would interview Robbie and in all probability tap his phone and have him followed. He dialed Robbie's number. He let the phone ring and when the answering machine kicked in, he hung up.

He strolled through a Rite Aid drugstore. Fluorescents glared from the ceiling, illuminating every corner of the store. He avoided looking at them. They blinded him. He wheeled a shopping cart to the men's toiletries. Teddy couldn't remember the last time he'd shopped for himself in a drugstore. Leonard filled in with blades, mouthwash, toothpaste, and shaving cream. He was so confused by the displays and the variety of brands that he couldn't even recall the shaving cream he used. No, they didn't have Clinique. He was

perplexed at the shampoo section but he was enjoying
the adventure, involved momentarily in the hysteria of
giant-economy sizes. He bought a small toiletry kit for
his shaving requirements, scanned the paperback
book section, and settled for *Time* and *Newsweek*. He
bought underwear, and caught sight of himself in the
mirror. He stared at himself and had the first con-
structive idea he'd had all day. He'd have to change
his appearance in some way to avoid immediate identification. He bought a bottle of Clairol Blonde and
some Just for Men. He'd grow a mustache, change his
glasses, and have Robbie buy him jeans and denim
shirts. He paid at the checkout counter, and placed his
possessions in his clothes bag.

He tried Robbie again from a nearby pizza joint.
Robbie answered the phone on the second ring.

"Why're you out of breath?" Teddy asked.

"I just came in," he said. "I heard the phone from
the elevator."

"Robbie, have the police contacted you?"

"No, why should they?"

"Is Lainie with you?"

"Yes, she's putting some groceries away."

Teddy thought for a moment. "It might be a good
idea for her to be with you. . . . Then the three of us
won't look suspicious."

"Dad, what's going on? Are you all right?"

"I'll explain everything when I see you. Just listen
for a minute. Can you leave your apartment by a
back way?"

"There's a fire exit."

"Will you and Elaine leave right now and take a cab
to a car-rental lot? Please ask her to rent a sports vehi-
cle in her name. A Ford Bronco or a Dodge Ram.
Something like that. I'll need a four-wheel drive. Have
her rent it for a month if she can."

"Dad, you're scaring the shit out of me."

"Just do as I ask. You leave by the fire exit, rent a car, and meet me."

"Where?"

"I'm in Boston, near a Rite Aid a block away from the bus station."

"Are you in trouble?"

"Yes, I am, but don't worry. I'm calling from a bar." He checked the take-out menu on the wall. "It's Dante's. Rob, how long do you think you'll be?"

"Maybe an hour."

"Robbie, whatever you do, make sure you're not followed. If it takes longer, I'll know you're trying to shake someone off."

"Dad, who's after you?"

"I'll explain later. Now be careful, will you?"

Teddy heard him muttering something to Elaine, and then she gasped.

"It's nine o'clock now. See you at ten, ten-thirty. 'Bye."

The handle of the training bag cut into his palm and made him wince. He hadn't realized how heavy the money was because he had been propelled by nervous energy. Dante's revealed itself as a meeting place for college students. Except for the bartender, he was the oldest person inside. Having lived for so long amid the luxury of his possessions, he had seldom ventured outside his own domain. Now he became acutely conscious of the shrieking rap in the saloon.

He found a table in the back, was asked by a young apron-clad waiter how many were in his party, and allowed to sit in peace when he said three. He ordered a double Stoli on the rocks and a sausage hero. The jukebox rotated from rap to hip-hop. The sounds bounced off his brain. The light at the table was dim, and he struggled to read the late edition of the *Boston Globe*, but found nothing about himself. If only he had the energy to travel the night, he might be able to cover his tracks and avoid capture. As he sipped his drink, a plan slowly evolved.

The police would assume that he would attempt to leave the country, but where would they assume he'd go? Brazil, Switzerland? If he could feed them clues to suggest that this was, in fact, the case, he'd have an opportunity to consolidate his position and effect a permanent escape. But where? It would have to be a place large enough for him to lose himself, one in which American money could be easily exchanged without arousing suspicions.

One summer, when he was a junior in high school, he and his father had driven across Canada on a fishing and camping trip. His father had saved up his vacation time at Carrier and they had spent a month traveling through the Northwest Territories as far as the District of Mackenzie. It had been the happiest time he could remember. He hadn't thought about it in years. It was beginning to come back to him The deserted landscape, the snow-covered mountains, the wilderness, small towns consisting of a bar, general store and post office, big rough men, many of them French Canadians, the wheat farms and gold mines around Great Slave Lake. They had driven as far north as Wager Bay, which led to Hudson Bay. Hundreds of small islands dotted the coastline. Most of them were inhabited by fishermen who went as far as the North Sea for their catches.

The prospect of an outdoor life among these people intrigued him. They seldom asked questions, accepting strangers at face value unless they proved untrustworthy. Wasn't that the perfect solution, rather than a city? The police would never expect him to go to a fishing village in northwest Canada. He still hadn't counted the money. But he was certain that there would be enough to buy a boat. He'd do it all in a small way and build a new foundation for his life.

He drew a crude map of Canada from memory and made a rough guess at the driving distance—somewhere around three thousand miles. He'd have to pick up a map of Canada at a service station. They'd have to cross the Canadian border that night. By morning, cars might be carefully checked by border-patrol police. The three of them could travel safely. He'd leave them in Montreal, and they could catch a plane back to Boston in the morning. Elaine would report the car stolen.

Robbie and Elaine headed through a group by the jukebox and he waved them over. His son stood over him, white-faced and twitching. Elaine's luminous eyes darted around. She bent down and kissed him.

"You smell delicious, Lainie. What time is it? My watch is broken. Anyone want a slightly used Patek Philippe?"

"We're not amused, Dad. It's ten-fifteen. We couldn't get here any sooner," Robbie said.

"Sit down. You're conspicuous standing. Did you rent the van?"

"Toyota Land Cruiser on my Visa." She touched his face. "Your head, Teddy. What happened?"

"I fell down a flight of stairs at the house." He hunched his shoulders, chilled. "Jesus, you can hang meat in here with this air-conditioning."

"Teddy, I think we've got to get you to a doctor."

"It looks ugly, but it's not serious."

"Dad, what is this all about? Why are we meeting in a place like this? And why're you worried about police?" Teddy's calmness belied the seriousness of his position, and Robbie could not conceive of any situation in which Teddy would be anything but master.

"We're going to take you to Mass General and you get checked."

"Robbie," he said, "a hospital won't help. I've committed a crime, and the police know about it."

"A crime!" Elaine was confounded. "What kind of crime could *you* commit?"

"Well, it involved Barbara."

Her name shook Robbie, and he broke out in a sweat. He didn't have the courage to look Teddy in the eye, fearing immediate exposure.

"Teddy, you're scaring us," Elaine said. "Is Barbara all right?"

"Barbara can go to hell," Robbie said angrily.

"Please don't ever say that about her," Teddy said in a perfectly controlled voice. "She's the innocent party. I love her and she isn't to blame. She did what she had to do."

"Which was?"

"I guess she called the police."

"Oh, Christ, Dad, you're not making any sense at all. Did you assault her?"

"No."

"Then why would she call the police?" Lainie asked.

"I assume to tell them that I was responsible for—" He looked into Elaine's innocent face. She was trembling. Teddy took her hand and smiled affectionately at her. "You're very pretty, Elaine. Would you like a drink?"

"Yes, please. Are you having a problem talking in front of me?"

"No, not at all. You're going to be a member of the family. No, no trouble at all. It's just that I didn't realize how young you really are."

Robbie signaled the waiter and ordered a round of drinks. He couldn't rush Teddy or push him around despite his newly born conviction that his father had lost his balance.

"I took a calculated risk," Teddy began, "and it didn't pay off. What I did was illegal but well intended. Christ, it all seems so reasonable now. Barbara needed psychiatric help, and I arranged for her to see a psychiatrist who was recommended to me. For a while she seemed to be making progress, but then things steered off-course badly for the two of us. I suspected that the psychiatrist was against me, and I had no way of knowing exactly what was going on. The more sympathetic and concerned I acted, the more anxious Barbara became. Try to understand how much I love her."

His son grimaced. "I took things into my own hands. I had to find out what was going on, so I got a man to steal her records from the psychiatrist's office. I just couldn't continue without hope. In the course of the robbery, the building's employee died. The police are treating it as a murder."

"I don't believe it."

"Well, Robbie, that's exactly what happened."

"For her!"

The moment Robbie had uttered the words, he regretted them. To the outside world, his father's behavior would appear inconceivable, but they hadn't met or been with Barbara. She was a woman who possessed a man. Her rampant sexuality combined with a sweetness and a directness were so formidable as to be irresistible. Barbara was a woman beyond charm and mere enticement, she embodied the dark fantasy embedded in men. That her powers were devoid of subterfuge produced a spontaneity and endowed her with the enigma of a goddess.

"Yes, and she's worth it."

Robbie, the new attorney took over. "Now wait a minute, how could the police know if you didn't tell them? The burglar didn't call or confess, did he?"

"I saw Barbara this morning and explained what had happened. She collapsed. I listened to the cassettes the doctor had made of their sessions. There were, of course, personal admissions that she would have only made to a psychiatrist. Honestly, all that interested me were her feelings toward me. Yes, what I did was unforgivable—at least from her point of view they were."

"Where were the tapes?"

"In my bedroom."

"Jesus, Dad! They can't go in and just search."

"Rob, they had a warrant. They clearly knew what they were looking for. They weren't on a fishing expedition. I hung around the doctor's building in the hope that Barbara would go to him and maybe the three of us could discuss it. Barbara never showed up. When I headed back to the house, there were squad cars on the sidewalk, double-parked. I managed to contact Leonard after they left and he was hysterical. Detectives came up to the office. They know about my plane, so there was no way of getting out."

Teddy was enveloped by shocked silence. After a minute, Robbie, struggling to remain calm, said, "You have some of the best attorneys in the country. Money isn't an issue. I'm going to call them right now."

Teddy held Robbie's wrist. "No, you're not. If I turn myself in, then Barbara will be exposed."

"As what?" Lainie asked. "What has she done?"

"Her personal life is not in the public domain and it never will be. It would've stayed that way if I hadn't been so suspicious."

Robbie rubbed his hand through his thick, dark hair. "I can't accept this. You're not going to be a fugitive and wind up busted in some tank town."

"On the contrary, Rob, I am a fugitive and I'm going to run for it."

"There has to be some way to make you see reason, Teddy. Please, don't destroy yourself," Lainie pleaded.

"I've thought it all out. Short of proving myself insane, I'm guilty." It was the first time he had used the word about himself, and he liked the sound of it, felt an enormous sense of relief. "You just don't know how relieved I am to admit that to both of you."

"But you weren't actually there when the man died," Elaine continued, as though offering him a reprieve.

"Ask the lawyer about my culpability."

"No, for God's sake, don't ask me! I know." Robbie swallowed his drink and jumped up excitedly. "Dad, it's your word against Barbara's. Maybe Barbara arranged the robbery. I mean, we can mount a defense of some kind that will cast doubt about the doctor and Barbara. And you can prove that you were elsewhere when the robbery was committed. Maybe Barbara took the tapes, gave them to you to exorcise her demons or whatever, had a change of heart and decided to blame you."

He did not know how he could comfort his son or how to restrain him.

"Who paid the doctor's bills?" Robbie continued in a calm, analytical manner.

"I did."

"Just suppose for a moment that the doctor *gave* you the tapes. He was found out and *he* had the burglary staged afterward. The important thing is to annihilate this guy's credibility."

Teddy raised his hand for silence. "Harvard can be proud of its law school ethics if this is the approach they teach. Robbie, Dr. Frere is blameless, and Barbara is without sin."

Robbie was about to indict her and himself just as Lainie cut across him.

"I believe you. I like her so much. She was a real

friend to me when Robbie and I came close to breaking up. Whatever she told the doctor—short of
murder—can't be so appalling."

"To her it was a tragedy and she blames herself."

"The police have the tapes?" Robbie asked. Teddy
nodded. "Leonard touched them?"

"I believe he left them on my night table. What are
you getting at?"

"A chain of evidence. You weren't there. The tapes
could have been planted."

"No, forget that. It won't play."

"Oh, Dad, I wish Barbara were dead, that you'd
never met her," Robbie said savagely, slamming his fist
on the table.

"Don't wish that. I've never been made so happy in
my whole life. By anyone. Nothing's ever meant more
than this year with Barbara."

"But you've sacrificed your life."

"Is there any other kind of sacrifice?" Teddy felt possessed by certainty, a new, deeper knowledge of himself, life, his motives. He saw his soul and tears of joy
welled in his eyes. "The two of you will live through
the scandal. They can't touch our money, Rob."

"Money, who cares about it?"

"I do. The two of you are going to have a very rough
time with the media and the police. Lainie'll ride it
out with you."

"Of course, Teddy."

She got up, sat down next to him and kissed him,
holding so tightly to his neck that it hurt and he had
to lift her hands. Robbie sat slumped over on the
other side of the table, bereft, and Teddy was reminded of a small boy suffering through a nightmare.

"I'm trying to figure some way out," Robbie said.
"There has to be something we can do."

"It's hopeless."

"I wasn't thinking legally. I was thinking of who knows what. How many people are involved, what records have been made of all this. There's the psychiatrist, Barbara, some detectives, possibly a man from the district attorney's office. Dad, we have political connections."

"They'll run for cover."

"Not if the price is right. It's a buyer's world. You always said that."

"There won't be any payoff. I've worked out a plan."

"Really? What kind of plan?" he asked skeptically.

"I'm going to disappear somewhere in Canada. I've got some money with me. Enough to live on for the rest of my life."

"Oh, stop this bullshit. For a minute I thought you were going to say just one sensible thing."

"Robbie, I appreciate your concern, but this isn't something I can buy my way out of, and if I could, I'd have to live the rest of my life in fear. The boys who committed the burglary are somewhere, and they'll read about this in the papers. Do you think they'd just ignore me, let me live happily ever after? In a crazy way I'm shaping my life for the first time in years. I exist, do you know what I mean? I've got a destiny to fulfill. And if I've learned anything, it's that I want to disappear, and if I'm lucky, I will."

"What if the police find you?" Elaine asked.

"I'll deal with that when I have to. But right now, I know I can get away. I've always had a sense of timing."

THIRTY-TWO

*T*EDDY WAS AT THE WHEEL OF THE TANKLIKE TOYOTA Land Cruiser. He enjoyed the feel of its power. Robbie was with Lainie in the capacious backseat. They had counted the cash. It came to $2.4 million. He had explained that Robbie was to sign the succession papers at their attorneys' office. He would now be in sole control of T. Franklin and Company. The security combinations of the office safe, which contained more cash, gold bullion, stock certificates, bearer bonds, and access to all of the offshore accounts Teddy maintained, would now also be under his control.

He had been clerking in Boston for a state supreme court justice. "Dad, what do I tell Judge Hanley when I get back?"

"The truth, a lawyerly version of it," Teddy said pleasantly. "He'll know by then that your father is a fugitive with a felony warrant on his head. It's his daily bread."

*T*EDDY DROVE TILL DAWN. SLANTING SHARDS OF purple-yellow light broke through the vast expanse of black sky, illuminating the low-slung hills weaving past them like a flock of birds migrating to some hibernal resting place. Elaine lay asleep, blanketed by her coat. In repose the two looked childlike, incapable of guile, arrested in some immutable posture of innocence.

Teddy was triumphant. They had slipped across the border without arousing suspicion, and the guard who had waved them through hadn't troubled to look at the couple in the back. Road signs informed Teddy that they were twenty miles from Montreal. Motor inns, lodges, guest chalets, barnlike concrete slabs that called themselves *suites* passed by in an endless stream.

It was almost six, and his eye fell on a shabby ma-and-pa motor lodge with individual cabins and vacancies. He wouldn't have to walk through a lobby. This sort of place would take cash. The car grated over the rough cast drive.

Elaine awoke first. "Where are we?"

"Just south of Montreal," he replied.

Robbie stirred, stretching his arms and rubbing his bleary eyes. His body ached after the hours of driving, and Teddy could see from the expression of surprise registering on his face that he couldn't quite remember where he was or the purpose of the expedition. He gazed blankly ahead.

"How do you feel, Dad?" he asked.

"I'm all right. I just need to shave and shower."

"I was dreaming about going up to fishing camp with you one summer at Lake George."

Teddy smiled at the memory. Shared history revealed a communion of emotion.

"Lainie, you and Rob had better register. Tell them your father's not well and sign me in if you need to as 'Conrad Hickman.' Try to get adjoining cabins at the back end."

He drove down the slip road running in front of the cabins and now became conscious of his exhaustion. In a few minutes he saw them coming. They were discussing something with great heat, but he wasn't curious.

"We're all set," Robbie said. "They took cash. We've got cabin eleven, which has two bedrooms."

"A winning number."

"Is it?" Robbie asked.

He opened the back door and lifted out the two cases. Elaine went ahead and unlocked the door of the cabin. It had a damp hothouse odor with an overlay of Pine Sol disinfectant; a queen-sized bed was in one room and through the communicating door two singles, a metal-topped dresser, and a small bathroom with a stall shower. Metal lamps were anchored to the night table, which in turn was braced to the floor—a perfect monk's cell, impersonal and inhuman, for outcalls of raw sex. He tried to imagine Laura in rooms such as this.

"To think you've come to this," Robbie said, with resignation.

"Calm down, Robbie." In a crisis, Teddy was always the unrepentant boss. "Maybe this is where I was always heading," Teddy replied. "I've had a good run for my money. It's time for another shooter. I'm going to get cleaned up, then Elaine maybe you'll"—he handed her the bottle of Clairol—"help me."

She looked at the bottles as though checking to see that they were up to FDA standards and shook her head. Her eyes blurred and appeared to fill with the world's sadness.

"You do know how to do it?"

"Yes, of course. But . . . Oh, Christ, yes."

"Nothing to fret about. Me going blond, Lainie?"

"It makes me sick," Robbie snapped.

"Oh, shut up, Robbie," she said angrily.

"I considered the same idea on the bus, but my destiny got in the way."

"What is your destiny? What are you *talking* about?"

"I'm talking about living and being reborn. I've never seen things as clearly as I do now." Teddy unbuttoned his denim shirt and stood in the doorway. His neck and arms were muscular and his barrel chest firm and powerful. He matched the role of outdoorsman he had selected.

"There has to be some way to fight," Robbie insisted. "You can't just go out into the wilderness."

"I can plead insanity," Teddy said with amusement.

He gave himself a close shave but left the thistle patch under his nose. He'd never had a mustache, not even as an experiment. The character of his face changed, fusing the ridges on his cheeks that made him look older, more reflective, creating a new point of interest. It was sparse still, but three days, a week, would give it texture. He wouldn't shape it; its unkemptness would provide folly, relieving the close-set gray eyes of moroseness and that hint of sharp-witted lambency that people found disturbing. He approved of the shower, which revived him. His fatigue disappeared as he dressed, and he called for Elaine. She came in carrying the bottles. He sat down on a stool and rested his chin on the sink top.

"We'll leave it on for twenty minutes," she said.

"Is it tricky to do?"

"No, you just watch. You didn't buy any cotton, did you?"

"Do I need any?"

"I'll use the washcloth."

"How often should I do it?"

"When the roots turn black. Every four weeks, probably."

"What's Robbie said?"

"He's against the whole thing. He wants you to go back and take your chances."

"What do you think?"

She dabbed some solution on the sideburns, then on the crown, and shook her head from side to side, the witness at an accident.

"How could Barbara do this to you?"

"What? Calling the police?"

"Not just that. Leading you on."

"You're wrong about her leading me on. She tried to remain uncommitted. I forced this. She was too weak to defend herself against me."

"You don't seem bitter."

"She gave me what I wanted. I'm alive, Lainie, and the truth is I love her more now than I did before. I can't hold her responsible for my actions. She had secrets that she couldn't tell me, and I refused to respect her privacy. At the time of the burglary, I was cavalier and indifferent to the man's death." He lowered his head over the basin. "Now I'm remorseful."

Teddy couldn't quite believe that he was the same man after Elaine shampooed his hair and then he towel-dried and combed it with a part. The transformation had the sudden, unexpected effect of a fatal illness that takes its victim off-balance, confronting him with a spectral unknown image of himself. The structure of his face had been altered by the sparse mustache and the creamy yellow color of the dye. His eyes were softer, and the strong, aquiline nose was less prominent, lending his face a vaguely uncertain character as though it had lost some of its function, like a guitar with a broken string. It was a disguise, and he embraced it, hoping that the softer, weaker man it represented would merge with his personality. Robbie looked away when he came into the bedroom, unable to face the apparition before him.

"Can we lock my stuff in the trunk and have some breakfast?"

Outside the cabin, the main highway was alive with cars and thundering eighteen-wheelers bound for Montreal and Toronto. Even in late August, the morning air carried a slow, lisping chill wind, but the sky was amber bright.

"Elaine and I'll go in first, Rob."

Teddy had combed the front of his hair over his forehead to shield his stitches and with the baseball cap, khakis and a new denim shirt, he was just another workingman. The restaurant was crowded with truck drivers bellowing cheerfully at the two elderly waitresses in stained blouses who rushed back and forth to the serving counter and skillfully stacked armloads of plates of ham, eggs, sausages, and pancakes.

Elaine found a table by the door, and Teddy looked over at the newspaper machine, expecting to discover his photograph on the front page, but the new edition had not arrived, and he sank down on the cold red vinyl seat with an audible sigh of relief. At the counter, two Canadian highway patrolmen lingered over their coffee and muffins. Teddy hadn't noticed a police car; then he saw a screen door that led to a rear parking lot, and he assumed that their car was parked there. Robbie glanced at the patrolmen as he entered, and he stood rigidly at the doorway. Teddy waved him to the table. At last he responded to Teddy's signal and came to them.

"For a minute I thought they had you."

"If you act as though you're guilty, people will assume you are," Elaine said.

"I think you were meant for a life of crime, Elaine," Teddy said good-humoredly.

"Big joke."

"What're you worried about, Rob? You haven't done anything, have you?"

Robbie had a moment of fear, wondering if Teddy knew about Barbara and him. Had she betrayed him? If Teddy accused him, he'd deny it and use the accusation as evidence to confirm Barbara's sick mind and her plot to destroy their family. And yet only a few days ago the two of them had conspired to betray his father. All true conspiracies, he reasoned, are designed by men and women in the act of love.

The waitress brought them toast, coffee, and Canadian bacon and poached eggs, which the three ravaged in minutes. Teddy's gourmandizing had never before been so perfectly rewarded, and he couldn't remember when he'd eaten with more appetite, Leonard's eggs Benedict notwithstanding. Teddy caught a glimpse of himself in the mirror behind the counter and decided that the new look suited him, softened the angles of his face.

To test his disguise, he called the waitress in a loud voice to demand more coffee and attracted the attention of the patrolmen, who sympathized with him and exchanged pleasantries about the service, which Teddy discovered was part of a long-standing needle match they conducted with the two waitresses, culminating in the waitresses' threat to bar them in the future. Robbie watched his father's banter with a mixture of terror and respect.

"Someone's bound to notice you if you keep this up."

"If I behave like a criminal, I'll be treated as one."

"The big cop stared at you."

"It's an occupational disease. They stare at everyone they don't know. It's something they're taught to do

during training." He patted Robbie's hand affectionately. "I'm going to leave now. Can I have the car keys?"

Robbie handed the keys to him under the table.
"Now, there are a couple of things to remember: First
of all, you haven't seen me, and I haven't tried to contact you. Second, can you think of some reason why
you'd be out of Boston for the night?"

"We drove to our summer house in Newport,"
Elaine said.

"Why would you do that?"

"Well, we're engaged, aren't we? We wanted to
spend the night there."

"Would anyone have seen you?"

"No, we only have a housekeeper when my parents
are there."

"Why didn't I drive?" Robbie asked.

"You had trouble with your car. And we rented the
Toyota."

Teddy detected a serious flaw in the plan that might
implicate the young couple. He left the table and went
to the phone outside the men's room. He flipped
open the yellow pages. A policeman came out, rubbing his damp hands together. Teddy smiled at him.

"Officer, do you know if there's a Toyota dealer
around here?"

The cop shook his head. "Yeah, up ahead, about five
miles on the south side. Maple Leaf Toyota."

"Any idea what the Land Cruiser is running?"

"Canadian or U.S.?"

"American dollars."

"Let's see, oh, I'd guess maybe fifty, fifty-five
loaded."

Teddy smiled at the obliging cop. When he returned chatting amiably with the officer, Robbie
averted his eyes and turned to look out of the window.

"How we doing, Dad?" Lainie said flippantly.

"Thanks to this gentleman, we've solved our problem."

Teddy paid for breakfast, left a ten-dollar tip, and the three of them headed for the Toyota dealer.

"God, Dad, have you got balls."

"So do you, and you'll need them as the new head of Franklin and Company."

"What're you going to do, Teddy?"

"Robbie's going to buy me a used car with low mileage."

"With cash?" she asked.

"Absolutely. I never heard of a car salesman who'd turn it down. You see, Lainie, if you report the rental stolen, sooner or later, there will be a pack of detectives and lawyers on your back asking ugly questions."

One hour later, Teddy stood beside a dark green Land Cruiser. He kissed Elaine, who held his hands tightly and began to cry.

"Teddy, you're my hero. . . . Oh, God be good to you."

"He's been very good," Teddy said, awkwardly, moving away from her, anxious to leave before he lost the small grip he had maintained on his emotions. Leaving them was more difficult than he had anticipated, and he was tempted to change his mind and go back with them. He edged away, opened the car door and touched Robbie's shoulder.

"Is there any way I can get in touch with you, Dad?"

"Let me get settled and I'll try to figure something out. If you see Barbara, be kind to her. She's the casualty."

THIRTY-THREE

$\mathcal{B}$ARBARA HANDLED THE INTERVIEW WITH THE DETEC-
tives without revealing anything damaging to
Teddy. Yes, they were engaged and he had been paying her psychiatric bills. She had no idea who the burglars were nor if Teddy had hired anyone. The notion
of Teddy being involved with the murder of Mr. Grant
was preposterous. It had now been established that
Grant had died of an aortic aneurysm and had some
months previously suffered a heart attack. Alex Hammond had offered, then insisted, that he accompany
her to the interview. She had declined. She had not
committed a crime. But more significantly, she wanted
to keep whatever lingered of her past intact.

"Then how come the tapes were found in Mr.
Franklin's bedroom?" Lieutenant Field asked.

"I have no idea how they came into his possession."

"You did call Dr. Frere after Franklin came to see
you at the United Nations?"

"Yes."

The detective was in his early forties, well dressed and with a pleasant, insinuating manner, but she was wary of him.

"What do you think happened, Ms. Hickman?"

"I haven't the faintest idea."

"You know Dr. Frere identified the tapes we found at Franklin's house." She remained unresponsive and would not allow him to lead her. "*One* of them is missing."

"I don't know how many there were, so one or ten of them could be missing."

"You're an extremely intriguing woman, Barbara."

He was taking a silky but prurient interest in her that she felt had little to do with the burglary or Grant's death. She had been hit on by experts and Field was gauche.

"Did you enjoy listening to the tapes?"

"It's part of my job."

"You and Howard Stern."

When she left, the smoldering late August heat hissed down Columbus Avenue. It was impossible to get a cab and she sat down on a bench at Lincoln Center, took off her heels, yanked out her Mephistos from her large bag, and changed. She continued to stroll past the west side's wondrous dueling gourmet markets and warring drug chains, until she reached civilization at Zabar's. She hadn't eaten all day and went inside, bought a smoked Scotch salmon sandwich on pumpernickel and ate it while she headed to Dr. Frere's office.

She had taken a leave of absence from the translation section. Her boss was sympathetic, but Barbara realized her days were numbered there. Now that Teddy had vanished, the gaping hole in her life had become evident and painful. She yearned for him and realized how deeply she loved him. But anger dispelled her grief.

Back in familiar territory, Frere's small waiting room, she idly flipped through a *House & Garden*, since the news magazines were already banqueting on Teddy's criminal mind and wealth. Through no fault of her indiscreet and voluble therapist, the media had referred to her as the mystery woman. Alex had informed the police that her life might be in danger if they released her name and with a powerful criminal lawyer on the record, they and the district attorney's office had offered her protection.

She was not afraid of Teddy Franklin; she feared for his safety, not hers.

Dr. Frere opened his office door and had an avuncular smile and radiated the professional warmth of a publicist. He clearly reveled in his place in the sun with the media who referred to him as "psychiatrist to the stars." He was in the public domain and loving it. If only he could enliven his recent interviews with the name of the woman who had been the object of Teddy's passion, he might be, elevated to *Rivera Live* or find himself on the panels of talking heads cherished by CNBC when a crime of passion was cooking, propelling world issues off the airways. Teddy's situation, parochial as it might be, was of greater interest than earthquakes in Turkey or the swamping rain of New York. Barbara realized that it was merely a matter of time before someone broke ranks and named her: The tabloids had a price on her head and Teddy was not around to buy them off.

"You weren't scheduled for this afternoon," Frere noted.

"But you found the time."

"My dear Barbara, I'm always here for you."

"And for *People, Newsweek, Time,* and every other rag. Time for your pet patient, of course you do."

He smiled coldly. "Are you criticizing my behavior?"

"I think you've interpreted that correctly."

"On what basis?" His attitude became guarded. "I know that you've hired a lawyer. He called to tell me never to mention your name in connection with this. Are you planning to sue someone?"

He had been careful to exclude himself. "No, I just want to be sure that my privacy is protected. Do you have a problem with that?"

"Naturally not."

"Then why the hell did you call the police when I trusted you with a personal confidence?"

He rose from his desk of dusty paperweights and a bullying, churlish aspect that he had kept hidden asserted itself.

"That could never be construed as a breach of faith, or betrayal of my loyalty to you."

"Really?" Despite the air-conditioning, she was in a controlled, sweating rage and flicked off the rivulet that had gathered above her lip. "The cops are listening to me spill out my personal life, my traumas on the tapes you made."

"I don't have the authority to advise them how to handle the evidence in a crime. You seem to be missing a cardinal point here, Barbara: a man was murdered. I had a legal and moral obligation to inform the police."

She wanted to slap him, kick him, beat him. "My attorney had access to Mr. Grant's pathology report. No one can ever prove that Teddy was responsible for his aorta exploding or that Teddy engineered the burglary. As I recall, you and your wife were blissfully spooning caviar into your faces at his expense at Le Cirque when the crime occurred."

"Then where is Teddy? Why isn't he here, explaining this to all of us?"

"He panicked because of me. And I'm to blame for

trusting you. If you think for a minute that Teddy's frightened of the police or anyone else for that matter, you're very much mistaken. I was his weakness. That's what defeated him."

"Barbara, I did my duty, obeyed the law and my conscience." She suspected that Frere was toying with her, setting her up for some unpleasant disclosure. "I saved you from a sociopath."

"Saved me?"

"If you went ahead and married him, he would have destroyed you. Men like Teddy Franklin have no sense of human worth or any value system."

"That's bullshit—psychobabble. A tape of *mine* is missing."

"I'm aware of that. I went through them with the lieutenant."

She sat silently, grim but dauntless, and this time, like him during their sessions, waited for the confession to emerge.

"It's the one dealing with Laura . . . and your adventure with the ladies in Boston."

"Ah, my adventure with the Boston ladies. A mysterious disappearance. Who gets it first, the *Globe* or the *Enquirer*? Maybe it'll crop up in London. Fleet Street papers serialize shit like that. 'A woman's secret perverse confession.' "

"Barbara"—Frere lit his pipe, expelled some smoke in her direction—"let's do what's best for you. I think under these circumstances, it would be appropriate if you considered seeking medical advice from another doctor. I can make a few recommendations."

"We're in agreement, finally. The purpose of my unscheduled visit was to give you notice and ask for any records still in your possession to be handed to me when I leave."

He nodded, but there was a suggestion of surprise

and she knew he had expected her to plead for reinstatement.

"Since we're about to close the book on this shabby episode, did you ever reach any professional conclusion about me?"

He sucked on his pipe, the avatar of Delphic wisdom and complacency.

"I have. You're immature and sexually dysfunctional. In a sense the reason you abstained from sex during your period in Europe—if you're to be believed—is that, like an alcoholic, you know that one drink is not enough and two are too many."

"You're suggesting that I'm a sexaholic."

"Your word, not mine. It seems clear to me that your fear of nymphomania is simply a cover-up and a defense mechanism inhibiting you from a lesbian lifestyle."

She began to laugh. "Oh, you poor man, you don't know shit. Laura led me on and fed me the poisoned pawn, which I accepted. But she did love me. If this was nothing more than a hustler's cheap trick, why did she commit suicide? And why didn't I? It would have been so easy. This was about betrayal, power, and control—not sex. Yes, I did love her and thought I could give her anything she wanted, but I didn't. If the two of us came out, what would have been the big deal? No one would have cared. This was Radcliffe in 1991!"

"Our work together is a process and ultimately something like this would have emerged."

"Not with you. Because you're incapable of a single insight. You're not a woman."

On her way out, Barbara was handed a bill for two thousand dollars by Frere's receptionist. "This was due last week, Ms. Hickman. Since Mr. Franklin is unavailable, I thought you might like to handle it."

"Thank you," Barbara said gaily. "Actually, I think your collection agency better deal with it. A strong letter to Mr. Franklin about lousing up his credit should do the trick."

Thirty-four

As Teddy sped along the highway on the Canadian Transcontinental Highway, he wondered why he hadn't years before discovered the physical pleasure of driving a car or thought of the cars he had bought and traded—Ferraris, Cadillacs, Rolls-Royces, Jags—as anything more than vehicles of conveyance, troublesome in cities and tedious for long trips. He kept at a steady fifty-five, which was five miles below the speed limit. He had his license and a display of platinum credit cards, but they were a deadly liability. Still, it was better to have some form of identification on him in case he was stopped. He listened to an all-news station retailing local mayhem. There was nothing about him.

Maybe he had been wrong to leave New York so quickly . . . and yet he felt an overriding joy in his new freedom. Although he was separated from Barbara, she had never been closer. The one fact of life he refused to face was that he'd never again see her, and he instinctively rejected it. In her own good time, when this had all become a half-remembered, seldom-recollected experience, he would find her, and she would forgive him. The idea gripped him.

On the outskirts of Ottawa he pulled into a gas station that was part of a shopping center. He had the car and the spare tire checked, filled up, and parked in front of a supermarket. At a newsstand he picked up the local papers, half a dozen paperbacks, and an old edition of the *New York Times*. At the bottom of the front page in a triple column he saw his name under the heading:

POLICE SEEK FINANCIER IN MURDER

Police today issued a warrant for the arrest of Theodore J. Franklin, chairman of the investment firm of T. J. Franklin and Company, in connection with the murder of W. T. Grant. Mr. Grant, a night employee, died during the course of a robbery on August 21. According to a police spokesman, Mr. Grant interrupted a burglary in the apartment of Dr. Paul Frere, a prominent psychiatrist. Records stolen from Dr. Frere were recovered yesterday in Mr. Franklin's Manhattan home. Dr. Frere was informed by an unnamed patient that these records were in Mr. Franklin's possession.

A police department spokesman stated that "Franklin is probably headed for South America. He has extensive business interests in Rio, Buenos Aires, and Caracas. Police of South America and Interpol have been advised of this development and have taken immediate action." Also questioned by the police was Mr. Franklin's fiancée. She was the last person to see Franklin before his disappearance.

Please see business section for reaction on Wall Street and Asian financial markets.

Teddy walked into the supermarket, slid a cart out of the rack, and pushed it down the aisle. He bought himself a variety of soups, including lobster bisque, cans of salmon, tuna, chicken, anchovies, biscuits, raspberry preserves, English marmalade, breakfast cereals, condensed milk, and two jumbo jars of Maxwell House instant coffee. He managed to break a hundred-dollar bill without arousing the checker's suspicions. He loaded his bags and got into the car.

He turned to the business section, which had a small, badly reproduced photograph of himself taken in the early eighties, which bore little or no resemblance to him as he was now. In the picture he was smiling, wearing a captain's hat on the deck of his first yacht. Beside him lay a five-hundred-pound marlin, which he had taken without the assistance of the crew, just off Dry Tortugas.

In collapsing the years to recapture the mood, he was astonished by his failure to identify with the smiling fisherman in the picture. It wasn't simply that he was no longer that man, but he could not conceive that he ever had been. The former image did not represent a division in his mind, an alter ego, but rather someone, as far as he could tell, who had never existed. And yet the facts of the story made sense, did not diverge from the truth of who he was, what he had done. He picked up a few sentences:

A. R. Pauley, executive vice-president, said that he could not believe his friend and associate had anything to do with the crime. . . . The firm's legal counsel indicated that he had not heard from his client, nor had a criminal attorney been engaged. . . . Mr. Franklin is a director of twenty-eight companies, traded on the New York Stock Exchange and has been active launching the IPOs of a number of online companies. . . .

Mr. Franklin shunned personal publicity and is reputed to be worth more than fourteen billion dollars. According to *Forbes*, this places him in the top ten wealthiest individuals. . . .

Teddy crumpled the paper, leaned out of the window and dropped it into a nearby garbage can.

They were writing about someone else, not him. His new persona, Connie Hickman, was heading for the Northwest Territories. He unfolded his road map and ran his finger along the transversal leading up to Yellowknife, on the eastern tip of Great Slave Lake. The name fired his imagination.

*A*T FOUR IN THE AFTERNOON HE REACHED A FAIR-sized town called Timmins, in central Ontario, and stopped for information at a service station. He realized how stiff he was. The mechanic he asked recommended the Sainte Marie Hotel. He cruised down the main street and saw cavernous holes and fenced-in stopes with *Danger* signs, vestiges of the gold and silver mining that had created this dismal atmosphere. This was hardscrabble land, untouched and unfettered by contemporary interest. The town—like many others—maintained its own uninfluenced rate of progress and to his city-wise eyes appeared centuries behind New York.

He needed to outfit himself and spotted a barnlike structure, McGee's Outdoor Clothes. A broad, muscular man, with a well-tended gray-speckled beard and mustache, thinning hair, pale blue eyes, and weathered skin that resembled corrugation on his neck approached Teddy with a welcoming smile. He wore jeans and a red plaid shirt.

"What can we do for you?" he asked with a chirp in his voice.

"Everything," Teddy said, conscious of the man's eyes on his crumpled seersucker jacket.

"You with the lumber camp?"

"No, I'm in mining."

"Oh, yeah, which company, Hollinger or the Dome?"

"Neither, I'm heading for Yellowknife. I'm with a gold-mining team."

"Been there before?"

"Yeah, years ago."

"Boyo, you're in for one hell of an ass-freezing winter."

There was a sharp, pungent odor of leather, hides, fur; on a long wooden display table there were warm shirts, trousers, turtleneck sweaters. Teddy strolled through the aisles, examining the merchandise.

"I need quite a few things," Teddy said from the back of the well-stocked store.

"Well, we got them. I'm Owen McGee at your service. They all call me Mac."

"Thanks. I'm just passing through."

Teddy bought long red underwear, half a dozen pairs of heavy corduroy trousers, ten shirts, five sweaters, a sheepskin-lined leather jacket, two dozen pairs of socks, two pairs of high boots, a wide-brimmed hat, and a wool stocking cap. The two chatted amiably for some minutes until it came time to pay. McGee experienced a moment's awkwardness, fearful that a checkbook was about to make its appearance, and the largest sale he'd made in months would evaporate into thin air. Had he misjudged this drifter? His suspense was relieved when Teddy peeled twelve hundreds off a thick wad.

"I'd watch out with that bankroll."

"Someone going to roll me for it?" Teddy asked, looking hard, the city killer, at McGee.

"You look able to handle yourself."

"I have so far."

"Got a gun?"

"No, do I need one?"

"You just might. I got a forty-five I could let you have for three hundred."

"Have you got ammo?"

"That's like asking a girl if she's got a pussy."

Owen McGee considered himself an explorer of the universe and he had waited a lifetime for this magical intervention. The flint of malice he concealed to strangers was ignited, fusing into bonhomie. Surveying this customer, he scented big money and an inexperienced fugitive scrambling for a sanctuary. McGee packed the clothes in a large cardboard box, and Teddy asked him to deliver it to the hotel along with a duffel bag he had also purchased.

"Well, it's been real fine meeting you, Mr. Hickman. How long'll you be in town?"

"Just overnight."

"I'll be by the hotel after I close. Are you doing anything tonight?"

"No, just a quiet dinner."

"Well, then, let me buy you a drink." Teddy looked uncertain, but McGee added insistently, "Sainte Marie bar, six."

In Timmins's oldest pharmacy *est 1879*, Teddy bought writing paper, some ballpoint pens, and envelopes. He forgot to ask for stamps. What he needed was a laptop, but there wasn't even a Radio Shack or a computer store around. This was catalogue territory. He made his way back to the hotel parking lot, removed his carryall from the trunk and entered a dimly lit lobby. It was furnished with a pair of chafed leather sofas, a rolltop desk for guests' use, and three easy chairs. The hotel had the atmosphere of a hunting lodge gone to seed. Moose antlers, a stuffed seal, and a snarling lantern-jawed mountain lion's head attested to the deadly accuracy of local hunters.

"I wondered whose car it was," a man with a custodial air said.

The hotel suited him fine because lobbies of the new motels and the larger hotels might be problematical. This place had no whirring computer or fax machine.

"I wanted to catch the stores before registering."

"Sign here," Teddy was informed.

"Cash or credit card?" Teddy asked, testing the waters.

"Fifty U.S. bucks would do me."

Teddy handed him a hundred. "You can give me the change in Canadian dollars."

"I could cheat you on the exchange rate."

Teddy smiled. "Cheat me? Well, I'll chance it. By the way, I'm having a package delivered from McGee's."

"I'll send it up." He handed Teddy a key. "That's on the first floor. Take a right. Given you a corner room," he added as though bestowing an unheard-of honor on Teddy. The room overlooked the small square in front of the hotel. It was furnished with Spartan simplicity, with a wooden dresser, mirror attached, so deeply tarnished that his image seemed like a psychic manifestation at a séance. He tested the mattress, which was thick and soft, and pulled down the spread, discovering heavy blankets and coarse linen. He washed his hands. Listened to the cistern's death rattle.

Despite his fatigue—and it was obvious to him from an eye twitch—he had a feeling of robustness and ease. His escape through the hinterland into this back-mining passage of the earth's core had so far gone undetected, and with instinctive certainty he knew that as he went farther north toward the arctic tundra and ice, he would be safe. Perhaps for a time he would be allowed to investigate the bloodied rents in the fabric of his life so that he could emerge with a purposeful existence.

He stooped over the mirror and snipped the stitches in his wound on which a blue black encrusted scab had formed. He pulled out the gut with tweezers, setting his teeth on edge, washed his hands with a bit of soap on the basin, blue-veined as Stilton, and went back downstairs, fortified by thoughts of a drink awaiting him and the prospect of an easy sleep.

The owner greeted him in the bar, advised him that the hotel was in the process of renovation and that new phones were to be installed in the spring as a final luxury, and asked him what he'd have to drink. He ordered a Smirnoff on the rocks and got a high-roller shot in a bucket. The bar was crowded, auguring a successfully run hostelry, and he noticed two slant-eyed, darkish-skinned women sitting at one of the booths with three broad-shouldered men, whom he heard mention a lumber camp and a breakdown at the sawmill. McGee came in, waved to several men in front of him, and clapped Teddy's shoulder. Teddy was pleased and hoped this instant familiarity would cure any local suspicion. Timmins was not a place for a vacation.

"I put the stuff in your room."

"Thanks. What about the gun?"

"It's at the bottom of the carton. Here are two boxes of cartridges."

"Do I need a permit for it?"

"Naw, only a target." He guffawed, waved his thick fingers at the owner, and ordered a round of doubles for Teddy and himself, which he paid for with one of the hundreds Teddy had given him.

"I haven't had this many hundreds since my last trip to Vegas."

"I wouldn't flash them," Teddy said, amused.

"The town's safe. It's round the lumber camps that you get your head chainsawed. If you don't mind me saying, you don't really belong to a mining team."

Teddy sipped his drink thoughtfully. Obviously his appearance and the cash had made him a curiosity, and he knew he'd have to be careful. Foolish of him to get himself trapped with McGee.

"I'm on the financial end of the operation."

"Aha," McGee said, holding up his glass to Teddy, "thought you might be. Well, good luck and good prospecting."

"Thanks."

"Didn't get the name of your outfit."

"I don't think you've heard of them."

"Try me," McGee insisted.

"Vulcan Financial Trust," Teddy replied glibly, remembering the name of a defunct tax shell he had taken over years ago. "We've got a claim, and it's up to me to decide if it's worth going ahead with or spinning it off to one of the other companies. It's a big investment, and we have to be sure."

"Makes sense," McGee agreed, signaling the owner for another setup.

He didn't like the way McGee was beginning to sniff around him, like a dangerous animal. For a moment he felt defenseless, cut off from his life source and his easy confidence with company presidents and bankers among whom he exerted power. McGee was part of the obscure, ominous millions who worked in steel mills, coal mines, car factories in Detroit; they bowled, drank cheap booze, beat up their wives, and their existence never amounted to more than a paycheck, and a mass-produced pine coffin. He'd seen and known men like McGee working alongside his father at the Carrier plant in Syracuse.

"Like them two?" McGee pointed to the two girls sitting with a French Canadian lumberjack.

"Not especially."

"We got some fine women in these parts. Most of the boys from the camps come down here for their ladies. We got some good Eskimo girls, Indians, and a bunch of Frenchies from Quebec that work here most of the year."

"You're not married?"

"Sure am. I still like it nice and steady any way it comes."

"It's a small town. Don't people—"

"Talk? All they like. But if you're a man, married or otherwise, you do your share of grabbing a little when it comes your way. Can't help it." He leaned across, and his breath was rank and sour. "In the winter, you'll feel little horns digging into your flesh."

"No AIDS here?"

"Ice kills it," he chortled.

Buttonholed, Teddy decided to buy his round and call it a night, but McGee, with his thick neck, his heavy, muscular arms, and his grip of iron continually digging into his forearm, had different plans.

"Let's finish here and hit the Palace."

"What's that?"

"It's the place, Conrad. Our own little dream palace," he said thickly. "Didn't imagine we had a dream palace up here, did you?"

"No, I didn't."

"We'll fix you up real well. 'Cause when you send up your crews to Yellowknife, I'll outfit them, look out for them. Oversee, as I like to put it. Make sure they have themselves a fine time when they fly into Timmins, so they'll be looking forward to the mine, especially when I tell them that there's good soft goods up there. Leave it to me. I'll look after them."

Teddy drank his vodka slowly. In the filmy bar mirror he had a split image of himself and Barbara at the Four Seasons, listening to Barbara's relaxed laughter, and then imagined the warm, soft, firm breasts against his chest, the honey taste of her nipples in his mouth, her tongue in his ear, the sweet magic of holding off and the warfare with his glands, as he desperately tried to visualize a horse race, baseball game, quarterback calling a play—in short, anything that would remove him forcibly from the viselike muscles inside her, and the fact that they were making love ecstatically and her saying, "Okay, I surrender," and his ease as the sperm shot out and he wallowed in her warm juices.

Outside, McGee held Teddy's elbow. The temperature had dropped to the mid-forties and he was unprepared for the cold. The night was bright, star-filled, and his dislocation was so severe that he might have been witnessing his own death. He followed McGee to a battered Ford pickup, rust-mottled with age.

"Where are we going?" Teddy again asked.

"Don't you worry!"

"But I am," he said firmly.

"Going to show you the sights, Connie."

"I'm too tired."

"Well, we're heading for the service station, Conrad. Seal-slick Inuits . . . some beautiful métis—that's our local half-breeds."

THIRTY-FIVE

THE INTERIOR OF McGEE'S PICKUP WAS CAKED WITH grease, the smell of a million smoked cigarettes, spent cartridges, and Teddy found no way to extricate himself. Outside of Timmins, the pickup slewed from side to side on a dirt road. He felt grinding bumps, potholes, and around him were deep stopes from the played-out gold mines. Behind the wheel McGee breathed heavily with excitement and Teddy listened with his inner ear to the night sounds of keening wolves, a deer herd pursued, the caw-caw of restless birds taking flight, and the distant tremulous toll of a bell somewhere in the wilderness beyond them.

The front wheel caught a rut in the road, and the car skidded down a gradient, coming to a halt on an angled shoulder. Teddy's head hung limply against the window. He blinked his eyes and discovered that they were on a parking lot where dozens of cars and trucks with wooden slats along the sides hung limply from the hillside.

"Perk up, Conrad. We're here."

"Where?" he asked, peering at the desolate expanse of land spread out like a graveyard and wondering dimly whether this was his last trip, and now McGee would rob and kill him, completing the pointless destiny that had been ordained by the invisible hand. Was this the end? Recognizing that he was no match for the big man, he'd still fight for his life, and he picked up a heavy metal flashlight that had rolled to his feet from under the seat.

McGee watched him and said, "Take it. We walk from here."

"But where the hell are we going?" he asked.

"Boy, don't you trust anybody? It ain't city nightlife, but it's the best we can do. It's the other side of the hill, and they don't want cops, even though they pay off, so you got to be checked in on foot."

The chill air woke him sharply.

"I'll hold the flash," McGee demanded. Teddy hesitated and reluctantly passed it to him. McGee directed it to the left of the hill. They walked for about five minutes, Teddy slipping as he moved uncertainly. A small frozen pond lay ahead, and they circled it, passed through a wooden stockade gate, where a man in a small shack with a shotgun slung over his arm stopped them. McGee turned the light on his own face.

"Oh, it's you, sir, Mr. McGee," the man said.

"This here is Conrad. If I'm not around, you look after him. He's a friend of mine. Going to give you plenty of business when his mining teams come up."

"Yes, sir."

They entered a compound that reminded Teddy of an army post. A large wooden one-story building flanked by a number of shabby cabins were illuminated in the northern light.

"Places like this are all illegal," McGee said. "We got these Bible Belters coming down on us from time to time, and the Palace closes for Christmas and Easter to prove it's Christian. Then when the men come into town, get drunk, start fights, and grab a couple of old ladies, the police shrug their shoulders and say, 'Well, there ain't no trouble when they're out at the Palace.'"

The walk had revived Teddy, and the bone-weary exhaustion left. He was grateful he hadn't been knifed in the car and felt a sudden jubilation by being spared.

They entered a large, deep room, where perhaps a hundred men and dozens of women were drinking, playing cards, and dancing on a small wooden floor. Music blared from big speakers located at the far end of the room. They stopped to watch a card game at a front table; it was lowball, with a fifty-dollar buy-in. At the table, the debris of poverty and violence were spread across the faces of the five men, squeezing their hole cards to cajole luck from her secret place.

"Want to sit in for a while?" McGee asked.

"Not just now."

At the long bar, which stretched the length of the room, men stood three deep, mulling their drinks and complaining of low wages, crooked logging and mining camp bosses who cheated them out of their bonuses, and the hopeless predicament of the working-man. Everywhere Teddy looked, he saw guns, rifles, long bone-handled hunting knives, the arbiter of unresolved arguments. He stood by the card table to avoid drawing attention to himself. After some moments he overcame his sense of impending disaster. McGee took an empty seat at the card table, placed a hundred in front of him, and exchanged greetings with the dealer, a red-bearded, tattooed angular man wearing a leather Harley vest. He had a tattoo on his thick bicep that said *Hell is home.*

They shook hands. "How're you, Mr. Salt?" McGee asked.

"Waiting for you, my man. You're just what we need, Mac, new blood."

Teddy edged away from him and found a place at the bar. He was seeing life, adding a new dimension to his sheltered existence, and he realized now just how secure and protected he had been in his fortress. He congratulated himself, silently toasting his instincts that had led him away from the city into the gut of a different society. He was among ordinary men. In order to recast his life, he had to dissociate himself from the sophistication of New York, emerging with a worldview that transcended all the money values that had formerly sustained him.

Power he would have again, but a different kind of power, a more rational introspective grasp of the realities. He would regain his manhood and find solace in the perfect, unbreakable image of love he would always retain for Barbara, who, despite her absence, was the center of his being. Rather than complain about the fall from a high place, he embraced the core of his identity. He felt young again.

Four women, all with yellowish complexions and Asian features entered. They were followed by a group of sniggering men, and they barreled up to the bar beside Teddy. The women had the imprimatur of whore, but now in the light, one of them was softer and unravaged. He guessed she was in her early twenties. She had waist-length coal black hair and yellow brown eyes, a short stub of a nose, arching eyebrows, and an artless sensuality. Her jeans were tight and she wore an embroidered western shirt and a sealskin vest over which multicolored beaded necklaces swaggered above her breasts.

She stood next to Teddy, drank Jack Daniel's neat, and the rest of the group broke away from her. She made no attempt to talk to Teddy or anyone else, and he liked her air of quiet self-possession.

"Can I buy you another drink?" he asked.

"Sure, if you like," she said.

The attentive bartender whipped over to them. When they were served, she made a sly gesture of thanks with the glass.

"Are you from town?" he asked.

"No, from Great Bear Lake. It's above Yellowknife."

"Are you living here now?"

"I guess. Where're you headed?"

"Great Slave Lake."

"Business there?"

"Yes, and in Yellowknife."

"Oh, gold. My husband was a miner."

"What does he do now?"

"He's with his creator . . . two hundred feet under the ground. Cave-in. Those big stopes in town are from the old mines, and the government claims they don't have the money to fill them."

"I'm sorry."

"So am I," she said without self-pity.

"How long ago?"

"Four months."

"And you came down here?"

"Two weeks ago. I had a baby girl."

"Is she with you?"

"No, with my mother. I've got no skills, except the obvious one. I'm learning a trade. I'm not much good. Won't be for another month till I heal, but still I'm picking up a little money."

Up close, she had a curious gentility, unmarked by her circumstances.

"Where are you living?"

"Oh, there are some cabins for the girls, and we bunk together."

"You don't like what you're doing, do you?"

"I'm earning a little money, and when I can hustle, I'll make more."

"Would you like to go home?" Teddy asked, flagging the bartender for another setup.

She gave him a penetrating look. "Sure, wouldn't you?"

He was startled by her reply, wondering if his flight was common knowledge.

Economics always intrigued him, and the financial mechanics of whoring was no exception.

"How much would you earn if you could work and had a good night?"

"A few hundred maybe . . . that'd mean probably two, three hundred. We split fifty-fifty with the house. We only do that kind of business Friday and Saturday. The rest of the week's lazy."

She accepted the new drink with a nod and belted it back. He slipped a hundred into her hand, and she stared at the bill, sighing deeply, uncertain what to say.

"I haven't earned it. I can't earn it right now. There's only one thing I can do for you."

"Maybe I don't want you to earn it that way. I'm enjoying talking to you."

"Me?" She shook her head. "What would an educated man enjoy about me, except the obvious?"

He dodged her question with one of his own. "If you had some money, what would you do with it?"

She pondered. "My dream is to head out to Nunavut. That's the new territory the Canadian government kicking and screaming gave us after years of legal battles. It became ours in April by treaty."

"Nunavut?"

"It means *our land* in Inuit. It's one of the last unspoiled parts of the world. Not that I'm a traveler. White foxes roam and herds of caribou. Out on the

Ellesmere Islands you can see the migrating geese breeding. Money'll come there from the big companies because of the mineral rights. In a couple of years, tourists will be flooding in. I'd open a shop in my town for ladies. I like clothes, and I can sew, and I'll be one of the first. I'd also have native artifacts. Some of my people are amazing artists. They carve scrimshaw whalebones and canes, beautiful soapstone sculpture and they make chess sets."

"How much'd a shop cost?"

"A fortune. I don't know . . . maybe ten thousand dollars. Sign a lease, get some credit so as I could buy direct and not have to hit the flea markets in Manitoba. More money than I'm ever likely to come by."

A vague, embryonic plan was forming in Teddy's mind that involved the girl. He wondered how much he ought to tell her. If she learned that she had to shield a man wanted by the police and that she might be eligible for a prison term, she'd probably panic. He still couldn't reconcile himself to the fact that he was prey. Accustomed to power, he was still making decisions.

"What's your name?"

"Deborah Connors. But I've always been called Deb."

In a good dress, rather than the jeans, she might pass for a respectable married woman. She wore a thin gold wedding band, so it was unnecessary to ask her to wear one.

"Would you drive up to Yellowknife with me, then go to wherever?"

Her deep-set eyes flickered with disbelief. What had begun as the usual bar conversation, aimless and time-killing, had taken an unexpected direction, which, in view of the seriousness and set expression of this man, as well as the crisp hundred-dollar bill that was now settled in a corner of her brassiere just under the belly of her breast so that she could feel it, might alter the course of her life.

"If you came with me, you'd be able to have your shop in Nunavut."

"If this is some kind of joke, it's a cruel one."

"I'll give you half—five thousand—in the morning and the rest when we got there."

"But why would you or anybody offer me that kind of money?"

"One of my rules is that you don't ask questions," Teddy said, as if talking to an employee.

She tried to detect the hint of a smile on his face, in his eyes, which would relieve the tension. She refused to believe she could be this lucky. But his face was open, and there was no deceit in his eyes.

"It's a sin to fool a girl like me. . . . Lots of men say things when they're drunk or want you to take your time with them."

"Do I sound drunk?"

"No, that's what scares me."

"*I* scare you?"

"I didn't mean it that way. You dream about something like this happening, like late at night when you can't sleep, but it doesn't ever happen. Not in real life." She shook her head. "Never. 'Specially to someone like me. I never had anything but bad luck." She took his hand. "It's not stolen, the money, is it?"

From the card table, McGee observed them and then strode to the bar.

"No, it's mine."

"You say it like it's really true."

"Will you come?"

She didn't have an opportunity to reply because a man's hand had reached over between them, seized her arm, and spun her around. Teddy looked into McGee's bloodshot eyes.

"She's real fine stuff," he said. "And I won eighty dollars. Drew me a bike. How much is it, honey?"

"Short time or what?"

"Well, I take it real slow." He rubbed the back of his hand over the cleft of her breasts. "Nice and soft." He turned to Teddy. "Something to grab hold of when you're sinking into the mud."

"I don't think she can go with you," Teddy said.

"Why not? She's for sale, isn't she?"

"She's with me," he said casually. There was a gradual meeting of eyes between the two men, and McGee withdrew. "I've paid for the night," Teddy added.

"Well, sure, Connie. You're fast."

An image of a large labor force crowding his shop, employed by this man, passed through McGee's mind along with other possibilities. "Oh, Connie, forgive me. I'll get myself another one. When the lights are out, they're all the same." He looked at his watch. "Be going in an hour or so. That all right with you?"

"Fine."

They watched McGee steer into a blonde at a table in the corner. The blonde nodded, then rose, followed by McGee, who swerved from side to side as he followed her outside.

Deb sighed nervously. "Why'd he back down?" she asked.

"He wants my business. I'm in room seven at the Sainte Marie. It's on the first floor. Meet me there at six tomorrow morning."

"I can go with you now. It's midnight, and the girls can knock off if they want to."

"All right," he agreed, thinking it safer to take her with him than chance locating her in the morning. He didn't know the roads, and she might change her mind or discuss her plans with one of the other girls, who would put her on her guard. He'd get her a room at the hotel and sleep secure in the knowledge that she'd be there.

"You wait for me here."

"I'll tag along, Deb."

"I'll grab my stuff."

Deb had a black-beaded sweater in a sling bag, which she threw over her shoulders, and they left by a side door, which led directly to the group of cabins he had seen earlier. Outside, the wind rasped through the pines. He followed her down a footpath, running behind the cabins. Through somber windows the brown bodies of Eskimo women wheedled men with chalky bodies. Teddy waited outside Deb's cabin. Through the doorway he caught the tarred odor of sleep, stenched flesh, and stale perfume. Deb shoved her clothes, what there were of them, into a backpack.

"I haven't got a car here," he said, remembering he'd come with McGee. "Can we call a taxi?"

"Not likely. It's not far. I'd be glad to walk if you don't mind."

He grabbed hold of the gypsy bundle, but she held tightly to it; then he touched her hand.

"I can manage," she said. When his hand remained on the handle, she surrendered it and said with childish discovery, "You're the real thing. My fortune's really changing."

*D*EB CHECKED INTO THE HOTEL FIVE MINUTES AFTER he went upstairs, then knocked on his door to tell him that her room was opposite his.

"Sleep well," he said.

She stood in the hallway staring at him, unable to believe that she was being dismissed. She lingered there, blocking the doorway, and he wondered how he could disengage himself without offending her.

She pushed her face close to his, and their knees touched, so that he was forced to give ground, and he stepped back into the small, dark room. She closed the door behind him, never taking her eyes off him, and he felt her soft, wet mouth on his cheek. She was unbuttoning her shirt with a free hand, and he heard the swish of her long hair as she swung her head forward. He backed away. She giggled like a young girl discovering the back of a car for the first time. He was about to protest when she placed her hand across his mouth, and he wondered if this route was part of the strange and muddy terrain of the uncharted landscape of his new life.

"You can't be paying me all that money for my dazzling conversation."

"Why not?"

"It don't make sense. You're a good-looking money man, and you could've brought a dozen girls with you."

"I decided against that."

"You're in some kind of trouble, aren't you?"

"Did we make a bargain?"

"Yeah, we did . . . but I want to know."

"I can't tell you."

"I lied before about not being healed. Connie, I don't have a baby. I just didn't fancy all them pig-eyed men. I'm not even married."

"The wedding ring?"

"It was my mother's. Keeps some of the vermin off me. My father was a drunken shanty-Irish gold miner with a lovely tenor voice and the temper of a grizzly. My mother was Inuit. So that makes me a méti. We were living out at Great Bear Lake when she walked out in a snowstorm one night and we found her in the spring thaw, still frozen. When the mine closed down, my father went up to Hudson Bay with some fur traders. I heard he was murdered."

Teddy reached out for her hand, but she was not emotionally engaged by her history.

"The Convent of Our Lady Queen of Martyrs took me in then. Let's see, I was twelve and wild. They did their best, but I broke away a few years later and ran into my mother's brother. I learned something about real life from my uncle and worked with him for a few years. He has a trading post and does boat rentals. But I was restless, so I scooted around the territories, working odd jobs, looking for some excitement."

"You're a survivor."

She smiled. "I shoot first and that's a fucking fact."

He switched on a lamp, and now with her in the room it was not so barren. She was small-shouldered, and the manner in which she moved them reminded him a bit of Barbara's habit of thrusting forward when she wanted to be emphatic. But desire was extinct in him, and he sensed for a moment, projecting himself backward, how Barbara must have felt by his advances. It wasn't a question of looks, skill, or even the encroaching smell of another human being—but simply an empty tedium, like waiting for a delayed plane circling an airport, existence held in a void, the dreadful empty parenthesis that isn't life or death.

"Do I turn you off?" she asked.

"No. You're a charming woman, but I lost someone recently. It's difficult to explain. I haven't got anything left. Not even for myself. I'm sort of wandering until I find out what to do, if I ever can find an answer. It's not just love, but a kind of sickness for her. I caught her the way you would catch a disease—like malaria—and I get chills, sick, and die when I think about her, and yet that's the only way I can stay alive. She's the host and I'm the parasite and we lived off each other."

Deb released her hold on him, and he sat down on the bed, head bent low as though about to retch.

"Love poisons all, not conquers all. That's what it's all about."

"Did she love you?"

"I thought so . . . for a time." He paused, looked up at her with bloodshot, tearless eyes that had something of childlike astonishment in them. "But then it vanished."

"Did you kill her?"

"Kill? Me? I don't kill people. I haven't got that quality in me. It might have been better if I had. I tried to be too clever, and that's anti-life, anti-love, anti-everything. You kill yourself by being too smart, playing percentages, guessing about people, instead of doing it the hard way. Learning, waiting patiently. Waiting for them to tell you in their own good time. I'm not a submissive man. I have to make things happen, and that means changing people if they don't fit in with my ideas." He laughed to himself. "Crazy, isn't it? To come up here, talk to a stranger . . . in the wilderness . . . spilling my guts. But I have to see if there are any guts left. Or if I'm like a paper bag that's sodden and is just going to have the bottom fall out. If that happens and I learn something, it'll be worth it. I'll know, you see. But if I stand up, survive, and that's what it's all about, surviving with what you've got, not what you don't have, then maybe I'll be able to make something of it all yet, and if there's nothing, then I haven't lost."

Deb leaned toward him as though frozen. Her hair over her eyes, a figure on a frieze, her open shirt exposing her lacy bra cup. She nodded her head.

"I don't think there's any question about it."

"About what?"

"Your guts. Good night."

"I haven't got a clock," he said.

"Who does, but we all get up, don't we?"

THIRTY-SIX

$\mathcal{I}$N THE SILENT EAST SIDE NEIGHBORHOOD, THE LA-
bor Day weekend loomed over Barbara like a
hidden bird of prey waiting to swoop down on her
from the rack of morbid clouds. It seemed as if there
had been a government order to evacuate Manhattan
and she took a gloomy walk down to Carl Schurz Park
where even the nanny-driven carriage traffic was ab-
sent. Some kids and apathetic fathers were kicking a
soccer ball around the grassy mounds and the occasional jogger puffed along the river path. Apart from
some stray freighters, and trap rock flatboats, the East
River itself had been abandoned.

She felt isolated, remote from herself, her surroundings. A mental picture of Teddy emerged in
her consciousness. He had his arms open, with a welcoming smile, embracing her as he waited with his
chauffeur for his temptress at his Rolls. She had ruined their lives and, in her desolation, grief over-

whelmed her. She had not been able to express her
love to him and now that he was gone, she offered it
to him unconditionally.

She was too despondent for tears but the confusion
of the year with him finally formed a cohesive pattern.
His was a straightforward courtship, but because she
had given the wrong signals, he had developed suspicions that led to uncharacteristic paranoid behavior.
His fear of a secret rival had a grounding. She had
acted as though there was another man, and she had
been cheating, which set off the entire chain of events
leading to the burglary. All she had to do was to have
admitted that there was no one but him. But she was
uncomfortable with the supremacy he had yielded,
baffled by her control, and at the bottom, she knew
she was unworthy of his devotion.

She sluggishly returned to her apartment, listened
to two messages from Alex inviting her up to Rye. His
offer for the house they had visited had been accepted
and an architect friend and his wife would be joining
them. She didn't want to see him or be cheered up.

She phoned Teddy's house and spoke to a mournful
Leonard. No, Teddy had not attempted to contact him.
But if he did, Leonard would give him her message.

On Tuesday morning, she shook herself out of the
doldrums and decided to act. She put on a pale
checked yellow linen suit that Teddy liked, and took a
taxi to the World Trade Center. She got out of the elevator on the hundredth floor and entered the kingdom of Theodore Franklin and Company. The
security personnel who had previously welcomed
her—"No matter what's going or who I'm meeting,
never keep her waiting," Teddy had ordered them—
regarded her warily. No one had countermanded his
order and they were powerless to prevent her from going directly into his office.

Behind the desk with its bank of humming computers, where she had first met Teddy, his son now sat talking to a group of executives, and Nancy, his father's assistant. Barbara encountered a silent expression of consternation from the group.

"This won't take long," Robbie said to them. "Nancy, I think Barbara has some kind of account that my father was running."

"She does, Robbie."

"Close it and write her a check so she can take it with her when she leaves. And tell the head of security that her visiting privileges have been revoked. Will you all excuse me for a minute?" The executives rose and left.

Barbara was neither dismayed nor embarrassed by this damage control. She had expected him to be unpleasant. Former fiancées were a contagious disease; it was universal.

"I'm a very dangerous threat. Maybe I brought a bomb in my handbag."

Robbie wore a blue button-down shirt, rolled up at the sleeves and a pencil-striped jacket hung on the back of Teddy's chair. She realized how comfortably he fit into this environment. Well, he was born to it, she thought.

"You were a dangerous threat," he said, glancing at the computers, "because he loved you."

"I didn't come to start trouble. I have one question. When you tell me where he is, I'll go and never see you again."

"I have no idea where he is."

"Is he alive?"

"I pray to God that he is."

"When did you last see him?"

"You said one question. I answered it honestly, like a gentleman, and I want you to leave."

She shook her head forcefully. "No."

"Haven't you caused enough trouble? You've ruined

my father, torn this family apart. Take your money and get the fuck out."

"I don't want the money. It's his. I have to see Teddy to explain."

"What, that he's facing prison and you called the police and will testify against him?"

"Dr. Frere contacted the police—not me."

Robbie frowned, then stared at her with disgust.

"You are a sick, depraved woman and everything you touch you devour."

"You know I actually believed that once. But it's not the case now. I love your father and I went to bed with you to spare Lainie. I seduced you psychologically because I really wanted your approval and I made the sacrifice of sleeping with you so that you wouldn't hate yourself or hold it against Lainie. I am what I am and I've stopped disapproving of myself and my actions."

He reacted with disbelief at her statement. "You *are* something."

"If you don't tell me where he is, I'll go to Lainie and spell out what happened and why I went to bed with you."

He was stupefied by the threat, and for a moment retreated, in the hope of defusing it. "You don't care who you hurt, do you?"

"Teddy wants me and I'm going to be with him."

"If I hear from him, I'll convey your offer."

"I believe you can do better than that."

He realized that she was serious and that they were both in play again, but people's lives and not chess pieces were at stake. He could not outwit her or submit to her demands. Suddenly, he overcame his emotional turmoil and saw the line of attack.

"Barbara, you're a very clever person and sometimes when people are as smart as you are, they overlook what's obvious."

He strode toward her and their faces were inches

away. The very fragrance of her was overwhelming and she seemed lovely, open, and without deceit. She waited with dread, but did not disclose anything or back away.

"Don't you think if my father wanted you to know, he would have called you?"

"He might be afraid that the police are tapping my line."

Robbie laughed in her face. "Let's get real. My father is a genius and he has good friends all over the world. Have you looked at your mail? Has your phone rung? Have you considered the possibility that he's escaped from your web? Maybe he got bored with business and making money and you and your box of tricks. Could it be possible that he's having a good time somewhere on a yacht with a martini in his hand and a beautiful woman beside him?"

Barbara turned away and glanced at the skyline as she had so often before, with Teddy's arm draped around her waist.

"Maybe he came to his senses and said: 'I've had enough. *I don't want her.*'"

She struggled within and at all costs knew she must not cry or give vent to her feelings. "I'd like to hear it from him."

THIRTY-SEVEN

*E*ARLY MORNING SOUNDS—THE GRATING OF TRUCKS over loose gravel, the squeaks of unoiled wheels, the soft-drinks driver wheeling cans to the service station—woke Teddy from his deep, untortured sleep. He rested on his elbow, still unaccustomed to the place, and for the first time since leaving New York the dissociation from his past was final. He went to the window, gazed down at the small, deserted square. He scanned the cloudy horizon and saw rain beginning to fall. A carpenter shop and hardware store were already open. He couldn't remember ever having been exposed to the quiet permanence of a sequestered town with its clear-cut division of respectability and corruption. In a big city like New York everything was intermingled in such a way that corruption existed alongside respectability—primary schools next door to exclusive brothels, bookmakers' offices across from hospitals, millionaires on Fifth Avenue's gold coast and a short distance away, the howling squalor of a slum with teenage junkies and murder the common threat.

In the doorway of the hardware store McGee and his card-dealing friend, Salt, were watching Teddy's window.

There was a knock on his door, and Deb, scrubbed and fresh-smelling, with just a hint of lipstick on her mouth, sauntered in.

"Good morning. It's five-thirty. We ought to get going," she said efficiently.

"I won't be long. Shower and pack my stuff."

"I'll do it."

"I bought some new stuff that's in the carton."

"I'll manage."

When he emerged from the bathroom dressed, he was impressed by the way Deb had organized him. She had packed his duffel and broken down the carton.

"I didn't know what you wanted to do with this." She held up the pistol and two boxes of cartridges.

"McGee sold it to me."

"Is it registered?"

"Does it have to be?"

"The Mounties can arrest you if they find it on you."

"Will I need it in Yellowknife?" he asked, now out of his depth.

"That depends on your friends, doesn't it?"

"What do you think?"

"I'm a passenger, remember." He frowned, and she was sorry for being sharp. "How safe do you feel?"

"That's difficult to say."

"Well, would you use it on a cop?"

"No, never."

She slipped it into her straw bag. "I'll carry it then. If we get stopped, I'll say I was a hitchhiker and I took it away from my boyfriend when he tried to shoot me. Might've been used in a murder for all you know.

'Specially since McGee sold it to you." He found himself respectful and amused by the survivor's cunning. "We can drop it in a lake."

She easily hoisted the duffel bag on her shoulder, and he was surprised by her strength.

"Let me," he said.

"It's not that heavy, and I'm used to carrying like a pack mule."

"Does that mean I'm not?"

"I didn't say that."

They laid everything in the back of the Cruiser.

As they drove off, Deb caught a glint of McGee and Salt in the hotel parking lot, staring after them.

THE TWO MEN STOOD SILENTLY WATCHING THE Land Cruiser drive away, then headed to the coffee shop on the corner.

"Where do you suppose he got the money?" John Salt asked.

"If I was a betting man, which I'm not, I'd guess it's Vegas money. He's very cool."

"The whore got to him first."

"Problem is, she's not a whore," McGee said ruefully.

"You didn't get a taste?"

"No, sir. She was saving it for a score."

"You think she'd play ball with us?" Salt asked.

"My guess is that bitch would sell her mother's eyes for a dollar."

WHEN HE WAS BEHIND THE WHEEL, TEDDY REMEMbered his offer to pay Deb. He squirreled through his vest and brought out a wad of cash. "Count out five thousand as a down payment."

She stared at the hundreds, shook her head, and

handed him back the roll. "I may be sorry, but I trust you."

"Millions wouldn't," he said.

"That's their problem, not mine. I mean, you could toss me any time you like and get back your money, so what's the difference if you hold it?"

"It's a pleasure to do business with you. I didn't know you were so smart."

"I wouldn't have been at the Palace if I was so smart. Would've got myself a rich shopkeeper back home if I had any sense."

"Why didn't you?"

"There was no one I was in love with."

"You *are* smart."

They had a vast breakfast of eggs and smoky caribou bacon at a diner, took out steaming containers of coffee, and at the adjoining service station she checked the front end and filled the tank.

"We ought to buy a gas can. This elephant looks like it gets seven furlongs to the gallon."

"That much?" he said with a laugh.

Deb looked younger than he realized, and he wondered if they'd be taken for father and daughter. He had added years to his age with his mustache, beard growth, and blond hair.

"Can I ask how old you are?"

"Twenty-two, so if you're worried about a jailbait conviction, you can be easy in your mind."

"I think we'd better say you're my daughter."

"If that's the way you feel."

"Your last name is Hickman. That's *H-i-c-k-m-a-n.*"

"Why'd you pick that name?"

"Just thought of it."

She mused over her coffee, sounding out the name, then turned to him.

"Is that the girl's name?"

"What made you say that?"

"Could be the way you move your mouth when you're lying. If you don't want me to know something, just don't tell me, but when we do talk, let it be the truth."

"I apologize. Her name was"—he stopped—"is Barbara Hickman."

"Older than me?"

"Yes, she's twenty-nine."

"Underneath the bleach job and the mustache you're not that old."

"Fifty, this November. If I live that long."

"I guessed about that. And she wouldn't marry you or whatever."

"Something like that."

"Why not? Wasn't that you couldn't afford it?" He laughed and caught her eye, and she giggled. "Oh, me . . . you flashing all those hundreds and me mentioning money . . . Sometimes I talk like the wrong end of a mule."

"She's—it's hard to explain—well . . . sick."

"Dope flipped her?" she said, touching her temple.

"Not that crazy. She's got problems."

"And you're suffering because of them, aren't you?"

He did not respond. "Let me ask you a few questions. Why'd you come with me?"

"Adventure, bucks—I got a nose for them—and I liked the smell of you."

"I'm flattered."

"I also had one foot out the door. I don't like that horny McGee or his partner, John Salt."

"Were they hitting on you?"

"Yes, sir. McGee and Salt own the Palace. And I wasn't whoring, just shilling and that pissed them off royally," she said, smirking at him.

The road they took skirted the main industrial

areas, brought them through farmland, wheat belts, dense, darkly shrouded forests of pine and cedar that covered the landscape like nails on a coffin. The road was excellent, but the wind shear rocked the car. They caught some rain squalls in mid-afternoon, ate cold white beans and tuna to save time, and reached Winnipeg just after six. He dropped her at a computer superstore, handed her four thousand dollars, instructing her to buy the most expensive Toshiba or Compaq laptop. She was not to ask or answer any questions or fill out any forms or registration cards. She was to carry it out herself and decline any offer of assistance.

"Never had this much money in my hands," she said, counting it twice.

"I guess you could vanish with it," he said.

She was cautious and doubtful. "They might ask questions about the cash."

"I trust to human avarice."

"Is that greed?"

"Yes, and it has eternal power."

He decided to leave the Cruiser in case his judgment was at fault and waited calmly outside the store. He spotted a tobacconist, went in, and bought a box of Cuban Coronas. He chatted with the clerk, bought a cutter while he was at it, and lit his cigar. He had a good vantage point of the computer store entrance. Ten minutes later Deb walked out carrying a carton. He followed her at a distance to ensure that no one was behind her and watched her try the locked van.

In a moment, he was behind her. "You scared me," she said. "I thought you lit out."

"I was stretching my legs."

"Well, avarice won the day. I've got about eighteen hundred Canadian dollars change."

"That's fine. Keep it for when I open a bank account."
"I never had one. I'm on a roll."

*B*ARBARA KEPT VIGIL IN HER APARTMENT, LIVING ON take-out food. She had not deposited the check that had been handed to her when she left what had previously been Teddy's office. Now a week later, she still had not opened the envelope. Apart from the infernal solicitations of phone companies offering her cheaper long distance rates, no one called. She sat in front of her computer, composing a letter of resignation to the UN, finally e-mailed her section chief and sent a hard copy by mail. She read *Bleak House*, the only Dickens novel she had missed, then cried her way through Graham Greene's *End of the Affair*. Teddy was gone and she was haunted by him.

*D*EB HAD SUGGESTED THAT THEY AVOID THE COAST because the roads were poor and snowstorms struck unexpectedly with wind gusts that sometimes overturned cars. They would turn north after Winnipeg, skirting Hudson Bay, and make for the northwest pocket through Saskatchewan. The rough new jeans, after itching for a while, wore smooth around the seat, and he was more comfortable. They split the driving, whipping through the rain forests and she was solid, experienced at the wheel.

Teddy felt alive, vigorous, and ravenously hungry when they reached the outskirts of the city and suggested a steak and a movie, which she agreed to enthusiastically. They found a small, comfortable family hotel on a side street in Portage la Prairie, south of Lake Manitoba. He was becoming an expert on the desperate amenities offered by sleazy, rundown dumps that called themselves hotels, and he knew after a minute in the lobby whether the place offered a decent room. The lobby, the appearance of the room clerk, and the bar—if there was one—were a clear reflection of the standards. Earlier that evening they had tried two or three more expensive hotels but encountered drunks and chambermaids who were part-time prostitutes.

He bought an evening paper at the newsstand in the lobby and waited for Deb, who was upstairs in her room; he felt more secure with her as a daughter. He scanned the paper, avoiding any lingering scrutiny of the financial page—what did it matter to him now?—and located a three-line squib sent from Caracas about local police on the trail of a T. J. Franklin, wealthy American financier, who had been sighted in the city. He closed the paper with relief, looked at the grandfather clock alongside the desk, which hiccuped seven o'clock. Finding Deb had been a stroke of luck, and he looked forward to spending the evening with her.

She came up to him from behind while he was still reading.

"Sorry I took so long, but I couldn't drag myself out of the tub. Kept adding hot water, and I forgot the time. My stuff's all wrinkled. Do I look a sight?"

"No, you're"—he broke off, imagining that he saw Barbara standing before him, blinked, and noticed that Deb's eyes had a kind of puzzled concern and were intent on his face—"very pretty," he mumbled.

"Aren't you feeling well, Connie?"

"I thought I saw someone I recognized. My mind's playing tricks on me."

"You're beat from all that driving."

"No, honestly, I'll be fine after I have a drink."

Three blocks from the hotel on a street twisting and zigzagging like a drunken man, they found the steak house the hotel manager had recommended. They had several drinks before dinner, and he ate with good appetite, but he couldn't help listening to the muted strains of familiar voices—Barbara, Robbie, Leonard, and Laura, who emerged as a shrieking Medusa—all coming at him as he watched a group of men and women at a Chamber of Commerce dinner.

Deb touched his hand, and it dawned on him that they hadn't spoken.

"The waiter's waiting for you to settle the check, Dad."

"I didn't see it."

"We've been here two hours," she said without complaint.

"Sorry, I didn't mean to be rude. My mind kept wandering."

"Don't apologize."

They walked down the street, past the local movie theater where a straggling line waited for *The Blair Witch Project*.

"I feel safe with you," she said.

"I wouldn't ever hurt you."

"You're a good man. You really are."

He gave a short, sardonic laugh. "If you knew me well, I wonder what you'd think."

"The woman who let you go is a fool."

"If it were true, it still wouldn't be any comfort."

"Whatever happens," she said, "I'll always believe that you're an honorable man, and I was lucky to meet you . . . and, Connie . . . I care about you."

He was tempted to slip his arm from hers, worried about physical contact and promises that couldn't be kept.

"I'm on a retreat . . . my final retreat, that's why I'm going where I am. When I was a kid, my father took me up here. There was something about the lake, Great Slave Lake, that got trapped in my memory. It's a good place to die."

"There's no such place."

THIRTY-EIGHT

HE MINERAL-RICH CANADIAN SHIELD, WITH ITS MYR-
iad chain of lakes, forests of birch and larch,
and craggy mountain ranges had a jagged, bustling
frontier spirit and revived the dormant sense of discovery Teddy had once possessed. With a heavy foot,
the trip from Timmins had taken five days through
the desolate uninhabited tail end of the sprawling, apparently never-ending country. The crazy cavalcade of
regions, taiga, forest, bare plain going russet, the
eighteen-hour days of sunlight, ice-jagged mountain
peaks enhanced the country's elusive search for identity. Occasionally, they would pass through a small village that was no more than a settlement, with a large
ramshackle general store, serving as post office, town
hall, and outpost of civilization. They usually managed
to find a small hotel or motel to spend the night, but
on the last night they had left it too late and were
forced to share a room outside Sandy Lake. There

were two beds in the room, and he let her undress and get into bed before coming into the room. He slept in long underwear because the room was frigid and the wind whined through the doorway all night.

Light crept through the sun-bleached curtains at five in the morning, and he awoke to find her dressed as usual and ready to go.

"Couldn't you sleep?" he asked.

"You've got a bad cough. Heard you all night. We'll stop at a drugstore and get you a cough mixture."

He dressed quickly in the gelid, drafty room, not bothering to shave, and they left before six. The dark green Cruiser was spattered with mud and oil streaks and gave just the right appearance. In Uranium City they located a drugstore, had coffee and doughnuts, and bought some of Mrs. Tarkin's Orange-Flavored Cough Linctus with codeine. It was the one Deb always used, and since she was wise in the ways of croup, whooping cough, and bronchitis—having suffered from all three at one time or another—he drank the mixture with assurance.

"I think you want to mother me," he said.

"It's not the only thing I want to do."

All along the shoreline of Great Slave Lake he saw signs posted, offering furnished cabins with fishing and central heating, and he jotted down several names with addresses in Yellowknife. The Lake itself from Hay River was shaped like a wedge, with small, rocky acclivities and some vegetation on the eastern side; there were numerous coves with cabins set back into the rocks, barely visible from the U-shaped road. From time to time he saw fishing boats, motor launches, and small ketches dipping precariously on the leeward side. The wind raucously tore through treeless hillsides, and there were frozen, isolated patches of snow on the rock-hard ground. Oil rigs hammered the northwest shore like giant black nails.

As they drove along the western perimeter of the lake, trees suddenly appeared. At first they were sparse growths, almost accidental; then closer to Yellowknife actual forests appeared. Despite the scattered industrial complexes they passed, Teddy was mesmerized by the beauty of the landscape: the vast expanse of dark blue water and the movement of boats became an optical illusion. Continuing straight ahead, he'd reach the North Pole, the top of the world, glaciers, icebergs in the Arctic Ocean, a metropolis of ice, a wasteland equal to his own. He played with the idea of joining a ship en route to the North Pole, but he'd probably have to wait until spring or summer because only icebreakers could get through in winter.

After parking the car on the main street of the town, he told Deb to check train times at the railroad station then to meet him outside. He had to avoid all airports. He asked a man in the street where he could find Slave Lake Realty and was directed to a wooden-front store next to the assayer's office. In the window a mass of plastic plaques announced to an indifferent populace a wide variety of bargains, from wooden-frame family houses priced at eighty thousand dollars to monthly rentals of boats and cabins.

His jeans, leather jacket, and prickly, stubbled face created the impression of a miner being relocated. The bearded owner, who shook his hand, explained that all rentals had to be paid in advance and that there were a good three weeks of fishing left before the lake froze. Teddy took the most expensive cabin on the western slope, three miles outside town; it was fully furnished and had kitchen utensils, three fireplaces, and could sleep eight. There was also a dock for the twin-engined cabin cruiser he rented. The boat and cabin came to fifteen hundred per month, and Teddy could judge by the man's smile that he had been overcharged. A month's security was required, and Teddy paid this as well as receiving a hastily scrawled map and the keys. There were no immediate neighbors in the vicinity; an Inuit handyman stopped by once a week with firewood.

The rustic cabin turned out to be well built and hidden in a thicket of tall pines, which could not be detected from the dirt road running just above it. It was set back in a rocky bluff and overlooked a small lake beach, more of an inlet, and the dock was half sunk, tilting up at an acute angle in the front so that he'd have to balance himself when he walked out. Along the shore were clumps of rock, shale, brown pinecones, and a narrow cave abutting into the lake. The water proved to be clear, and warm in the shallows and lime green with schools of minnows swimming feverishly around a chain of rocks.

"I like it," he said.

"When I'm gone, it'll be more private. You'll be completely on your own."

He opened the front door, lifted his carton of groceries, and waited for her to go in first. A narrow hallway brought them to the living room, furnished with an old leather sofa, a rocker, a small table by the char black hearth. Half a dozen old plates with painted scenes decorated the wall by the fireplace; there was also a warped, teetering Welsh dresser with old-fashioned multicolored glasses behind its glass window.

"It's lovely," she said excitedly. "Needs a cleanup, that's all."

He followed her into the kitchen, where she tested the open range, discovered it in working order, and marveled at its size. There was a back door with two bolts that opened onto a small garden, where one of the former inhabitants had made an effort to grow vegetables. Molding cabbage heads were strewn in the pathway as though victims of an Oriental execution. He started to put away the food, but she stopped him.

"Just bring everything in, and let me clean first. I'll put it all away."

Upstairs he located two bedrooms, both with double beds, new mattresses, sheets and blankets in a large storage cupboard on the landing. He opened the windows, and gusts of lake wind scattered the dust. Lived in, it would be comfortable, fine for him. The front bedroom had a view of the lake through flickering pines, leaning forward for a glimpse of evanescent sun. A dresser, small trestle table, straight-back chair, kerosene lamp on a bedside table. He'd have to make a list and go into town the next day, whatever it was, Friday or Saturday, and purchase supplies. He heard an explosion and rushed to the foot of the stairs.

"It's all right," she shouted. "I had to start the boiler."

Thank God for talented people, he thought.

"Okay . . . scared me."

Not exactly the lord's manor in East Hampton, but secret and habitable, a place to regroup his forces.

She'd found several bottles of detergent in the food carton that he had no recollection of purchasing, and by seven that evening, with a crackling fire in the room, the cabin had the atmosphere of a lake holiday for lovers. She didn't fish around for compliments and was embarrassed when he seemed pleased with the eggs and sausages she made for dinner.

"It's all right. I'm being well paid, aren't I?" she said, for the first time captious and miserable. "You'll have it all to yourself soon."

He poured a couple of drinks into mugs, offered one to her, but she wouldn't accept it, and he placed it on the table beside her.

"Don't you want to go back?" he asked.

"Only if you send me."

THIRTY-NINE

BY THE MIDDLE OF SEPTEMBER, THEY HAD SOMETHING of a routine. Deb possessed a cheerful, but remote, efficiency and easily opened a bank account, skillfully changed U.S. dollars into Canadian, set up utilities and found an on-line server. She attended to these tasks, using her name. She was the flawless bandit's bride, respecting his privacy, as well as being a wondrous housekeeper. He taught her how to use the computer in a few days and an addiction was born.

"Beats gambling."

"You can do that on-line, too," he said.

Since he could not use his credit cards, and her Visa was maxed out, he had her pay it off and FedEx a five-thousand-dollar cashier's check to them. This gave them some breathing space and enhanced her credit limit, which was raised a day later. He kept track of the world and financial kingdom he had abdicated. He came to the conclusion that the police were not clowns and that somewhere an inquisitive detective would be tracking him. Teddy knew he was big game. Robbie's Internet server might be monitoring his e-mail, but he wondered if Barbara was also under scrutiny.

His capricious, impulsive flight had paid dividends. He had discovered his Eden. At the northwest corner of the lake, he visited Sah Naji Kwe, a wilderness spa, bathed in marine glacial clay, had a massage, sometimes had dinner there or at the Yellowknife Inn with Deb. He embraced his new freedom, hiking and fishing. In the evening, from the front of the cabin, he watched the arctic terns and eagles glide while she bathed naked, unself-consciously, in the warm shallows. He caught the tail end of the aurora borealis; the light greenish pink bands of light swirled and dipped like a corps de ballet in the sky when the charged solar particles embraced the earth's atmosphere. He stood entranced by nature's light show.

Deb tied a bath towel in a sarong and stood beside him. She had used all of her sexual wiles to draw him closer, but he remained in a dreamy state, deeded to another woman who might be an abstraction in their common setting, but for him she was tangible and he was breathing the ghost's air from time gone by, the captive of her aura. Never for a moment did he miss his life in New York. But within him the yearning for Barbara cleaved at him and Deb could not vanquish her presence and the unspoken rivalry.

"God's fingerprints," she said of the coruscating light, bowing her head in benediction.

Teddy did not trust the bank safe-deposit boxes. If he had to escape quickly, he needed easy access to his money and he decided to hide it near the cabin.

After an early morning of fly-fishing, he climbed up a rocky butte and located an abandoned mine shaft about a quarter of a mile from the cabin. He had taken a flashlight with him and wove through the mouth of a cave, exploring the recesses. Overhead, jagged zinc-veined rock hung low and a strong acidic tincture permeated the air. There was a high vaulted interior, dusky red sediment, and weird icicle-like stalactites hanging from the roof, which in some instances had formed pillars with the stalagmites thrusting up from the floor. As he flashed the light he could see a serpentine of chambers. He found a rusted shovel and an old railway spike and cautiously began to dig. He made a small trench and decided that this might be a good place.

When he returned to the cabin and removed the carry bag from the locked cupboard, Deb knew what he was doing, and to avoid suspicion turned her back.

"I'll run into town to shop at the market. Anything special you want?"

"See if you can get some fresh coffee beans. If they've got Kona, buy a few pounds."

"Eye-round of beef for dinner?"

"Perfect."

"I'll take my time."

*D*EB CRUISED THE COVERED MALL NEAR THE CAPITAL. She had never had so much money and the giddy freedom to buy whatever captured her eye. He never asked for an accounting. But Connie's reluctance to be intimate wore at her, affecting her confidence. Was her skin too coppery? Did she give off an odor that was distinct to Inuit women? In the month they had been together, he had never revealed any prejudice and frequently hugged her with paternal fondness, or as she sat at his knees he stroked her hair and told her she was beautiful. He never spoke of the other woman. She had come to hate this woman, who had destroyed the possibility of a life with Connie. She knew with increasing hopelessness that she had fallen in love with him.

In a lingerie shop, she bought a white silk nightgown, embroidered with pink angels, and a matching robe for three hundred dollars; bikini panties in a variety of colors, and several different bra shapes. She toyed with the idea of having her hair cut, but she was Inuit and this emblem of her birthright as well as the looming arctic winter dissuaded her from such a sacrilege.

When she returned to the car park, her arms filled with bags, she stopped short at the Cruiser.

"Does Madam require help with her shopping?" McGee waved his arm in a mockery of a bow. "Mr. Salt, please assist the lady."

"Certainly, Mr. McGee. I'd like to fire about six loads up her butt."

"Mr. Salt, you're in the capital city of the Northwest Territories and we don't like behavior like that."

Until the two had spoken, she thought for a moment that they might have been civil servants who worked at the capital building in Yellowknife. They were both in suits and ties, clean-shaven, wearing lace-up brogues, and the morbid scent of a musky aftershave embraced her.

"Been watching me?"

"Ah, Deb girl, this is a miraculous coincidence," McGee said, seizing some carry bags from her. "What's next, Paree? London? Skiing in Switzerland."

"She should do fine there with snowshoes," John Salt said with a harsh snigger, "burning daylight on her dogsled."

"Born to the slopes."

"Get out of my way," Deb said, calm on the outside.

"We must discuss your present situation," McGee said. "It's commerce, Deb. God almighty, girl, our mother lode has come in."

Salt opened his suit jacket, and hooked on his belt loop in a sheath was an ivory-handled skinning knife.

"Yes, ma'am. Life is a trading post. So while Mr. Moneybags is still having his siesta with his pecker drier than Eskimo firewood, haul your ass to the bar at the hotel and we'll buy you a Crown Royal."

She was dumbfounded when McGee slapped at the air, close to Salt's nose and said in a sham military dressing-down to a recruit, "Salt, Mr. Theodore J. Franklin's lady doesn't drink the pride of our rye whisky, she only drinks champagne."

*W*HEN DEB RETURNED TO THE CABIN, TEDDY HELPED her in. She laughed and veiled the worried expression. Once inside her eyes darted around.

"You're a little late."

"I went on a shopping spree. I guess it's in my blood."

"You're a buyer, not a shopper now. I found a cookbook and read an article about roasting. I turned on the oven to five hundred. I'm going to cook dinner for *Madam*."

"What did you say?" she asked with a shiver.

"What's wrong?" Teddy asked.

"Oh, nothing. Somebody tried to get smart with me. I guess I'll always look like easy pickings."

"Don't be silly."

"I checked and can't catch a train till the day after tomorrow. There isn't a main station until Edmonton. I can pick up a connection there and change a few times and get to Churchill by Saturday."

"What's this about?"

"I'm afraid I overstayed my welcome." She hesitated, lowered her eyes, and warily asked, "Do you really want me around?"

"Yes. I love having you here."

"Do you? I wish you showed it more."

He lifted her chin and put an arm around her. He didn't take the conversation any further, fearing the implications.

"Do you really want to go to Nunavut?"

One of the world's experts in negotiating everything but love studied the cast of her face and waited. He was patient and in a good martini mood. He had been making them better than Leonard at home.

"Who knows? Maybe I should head down to Winnipeg. Find myself a cozy bar and work as a cocktail waitress. If I get lucky, I'll pick up a married man, give him what he doesn't get at home, and maybe he'll look after me, leave his wife, then get Sunday-morning sorrows when he misses the kiddies, and I'll be back where I started—a home wrecker. Sound sorry for myself, do I? Well, I'm not. I just don't care. I have no purpose. There are women drifters as well as men. Maybe that's what I am. Oh, Connie, you don't want me."

Teddy sipped his drink in silence, worried about committing himself. She bolted the door, checked the rear—someone accustomed to fending for herself, equipped for adversity in a soulless universe. She dashed upstairs, leaving the bags and he unpacked them. He listened to Deb crying, powerless to go to her room. He opened the front window, and the sounds of lake and wind drowned her out. Perhaps she'd be gone in the morning in silent, accusing grief.

When he was certain Deb was in bed and asleep at three in the morning, he placed the money on the living room table without a note. He had held out ten thousand dollars. Nightmares were private adventures, and Barbara belonged to him; she always would be there for him in the dark, the final gasp, the long sleep.

Since going on-line, he had been struggling with the idea of contacting her. Would she alert the police immediately or not? Were they having her Internet server snoop through her mail? Did she ever want to see him or was she at peace with him out of her life? Whenever he tried to resolve this dilemma, he foundered. When he switched on the computer, a plan began to emerge.

*B*ARBARA SAT ALONE IN THE LIVING ROOM. GUILTY thoughts of Teddy spiraled through her mind. The dead flowers of his old bouquets lingered in the air, musky, half remembered, and she was filled with a torpor, a sense of aimlessness that she was unable to overcome. She had persuaded Alex's physician to prescribe Seconals for her. The pills were on the mantelpiece next to Laura's photograph, and every now and then she would find herself staring at them.

What she determined, after hours of groping, during which her life, in slivers, splinters of people, and felt experience, appeared as though on parade, was that she wanted to do the right thing, and the right thing was a question of moral capability. Would it be better for Teddy if she ended her life? Would it make him happy, or was it the strain, the conflict, the antagonism that had fused them? Perhaps what she'd resisted all along was the fuel, the current of life.

She pushed herself up from the sofa, leaned on the mantelpiece. Laura smiled down at her, a citizen of an unidentified planet moving somewhere in the stellar void of frozen space and arrested time. Where was the vision, where the revelation, the final knowledge? Do people have the first claim, or is it life itself?

She picked up the bottle of pills, clutching the bottle to her as though embracing a lover.

Without a job, or the sessions at Frere's office, and Teddy on call, she had nothing to do, no one to see, and nowhere to go. The police investigation had come to a standstill. Without Teddy she found herself in a vast expanse of unoccupied space. What she understood for the first time—all along she had ignored it, a believer in revelation rather than simple, common sense—was that Teddy was her friend in the truest sense of friendship and that in renouncing him, she had given up her claim to the presumption of character.

She replaced the photograph of Laura with one of her and Teddy that Leonard had taken of them on the roof of Teddy's town house in the spring. She noticed something in his eyes, the way he looked at her, through her, which infected her with harmony, breached her defenses, made her think that he had found a belief that went beyond her and his own mortal awareness. She had never seen anyone look at her with such adoration.

As a solemn, fateful act of contrition she had started to go to church, which, in spite of the temporary solace it provided, only served to prove to her that she was without faith, merely another of those lapsed Catholics who want expiation, move their lips, genuflect, observe ritual, but give nothing. It had been a confrontation of many things, uncomfortably direct, exposing her to herself, and as she made her way down the aisle to the altar for the seventh day of her novena, she thought she understood herself. The church, a small, dark place, locked between apartment houses on Eighty-third Street, and usually deserted between two and three in the afternoon, had simply been a place to go to, and even though the novena was for Teddy, she had been praying for herself.

Candles flickered from the drafty passage leading

from the priest's quarters to the altar, and in the moving flames she saw the method of exorcism. The church had resorted in the past to days of fast, the scourge, the missal, confusion, but none purified as supremely as fire. She held her hands over the candles, and flames scorched her skin. Closer and closer to the flames she moved until it was not clear which was flame and which the fingers of the hand. United in a victory of pain that no longer was pain, she stood transfixed in an ecstasy of incense, a statue of Christ above her sharing, she thought, her sweet act of piety. The purity of Teddy's love—and it had seemed a form of derangement, wolflike in its aberrance, encompassing her as securely as barbed wire—had been protective, had informed her of love that she had rejected. But now it ate at her, reaching into her soul, removing her past, releasing her, the fuel for the flame, and she felt secure and at last at peace. She looked at her hands. Her shirt sleeve was singed, but her hands were unmarked from the candles.

*W*HEN SHE RETURNED TO HER APARTMENT, SHE opened a bottle of 1990 Ponsot Chambertin left over from her father's collection, sniffed the cork, but did not decant it. She poured herself a glass and drank it greedily. She had picked up some pâtés, cheese, and vegetables at the market after church and fixed herself a plate. She had made a decision. She would write to Jules LeClerk, her former employer in Bordeaux, and ask if he or any of the vintners had an opening for her.

With the bottle of wine and plate of snacks beside her, she went on-line. She had Jules's e-mail address and she was in the mood to chat, plunge herself back in the wine trade and return to France. Nothing of her period in New York would be known there. She would reinvent herself again as she had after Laura's suicide.

She saw that she had some messages on her home page, typed in her password, VINTAGE, and said "Shit" when she saw she'd been spammed. She highlighted the ads but held off deleting. One message said *Krug '59 Available,* which aroused her curiosity. She opened the e-mail and read:

> A rare case of Krug '59 *grande cuvée* from the Conrad Hickman estate has surfaced in an unlikely location. As I am aware that you are a lover of this great champagne, perhaps you would like to have an opportunity to test its resiliency. D. Connors.

For a few minutes, Barbara's mental faculties were diminished and she sat staring at the message, the unfamiliar Internet address. She held her wineglass, sipping at it.

"Teddy, you're alive," she whispered. "I love you!" She instantly replied to the sender:

> Because of this great wine's scarcity, uniqueness, and my own selfishness, I would be unwilling to share its secrets with anyone. I would LOVE to test its resiliency. Advise details of tasting.

> Your Vintage.

FORTY

$\mathscr{B}$ARBARA FOLLOWED THE INSTRUCTIONS, WHICH AR-
rived shortly after her reply. She swiftly packed a
change of clothes, toothbrush, photo ID, passport,
and credit cards in a small carry bag. Tiptoeing out,
she quietly closed the front door and waited for the
bolt to catch. She had worn her running shoes and
she sprinted over to York Avenue and hailed a cabby
outside the all-night Greek diner on Eighty-sixth
Street and he drove her to Kennedy Airport. She paid
cash for a one-way ticket to Burlington, Vermont, and
caught a plane that had one stop in Boston. She arrived in Burlington at 6:00 A.M., and rented a Hertz
car from a sleepy attendant. She picked up a beige
Toyota Camry and studied the map.

At nine she was waved through the Canadian border and following the road signs arrived at the airport.
She dropped the car off at the long-term parking and

went to the international terminal at Dorval Airport. At the British Airways desk, she showed her passport and driver's license and picked up the ticket that D. Connors had paid for. She had no idea who this person was and assumed it was Teddy's alias.

She went through immigration and at the gate received a boarding card. She found a croissant shop and had coffee while travelers began arriving for her flight. At noon, when the flight was called for boarding, she made her way back out through security, descended the escalator, and bolted out of the terminal.

She took the shuttle to Air Canada's domestic terminal and purchased a ticket to a place she had never heard of before. It was called Yellowknife. She had two hours to kill before the flight and bought the local paper.

Once aboard the plane, Barbara cautiously roved over the faces of the passengers, wondering if she could pick out a detective. If someone was following her, she assumed it would be a woman. As the de Havilland taxied down the runway, she picked up the airline magazine from the pouch, scanned the flight map at the back, and learned that she was heading to the District of Mackenzie in Canada's Northwest Territories. She never drank when she flew, but this time when the flight attendant asked what she would like, she took out a twenty-dollar bill.

"Vodka. I'll take a bunch of those miniatures."

*T*EDDY HAD GOTTEN INTO THE HABIT OF RISING AT first light and at the window he heard the ratchet of an icy rain, but he still got out bed and enjoyed cleaning up early. Deb came into the bathroom.

"I'll need some money," she said as he was wiping off shaving cream from his ear.

"Sure. How much?"

She held up the .45 and Teddy backed away. "Your gun has no firing pin."

He was incredulous. "How can that be?"

"It was removed by the man who sold it to you."

"That goddamn McGee."

She nodded. "Two rules up here. Dress warm, no matter what the weather, and never buy a gun from a stranger unless you fire it first."

Her face had a morose cast and he was disturbed by her behavior, which matched the sharp stalks of rain that had been falling, hacking at the lake like machetes. The clear water now seemed to have a coating of gunmetal. In the sky the geese had taken flight, flapping over the lake and leaving the lame chicks. He detected an ambivalence in her attitude, but the prospect of making further inquiries struck him as a dangerous choice. He decided to play the hand in silence and accepted a mug of black coffee with a nod, slapped his cheeks with aftershave and slipped on a black corduroy shirt.

"I'd like to take a thousand off the ten you gave me."

"Is that the going price for a firing pin?"

"No, for a Winchester Pump."

"Are you going hunting?"

"Maybe."

"What about a license?"

"There are people up here I've dealt with before."

"I see."

She looked at her watch. "I'm going over to Great Bear Lake. I'll try to be back before dark." She twirled the automatic like a gunfighter and shoved it into her belt.

"You handle that like an expert."

"I've been shooting since I was five, skinning caribou and tracking deer. In case you didn't know, this is also bear country."

She put on a yellow slicker and he followed her downstairs, then outside, and stood on the porch as she sloshed through the puddles.

"Deb, have I got a problem?"

"Not with a twelve-gauge, Mr. Franklin."

He was frozen by the sound of his name. Even the syllables had a foreign meter. No one had used it since he had escaped from the police outside his house in Manhattan.

"Deb, I don't want anyone hurt. I've taken that road before."

"Don't open the door to strangers."

He grabbed a loose piece of boat tarp on the porch and covered himself in it. He caught a puddle up to his ankles and leaned in on the driver's side when she started the engine.

"Deb, she's coming in tonight."

Deb lowered her head on the steering wheel, then pounded the dashboard.

"Theodore, I wish the hell you'd trusted me."

"It's Teddy, and I do trust you. I always will. All this time, I wanted to tell you, but I thought if I were arrested and you didn't know who I was, then you couldn't possibly be accused of aiding or abetting me."

Soaked, he rushed to the passenger side and got inside. Her hissing, angry breath clouded the window. He moved close, held her in his arms, and her mouth suddenly sprang against his and she kissed him in the wrath of passion.

"Don't you understand anything? *I love you.* I don't want any harm to come to you. This is outlaw country. People vanish, freeze to death in the tundra, and neither God nor man hears about it or asks questions."

"Barbara's coming."

"You said so. You catch up with her on the computer?"

"Yes. I sent her an e-mail."

"She bringing the cops and extradition papers?"

He had a sense of anguish, torn between Deb's pessimism and his own conviction that Barbara would not give him up in this way and that they could have an honorable break. Nothing would be withheld from his side of the table.

Through the foils of rain she scanned the lake for the men. "You're worth killing."

"I didn't know there was a price on my head. I looked up every news story on the Web and didn't see that there was a reward out for me."

"You forgot trophy and the fame that gilds the hunter."

He realized that his preoccupation with Barbara had made him less vigilant. "Have I done something dumb or been careless?"

"No."

"Do we really need a gun?"

"You said you trusted me."

Teddy reflected for a long moment. If he were arrested, there would be no way he could use the money he had hidden. He would be extradited and short of sending Robbie up to retrieve it, it would be lost. He knew that Deb cared deeply for him and that her position was not unlike his own had been with Barbara.

"Let's take a ride before we buy a gun."

*A*CROSS THE LAKE SHORE, ENSHROUDED IN THE GRAY vagaries of mist, hollow echoes of terns diving into the water for baby pickerel eerily mixed with the wind lashing the heavy spruce branches of the forest. McGee dozed fitfully behind the wheel of a Jeep while Salt, squinting and red-eyed, trained a pair of binoculars on Teddy's cabin. They had been watching all night. Salt coughed through the bitter fumes of stale smoke and spat out the lukewarm sour coffee that had turned syrupy in the thermos.

"They're driving off, Mac."

"What?" McGee asked, with a peevish whine. "Did Deb send a signal?"

"It's pissing rain. I don't think she knows where he's got the stash yet."

"Well, she damn well better find out before we march right in and take the chainsaw to him."

"She'll find out. She's one sharp puss. I'll tell you, soon as we get that money, I'm going to lay one into that bitch. Had the hots for her since she wiggled into the Palace."

McGee gave a boisterous laugh. "After this, you'll have enough money to drill anything walking in Quebec, so don't be building an attachment to this Eskimo."

"A one-timer and that's it."

"It better be," McGee said authoritatively, "because we're going to have to put her down too."

John Salt had been an itinerant cardsharp and bunco specialist until he hooked up with Owen McGee some five years ago and now he had the prospect of a grand future with this crafty businessman.

"Mac, are you in earnest about moving up to Nunavut?"

"That's a definite yes. Last April, the dumb Canadian government gave these savages three-quarters of a million square miles. What are they going to do with the silver, zinc, and gold up there? The oil deposits. Who's going to clothe and feed the new settlers? Build houses? Who's going to see that the men have a good time? Who's going to sell the sealskin and the white fox?"

Salt shook his head in wonderment. "Who, Mac?"

"Owen McGee and his first deputy, Mr. John Salt."

"I'm honored, sir," Salt said with fervor. He looked

at the dashboard clock. It was now seven. "I'm hungry. How about we head into town and get some breakfast?"

"A shower would suit you first."

"Sure thing. I better stock up on some Old Spice while I'm there."

*F*ROM THE ENTRANCE OF THE LAKE-BUTTE CAVE, Teddy surveyed the rock-faced shoreline, slate-black, jagged, the toothless smile of an old man. Cabins spotted the hills like pockmarks, and in the distance trucks brimmed with grumbling men on the way to the gold mine. After the rain, spurs and wires of sunlight, like metallic alloys, grazed the lake in the coming winter light. The wind lowed over the lake, and reverberations of oil dredges pumping into the rocky ground from the distant shore sounded as though fissures of ice were cracking. The howl of foraging bears came from the forest when Deb emerged.

"A fortune," she said in a daze. "How is it possible to make so much money?"

Teddy smiled at her. "It's a secret."

"Tell me."

"I've never really analyzed it. But some people are born with gifts for painting, composing music, singing. I look at a balance sheet, visit a factory, meet the people running it, think about what they're making, and somewhere along the line I make a mental connection. If it's a consumer product I say to myself, 'Can I *see* people using it, needing it?' If it's a specialized industry—I mean, when they're starting up—the Internet, computers, electronics, biogenetics—I try to imagine its effect on the global economy. Will it create new jobs? How does it all fit together? I'm always thinking ahead. Should a company be developed, then sold off to a giant, or do I take over the giant and form a worldwide conglomerate? That's it. You know the secret."

She leaned her head on his shoulder. "You're a piece of work, Teddy."

Deb did the driving, weaving along the hilly, rutted back roads, until they arrived at Hornby Bay; the northern cusp of Great Bear Lake. There was a fishing hut, a rambling log cabin and bizarre tentlike structures that looked as though they had been made from some kind of animal skin. Deb pulled into a muddy wedge around the side where a squat man in shorts and a black butcher's apron was skinning a caribou. Beside him was a plastic table where a haunch lay in a bed of salt.

"Where are we?" he asked when she cut the engine.

"My ground."

She burst out of the cruiser and dashed over to the man who stood back, wiped his hands on a rag, then smiled through a mouth of teeth that were as pointed as a chisel. Deb bowed to him. Teddy got out slowly in this no-man's-land. He listened to them talking rapidly in a foreign tongue and making hand signs. The man squinted at him, his gaze lingering, then with a swagger he turned away and went inside the building with Deb.

Teddy peered through the rear window when he heard the grinding of a machine. It was a dimly lighted workshop, filled with a wide variety of tools. Standing over a vice with goggles on was the man. Sparks flew from an electric saw as he cut off the barrel of a shotgun. Deb was beside him. In a moment, he put on rubber gloves, picked up a file and smoothed out the lips of the barrel. He removed the goggles and expertly stripped the .45. He roved around his workbench with tweezers and found something Teddy could not descry. Teddy moved away from the window and returned to the front of the building.

In a moment, Deb emerged, carrying the .45 and sawed-off shotgun. She had on a walrus-skin bandolier filled with ammunition.

"My uncle said to send his greetings. He wants to clean up before shaking hands with you." She handed Teddy five hundred-dollar bills. "Your change. I got a family discount."

"I don't want the money. It's yours."

"Okay. Let's check these suckers out."

Teddy followed her to a small clearing in the woods behind the tents. There, on a pair of tree stumps were some grimy oil cans. She paced off about sixty feet, turned and rapidly fired the .45, then, without pausing, bombarded the target with the shotgun. He found himself applauding the display of accuracy, and her laughter pealed through the silence.

"I told you this was bear country."

Emerging in shorts and still wet from his lake bath, her brawny uncle toweled himself off.

"This is Teddy, Uncle."

He vigorously shook Teddy's hand. "Excuse the mess," he said. "I was getting ready to smoke some meat. We plan for winter early up here."

"It's a pleasure to meet you. Your niece has been a great friend to me."

"She told me that you're a gentleman and you've treated her very well and with respect."

He opened the flap of a tent and inside were a variety of watercraft.

"This is the best of them, Deb," her uncle said, pointing to a kayak from a group in various stages of construction. "The frame is whalebone."

She observed Teddy's puzzlement. "It's called a *umiak*. That's an open one for women. Uncle, I want a closed one."

"Are you sure?"

"Yes."

She lifted the kayak easily and her uncle helped her tie it to the roof of the Land Cruiser. She embraced her uncle with noticeable formality, but the shimmer of affection between them was evident.

She lifted the rug in the back and set the weapons and ammunition below it, then covered it with some tarp, her uncle scrutinizing her every movement.

"Man or beast, I wouldn't like to be at the other end when Deb's agitated."

Teddy heeded the warning, and as they began to drive away, she smiled sweetly at him.

"What's so funny?"

"Oh, my uncle, always trying to scare away men. I guess that was one of the reasons I hit the road. Everyone who came near me was terrified of him. His name in English is *whale killer*."

FORTY-ONE

_J_UST AS AN APOCALYPSE HAS ITS MOMENT OF GREATEST intensity, like the ultimate, demonic transcendence of the tsunami caught at the height of its swell before it obliterates all in its path, so Teddy captured a vision of truth when Barbara appeared. It was just past midnight in the crowded bar of the Yellowknife Inn, and he and Deb were cloistered in a booth next to the fire exit. The Land Cruiser was parked just outside in case Teddy had to escape. Deb would cause a commotion and try to allow him to clear out.

Barbara threaded her way through the layers of rowdy drinkers, carrying a tequila shooter like one of the guys. Deb gloomily scrutinized this woman. Even in her bearing, she carried a certain exotic foreignness that was natural and delicate, Deb thought as she approached her. Yes, Teddy's goddess was exquisite.

"Do you happen to drink champagne?" Deb asked.

Barbara was startled, then nodded. "Yes, Krug."

"Have you checked in?"

"A little while ago." Barbara immediately sensed her rivalry. "Are you D. Connors?"

"It's Deb. What room are you in?"

"Three-eighteen. Here's the other key." Barbara furtively handed it over. She had a penetrating awareness of Deb's powerful physical attributes. "I'm glad my friend found such attractive company."

"Obviously, it wasn't good enough for him or he would have kept it," Deb replied in an acidulous tone. "I don't know what you've done to him, but he's been hurt enough. So don't whip him."

"I have no intention of doing anything like that."

"Are you sure no one followed you?"

Barbara's fatigue turned to repressed anger, but she restrained her combativeness, for the antagonism had become evident. "I honestly did my best to follow instructions. I kept my eye on the passengers on the flight—men and women—and took the bus at the airport."

"Okay. But I swear there'll be hell to pay if some Mounties wander in and bust him."

"You're his protector."

"I damn well am."

Barbara's eyes anxiously scurried among the faces at the bar and she had no inkling that Teddy was present. "Is he here, or hiding out?"

"At the table by the exit."

Barbara's stood rigid when she gazed down at the bearded, blond-haired, tanned man in a blue plaid shirt, work boots, and a sheepskin vest. She had no idea he would be so vigorous and she would not have recognized him.

"It's good to see you," he said softly, rising.

Tears shimmered in her eyes. "You, too."

In the two months since he had vanished, Barbara had undergone physical changes, as he had. She had a

gaunt frailty that aroused all of the tender emotions
he had secreted. Teddy took Barbara's hands and realized that although he had considered his relationship
as the fruitless pursuit of an illusion, Barbara's presence sparked the uneasy whims of the flesh. Neither
absence nor flight could rescue him from the intoxication of his craving. The rancor of love and its endless humiliations entrapped him.

"I'll see you in a while, Deb."

Deb uneasily shifted her gaze to the room. "I'll be
outside and keep an eye out," she said, then reluctantly elbowed her way through the bar.

Barbara's manner toward him after the first few
speechless minutes was a mixture of uncomfortable
concern and fear. Her face was bloodless, and her
hands had the chalk white color of illness, so that for
the first time he was aware of the dark blue veins. In
her eyes he detected resignation, a retreat from battle
that alarmed him, and she—not he—had become
passive.

About to say something, he stopped, and they sat
staring at each other, with no attempt by either to
turn away.

"The day I ran away . . ." he began, then lost track of
what he wanted to say.

"Yes?"

"I terrified you. What I mean is that you thought I
was going to hurt you. I had no intention of injuring
you, and I'm sorry for frightening you."

"I've spent my life stepping over bodies."

"That's not true, and you know it. You're a decent
woman, and that's what defeats you. You can't accept
it. You want to believe that you're evil and destructive,
but you were victimized by your feelings."

"Teddy, don't be magnanimous. I don't deserve it."

"That's about the last thing I'm guilty of."

"Well, you are Teddy, I've never been up to your standards, or deserved you. I had a prince, and I turned you into a criminal. You know, looking at you now, Teddy, you've never been more desirable to me. There wasn't a second of the day that I didn't want you, when I wouldn't have given everything to have you make love to me, and now, I get the sinister feeling that you don't want me."

"Don't sell yourself short."

"You're reassuring me, and the point is, I should be reassuring you. I was never truthful with you. When we made love, you satisfied me. You made me happy, but I wouldn't admit it to myself."

"Why not?"

"I was afraid it was a weapon you'd use against me, so instead I used it against you. Oh God, I wish I had the capacity and the depth to feel sorry for myself."

He preferred silence, the perfect communication of looks, gestures, the movement of her hands, the listing motion of her eyelids, which told him more accurately what was in her heart than words, which he came to regard in connection with her as the double agent of thought. If only they could break through the layer of sounds disguising emotions, they'd find the center. Silence frightened her, and she gabbled on, but he took in little except the fact that she was in a panic.

"Aren't you talking?"

"I've dreamed about the sound of your voice," he said.

"Teddy, can you forgive me?" Barbara asked.

He reached out for her hand. "I was at fault, Barbara, not you."

She laughed bitterly. "I now realize that everything I did was aimed at destroying my love for you. Teddy, I felt I was unworthy of it. I didn't know how to accept it, or your generosity, your caring. When I think of what you did for me, how you pulled me together, got me on my feet, I hate myself. I'm so mortified." Her head fell against the booth rest and she sobbed. "I ruined you, forced you to become a criminal."

"Confusion was the enemy."

"But there's a way out, darling. Please, please, will you marry me? If you do, I can't testify against you."

He was astounded, startled by the offer. "That sounds like a business transaction and I'm the last man anyone—especially you—should negotiate with." He shook his head, bemused. "That doesn't sound very romantic. In any case I don't need a shield. I've decided that I'm not going to keep running."

She embraced him. "I've spoken to a criminal lawyer who knows you. It's his opinion that all they can convict you for is conspiracy to commit burglary. You'd pay a large fine and be given probation. The man who died—Mr. Grant—his aorta burst. It could have happened any time."

"Really," he said sardonically. "If the two boys hadn't been committing a crime I masterminded, would he have lived for another day, another hour, another minute?"

"No one knows for sure."

"Would his daughter have called me a murderer when I spoke to her? I paid her conscience money. I hope she files a civil suit and winds up with every penny I've got.

"You see, Barbara, what I did was unconscionable. A man died so I could satisfy my need to know about what was going on with you. How I stood with you. *Information*, a lot of good it did me. You don't have to worry about the tape of you and Laura—your confession. I destroyed it."

"Oh God, Teddy. What horrors you had to endure."

"They were yours and they became mine."

"I want you to know that I didn't call the police. I was

hysterical and I phoned Dr. Frere asking for advice. *He* brought the police into it. I never betrayed you."

"We betrayed each other."

She was mournfully silent. He took out a handkerchief and wiped the tears off her cheeks.

"I'm going back with you and I'll plead guilty. There won't be a jury trial. I'm not going to weasel out of this. I've accepted the fact that I'll be going to prison. You see, Barbara, I'm an example for people. It'll never be any good for me—for us—if I don't do the right thing this time."

She was awed by the dignity and the grace of his declaration.

"I'll do anything you want," she said.

"It's what you want, it always was."

She turned her face to his and he kissed her. "I want to be with you, Teddy."

He took her hand and pressed it against his lips, then rose and slipped into a leather jacket.

"Where're you going?"

"To say good-bye to my friend." He took the second key. "Why don't you go to the room and I'll be up as soon as I can. Oh, call your lawyer friend and have him inform the DA in charge of the case that I'll be surrendering tomorrow."

The snow-riven arctic night bespoke an early winter to the Northwest Territories, and Teddy's breath came in puffs of smoke as he approached the Land Cruiser. The engine was running, and Deb turned the heater on high when he got in the passenger side. Faced with the futility of the situation, she radiated a benevolent resignation.

"I'm not glad you got your lady back."

"In some ways I wish it could have been different. I'm going to leave. I have to face the consequences, Deb."

"No, you don't. You choose to and that makes the difference."

He held her in his arms and she wanted to shriek, but endured her chastisement with an impassive mask.

"Deb, you probably know this now. I have a great fortune, and the money I took with me isn't crucial to my survival and it wasn't stolen. I want you to have it. You can start a business in Nunavut, build something that can help your people."

"I'd rather burn the money if I could have you. My heart is shattered," she said dry-eyed, numbed by defeat.

"I know what's best for you. You'll meet someone your own age and have a family."

"Probably that'll happen, but there will never be anyone but you."

He leaned over and kissed her. "I'll get my stuff out of the cabin in the morning."

She switched off the engine and handed him the car keys.

"How're you going to get back?" Teddy asked.

"I can use a little air. I'll walk."

"Deb, I won't need the Cruiser after tomorrow. You take it. I'll come by and pick you up in the morning and you can drive with us to the airport."

"Good-bye, Teddy."

She watched Teddy return to the hotel, sighed despondently, snapped the interior lock and slammed the door. As she turned, a cold gun barrel was pressed against her temple.

"I filled out a withdrawal slip, Deb. I think you better honor it," McGee said.

"How's my favorite Eskimo?" Salt asked. "In the mood to rock 'n' roll?"

"If you ever want to see a penny of the money, get the damn gun out of my face."

"Come on, let's get moving. My Jeep's over there," McGee said.

"Where's Mr. Gold Dust?"

"I gave him a sleepover pass," she replied.

At the Jeep, Salt patted her down and she raised her hand to strike him.

"Nothing personal, young lady, just want to see if you're packing."

She attached the seat belt and felt Salt's sour, humid breath spray on her neck from the backseat.

"Where to, Deb?" McGee asked.

"Great Slave Lake."

FORTY-TWO

*T*HE WIND GRUNTED WITH THE WEIGHT OF SNOW, flailed and thrashed the saplings on the hillside and the ghostly lamenting cries of a downed caribou at the mercy of a pack of timber wolves carried up to the butte from the lake beach. Rather than walk through the hilly path, McGee had recklessly tried to drive on four-wheel up to the cave. The Jeep hung like a spider on the rocky plateau. Beads of snow gathered like parasites on the windshield.

"You jackasses ever listen to a woman?" Deb asked.

"We better get out here."

"Carefully," she said.

McGee cracked the door and as the interior light flashed on, there was a thunderous report as though a lightning bolt had struck. Deb screamed and leapt up from her seat. In the confined cell of the car the smoky stench of cordite and gun gas was overpower-

ing. Owen McGee slumped over the wheel, the back
of his head a hollow cove of blood and gristle.

"I'm John Salt. I'm a somebody! And for once sitting in the backseat suited me." She was shocked by
the unyielding menace in his voice. "That bastard
McGee's been down on me since we met. Treating me
like a scrounging pack dog. Now, sweetheart, let's get
the money."

"You're going to kill me too."

"No, I'm crazy about you, babe. We're going to have
a good time together. Open us a Palace up in Nunavut
and rule the province. The king wants his queen."

"You're sure."

"Look, I got a full house, so just throw in your cards."

"Okay. Have you got a flashlight?"

"In my hand. Now as you suggested, let's be careful
and please don't think of trying to make a fool out of
me. I can see in the dark better than a snake."

As they cautiously eased out of the rocking Jeep,
they were just below the cave entrance. The Jeep stabi-
lized and she took out a penlight and walked ahead
with his beam illuminating her path.

"Two million four hundred thousand. I have to give
you your due, Deb."

"I was looking for that big score—just like you and
McGee."

"I figured that's why you weren't giving it away like
the rest of those métis in Timmins. I have lived by a
ruling faith since I came up to the Territories: Follow
the pussy and it'll map treasure island."

"Mr. Franklin's going to be very upset when he finds
his money gone," she said as they climbed into the
cave. The flickering shadows cast by the flashlight
formed a wrathful ballet of formless shapes, and the
sour-acid effluvium of thousands of years was crystal-
ized in the cold.

"According to what I've read about him, he won't miss it. He'll have enough on his plate when the police find him." Salt paused and sniffed the air. "Funny odor in here. Like meat."

Deb picked up the shovel she had used earlier to bury the money and began to dig.

"It looks like I've forgotten my manners, letting you do all the work," Salt said, "but I promise to make it up to you later. I'll do you royally from head to toe."

"With your skinning knife?"

Salt laughed. "Have a little faith in human nature."

As she continued to dig, he was seized with a fit of sneezing.

"That stink is like barbecue. . . ."

She reached the cache, yanking the handles of the heavy sports bag up to her ankles. She unzipped it and took out a stack of hundreds. She handed Salt some bills and he howled with delight.

"I'm rich."

"Not *us*?" Deb asked.

"Deb, I'm afraid I'm going to have to find a replacement. A witness to a killing is like a hand of aces and eights." He sniffed the money, trying to detect the source of the rank smell. "Is it the money that stinks?"

Behind him a man's voice. "No, it's me, Mr. Salt. I've been smoking caribou all afternoon. The odor clings. You'll never have to look over your shoulder again."

"Maybe where you're going you'll learn to treat a woman with respect," Deb said.

Deb's uncle, the whale killer, fired both barrels of the sawed-off shotgun.

_A_ T SEVEN THE NEXT MORNING, GREAT SLAVE LAKE took on a leaden cast and the sun dusted it from the east like a parsimonious trader counting fool's gold. Patches of fresh snow hung limply off the rock face above and at the shoreline the skeleton of a caribou outlined the architecture of its death. The north wind kept up an unremitting growl. Teddy pulled the Land Cruiser into the familiar spot by the side of the cabin he had rented with Deb. He was surprised to see her uncle sitting on the porch rail.

"Who is he?" Barbara asked.

"Deb's uncle," he said.

"Is everything okay? Do you want me go with you?"

"No, darling, stay put. I won't be long."

On the porch, the whale killer was smoking a pipe and drinking coffee.

"Good morning, sir."

"Morning. I came to say good-bye. Is Deb around?"

He pointed to a lone figure paddling a kayak out on the lake. Teddy narrowed his eyes and made out a golden splash on the horizon, then it was swallowed by cloud and speckled sunlight.

"She packed up all your stuff."

"Why isn't she here?"

"She doesn't like to lose. Always been that way. Your money's in the bag, Mr. Franklin."

"It was a gift to her."

"Deb didn't care about the money, you know that." He peered at Barbara in the car. "She hoped you might change your mind."

Teddy turned for a moment and looked at Barbara. "I'm going back. The money is for Deb."

"Are you sure of that?"

"When it comes to money, I'm always sure."

Her uncle bowed his head. "I thank you on her behalf."

Teddy and the whale killer carried his bags to the Cruiser and shook hands.

"I wish you a safe voyage back to civilization, Mr. Franklin."

"I don't know that it's civilization."